A TIMELESS LOVE

"Who are you, Kayla Fairchild?" Ben asked, nuzzling the spot below her ear.

"I'm an artist," she blurted. She gestured to the sketches on the table.

Bracing his palms on the table, Ben studied the sketches, flipping one, then another. "These are incredible," he said. His skin suddenly flushed red and Kayla glanced down. It was a sketch of Ben.

Kayla reached past him, turning over page after page: Ben atop his horse the day she met him; Ben watching her teach, leaning on the fence rail outside the Andersons' meadow.

"You knew I was there?" he asked cautiously, not looking at her.

"I always know where you are, Ben."

His gaze flew to hers.

"Don't you feel it?" she whispered. "This connection we have?" She had traveled back in time for a reason. She was sure of it. Whether it was to find the love of her life or not, she couldn't know, but she was definitely here for Ben. To love him? Or leave him?

from "Summertime Blues," by Amy J. Fetzer

TIMELESS SUMMER

ROSALYN ALSOBROOK BARBARA BENEDICT
JANICE BENNETT AMY J. FETZER
KATHARINE KINCAID JOAN OVERFIELD

ZEBRA BOOKS
KENSINGTON PUBLISHING CORP.

ZEBRA BOOKS are published by

Kensington Publishing Corp.
850 Third Avenue
New York, NY 10022

First Printing: August, 1995

Printed in the United States of America

CONTENTS

The Gift

Rosalyn Alsobrook

One

If there is truly a power in heaven, please, help me. Please take away this pain.

Still dazed, Crissy Townson lay pinned inside the twisted wreckage of her car. Only minutes had passed since her car slammed into that last tree and already she was racked by pain.

Please. Don't put me through this. I can't bear this kind of pain. Please. Take away everything I ever owned or ever wanted, just please do something to stop the hurt.

She tried again to move, but couldn't. She was trapped face down against the buckled floor of her car by some twisted part or the interior, her cheek pressed into a wet carpet.

Fear shot through her when she realized the wet in the carpet was blood. *Her blood.* Where was she bleeding? She had to know. She tried to move, but the wreckage held the back of her neck in a firm grip.

Gritting her teeth hard, she tried again. Her head moved just enough for her to glimpse one arm and the lower part of her body where most of the pain was. Her breath lodged in her throat when she saw her leg. The broken dash had sliced it almost in half. Her foot and ankle dangled awkwardly from the seat, nearly severed from her leg. Her white Reeboks were soaked with dark red blood.

Crissy stared in horror for several seconds before letting loose a piercing scream. Terrified and now understanding the severity of her pain, she yelled again for someone to help her—but the effort made her dizzy. White shadows pervaded her vision, making it hard to focus.

Knowing she would soon pass out, she listened for a sound to indicate somebody had stopped to help. Someone who had seen the accident. Or even somebody less seriously injured from the other car.

But when she heard nothing but a gentle breeze ruffling the leaves of the huge oak tree propped over her car, she closed her eyes and whimpered. *Please, somebody help me. Before I bleed to death. Please, don't let me die.*

She listened again for a sound.

Again nothing.

There would be no rescue.

She would die right there, all alone, with only her uncle Jack to remember her. She felt a sharp pang of regret, knowing she left no one else behind. No husband. No children. No parents. Not even a lover. She was only thirty-one. There should be plenty or time for love, marriage, and children. But now there wasn't. She would die young and alone, her only real friends the employees who worked for her.

Trembling, she wondered what would become of her health spas. They were her life's work. Would Uncle Jack find someone capable of running them? Or would they be too much for him to manage in addition to his medical practice? Would any of her "Reductions" spas exist a year from now, or would they be sold to a new owner and renamed? Would that leave her friends suddenly without jobs?

It was all so unfair.

She shivered, cold despite the August heat, and wondered what death would be like. Would that part be as painless as she hoped? Or would it be worse than what she felt now? When she slipped into the timeless void, would her parents be there waiting for her? Or would she face the hereafter alone?

She felt colder still when the heavy, white shadows turned murky gray, but relaxed into the comforting darkness as it settled around her. *Dying is okay,* she thought, relieved that there would be no more pain. Just as her eyelids closed so she could slip away, a sudden, bright blue light filled the car with a soothing warmth that lasted barely a second before the cool darkness returned. She welcomed the coming sleep.

She hardly noticed the second flare of blue light.

All was quiet when Crissy awoke warm, dry, and disoriented. It was too dark to make out more than shadows and shapes, but she could tell she was inside a small room. But where? Inside a St. Louis hospital maybe? Yes, that was it. She had been in a car accident. She remembered that now. She would have to be in a hospital. Probably the same hospital where her uncle was on staff.

A quick study of the shadows let her know the room was not small enough to be an ICU cubicle. It had to be a private room. How amazing to have come out of that wreck well enough not to need the close, individual attention of an Intensive Care Unit. Or was she asleep long enough to have already spent her time in ICU?

Lying alone, surrounded by darkness, she turned her groggy thoughts to the past. She tried to remember her rescue, but couldn't. Nor could she remember having been admitted into the hospital or spending doubtless hours in emergency surgery. Or eventually being brought up to that room. What she *did* remember was the accident. And she remembered the incredible pain that followed. A pain so sudden and so severe she thought she could not bear it. A pain that had caused her to scream out loud like a small child when usually she was strong when it came to such matters.

Oddly, she felt no pain now.

Glad of that, she tried again to recall the incidents following the accident, but it was all so hazy.

Quietly, she listened for hospital noises. Hearing none, she decided she was nowhere near the nurses station. *Good.* The silence would allow her a better chance to sleep. And to think back to the soft, distant voices calling to her in her sleep. Sweet, calming voices echoing in the darkness. She couldn't remember what the voices said, only that they knew her name and sounded wonderfully reassuring. Probably the voices were those of the doctors and nurses who had taken care of her in Emergency. But she could not be sure.

Determined to remember, Crissy continued sorting through muddled snatches of memory until finally an image cut through her thoughts so stark and so frightening, it caused her heart to slam hard against her chest.

Suddenly, she remembered the source of all that pain. Her leg. She'd lost her left foot in the accident. Her pulses raced with brutal force, the image now vivid inside her brain.

Tentatively, Crissy wiggled the toes of that left foot and was amazed that she still felt no pain—at least not in her leg. She did have a dull, throbbing ache along one side of her head, but her leg felt okay. She could not imagine what sort of medication her uncle had her on, but she knew it had to be some powerful stuff to keep the pain of a nearly severed foot at bay.

Either that or her pleas to heaven had been answered, because although she was incredibly woozy, at the moment her only pain amounted to little more than a mild headache. Again she wiggled her toes and realized by the way they rubbed against the sheets her foot had been successfully reattached. Had her uncle performed the surgery? Or was it someone else?

Not certain where the light switch was, she felt in the darkness to count the tubes threaded into her arms. It amazed her to find no i.v. despite how much blood she must have lost. How long had she lain there?

Exhausted but pleased the pain had proved so short-lived, and not caring in the least that her brand new car was now totalled and lying in a wrecking yard somewhere, she succumbed to the medication and slept again.

It was hours before Crissy awoke again, prodded from her deep, hazy sleep by a soft male voice. A name was called out repeatedly. "Lahoma? Lahoma? Can you hear me?"

Crissy opened her eyes to find a kind-looking older gentleman leaning over her, peering into her eyes. Although the tall, gray-haired man wore no white coat over his white shirt and gray trousers, nor a hospital badge on his pocket to identify himself, she assumed he was a doctor.

That was confirmed seconds later when an elderly woman wearing what looked like a white surgical cap with ties to hold it in place and a long-sleeved, floor-length black dress with an equally long white apron, paused inside the door and queried, "Dr. Mack? Did you call me?"

Crissy arched a questioning eyebrow. Why was the woman dressed so strangely? *What kind of hospital is this?*

Upon seeing Crissy's eyes were open, she looked pleased. "Is she going to be all right?

Still addled by the medication she'd undoubtedly been given, Crissy did not try to make conversation. At the moment she had enough trouble just following the actions of these two.

While the nurse hurried forward for a closer look, the doctor continued to probe and prod. When he poked at the side of Crissy's head behind the hairline, and her only response was a grimace, he smiled. "Looks like she'll be just fine. Even though she still has that big knot on the side of her head, I don't think she cracked the skull after all. Neither pupil looks more dilated than the other and she has followed my movements since she woke. Tell that deputy outside that he can go get Sheriff Walters. Since she seems to have very little pain, I'll let him talk to her for a few minutes like he wanted."

The nurse finished plumping Crissy's pillows then rushed from the room, her long skirts swaying animatedly behind her.

Thinking Sheriff Walters wanted an accident report, and more than willing to tell him about the little white sports car that pulled out in front of her, Crissy did not question the doctor's willingness to let the sheriff in. What she did question was his assessment of the damage.

"But what about my foot?" she asked, glad to find her voice.

"Which foot?" His eyebrows rose with concern.

"My left foot."

He pulled aside the bedcovers and examined the leg. "All I see is a small bruise, and even that hasn't seemed to cause you much misery." He pressed the injury to prove his statement.

Remembering the blood and the excruciating pain that had led her to the discovery of her missing foot, Crissy sat up and looked for herself. She found he was right. Only a bruise, and not even a bad one at that. No indication of even a small cut.

Bewildered, she sank back into the freshly-fluffed pillows.

"I have to admit though, you really had me worried there for a while," Dr. Mack continued as he smoothed the bedcovers back into place. "You hit your head on that counter pretty dang hard. What caused you to fall like that? Were you pushed? Or did you slip on something?"

Crissy stared at him, perplexed. His questions made no sense. "I don't know what you're talking about."

The doctor nodded, then looked at her encouragingly. "I've seen this sort of thing before—amnesia, probably brought on by the sheer horror of what you witnessed. Your mind has decided to block out everything until it is ready to handle the implications. I can certainly understand that."

A movement across the room caught Crissy's eye.

The sheriff, a tall, exceptionally handsome guy who wore black trousers and a light blue cotton shirt that bore a scuffed badge where a pocket would normally be, had entered in time to hear what the doctor said about her blocked memory. He glared at her, as if he did not believe it—or did not *want* to believe it. He was probably worried she wouldn't remember the accident.

"What do you mean she's blocking out everything?" he asked in a voice so low and menacing it sent chills down her arms.

Crissy focused on the strong lines of his face, ready to explain that even though some thoughts were still sketchy, she had not blocked out *everything*. She still remembered the events leading to the accident and the accident itself.

But for now he was too busy talking to Dr. Mack.

She listened patiently while the doctor explained to the angry sheriff that he believed her. But just because she could not remember the incident at that particular moment did not mean the memory was gone forever.

"Look, Gil, I've seen this sort of thing before," the doctor told him. "Back during the war. In time, it should all come back to her just as clear as ever. She can probably still be a witness. Just maybe not right away."

The doctor, obviously aware of her baffled and somewhat peeved expression, turned away from the sheriff and spoke again to her. "I think you should be warned that you are probably in very grave danger. Even though you can't remember anything now, whoever murdered Thomas Walters doesn't know that. And even if he did, he might not want to take the chance that your memory won't return. I'm sure he knows you're the only one who can possibly identify him."

Having no idea what he meant and for the moment not really caring, Crissy asked, "Can I please see my uncle, Dr. Jack Owen?"

Both men looked at her, perplexed.

"Please, would you just see if Dr. Owen is in the hospital. I'm his niece, Christina Townson. He'll want to know I'm awake."

"This might be more serious that I thought," the doctor told the sheriff, who by then glowered at Crissy with more hatred and hostility than she had ever seen in a man. "Lahoma doesn't just have memory loss, she's also having delusions. I wonder where she came up with the name Christina Townson? Never heard of anyone with that name, at least not around here."

"Maybe it's the medicine you gave her," the sheriff suggested while the doctor bent forward again and pushed her hair aside to reexamine the bump on the side of her head.

Dr. Mack frowned. "I don't think it's the medicine. She's had time for most of that to wear off, and she seems perfectly alert." He stood again and stroked his chin. "It could be there's some inside swelling slowing the blood supply to the brain. That could also explain why she went into convulsions and stopped breathing for a couple of minutes there."

Crissy's mouth flattened. The two acted as if she weren't even there. Typical male behavior, she thought, then crossed her arms, wondering why she bothered to put up with it. While listening to the doctor and sheriff discuss the different possibilities, the deep wail of what sounded like an old-fashioned train whistle drew her attention for a moment. Startled by the odd sound, she glanced first at an open window filled now with brilliant sunshine, then at the room itself. What kind of hospital room had open windows with heavy black screens, antique furniture, no major medical equipment, and glass oil lamps instead of electric lights? Curiously, she noted there was no overhead television, no adjustable service table, not even a sink for the doctor to wash his hands, just a porcelain pitcher set inside a large bowl on top of a nearby dresser.

Looking down, she became more perplexed. Instead of hospital issue, she wore a white cotton nightgown with long, loose sleeves trimmed with tiny white ribbons and narrow bands of lace. Her hair hung just past her shoulders, longer and even a shade darker than it should. She decided her hair probably looked a little darker because the gown and sheets were so white. And because her skin was still very pale from the accident.

"What kind of hospital room is this?" she asked as soon as the two men finally finished their discussion. She had heard of such cozy rooms in the maternity ward, where they wanted to make the mothers feel more at home, but she'd never heard of such rooms in the trauma wing. She could see where it had its advantages. The atmosphere was certainly calming.

"You don't remember, but this town is too small to have a real hospital," the doctor answered patiently. "You're in a spare bedchamber I keep for my patients in my home, and for now there is a deputy stationed in the hall outside your door—for protection. The sheriff doesn't want to lose his only witness."

Crissy blinked. *Protection? Only witness? Of what?* Was the doctor trying to tell her that car pulled out in front of her on purpose? Was the accident part of an attempt to kill someone? Her? Or the person who sat in the passenger seat of that little white car? She remembered an earlier mention of someone named Thomas Walters being murdered.

"Was someone killed in the accident?"

"That was no accident," came the sheriff's cutting response. He glowered at her with a hard, judgmental gaze, clearly unconvinced she had lost her memory.

Crissy wondered if she had lost her mind. She touched the lump on her head and considered the doctor's theory about the lack of blood to her brain. Maybe it *was* that lack of blood that caused her to have such strange hallucinations's.

The handsome sheriff glanced briefly at the doctor, but quickly returned his gaze to her. "Doc, can I have a moment alone with her? I think I need to warn her about the very real danger she's in, and I'd rather do that in private."

"Sure, Gil," Dr. Mack responded. "I'll be right outside."

The second he left the room, the sheriff stepped closer. His anger intensified.

"Listen up," he said in a voice as grating as his gaze was determined. "I don't have the time or the patience to play any of your games. They aren't going to help you anyway. I already know that you were involved in the bank robbery and the *real* reason my deputy is outside isn't for your protection. It's to make sure you don't try to escape." His gaze narrowed. "So don't even try."

Crissy was too stunned to reply. With open-mouthed disbelief, she watched while he leaned over her bed so close she could see the silver flecks in his blue eyes and could smell the clean scent of his bath soap. Although not exactly comfortable with the expression on his face, she did like the pale color of his eyes and the firm shape of his mouth. She marveled at what a truly handsome hallucination her injured brain had created. He looked to be about as perfect as a man could get. Too bad she hadn't done as well when creating his attitude.

"I sent the doctor out because I want to make you an offer," he continued, his anger so evident now it sent very real shivers through her.

Bracing himself with an arm on either side of her, he positioned his face only inches above hers, giving her no choice but to stare into those uncanny blue eyes. Her heartbeat doubled, but she wasn't sure if it was because of his anger or because he was so incredibly attractive.

"I'm giving you two choices," he continued, unaware she was paying more attention to his expression than his words. "Either agree to be a witness against the man who pulled the trigger, or go on trial for murder."

"That's a choice?" she asked, wondering why one option

wasn't just to send this whole situation back into the far regions of her mind from where it had come.

The muscles in his arms tightened as he lowered his face closer still. He obviously did not care for her impudence.

"Look, Lahoma," he said through tightly clenched teeth. "You and whoever else was involved in that robbery made a big mistake when you killed my brother. I'm not letting up until Tom's death is avenged!"

"My name is not Lahoma," she corrected, while still absorbing the fact that his brother was the guy killed. It was all so confusing. Was Tom the passenger in the car that pulled out in front of her? Or was he some fictitious character in this strange dream? And what did a robbery have to do with anything? "I told you. My name is Christina. Christina Townson. My friends call me Crissy. *You* may call me Ms. Townson."

Ignoring the implication, he glared at her. "Call yourself whatever you want. But the fact remains that you are my prisoner whether other people realize it or not. And I haven't told anyone yet about your involvement. I'm leaving that open as part of the incentive to be a witness. No one has to know but me."

His tone calmed. "All you have to do is name the culprit, tell me where I can find him, and then act as a witness against him. In return, I'll see to it that you are never linked to the crime. Your grandfather, the doctor, and everyone else in this town can go on believing you were just some unfortunate bystander—someone who happened into the bank at the wrong time."

Still thinking it was all a bad dream induced by pain drugs and a vivid imagination born of having watched too many old westerns, she crossed her arms and told him to go away.

He refused to budge. "I'm not going anywhere until you tell me who shot my brother."

Confused and a little frightened that things had taken such a nasty turn, she tried explaining that she was not involved in a bank robbery. "And I sure wasn't around any shooting. I'd remember something like that."

The sheriff refused to believe her. "All I can say is that you'd better have a rapid memory recovery, because I am determined to find the man who killed my brother," he told her coldly. "Since the posse lost the murderer's trail after he slipped into Glade Creek, you are the only hope I have now of finding him. You *will* help me or suffer the consequences. And you *will* give the testimony I need to see that he either hangs or spends the rest of his life in prison. My brother's killer *will* be punished for what he's done."

He stood erect again, folded his arms across his broad chest. then continued. "You really have little choice. Unfortunately for you, my brother lived just long enough to tell me that you were not just a customer in the bank. You signaled to the outside that the bank was empty, then helped gather the money into a large valise while a man with a bandanna over his face held a pistol on him. Tom also said you would have gotten away with your tall, dark-haired, bank-robbing friend if you hadn't slipped on a pencil and fallen against the counter, knocking yourself out cold. It's true, you may not have done the actual shooting, but you know who did."

"I have no idea what you're talking about." Was this guy nuts? Or was *she?* She frowned, wondering when she'd finally wake up. She'd had just about enough of this.

"Oh, but you do. Even though I don't quite have the evidence yet to prove you participated in the murder itself, I *can* prove that you helped with the bank robbery." His hands curled into tight fists. "Not only do I have the testimony of a dying man who was known for being as honest as the August sun is hot, there was a handful of money on the floor beside you. Even if I can't prove you were partly responsible for Tom's death, I can still put you away for a long, long time. Robbery is as illegal as it ever was, and unless you cooperate, lady, you are headed to prison for at least ten years. It'll be 1886 before you see the light of day again."

His lips pressed into a scornful sneer, obviously pleased by the way that last comment had made her blink. "So, tell me, how is your memory now?"

Crissy's mouth flattened. She still believed the scene unfolding before her was the effect of whatever medicine she'd been given and that eventually she would come out of it and be back in the real world again. Even so, she also knew that when she did, she would have to face the magnitude of her real injuries. And because she knew none of this was real, she did not let the fact that he had just insinuated the year was 1876 bother her. Nor the threat of having to spend ten years in jail. She'd be awake long before then. Awake and back in her own world where every luxury awaited her.

Tired, and ready to drift into a deeper sleep—one that bore no more angry images and no unreasonable threats—she again told him to go away. "You don't scare me one bit."

"Okay. I'll go away," he agreed, already headed toward the door. "But I will be back this afternoon, right after my brother's funeral. You are my only hope of capturing the man who murdered my brother. I won't leave you alone until you finally promise to help me." He paused at the door, looked at her a long moment, then stormed out of the room.

The loud clomping of boots on a wooden floor was followed by the softer scuffling of shoes, and the doctor reentered. "I feel like I should apologize for the sheriff's brusque manner," he said, then glanced back in the direction Gil Walters had just taken while he continued toward Crissy. "I don't know if you remember, or if he told you, but the banker who got shot was his brother. Gil is usually a very nice fellow, but he is carrying around a huge load of anger and frustration right now because the posse lost the trail so early. You are his only hope of ever finding out who killed Thomas."

Bending, he took another look at her head injury. "It appears God indeed heard your prayers, young lady. As swollen as that knot is right there in the center, I'd think it would be a lot more tender than that."

"My prayers?"

"Yes. When the sheriff first carried you in here, you were muttering something about how bad your pain was. I think you were pleading with God Himself, to make it stop." The doctor straightened after a moment then headed toward the dark blue porcelain water pitcher. "You even tried to strike a bargain with the powers that be. You agreed to give up everything you ever had or ever wanted if the pain would just go away. Remember that?"

Crissy nodded that she did, though not word for word.

"That's why I used such a strong drug at first." He poured a few inches of water into the accompanying bowl then opened the top dresser drawer and took out a white cloth. He dipped the folded cloth into the bowl then squeezed out the excess water. "I thought maybe the injury was worse than it looked. Figured maybe you'd cracked your skull when you fell. Especially after you went into convulsions and stopped breathing." He shook his head in amazement then headed back toward her. "I really thought you were dead. But just as suddenly as you quit breathing, you started again. It's a true miracle you're still here."

Carefully, he pushed her hair out of the way and turned her head to the side so he could place the cool, wet cloth over the injury. "But I wouldn't worry too much about your memory loss. Everything will return to you eventually. Are you hungry?"

"No," she answered honestly. "Not at all."

"Thirsty?"

"No."

"Let me know when you are. For now though, you need your rest." He started toward the door. "Get some more sleep. I'll come back this afternoon to check on you."

Glad to be alone again, and exhausted, Crissy unbuttoned the top buttons of her gown to give her more comfort then closed her eyes and did exactly what her imaginary doctor told her to do. She slept.

Later that afternoon, Crissy awoke again. Opening her eyes slowly, she prayed for normalcy, but the hallucination persisted. Disappointed, but feeling more clear-headed than before, she glanced around the uncomfortably warm room and saw that nothing had changed except that less sun flooded the tall, guillotine-style windows.

Pushing her sleeves high onto her arms, she plumped her pillows then sat studying her surroundings, amazed by the detail. She decided the hallucination was a lot like being inside a poorly scripted movie when, minutes later, the doctor knocked then entered again, now wearing black dress trousers with a matching coat, a white shirt, and a black ribbon tie.

"Sorry I haven't been in, but I decided to go to Tom Walters's funeral. Hope you didn't think I forgot about you," he said, his tone as cheerful as his smile. "How you feeling?"

"Hot. And frustrated that I'm still here," she admitted. "I expected to find myself inside a nice, air-conditioned hospital room by now."

"Air-conditioned?" the doctor repeated with a quizzical frown.

"Yes, you know. Nice and cool."

He shrugged as if he had no idea what she was talking about, but did not question her further. Instead he plucked the damp cloth from her pillow where it had fallen and tossed it aside. "How's the head?"

Crissy smiled when she realized there was no pain. "It quit hurting."

"Good." He pushed the hair back out of his way again. "I see the swelling has gone down some. Does it hurt when I push against it?"

"A little."

"Can you tell me your name yet?"

"Yes, my name is Crissy Townson."

He shook his head, but his expression remained optimistic when he dropped her long hair back into place. "Don't worry, one of these times you'll wake up and remember that you're really Lahoma Reed. By the way, I sent for your grandfather, but he wasn't out there. We'll try again later."

Crissy considered asking questions about this Lahoma Reed with the missing grandfather, but decided she really did not care to put her brain to work trying to figure out this new identity she had created.

"I'm hungry now," she told him, thinking she might as well dream herself up a nice hot meal while waiting to fully awaken.

"Good. I'll go tell Minnie to bring you something to eat."

"Is Minnie your nurse?"

"Oh, that's right. You don't remember," he said, apologetic. "No, my nurse is named Ruby. She's also my wife. Minnie is my housekeeper who, fortunately for you, happens to be one of the best cooks in all of Gladewater."

She blinked again. Gladewater? She never heard the name

before. Thinking it pointless to psychoanalyze her own hallucination, she did not question him further. Obviously she had reached so deep into her memory that she had come up with discarded facts for some of this.

Tired of lying flat and no longer feeling drugged, Crissy waited until the doctor left the room then tossed back the covers and slid out of the bed. Pausing to test her legs to make sure they were strong enough after all she'd been through, she felt a moment of dizziness, but not enough to force her back into bed. When the dizziness passed, she stepped over to the open window and stood in the warm rays of the summer sun, allowing a brisk breeze to billow the lacy curtains on both sides of her.

Through the coarse window screen she saw a beautifully kept flower garden filled with petunias, roses, and marigolds, all splashed with intermittent patches of shade and sunshine. Leaning against the frame and thinking what a wonderfully peaceful turn her dream had taken, she watched a pair of cardinals flit from tree to tree while waiting for her imaginary breakfast. She was more than a little annoyed when the tray was eventually brought by the only hostile person in her accident-induced coma—Sheriff Walters.

She turned to look at him. Stretched across his broad shoulders was a black dress coat and white shirt with a black string tie. Hugging his long, lean legs were black trousers pulled taut over a pair of dark brown boots. He looked even more like something straight out of an old western movie. His thick, dark brown hair, which that morning had been combed neatly away from his face, now fell across his forehead in soft layers. The tousled locks gave him an attractive yet rugged look. Crissy felt a pang of disappointment when he raked it back into place with his free hand.

"I see you're out of bed," he commented, still headed across the room. "How's your memory?"

Crissy was not surprised that was the first question out of his mouth. "Well, I certainly remember *you* if that matters," she replied while watching him set the tray down on the table beside her bed. She thought it odd that she could smell imaginary food.

"You do remember me?" He studied her carefully.

"Yes, from this morning. You're the jerk who threatened me."

"That's not what I meant," he replied, his expression stony. "I was talking your memory of the holdup. Are you ready to tell me who your partner was and where I can find him? The longer you wait, the better his chance of getting clean away."

When will this nightmare ever end? She'd grown tired of these senseless accusations.

"Speaking of away, why don't you go there?" she muttered, shaking her head. "You aren't even real."

When Crissy first got up she'd planned to have a look at that lump on her head in the small mirror across the room, but she decided against it and tossed herself back into bed with a bounce, glad when that foolishness didn't cause her head to hurt again.

Angered by her impudence, the sheriff leaned over her again. Propped up with one hand, he captured her jaw firmly in the other. His gaze dipped briefly to the unbuttoned yoke of her nightgown but did not remain there long. She could tell by the redness below those incredibly long eyelashes that the guy had been crying. That fact surprised her.

"Oh, I'm real all right," he said with certainty. His fingers dug painfully into her tender skin. "I'm about as real as a man can get."

Crissy stared at him, startled to feel his strong grip. Confused, she lifted a hand to touch his angry face and became more perplexed when she felt the warm curve of his cheek, freshly shaven beneath her fingers.

"But you can't be real," she complained, frowning more out of confusion than because of his painful grasp. "None of this is real. It can't be."

The muscles in his jaws tightened until they became granite beneath her touch. His blue eyes glinted like dark steel. "Quit pretending you're so addled by your injury that you don't remember who you are or what you did. It isn't working. I *know* you, remember?"

She lifted a challenging eyebrow and met his gaze. "If you know me so well, then who am I?"

"Lahoma Reed," he answered without hesitation. "The woman I *almost* married."

Two

"Almost married?" Crissy asked, intrigued by her own inventiveness. "What happened?"

Gil's expression changed from anger to uncertainty.

"You tell me." Though he continued to glare at her, he dropped his hand from her jaw and stepped back. "All I know is that everything seemed fine until about two weeks ago when you suddenly came into my office and told me I was to quit paying call on you—but gave no reason why. At least not one I understood."

His heavily lashed blue eyes narrowed just enough, she noticed. "Not long later, I was told that someone else had already started calling on you, but I could never find out who. I suppose it was the same man you're now trying so hard to protect. Who is he? Where did you meet him? And why'd you think you had to be so secretive about him?"

He raked his fingers through his dark hair. "If you'd found someone else, you should have just come out and told me so. Didn't you know that someone would eventually see him riding up to your house and come tell me? Did you think I'd never find out the real reason you wanted me out of your life? Or did you just not care?"

"Look, fella, I have no idea what you're talking about," she replied. Her fingers touched the area of her face where his warmth still lingered. "I am *not* protecting anyone."

Gil threw up his hands, clearly disgusted. "To think, I believed you to be such a caring, decent woman. And I am usually a very good judge of character—but, lady, I misjudged yours completely. I guess I should just be grateful you decided to toss me aside as early as you did."

"I guess so," she responded, returning his angry glower with one of her own. She did not like being insulted, even by a figment of her own imagination. "At least you're willing to give me credit for having done *one* smart thing—tossing you aside."

Gil looked as if she had just struck him a physical blow then lashed out again. "I have to wonder now if that late husband of yours didn't catch cholera and die on purpose. He probably found out what a cold-hearted manipulator you really are and decided death would be easier than having to live with you forever."

Though that last remark made no sense, it made her angrier still. "It just so happens Mr. Smart-guy that I have *never* been married. Ever." Oh, there had been a serious relationship or two during the last several years, but nothing that ever led to talk of marriage. She had yet to find a man who proved more attracted to her than to her over-abundance of money.

Gil looked as if he'd just caught her in a lie. "Oh? So you admit you lied about that, too?"

"I admit nothing of the sort. I never told you I was married."

"Oh, yes you did." His boots clicked twice on the hardwood floor as he moved a couple of steps closer. "When you first came to Texas to live with your grandfather three years ago, you told everyone in this town that you were a new widow. You told us that your husband of two years—some foolish soul by the name of Robert—had died of cholera during an epidemic earlier that summer. That's why I didn't ask to call on you right away. I figured you'd probably need time to get over your grief." He crossed his arms, straining his black coat with bunching muscles. His face hardened with intent. "I can produce any number of people who will attest to *those* facts."

Crissy decided to let that particular argument drop. She had too many other matters on her mind at the moment. "And were you ever married?"

"You know I was," he replied, his expression suddenly more hurt than angry. "I already told you about Iris." The harsh lines near his eyes softened just before he lowered his arms and looked away. "We were married barely a year when she died trying to give birth to our stillborn son." He ran a hand over his arm as if suddenly cold.

Glimpsing Gil's vulnerable side for the second time, Crissy's antagonism dwindled. *So the guy has human qualities after all.* "When was that?"

"Six years ago." He paused then let out an exasperated breath and turned to glare at her again. "Will you stop pretending you don't remember anything from the past? I already told you, I *have* to have your help or that man is going to get clean away with murdering my brother. How can you keep protecting someone who could just up and shoot a man like that? Especially a good man like Tom."

Crissy crossed her arms just as defiantly as he had moments earlier. "And I already told you. I'm not protecting anyone." *Why can't that one simple fact register with this guy?* "And I am not suffering from memory loss. At least not about any of that."

"You admit to not having memory loss?" Gil's eyes widened with renewed hope. He moved closer. "Are you finally willing to tell me who killed my brother?"

Crissy shook her head then dropped her arms onto the bed again. "I wish I could tell you. But the truth is, I don't know."

"La-hom-a." His blue eyes glinted with warning.

"That, buddy, is exactly the key to your whole problem," she responded with a quick wave of her finger. "My name is not Lahoma. My name is Christina. And the sooner you let that one little fact register inside that incredibly hard head of yours, the better it will be for both of us."

He stared at her a long moment then reached up and loosened his black string tie with several hard jerks. "So that's the way it is. You're going to go on protecting the culprit even though you know he killed an innocent man in cold blood."

"I told you I'm not protecting anyone," she repeated, this time more tired than angry. She had grown weary of arguing with this tall, handsome, overbearing figment of her own imagination. "I simply don't have the details you want. If I had them, I would give them to you, if for no other reason than to get you out of my head once and for all."

He expelled a short breath. "I wish I could believe that. But I don't."

"Fine," she replied with an angry toss of her head, a defiant gesture that resulted in a brief stab of pain. She grimaced at the grim reminder of her injury. Frowning, she touched the lump on her head but found the swelling almost gone. Wondering if it had started to bruise yet, she wished now she had gone ahead and looked at it in the mirror. "Believe whatever you want. Just do it somewhere else."

Before Gil could offer another angry retort, the door swung open and in walked Dr. Mack, no longer wearing his coat or tie. Smiling, he cut his gaze from Crissy to Gil, then back to Crissy. "So how was the food?"

Gil backed away at the same time Dr. Mack stepped over to check her tray. When he noted she had not eaten even one bite of the food brought her, he frowned and handed her an already buttered roll. "Here. Eat at least that."

Obligingly, Crissy accepted the roll, tore off part, and plopped it into her mouth. Finding the moist bread amazingly delicious, she quickly tore off another piece and another until the entire roll was gone. Reminded of her hunger, she turned her attention to the rest of the food. She tried not to feel too self-conscious while she ate, knowing the sheriff stood across the room watching her every move. Even though she knew the food was not real, it tasted real, and at the moment that was all that mattered.

She savored every bit and tried not to feel disappointed when minutes later Gil spun about and left without speaking another word.

That night, not long after the doctor and his wife had traipsed upstairs to bed, Crissy lay in the darkened room, staring at the shadowed ceiling ten feet above her head. Trying to make sense of it all, she wondered why she could not wake up and what she would face if and when she finally did. She knew her injuries had to be very serious since she had been kept drugged that long. Or was it more than drugs that prevented her from resurfacing into reality? Had she slipped into some sort of coma? Was that why she couldn't force herself to wake up?

Crissy wrinkled her forehead, thinking. If she was that seriously injured, perhaps the real problem was that she didn't *want* to wake up. She hated pain. Always had. Even as a child. And being in a coma protected her from whatever pain she suffered—at least for now. She should be grateful.

But on the other hand, she knew she could not continue living in this make-believe world forever. Or could she? The thought frightened her. So much so that when she heard the door creak and watched while Sheriff Walters's broad shoulders moved to fill the partial opening, blocking much of the light from the hall, she was actually relieved to see him. She welcomed the distraction.

"Sheriff? Is something wrong?" She thought it odd he had opened the door without knocking.

"I don't know." He lit one of the four frosted lamps near the door. It gave off just enough glow to see the inside of the room. After lighting a second lamp, he glanced at the windows, then scanned the shadows. Having found nothing of apparent interest, he pushed the door shut then walked over to her bedside and gazed down at her with a most disturbing look in those opulent blue eyes. It was a look Crissy had seen before, though not all that often, and most certainly not on him. It was a look of longing.

"Why are you in here?" she asked, feeling extremely uncomfortable to have the tall, handsome man standing over her and looking down at her like that—*imaginary or not.*

She swallowed, then dropped her gaze and noticed he had removed his coat and tie. He now stood with the collar of his white shirt unbuttoned, allowing her to view the small patch of curling black hair at the base of his suntanned throat. Wide, black suspenders shaped the loose-fitting shirt against his broad shoulders.

"I thought I heard a noise outside," he answered, his voice surprisingly concerned. "I just wanted to make sure you were all right."

With his anger seemingly forgotten, he sat down, the side of her bed giving way to his weight. He smiled sadly while his gaze moved wistfully across her face. "You know, I'd forgotten just how beautiful you are lying in bed with your hair down like that, your face bathed in lamplight."

Crissy's first thought was to ask him how he could possibly know what she looked like lying in bed, lamplight or not, but realized that would only antagonize him again—and for some reason she did not want to do that. She had nothing to gain by stirring up more hostility. Instead she smiled. "That was a nice thing to say."

He responded by reaching out to touch her hair lightly with the tips of his fingers. He looked so lost and forlorn, like a child uncertain of the future. It was hard not to comfort him.

"I know now what a fool I was to have ever believed it," he continued with no trace of animosity in his voice. "But I really thought we had something special between us." The long tresses of her hair slid through his fingers like dark silk while he peered again into her eyes. "I really thought you wanted to marry me. I know we haven't known each other all that long, but I had developed such strong feelings for you. I still find it hard to believe you'd willingly do anything to hurt Tom. Not the way you two got along."

"I've never willingly done anything to hurt anyone," she stated honestly, slowly becoming lost in the probing depths of his glittering blue eyes. How glad she was to see no anger there. "And I truly am sorry about what happened to your brother."

Enjoying the tender moment, her gaze stole over his features, wandering from the strong lines that shaped his mouth and his cheeks to the thick fringe of eyelashes that surrounded his pool-like blue eyes. Eyes that tugged at her from somewhere inside. "I hope you believe that."

"To tell you the truth, I don't know what to believe anymore." A tiny notch creased an otherwise smooth forehead. "First, you told me you loved me and promised to marry me as soon as you'd seen that your grandfather's cotton crop was in and that he was set for the winter. You even let me make love to you. Then suddenly you just up and announced I couldn't call on you anymore."

Hurt deepened those incredibly blue eyes. "Then, earlier today you tried your darnedest to convince me that you don't remember anything at all about what happened yesterday, yet now you tell me you're sorry my brother is dead."

Finding the mere suggestion of ever having made love to this amazingly handsome man quite enthralling, Crissy wanted to hear more. Since what happened was all just one long dream, she knew she would not be held accountable for anything she said or did.

That made the situation all the more interesting, if not downright arousing. All her usual inhibitions were tossed to the side.

"Just because I don't remember what happened at the bank— or the fact that we've made love—doesn't mean I can't be sorry you are in so much pain. I don't have to have such memories to see that you loved your brother very much."

Gil blinked back sudden tears and Crissy's heart went out to him with a rush. She pushed the bedcovers aside and sat forward on her knees so she could follow her unexpected urge to touch the strong lines of his face. She trailed a finger lightly across the firm curve of his cheek, wishing again that he was real and not just some gorgeous figment of her imagination.

Her heart raced at the thought. "I don't like to see anyone hurting as much as I see you hurting right now."

Gil closed his eyes, clearly fighting a desire to believe her, yet at the same time needing to be comforted. "Lahoma, I was there this afternoon when they lowered Tom's coffin into the ground and I stayed until they had covered it with earth and packed it down. But none of that seems to matter. Even though I stood right there and watched him be buried, I still can't accept the fact that he's gone. It all happened so suddenly. Too suddenly."

A tear pushed past his closed eyelashes and trickled down his cheek, causing an ache inside Crissy so strong she wanted to cry along with him—and almost did.

"I just can't accept the fact that my brother's gone."

"I know." She moved closer and caressed his face between her palms. "I felt the same away about my parents. One minute they were there, alive and happy, and the next minute they were gone."

Gil's eyelids parted and he looked at her suspiciously. "You can remember your parents' deaths, but you can't remember my brother's?"

Not wanting him angry again, she answered simply and honestly. "Some things I can remember and some things I can't."

He paused a moment, then tested her. "What do you remember about us?"

"What should I remember?"

He looked saddened again. "That until a few weeks ago we were very much in love. Or at least I was."

Crissy liked the way those words warmed her right to her very toes and leaned closer. Her heart hammered fiercely at the mere thought of a man like Gil Walters thinking he might be in love with her. She bent lower so she could see his face better. "What else should I remember?"

When he did not answer right away, she dampened her lips with a quick dart of her tongue then prompted again. "You said we made love. What was that like?"

Caught up in the moment, she ran her fingers over the shape of his face then dipped forward to kiss him lightly on the corner of his mouth. Surprised by her own boldness, she could not remember ever having felt so aroused. "Show me what it was like between us."

When all he did was look at her oddly, she gave further encouragement. She had to know what it was like to be closer to this man. "Maybe if you kissed me it would help unlock some of the memories you think I'm suppressing."

A tiny muscle twitched near the back of Gil's jaw. He studied her a long moment, then slowly his mouth moved closer. A ribbon of heat swam up from her toes and curled gently around her heart when he pulled her into a strong, firm embrace.

Fully aroused, Crissy drew a sharp breath and braced herself for the onslaught of emotions she knew would follow. Anticipation tumbled through her while ever so slowly he tilted his head then touched his mouth to hers.

The kiss that followed was every bit as magnificent as she'd expected. At first gentle and probing, it quickly intensified until it became the most powerful kiss she had ever experienced. Her body filled with a tingling wave of heat that left her both light-headed and physically weak—and made her want more.

Gil's lips continued what could only be classified as magic on her willing mouth until she moaned softly in response. Her eyelids drifted closed so she could better enjoy this passion that had so suddenly burst to life inside her and had taken complete control over her senses.

When she brought her hands up to caress the back of his neck, the kiss intensified even more. Her heart drummed wildly while she wondered how far the kiss would advance. Did Gil enjoy it enough to allow it to take them to the ultimate of heights, or would he pull away after only one kiss, or maybe two? Though normally reserved in such matters, her body ached with the hope he would not pull away at all. She longed for Gil to take this new-found passion as far and as high as it could possibly soar.

Ready to explore the pleasures this guy offered her, and knowing she would not have to deal with any consequences later on, she met the hungry kiss with eager abandon. She slid her arms from the strong column of his neck to his broad shoulders then pulled his body closer, an action that generated an even stronger wave of passion inside her.

With their bodies melded together, Gil lay back onto the bed, bringing her down with him. Feeling her breasts flattened against his strong, muscular chest, Crissy met his kiss with eagerness and furor, especially after his hands found their way to the buttons of her nightgown. There he fumbled with the buttons until the front parted wider for him. Crissy felt immediate disappointment when he gently pushed her back by her shoulders and broke the kiss.

His eyes remained black with desire while he studied her flushed face. "God, I've missed you. Deny it if you want, but you belong in my arms."

At that moment Crissy had no desire to deny any such thing. If anything, she agreed with him. Her body burned with a heat so profound, she reached immediately for the tiny buttons that held his shirt together. As soon as they were undone, she slid a hand inside the opening and ran her palm over his taut, warm skin.

Gil responded with what sounded like a wounded growl then lowered her on top of him again. His kiss became even more ravenous than before.

Although she never would have thought it possible, the burning ache deep inside grew stronger still. She responded to the wild pleasure by dipping the tip of her tongue into the velvety softness of his mouth. She yearned to taste him as much as feel him, and moaned again when he felt for her breasts through the thin material of her white gown.

Needing breath, Crissy broke away and gasped aloud. Propped by arms braced on either side of him, she arched her back while his fingers sought and found the hardened nipples, then played with them gently. Pleasure coursed through her, making her want more and more. She whimpered in response.

"Is your memory returning?" he asked, his voice but a deep growl. He lifted his head to nip lightly the base of her throat and at the same time he dipped a hand inside the gown to touch skin instead of cloth.

Crissy bit deep into the sensitive flesh of her lower lip when his fingertips first brushed those same hardened nipples. The resulting shaft of pleasure was so strong it made her want to rip the cumbersome gown from her body. She pulsed with a sweet agony only he could relieve.

"Don't talk about that now," she moaned, desperate with need. She could not bear this gentle torment any longer. "Just make love to me."

"No, not until you admit to me that you remember," he coaxed and continued to tease the sensitive breasts with his fingers while lifting up to trail another group of kisses down her neck. "Admit that you remember telling me you love me and that you remember our having made love together—and that you remember who murdered my brother."

Crissy drew in several quick, needed gulps of air, so overwhelmed by desire she could hardly think. "But that's not fair."

"Oh, but it *is* fair. It is *very* fair."

She looked down at him, pleading with him to understand. "Not when there's nothing there to remember."

Gil's passion came to such an abrupt end that it left Crissy off-center and angry. And confused to find herself suddenly abandoned on the bed while he paced the floor only a few feet away, his shirt still open and a large mass of crisp, dark body hair exposed to her view.

"You have to tell me his name. I have to know who killed my brother. Why can't you understand how important that is to me?"

"But I do understand how important it is to you. I just don't happen to know."

He glared at her, his eyes black with rage. "Is what you feel for *him* that much more important than what you feel for me?"

Crissy pressed back against her pillows, pulled the front of her gown together, then jerked the bedcovers to her chin. "All I feel for you at this moment, Gil Walters, is anger."

He squared his shoulders. "Well, at least it's a mutual feeling." He stopped his pacing. "Have it your way. Don't tell me what I want to know. I'll find out eventually anyway. Somehow. And when I do, and I finally bring in that murdering outlaw, maybe you two can share the same jail cell." His eyes narrowed into two slits of glinting steel. "Would you like that, Lahoma? Would you like to share the same jail cell with your latest lover?"

"Get out of here," she replied, pointing toward the door with a trembling hand, still overwhelmed by the very real desire she felt for this man. "Get out of here and leave me alone."

He glowered a moment longer then punctuated each word he said with short finger stabs to his palm. "Well, it's a damn good thing you like being alone so much, because after the jury in this town gets through with you, that's exactly what you will be for a long, long time." He then stalked toward the door where he stopped long enough to extinguish the two lamps.

Crissy knew it was a cliche, for she had heard it in nearly every western she had ever watched as a child, but for the life of her, could not stop herself. "Sheriff, there hasn't been a jail built yet that can hold the likes of me."

She found grim satisfaction in the way his broad shoulders stiffened. She watched with a pleased smirk when he gave her one last angry look then hurriedly yanked the door open, stepped through, then jerked it closed behind him.

Again cloaked in darkness, Crissy settled deeper into her pillows, puzzled by the strange yet powerful feelings she felt. Not long later she heard Gil drag his chair closer to the shut door. She thought about how very angry he had become. All because she did not remember something that never happened. It hardly seemed fair.

Sighing sadly, she touched lips still warm from kissing him and realized that if he *were* real she would be *very* attracted to him. Enough so she might eventually consider making love to and even marrying a man like him. She smiled over the thought of what her uncle would say to that. He had been after her to marry someone, *anyone,* for years now. He was tired of worrying about her. Tired of her being alone.

Her smile deepened. Uncle Jack would want her to analyze everything going on inside her head right now so she could find the deeper meaning behind it all. Her uncle was like that. Always wanting her to see all sides of every issue. Much like her father had. Such pragmatic people, her family.

With a tired sigh, she rolled over onto her side and closed her eyes and was almost asleep when she heard a tiny popping sound outside one of the windows.

Blinking awake, she rolled to face the windows, but it was too dark to tell who or what made the noise. All she saw was a dim shadow as it moved across the coarse metal webbing that passed for a screen.

"Who's there?" she called out softly, not wanting to alert the sheriff sitting guard outside her bedroom door. Real or not, she'd had enough arguing with that guy for one day.

"It's me," replied a deep, husky male voice. "I've come to get you out of here."

Crissy sat up and watched curiously while a silhouette gently pulled the bottom corner of the screen loose then curled it out of his way. If not still dreaming, she might have been afraid. Instead, she sat fascinated by how real everything seemed—and how amazingly detailed. She could even hear the rustle of the night breeze through a tree outside her window.

"Come on," he coaxed as he crept across the wooden floor toward her. "Get out of bed. I got two horses waiting just down the street."

Instead of obeying, Crissy found a match and lit the nearby table lamp and was immediately impressed by how handsome her rescuer was.

She studied him a moment and decided that this guy was almost as gorgeous as the one seated outside her door, though not nearly as overtly masculine. He was tall, but not quite as tall as Gil, and his black clothing hugged a far less muscular frame.

Her savior held out a hand, beckoning anxiously for her to join him. "Hurry, before that sheriff comes back from the privy and catches me in here." He cut his gaze to the door.

"Oh, so *you* are the one who shot the sheriff's brother," she commented, putting the facts together as quickly as her sleepy brain would allow. The plot, or rather the dream, thickened. "Do you by chance have a name, Mr. Rescuer, sir?"

He looked at her, puzzled. "You know my name." The muscles in his lean face tightened and his green eyes glinted as he took another step closer. "What are you trying to pull here?"

Annoyed by his sudden show of anger, she lifted her chin and met his gaze. "You're wrong about that. I don't know your name. But I am perfectly willing to give you one if that's what you'd like." She drummed her fingers on the sheet to show her impatience. *"Butt-head* seems rather appropriate to me."

Angrier still, he lunged forward, grabbed her by the arm, and twisted it painfully. "Quit playing games and get out of that bed. You know very well that my name is Drake Stephens and you also know what harm I can do. That's why you're *here.* Remember?"

Confused by the pressure she felt, she slapped his hand away. "Let go of me."

He grabbed her again, then with a quick movement produced a large knife from inside his black clothing. "I said to get out of that bed. You're coming with me."

Thinking an apparition could not really harm her, at least not fatally, she shook her head then wrenched her arm free again. "I'm not going anywhere with you."

"Oh? Have you forgotten about your grandfather?" His lips curled against clenched teeth. He took a swipe at her with the knife, cutting the sleeve of her gown. A red stain formed immediately.

"My grandfather is dead," she answered. For the first time since the accident, she considered the possibility that everything happening around her was real. But that was impossible. She pressed her hand over the stinging cut and felt the dampness beneath her touch.

"He isn't yet, but you keep this up and he *will* die—slowly and painfully."

Crissy decided to cooperate. Real or not, she did not care to suffer any more pain, and she most certainly was not prepared, emotionally or otherwise, to deal with any situation in which her grandfather might be hurt. "Okay, okay, I'm coming."

Reluctantly, she tossed back the covers, and with nothing to put on her feet and no robe to cover her gown, she padded barefoot across the wooden floor.

Not until they sat astride the waiting horses, headed out of a rough and tumble town that looked like something straight out of an old *Gunsmoke* episode, did the apparition bother to speak to her again. And then only because she spoke first.

"Why am I with you?"

"Did you really think I'd leave you there and take the chance of you testifying against me?" he asked. Despite the darkness, he kept both horses moving at a brisk clip.

Playing along, she answered, "No, I guess not."

After studying him a minute longer in the pale, silvery moonlight, she ventured, "Where are we headed?"

By then, Crissy's arm had stopped bleeding, but because the blood-soaked material over the cut felt sticky against her skin, she tore away most of the sleeve and tossed it to the ground while awaiting his reply. In afterthought, she realized that if what was going on around her *were* real, she would have just left a clue for the sheriff to follow.

For some reason that was a comforting thought.

"First we're riding out to collect your grandfather, then we'll head on out of the state." Because he was busy trying to make out the tree-shadowed road ahead, he didn't notice when she tossed away part of her sleeve. "I guess we'll head to Louisiana since it's closest."

"Where exactly is my grandfather?" she asked, gazing off at a moon-bathed hill, trying to imagine what the wooded surroundings looked like in daylight.

"Where no one can possibly find him," he answered then pushed his hat back. "I've got him where not even that lousy sheriff of yours would think to look."

Crissy fell quiet after that. She looked forward to the unlikely prospect of visiting with her grandfather again and rode peacefully for the next few hours, thinking of what a treat it would be to see him again. Or to see both her grandfathers again, even though one had died so early in her childhood she barely remembered him.

After riding until her back and thighs ached, it having been years since she rode a horse, they finally approached a run-down house and barn. Tall, leafy trees loomed over the gray, dilapidated buildings, cloaking them in ghostly shadows that wavered in the night breeze.

An armadillo nudged through the tall weeds and the not-quite full moon slid behind a cloud just before she drew her horse to a stop beside Drake's. Uncertain of his plans she waited until he climbed down, tethered his horse, then turned to assist her.

"So, where is my grandfather?" she asked, as soon as her feet hit solid ground. Her legs felt as if they were still bowed around the horse's back while she took a few exaggerated steps to stretch them.

"Follow me," he told her, already headed toward the barn.

Seconds after they entered the musty darkness of the lofty wooden barn, Drake lit a nearby lantern, illuminating the inside of the raftered building with an eerie glow.

Crissy glanced around the near-empty building and was disappointed to see an old man she did not recognize asleep on the moldy, hay-strewn dirt floor. But even though she did not know the scrawny old man, she was plenty angry to see his left leg shackled to a support post and to learn that he'd had nothing to eat or drink for the past several days.

"Why would you do something like that?"

"To keep you in line. Remember? I warned you that if something went wrong with the robbery and we both ended up conveniently caught, your grandfather was as good as dead. If you hadn't cooperated, this man would have starved to death."

"That's cruel," she complained, already moving forward to

find out if the old guy was all right—for even though this might not be real, it *felt* real, and she had to go with that. "How could you do something so mean?"

The old man rolled his head to look at her but did not attempt to lift it off the dirt floor. Twigs of hay and clumps of dirt clung to his unshaven cheek.

"Look at him, he doesn't even have the strength to sit up." She knelt beside him and brushed his long, white hair away from his dirty face and felt a strong surge of compassion when he attempted to smile his gratitude. This man needed her help.

"Have you no heart at all?" She glanced down at where the trouser leg had been torn away so a metal cuff could be fitted just above his bleeding ankle.

"Shut up, Lahoma," Drake warned. "I don't want to hear that from you."

"Well, you're going to *have* to hear it because I'm not about to shut up," she said, angry. "Not until you produce the key and unlock this shackle."

He stepped closer, his shadow falling across the old man's legs. "I said to shut up, Lahoma."

The lantern light illuminated Drake's gaunt face at an angle that gave it a disturbing, demonic quality. How she ever thought this guy attractive was beyond her.

His expression hardened. "I don't want to bother with him right now. Lie down, Lahoma, and get some sleep. It will be daylight soon and I plan for the three of us to take off just as soon as it's light enough to see."

Crissy considered correcting her name, but decided it wasn't worth the effort. If Drake wanted to call her Lahoma like Gil did, so be it. But she refused to let him continue to hurt this man.

"I'm not sleeping until you've taken off that chain."

"Do you think me a fool? I'm not about to let that man free. Do you think I don't know that he's the only reason you're still with me? No. The chain stays."

Aware that the old man had had to urinate in the same area he was forced to sleep, Crissy pleaded once more for his welfare. "At least you could move him to a cleaner area."

"Woman, don't you understand plain English?" Drake enunciated, furious with her, but all the while unlocking the chain. "I told you I didn't want to bother with him, and I don't. Haven't you figured out yet who's in charge here?"

After allowing Crissy enough time to help the man to his feet so he could move to a cleaner area, he quickly wrapped the end of the chain around another support post and locked it. "There now. Will you finally shut up and let me get some sleep?"

"I'd feel better if he didn't have to have that chain around his leg at all. Look how the cuff is rubbing his leg raw. You really should set him free."

"Set him free?" He shook his head at such a ludicrous thought while he quickly gathered several old horse blankets and laid them one atop the other. "And have you two sneaking out of here the second I fall asleep? I don't think that would be too smart."

Drake pulled an old, torn saddle off a nearby railing, dusted it with his hand, and placed it at one end of the makeshift pallet. "I'm smart enough to know that by keeping him chained like that, I hold you both prisoner."

Still glowering at her, Drake snatched off his hat, set it on the ground beside the pallet, then raked his hands through his long brown hair. "Just remember one thing, Lahoma. If you try to run away, I *will* kill your grandfather. His life is still in your hands."

The old man lay on his side, scowling at Drake but said nothing to him.

"Now get some sleep. Both of you."

Drake brought the horses inside, then, without unsaddling them or extinguishing the lantern, he lay down on the pallet with his knife shoved inside his waistband and a rifle tucked up under the bedding, all within easy reach. "You're still awake over there. I thought I told you two to go to sleep."

"Can I at least go get him a drink of water?"

"You do and I'll shoot you both. Now go to sleep."

Exhausted and angry, Crissy sat down on the cold, silted dirt floor and leaned against a rough, planked wall. Eventually, she slept.

While dozing, the images inside her mind took a fresh turn. Suddenly she was in her car again, speeding along the shaded two-lane road, the summer wind whipping through the open windows, a small white car off in the distance. The car waited until she was nearly upon it, then, with excruciating slowness, pulled out onto the road in front of her. Like before, she turned the wheel as sharply as she could, but still clipped the back of the other car. Suddenly she was airborne again, smashing headlong into one tree, spinning about, then slamming hard into a second tree. Then a third. And a fourth. All the while the car she'd bought just two days earlier folded around her.

If it hadn't been for her seatbelt, she would have been thrown out the window. She was sure of that. But even with the belt holding her in place, she still suffered blow after blow from the crumpling car.

With vivid detail, she remembered blacking out, but coming to again as a result of the pain throbbing in her leg. Again she lay inside her car, pinned face down to the floor by some unseen part of the interior. Again, there was a sudden flash of bright blue followed by a gentle darkness filled with soft, beckoning voices. Voices she still didn't recognize—but at least this time understood.

"Your prayer has been heard and will be granted," said one deep voice, high above her head.

"You will not die," a second soft voice echoed from a different direction.

"Your offer to give up everything is acceptable," chimed still another.

"It is decided. You will be delivered from the pain and allowed to remain on earth awhile longer. It is an extraordinary gift. Make good use of it."

"Do only that which you think is right, and care not again for the material things you surrounded yourself with, for they will be gone."

"Accept your new fate without question," chanted the final voice, echoing softly.

A second flash of brilliant blue light brought Crissy awake with a start. Her heart hammered wildly inside her chest.

Three

Gil sat impatiently outside the bedroom door, waiting for Dr. Mack to come downstairs and check his patient. After what happened earlier; he refused to enter the bedroom alone. He could not afford another outburst of restless anger. It was too important he convince Lahoma Reed to name his brother's murderer, and he knew he would never accomplish that through anger or impatience.

Tapping his thumb on the scrolled arm of the scant wooden chair, he alternately watched the cabinet clock perched on a small table at one end of the hall and the empty staircase near the other. Finally just as the sky turned color outside, he heard a rustle in the room directly above him. Not long later, Dr. Mack appeared on the stairs.

"Good morning," he said to Gil. He glanced down to make a final adjustment to his black suspenders while headed toward him. It still being early morning, he had yet to put on a coat. "I see your deputy hasn't come by to replace you."

"No, not yet," Gil responded. Standing, he stretched first his long legs then his aching back. He wished now he had accepted the doctor's offer of a more comfortable chair. "But then I don't expect him here until at least eight o'clock." That was hours yet.

"Have you looked in on the patient yet?"

"Not since last night when I thought I heard noises outside," Gil answered honestly but without providing any of the particulars. His pulse quickened at the enticing memory of what almost happened. "She was fine then."

"Good." Dr. Mack turned toward the back of the house and

breathed deeply. "Smells like Minnie's cooking up a batch of bacon for breakfast. Hope we're having scrambled eggs, too. I'm hungry as a bear." He gave a loud smack of his lips as he reached for the doorknob. "But first I guess I'd better make sure Lahoma rested well. Maybe by now she's gotten back some of her memory and can finally tell you something about the man who killed Tom."

About to face Lahoma again, Gil smoothed the front of his crumpled shirt then moved into place behind the doctor. He fastened his gaze on the area where the bed would be when the door swung open and was surprised to find it empty.

"Looks like she's already up," the doctor said. He glanced back at Gil curiously then stepped inside the door.

Gil followed, scanning the room as he did. When he spotted the pushed out window webbing, his anger was immediate.

"She's escaped!"

Dr. Mack looked at him puzzled. *"Escaped?* From what?"

Gil did not answer. He was too angry to answer. Instead, he rushed to the window to see if by some remote chance she was still in sight.

"She's gone." He shook his head, unable to believe his own stupidity. "She slipped out that window as easy as you please."

"Gil?"

Feeling both betrayed and foolish, Gil turned to the doctor who stood beside the rumpled bed, scowling. "What is it, Doc?"

"I don't think she left of her own accord. I think someone broke in and forced her to leave. There's blood on her sheet and on the floor."

Gil's heart twisted at the mere mention of blood. *Lahoma's blood?* He crossed the room to see for himself. "Where?"

"Right there." The doctor pointed to the brown patches.

Gil's anger dissolved into fear and confusion. There was not enough blood to worry she was near death, at least not yet, but there was enough to indicate she had left unwillingly.

His heart hammered with brutal force when he realized the real reason Lahoma had refused to tell him the name of the man who killed his brother. She was not protecting the killer as he first thought. She was protecting herself, afraid the man would come back and hurt her.

Which obviously he had done.

And by not having believed her or protected her, Gil was responsible.

Crissy's pulse drummed a hard, frantic rhythm inside her sweat-soaked body. Frightened by the vivid dream, she glanced down at her hands and for the first time thought she detected a difference, however slight. Alert now to a possibility that everything happening was indeed real, she noticed her fingers looked a little longer than before, and that her hands were not quite as tan. Next she studied her arms, and after examining the knife slash, which showed slight signs of infection, she realized they were not as freckled as before and maybe not quite as long.

Stunned but still doubtful, she lifted the ragged, blood-splattered hem of her night gown to search for the childhood scar on her left knee, eager to prove she was imagining things—that no such changes had taken place. Panic pulsed through her when she discovered the jagged scar was not there.

Still not convinced such a change possible, she felt her face with her fingers; searching for similarities more than differences, but could not tell much merely by touching. She needed a mirror. She had to know if her face had in any way changed.

Glad Drake was still asleep and thinking there might be a mirror inside the old house, Crissy quietly stood. She tip-toed across the damp, cool earth to the barn door; knowing if Drake woke and found her trying to slip out the door, he'd think the worst. Blood rushed through her with incredible force as she slipped past him without a sound, but her pulse screeched to a sudden halt when one of the horses whinnied then shifted its weight.

Drake stirred, muttered, rolled over—and continued to sleep.

With that danger past and her pulse pounding so hard she could hear the sound in her ears, Crissy released the breath lodged in her throat. Slowly she parted the double doors. A creaking hinge made her legs quiver and her chest felt too small to hold her racing heart, but when even that noise did not rouse Drake, she slipped quietly outside.

She hardly noticed the first pink rays of the coming dawn or the scent of misty pine as she stole quickly across the neglected yard. Because the now ragged hem of her nightgown fell several inches above her ankles she did not have to bother lifting the material out of her way, but did have to be careful of sharp rocks and sticks.

Finally across the yard, she climbed onto the rough-planked porch of the battered old farmhouse and peered through the slats nailed across the largest window. Except for a broken chair and an overturned wooden box, the house looked empty. And if dust was any indication, the house had been empty for quite some time.

Disappointed to find no furniture, but still needing to prove that the strange dream meant nothing—that she was still herself and not someone else—she pulled hard on one of the wide planks nailed across the tall window. The protective board snapped off with amazing ease and exposed enough glass to reveal her re-flection on the darkened pane. She sucked in a sharp gasp and stared with disbelief as she touched a quivering hand to her cheek.

The face was not hers.

Blinking, she leaned forward for closer examination and no-ticed that her once pale green eyes were now dark brown and much larger than before. Her once slender face looked wider, her cheeks rounder, more shapely, and her hair was not just a shade darker, it was also thicker. She stared at an attractive mouth that looked fuller than before, then ran the tip of her tongue across her lower lip and blinked again when the reflection before her did the same. The image she saw was that of a beautiful stranger. Yet somehow she knew that beautiful stranger was her.

Stunned, Crissy stepped away from the window. Her heart sank like lead. She was not lost in some drug-induced hallucination after all. Everything around her was *real*. She really *was* off somewhere in Texas, trapped in the year 1876.

But that didn't make sense. Why would she be in Texas? And why in the year 1876? And why in someone else's body?

Patting her bare foot on the roughened floor in stunned, angry confusion, she glanced down at her body again. So similar yet now so very different. How could she not have noticed that the curves of her hips were rounder and her breasts a little larger? But even if she had would she have made the connection? Would she have believed it? Until that dream, would she have accepted it as real?

Bewildered, she shook her head to clear it of these strange thoughts, then again lifted her gaze to her surroundings. She still did not want to believe such a thing had happened, but at the same time could not prove that it hadn't.

She stood on collapsible legs and touched her face again, reminded anew of the changes. She wondered how she might go about undoing what had been done. Was this change permanent? Or was there a way to put things back the way they were? The way they should be—back at the tail end of the twentieth century, living a life of relative luxury.

She curled her hands into tight fists when she remembered one of the voices telling her to accept her new fate without question. *Without question.*

Her heart raced frantically, fearfully. It was clear now. She would not be waking up in some spotless hospital room to face her injuries after all. She was *already* awake. *This* was reality.

Trembling with the realization that everything from her past was now gone—her uncle, her business, her car, and her parents' estate—she stepped out into the yard. She stared at the dilapidated barn now framed by an awakening blue sky, then at the tangle of weeds and grass standing in places as high as her knees, then at a long, narrow water trough filled nearly to the top with rain water, and knew it was all as real as it could be.

At that last thought, her eyes widened more. That meant that Drake Stephens was real, too. As was the situation with the old man. And the bank robbery.

Frantic and at the same time angry to find herself in such a strange and dangerous situation, she spun about trying to decide the best direction to run. She had to get out of there—*before*

Drake woke up. She had to be free to figure out some way to return to the time and place where she really belonged.

With that thought, she hurried toward a small path that veered off into a nearby patch of woods, but stopped at the edge of the yard when she realized there was no known way for her to go back to where she was—or *forward* as it were. She'd been placed there by powers she didn't fully understand.

There was every chance she could be stuck in the late 1800s for good.

Frowning, she tried to remember what else the voices had told her, but was too frightened at the moment to remember. With her heart still hammering hard, she spun about and tried to decide what to do now that running seemed out of the question—especially when she didn't even know where she was or what direction she should take.

Crissy chewed nervously on the edge of her lip, aware she was in some serious trouble. Somehow, as a result of the accident and her impulsive bargaining with the powers that be, she had been transferred into the body of someone else—someone who had obviously helped rob a bank and murder Gil's brother. Her throat tightened as she looked down at her still trembling hands with disgust. Were they the hands of a murderer?

Trying to get a better grasp of the situation, Crissy wondered just how involved she'd been in that robbery and killing. Was she destined to spend the rest of whatever life she'd been given in jail for something she knew nothing about? Again she considered running, but stopped when it dawned on her that if she did run away, Drake would make good his threat and kill that helpless old man inside the barn. If that happened, she'd be guilty of having helped murder *two* people. She could not bear the thought.

She had no choice. She could not run. Would not run. Not until that gentle old man was safe. Somehow she had to convince Drake Stephens to set him free.

Aware now that Drake held her prisoner as surely as if he'd chained her, too, Crissy wasted no further time on thought. She scooped water from one of the animal troughs with a pan lid she found lying on the ground and returned to the barn to give the old man a a drink.

Careful not to rouse Drake who still slept fitfully on his make-shift pallet, she woke the old man quietly and helped him sit up and take a long drink. By the time he'd gulped the last of it, some of his strength had returned and he was able to sit alone with his back propped against the same support that held him prisoner.

"Thank you," he rasped in a throaty whisper. He looked at her with pale, grateful eyes that were neither blue nor green. "And I am so sorry."

"Sorry?" she asked, also whispering, for she did not want to face Drake yet—not now that she knew he was real. "For what?"

"For what you've had to go through because I was just too blame old to fight that lowlife, no account varmint." He cut an angry gaze at Drake, but when he looked at her again, it was with sad, caring eyes.

Crissy was touched by his apology and by his sincerity. That made her more determined than ever to see this man safe. "Don't worry about any of that," she said, feeling a strong need to comfort him. She touched his stubbled cheek with her fingers and felt an ache deep in her heart that made her wish he really was her grandfather. "You just worry about getting out of here."

He attempted a weak smile. "I want you to know that I don't believe you had anything to do with Thomas Walters's murder like that mongrel said." He gestured toward Drake with a short, angry thrust of his chin. His hazel eyes narrowed. "I know you better than that."

"Thank you," she said, glad to know that whoever she had become, at least one person still respected her. "But for now we have to concentrate on getting away. We need to find some way to get your strength back."

She glanced around, then noticed the saddles and gear still on the horses. Putting a finger to her lips to caution for quiet, she tiptoed to the horses and checked the various pouches. Although there was no human food to be found, two of the small bags tied onto the saddles were filled with raw oats.

Grabbing two heaping handfuls; she headed back toward the old man. Her legs nearly gave out from under her when she heard

Drake mutter her name before she made it halfway. With eyes
wide and heart racing: she turned to face him, wondering how
she would explain having stolen food obviously meant for the
horses and was relieved to discover his back was to her. He'd
muttered while rolling from his back onto his side.

Letting out a trapped breath, she quickly returned to the old
man's side.

"Here," she told him, whispering more softly than before.
"Eat this. It's not much, but won't hurt you and should help you
get back some of your strength."

"Lahoma, you are as resourceful as that half-Indian grandmother you were named after," he told her with a proud smile,
then ate obligingly.

Aware now that she had somehow become this Lahoma Reed
everyone kept talking about, she considered asking him something about the grandmother he mentioned. But before she could,
Drake awoke with a start.

She turned in time to watch him blink several times then scowl
at her when he propped up on one elbow.

"Oh, what a touching scene," he commented, his voice gruff
and cutting as he pushed himself into a seated position. "You
kneeling there, trying to comfort your poor, ailing grandfather."

He reached beneath his bedding and pulled out his rifle, an
action that put Crissy on immediate alert.

"Get away from him," he said then glanced at a small, dirty
window near the double doors. "It's daylight now. Time for us
to get a move on."

He rolled to his feet, checked to make sure his knife was still
tucked inside a hidden sheath, then headed for his horses.

Seeing both anger and fear in the older man's eyes, Crissy
reached out to pat his hand reassuringly.

"Damn," Drake muttered more to himself than to either of
them. "I forgot to feed those animals last night before I fell
asleep." He tilted his head while he considered that. "No time
to feed them now. They'll just have to wait until later."

Turning to face Crissy again, he pulled a small key out or his
shirt pocket and pitched it to her. "Here, unlock the old man
while I take the horses outside and let them get a drink." He

reached for the reins, then cut back to her with an angry glower. "And don't you or your grandfather try anything foolish. I'll be right outside that door with this rifle loaded and ready." He held the weapon high to verify the danger. "I'll gladly shoot you both if you try to make a run for it.' He paused a moment then shook his head and chuckled at his own foolishness. "As if that starving old man could run anywhere."

Clearly amused, he led the horses outside and left Crissy to unlock the man's chain, first at the post, then from around his leg. Her heart went out to him when she saw how bloody and raw the metal cuff had left his ankle.

"Can you stand on that leg?" she asked, not at all sure he could.

"I think so," he said and frowned with determination while Crissy helped him to his feet. He tested his weight on the injured leg then grinned. "See there?" Now that he no longer whispered, Crissy detected a definite Texas drawl. "I'm fit as a worn-out fiddle."

She wanted to laugh and would have had Drake not chosen that moment to reenter the barn. The water that wet the dark stubble on his face let her know he'd taken time to wash at least his face. And the way his hair lay smooth again showed he'd also combed through his hair.

"You two get a move on. The horses are nearly finished drinking and as soon as they are, we're riding out."

He walked over, took the man who was supposed to be her grandfather by the arm, and pulled him roughly toward the door

Crissy's anger returned immediately. How could anyone treat a sweet, gentle man like that?

"Come on, Lahoma, we don't have all day," Drake shouted back over his black-clad shoulder just before he and the stumbling grandfather disappeared outside.

Reminded again just how real and how dangerous the situation was, Crissy thought about the torn piece of sleeve she'd tossed on the side the road the night before. Glancing down at the angry, red cut on her arm, she hoped that the sheriff would spot the bloodied piece of cloth and have enough sense to know it was hers, and also enough skill to follow the horses' tracks all the way there.

To provide a similar clue should they be gone by the time the sheriff finally arrived, she tore a small piece of lace off the skirt of her tattered gown and dropped it on the barn floor in plain sight. She then hurried outside to join the others so Drake would have no reason to discover what she'd done.

With the horses finished drinking and still saddled, Drake turned to watch as she approached. He gestured to the black horse she'd ridden the night before with a quick swipe of his arm. "Mount up. Both of you. Joseph, first."

Hoping to leave the man, Joseph, safely behind, Crissy frowned as if annoyed, then gestured to him with a brisk flick of her hand. "Why are we taking him along? Look at the way he's leaning against that fence. He's so weak from lack of food and water he can hardly stand. I'll just end up spending most of my day struggling to keep him in the saddle. We'd make much better time without him."

Drake looked at Joseph then at her and rubbed his chin.

Aware he was considering the complaint, she went on, "You said yourself we have no time to waste. Taking him along will just slow us down."

"You could be right." He cut his gaze from Joseph to her then back to Joseph. "And we do need to make good time today." Finally he nodded. "Okay, your grandfather stays here."

He walked over to the fence where the frail man supported his weight with two spindly arms and wagged a finger in his gaunt, stubbled face. "Look, here, Joseph Mackey. I don't want any trouble out of you." He gestured toward Crissy with a backward jerk of his hand. "You just remember that I have your grand-daughter and will hurt her plenty if anyone tries to come after us. Do you understand that?"

Joseph nodded that he did.

"Good," Drake replied then smiled happily, obviously pleased with himself. "As long as you understand, I guess it is safe to tell you that there is a little community called Bethel only a mile southeast of here. When you feel up to walking, you can go there for help. Just don't tell anyone which direction we took. And don't tell them anything about where we're going. If you do, and somebody catches up with us, your granddaughter won't live to see jail. I'll kill her on the spot. So watch what you say."

Not trusting Drake to have told the truth about the nearby community, and knowing the man did not have the strength to walk far, Crissy waited until she was again on her horse and riding one step behind Drake's before she turned to look back at Joseph Mackey and mouthed the words, "Stay there."

Remembering how determined Gil Walters was to find his brother's killer, she felt that eventually their trail should lead the sheriff to that old house and barn. Her heart fluttered at that last thought, aware now that if Drake was real, and Joseph was real, and her situation was real, that meant that Gil was real, too.

That thought alone gave her new hope.

Dressed in the tattered white gown with her hair steaming down her shoulders in desperate need of a combing, Crissy rode the first hour in silence. While absently working her fingers through the ends of the thick, tangled tresses, her thoughts strayed to possible ways out of her present dilemma. Several ideas presented themselves, but none seemed logical enough or safe enough to try.

While her horse continued to clomp along one step behind and to the side of his, a bushy-tailed gray squirrel assumed an alert stance just as the two horses approached a fallen log where it played. But Crissy remained too lost in thought to notice.

She was too busy trying to grip the that fact she was now in someone else's body, trapped in another time period. As incredible as it seemed, she was no longer Christina Townson, the wealthy daughter of the late Dr. Roger Townson, the niece of Dr. Jack Owen, and the sole owner of an exclusive chain of exercise clubs. She was someone else entirely. Someone about the same age called Lahoma Reed. Someone with a dear, sweet grandfather and a half-Indian grandmother. Someone who for some reason unknown to her helped Drake Stephens rob a bank and maybe even kill a man.

Her heart sank as she realized what she had been forced to give up, a life of ease and luxury, a life in which she could have, and *did* have practically everything she ever wanted. It was all so unfair. But at the same time she remembered the pain she'd felt, the horror she saw, and her desperate plea to live. She also remembered promising to give up everything she had if the pain would just go away.

At first Crissy had felt angry over what happened, but eventually she realized she had no right to be. She never stipulated any terms to her desperate plea. She never stated that she wanted to continue living *in the same body* as before—only that she wanted to continue living. It had never occurred to her such stipulation was needed. But then, never in her wildest dreams would she have believed such a thing possible.

She looked again at the body she'd been given and wondered what happened to whoever had been inside that body before. Was the real Lahoma Reed gone forever, or had they simply traded places? Perhaps Lahoma had awakened to find herself in a modern hospital room, Uncle Jack seated nearby, worried sick. What would she think when she discovered how incredibly wealthy she was? Or perhaps that other body had been left vacant and Christina Townson was now dead. She shuddered at the thought, then realized what a remarkable gift she'd been given.

Although she might not be in the best of situations at that particular moment, she was still alive. Had she not been given the second chance, she might very well not be—and life in itself was important.

She looked up into a sun-filled sky and thought of Gil again. Smiling, she realized he was the most pleasant aspect or the whole situation. She hoped he would spot the pieces of cloth she'd left behind then come find her. Her heart fluttered as thoughts of how she might reward him for saving her from Drake flitted across her mind. Now that she knew the wildly attractive sheriff was real, which meant the strong feelings she felt for him were also real, she was willing to do whatever it took to make him a lasting part of her life. She smiled wider, knowing that although she no longer had the material things she'd owned before, there was a good chance she could end up having something even better. She remembered hearing him say that he'd once loved her, and that memory alone made her feel all warm and tingly inside, more so than she ever expected.

"What are you grinning about?" Drake asked, having glanced over his shoulder and found her rocking pleasantly in the saddle.

"Nothing," she answered, quickly sobering. Then, for no reason other than she felt it was what he wanted to hear, she added, "Just thinking of what we'll be able to buy with all that money."

His eyebrows arched with obvious disbelief. "You aren't still angry with me for the way I forced you to help me?"

"Not anymore," she answered, aware she must have been before. "Not now that I've had more time to think about it."

He looked very pleased by that response but didn't say more. After a few minutes of silence, Crissy commented on their direction. "Aren't we headed south? Isn't that back in the same general direction we came? I thought you said we were headed for Louisiana."

"We will be, eventually," Drake answered. "But first we're headed for Glade Creek just outside town. That's where I hid the money. I didn't want to take the chance of getting caught with it, so I buried it under a huge pile of leaves before going back to get you."

He glanced at her again. "But because I don't want to end up head to head with the sheriff or any of his men, who will be hot on our trail by now, we're taking the long way around. As soon as we've collected the money, we'll head on over to Longview where we can dump these horses and buy train tickets to Shreveport."

With no intention of taking off to Shreveport with him, and at the same time wondering how he planned to get her on a train dressed like a ragged waif, Crissy again considered a possible escape. She would wait until they'd traveled farther from the abandoned farm where they had left her grandfather—where Drake had indicated he could easily return should he *need* to— then make a run for it. Waiting would also give Gil more time to get there and ensure Joseph's safety.

Her heart hammered while she plotted her escape. With Drake riding just a little ahead of her like that, she should be able to get at least a small head start on him. Maybe that would be all she needed.

With that plan in mind, Crissy rode along quietly. After several more minutes, Drake spoke again.

"I want you to know that I never meant to kill Tom Walters. I really had no choice. I know you weren't close enough to see, but right after Tom recognized me, he pulled a pistol on me. I had to shoot him."

Crissy frowned knowing at least part of what he told her did not ring true. Tom never recognized Drake. If he *had,* he would have told Gil. Hers would not have been the only name to pass his lips before he died.

"Do you think he would have shot you?" She studied him closely.

"He would have tried," Drake answered with a defensive lift or his chin. "And I couldn't take the chance of being hurt. Not with all my plans finally coming true."

"Plans?"

"To get my hands on the money we need to get married and live in style." He looked at her grimly. "And we *are* still getting married, just as soon as we're a safe enough distance away."

The thought of marrying a man like Drake sent chills through Crissy, but she decided not to say anything to anger him. Not if she wanted to catch him off guard later. "Where? In Shreveport?"

"Probably," he answered then fell silent again.

Tired from all the physical and emotional exertion, Crissy let the matter drop. Her thoughts eventually turned to her uncle and how much she needed him and missed him. At that moment, she wanted nothing more than to return to the twentieth century where she could be safe again. But when she remembered how near death she'd been, she decided she should be grateful for what life she now had. At least she had no injuries other than the stinging cut on her arm and the dull, drawing ache in her thighs and calves from having ridden too long.

Still, she wished she could hurry and find a way out of her trouble so she could turn her energies to figuring out just how to deal with living in such a strange, new world. After that, her thoughts turned again to Gil Walters, causing her pulse to quicken when she realized how desperately she hoped the tall, handsome sheriff figured into whatever the future now held for her. The exhilarating memory of his gentle touch and of his tantalizing kiss stirred her imagination and sent her heart soaring—and gave her all the more reason to try to escape Drake Stephens.

"Almost there," Drake said, temporarily yanking Crissy's thoughts from the possibility of a future with Gil.

Drake steered his horse off the narrow dirt road and started through a small thicket, clearly expecting her to follow. Crissy's heart vaulted, aware the time had come to make her break. She let her horse fall further behind and was several yards away when Drake reined to a halt near a rambling, shallow creek.

Crissy waited until Drake had dropped to the ground and was busy uncovering the satchel of money before turning her horse and prodding it into a dead run.

Four

"Lahoma!" Drake shouted the second he realized what she'd done. "Lahoma, come back here." She heard rustling then his footsteps on the hard ground as he bounded again for his horse.

Having no idea where she was or where she was headed, Crissy allowed the horse its head. She knew Drake would take only seconds to remount and head after her. She had to make every one of those seconds count.

"Lahoma, I said come back here!"

Holding the reins with one hand and the saddle with the other, Crissy concentrated on not falling off, unaccustomed to riding a loping animal. She knew if she fell she'd be immediately trampled by Drake's horse.

Her heartrate vaulted again when seconds later three shots sounded in rapid succession. But either Drake hadn't really aimed at her or he was a terrible gunman, because none of the three shots met their mark, and the sound caused her horse to run harder still.

Leaning forward to make less of a target, she continued to hold on for dear life. She didn't dare look back for fear she would lose her balance, and desperately hoped that she was putting distance between them. But scant minutes later his horse overtook hers and he snatched the reins right out of her hands.

"That will cost you, Lahoma," he said after pulling both horses to an abrupt halt. Holding her reins in a death grip, he glowered at her then bent forward to catch his breath. "That will cost you dearly."

With both horses now winded and the money satchel safely

tucked inside his saddlebags, Drake headed down the tree-dappled creek toward a nearby farm house. Although the house and outbuildings were well kept, which meant someone lived there, only a cow in the barn answered when Drake called out their arrival.

"Looks like no one's home," he said unnecessarily, then quickly dropped to the ground and led both horses to a nearby water trough where they drank greedily.

Crissy stayed in the saddle, terrified of what Drake might try in retaliation for what she'd done, while he poured the feed he carried onto a board for the horses to eat. When he finished, he pointed to the ground and ordered her down. "I haven't eaten since early yesterday morning. We're going inside so you can cook us up something to eat."

Seeing how angry he still was, Crissy knew better than to object. Quietly, she slid to the ground and headed toward the house, wondering which window he'd break to get in. To her amazement the house had no locks, and even if it had, the windows had been left open. Entry proved as easy as turning a doorknob.

Inside, Drake set the money satchel and his rifle atop a work table then watched while Crissy moved about the kitchen contemplating how to make use of the huge iron stove and the different food items she found stashed inside tall canisters. Being part of the microwave generation, she rarely cooked anything from scratch and *never* without a recipe. Peeking inside cabinets, she worried what he might do to her if she didn't produce something edible. Finally, she opened a large, upright wooden box that obviously passed as a refrigerator and found several eggs and a half-filled pitcher of milk inside. She decided to make scrambled eggs.

"Could you light the stove for me?" she asked, knowing she'd never figure out how, then proceeded to search for a small pan to cook the eggs.

"I've been thinking," Drake said, coming toward her instead of heading for the stove. "While we're here, we should try to find you something more suitable to wear." He pointed to a door on the opposite side of the room. "Let's see if the lady of this house has anything you can wear."

"But I thought you were hungry." She gestured to the eggs, thinking he might be in a better mood and be more likely to relax his guard again if he'd eat.

"Finding you clothes to wear is more important. Look at you. We can't go into Longview and board a train with you dressed like that." There was enough anger in his expression to prevent her from arguing. "People would ask too many questions."

"Okay, I'll go see what I can find while you light that stove." She headed toward the door he'd indicated, not at all surprised when he followed only a few steps behind.

Down a short hall and to the left, she found what was obviously the master bedroom and entered. Seeing no closets, she headed for a tall cabinet and opened the double doors. Inside she found several garments on brass hooks and pulled them out to have a closer look at them. Some were readily identifiable as dresses, skirts, or blouses. As for the others, she could only guess their use.

She held several up to try to judge their size. Obviously the woman who lived there was not much larger than she was.

"Try that one on," Drake said, pointing to a long pink garment with white ruffles and white sleeves. "That looks about right for traveling."

"Okay," she said agreeably, then waited for him to step out of the room. When instead he walked over to a tall four-poster bed and sat down, her heart thumped hard inside her chest.

"What are you waiting for?" he asked then rested his hand on the knife handle half-hidden inside his waistband. The same knife he'd cut her with the night before.

"I was hoping you'd step out into the hall," she said, her skin crawling at the thought of having to undress in front of him.

"And have you try to escape again?" He snorted at the thought. "There isn't even webbing on those windows. Hurry up and try that thing on."

Afraid to argue, Crissy draped the pink and white garment over a nearby rocking chair then reached back into the cabinet to see if there was anything that looked even remotely like underwear.

She felt Drake's gaze follow her every movement while she pulled out several more items and tried to decide what was what. Eventually she found enough underclothing to cover everything she considered vital, and was about to try to slip the chemise on under her gown when he shouted at her.

"Take the gown off first."

Crissy saw the desire glinting in his green eyes and shifted nervously. "No. Not with you staring at me like that."

Drake's gaze darkened as he slid off the bed. His hand still cupped the handle of his knife when he moved closer. "I said to take off that gown."

"And I said no." She met his gaze bravely, though inside she felt like jelly. "I won't."

"Oh, yes you *will*." His lips peeled away from clenched teeth as he moved closer still. "You will take your clothes off for me just like you took your clothes off for Gil Walters two months ago. You are not going to put me off any longer."

Aware he meant to do more than simply watch her dress, Crissy backed away. She glanced at the open windows and realized they were her closest means of escape.

Still backing away; she tried to get her bearings enough to figure out which direction the horses would be from there. "I don't know what you are talking about."

"The hell you don't." His eyes narrowed. As if sensing her plan, he cut at an angle that placed him between her and the windows. "Quit pretending to be so pure and innocent. I know for a fact that you already gave your body to Gil Walters. Willingly. And you will now do the same for me." He continued to move toward her, backing her against a wall. One hand stretched out while the other quietly slid the knife out of the sheath hidden beneath his belt. "Willing or not."

Remembering just how sharp the knife was, Crissy glanced around for something to use as a weapon, but there was nothing in that area of the bedroom.

His grip tightened as he turned the knife so the tip pointed out. "You didn't know it, but I was there that day you two slipped off to have your private little picnic just outside town. Knowing he was the one courting you instead of me, I followed, then watched with disgust while you two peeled each other out of your clothes and made love right there in the field. I swore then that one day you would do the same for me." A muscle in his jaw jumped spasmodically. "And, Lahoma, that day is today. You may not *love* me the same way you say you love him, but you will *make* love to me the same. You will do for me everything you did for him, but with one difference. In the end, you will marry me." Only a few feet away, he gestured to her gown with a flick of the knife. "Off with it."

More angry than afraid, Crissy spied a metal penny bank on a dresser across the room and decided that should make a pretty good dent in his head.

Not wanting to alert him to the plan, she took a deep, calming breath, then lifted her hands to the buttons of her gown. While pretending to be unfastening the garment, she started across the room, but he grabbed her by the arm and stopped her.

"Where do you think you are going?"

"To see if I can find a brush," she answered with amazing quickness. "So I can brush my hair for you."

"I don't need your hair brushed." Impatiently, he made a grab for the front of her gown, then jumped back when a shot rang out, splintering a wall only two feet away. "What the—"

Startled, Crissy gasped then turned to see who had fired the shot. Relief flooded her to her very soul to see Gil standing just outside an open window, smoking pistol in hand.

"Drop the knife and step back, Drake," he said, then he carefully pulled himself up through the window.

Reluctantly, Drake tossed the knife in Gil's direction, took only a couple of steps back, then waited until Gil was inside the room headed toward him before lunging forward, snatching up the knife again, and making a fresh grab for Crissy, catching her by the arm.

Aware that Drake did not have a good hold on her, and refusing to let him have any advantage over Gil, Crissy jerked free and dove for cover behind the bed, striking her head in the very same place as before on the jutting corner of a window ledge when she did.

Caught in a vacuum of pain so overwhelming it would not let her breathe, she crawled under the bed where she'd be safer but could still watch what happened, then grasped her stinging head with both hands. The pain proved so immediate and so blinding she could barely see past the gray haze when Drake scrambled through the door and darted from sight.

Gil shot again and missed. Then, while she watched him squat low near the door and fling himself into the hall only seconds behind Drake, she slipped into the a void of now familiar darkness.

A tiny flicker of light stirred in the distance. Crissy tried to wake up but couldn't. She heard her uncle's voice calling her from somewhere far away and attempted to respond, but no sound came forth. Although she could not open her eyes or move her hands to feel, she knew she was lying on something cold and hard—*like an emergency room or an operating room table.*

While she continued her struggle to surface from the dark, curling gray haze, she sadly realized the whole thing had all been a dream. Just one long, strange, but oddly compelling dream. She had never really gone back in time. Never really took over someone else's body. Never really met and fell in love with a tall, handsome man named Gil Walters. It had all been some drug-induced dream like she'd originally believed. The only *gift* she had received since the accident was that of sedation, to help her through her time of pain and initial healing.

Disappointed and angry, yet at the same time relieved to finally have a reasonable explanation for everything that happened, she tried again to force her eyelids apart, but they refused to open. Instead, she felt the darkness pulling at her again and she slipped willingly back into it.

Her uncle's voice faded in the distance.

When Crissy tried once more to surface from the darkness, she was no longer lying on something cold and hard. Instead, she felt herself wrapped in softness and warmth. There were muted voices talking to each other nearby. Although none proved quite discernible, she knew they were not the voices of angels. These were the voices of real people. People in charge of her care.

With a heavy heart, Crissy opened her eyes, expecting to see her uncle and several nurses hovering nearby. She was pleasantly surprised when, instead, she saw Gil Walters leaning over her, looking deeply concerned. She glanced past him and her heart soared even higher. She was not in a hospital. She was still inside that farmhouse—only now she was lying on the bed instead of on the floor *under* it. Trembling with joyful disbelief, she cut her gaze to a clinking sound and saw Dr. Mack mixing medicine into a small glass of water. Beside him stood an unknown woman who looked not much older than she was.

Crissy blinked, then looked at Gil again, so thrilled the past few days had not been a dream she was about to burst. "What happened?"

Gil smiled, clearly relieved she was well enough to speak. He touched her cheek with the curve of his palm, sending tingles of elation through her.

"What happened is that you hit your head again," Gil said with a perplexed grin. "Same spot as before, only this time you broke the skin and had to have a few stitches."

Crissy lifted her hand and felt the small bandage. The area was extremely tender to her touch. "What about Drake? Did he get away?" She looked down to see if Gil was injured, relieved to find he was not.

"No. We caught him," Gil assured her. He explained, "I was not alone when I followed you here."

"You followed us?"

He nodded and gently brushed a strand of dark hair from her face. "I was following the tracks leading out of town on a road not far away when I heard gunshots over by Glade Creek. Thinking they could have something to do with you, I decided to check them out and arrived just in time to catch a glimpse of him leading your horse by the reins toward this house. I waited for the two deputies riding with me to catch up, then we advanced on the house together." He looked chagrined, almost apologetic when he admitted, "I was supposed to wait until the other two had had plenty of time to enter the house from the front, but I just couldn't do that after I looked inside and saw what Drake was about to do. I had to try to take him by myself."

"I'm glad you were there," she said, smiling gratefully up into the face of her hero. She tried not to think about what might have happened had she been forced to fight Drake alone.

"So am I," he replied, then grinned. "I'm also glad I waited at least long enough to overhear some of what was being said between you two."

She frowned at such an odd statement and tried to remember the conversation. "Like what?"

"Like Drake's comments about who you really love," he told her, his blue eyes twinkling. "I know now that what you did in town, you did because you had to, not because you had fallen in love with someone else and were trying to please him. Drake eventually admitted, albeit reluctantly, that you never wanted to cooperate with him at all. But after he kidnapped your grandfather and threatened to kill him, he left you little choice but to do his bidding. The only reason you helped him rob that bank was to save your grandfather's life."

Crissy nodded. That was pretty much the way she had it figured. "And *is* he safe now?"

"By now he is. After Drake told me where I would find him, I sent Mrs. Hinze's husband over to get him and bring him back here. He gestured to the woman standing quietly near the doctor, obviously Mrs. Hinze.

"Lahoma, I want to apologize for every wrong thing I thought about you. I was very upset about my brother and wasn't thinking straight. Can you ever forgive me for believing you could have ever had a hand in Tom's murder, and for having threatened you the way I did? I should have known you could never toss away our past like that."

Glad to know that the person's body she had entered really was not such a bad person after all, and having fallen deeply in love with Gil in the short time she'd known him, Crissy smiled brightly.

"Yes, I think I can manage to forgive you if you can accept the fact that I really *don't* remember everything from our past just yet." Crissy decided pretending amnesia would be easier than trying to convince him of the truth—that she was there as a result of a very special gift. Maybe one day she would try to explain it all to him, but for now, she'd let matters be.

"Yes, I can accept that now," he said, then took her hand in his. "And I will do everything within my power to see that eventually you remember it all."

The doctor, seeing the looks of adoration in Crissy's and Gil's eyes, motioned for Mrs. Hinze to step out into the hall with him.

Gil waited until they were alone then bent forward to kiss Crissy gingerly, first on the cheek opposite her injury, then on the mouth. "Is there any chance you've forgiven me enough to again consider marrying me?"

Crissy stared at him, amazed. Her heart soared to new heights when she realized just how wonderful this gift was. Suddenly she had no desire to go back to the twentieth century. No desire to have any of those material things back in her life.

Oddly enough, she had everything she ever wanted right here. She just didn't know that until now.

"Yes, Gil, I'll marry you," she told him, then quietly added, "Just as soon as my grandfather's cotton crop is in and he's all set for the winter."

About the Author

Rosalyn Alsobrook, who is married to her high school sweet-heart, lives in Gilmer, Texas. She has two sons and one grand-child. Rosalyn's newest time travel romance, *Beyond Forever,* is currently on sale at bookstores everywhere. She is also the author of the time travel romance, *Time Storm,* and a number of historical romances.

Whispers in the Night

Barbara Benedict

One

"What am I doing here?"

Whispering to herself, daunted by the eerie quiet of the place, Julie Ward stared at the ornate iron gate with a mixture of excitement and dread. Down that secluded driveway was her miracle house, a shining symbol of the start of a new life. Yet it was hard to hope and plan when amnesia clouded her future, when she never knew when ghosts from the past might pop up to haunt her.

Gripping the steering wheel of the convertible, she tried to peer through the thick stand of oaks and maples guarding the drive. Last night, she and her roommate, Gwen, had tried to envision the house she'd so unexpectedly inherited, but none of their imaginings included this tree-lined drive and huge iron gate. Dangling by a lone remaining screw, a rusted name plate spelled *Delange,* the name of the unknown benefactor who'd left Julie this house. Was William Delange one of her ghosts, she wondered, or just a crazy old man who'd taken pity when he'd seen her bewildered face displayed in the media?

"Who are you?" she asked the face in the rearview mirror. She often felt as if her blond hair and blue eyes belonged to a stranger, the woman the media trotted out for public scrutiny. After two years, she'd yet to get used to the borrowed identity— Juliet, after the kindly lady who'd found her wandering in the streets of New York, and Ward, as in ward of the state.

Who needed a past? Gwen would say, offering to share her huge family with its umpteen cousins. But watching them interact at each holiday made Julie feel increasingly lonely. Surely, she too must have roots somewhere—people who loved her—and she had to grasp at any straw to find them. Gwen might call it wishful thinking, but Julie clung to the hope that old Mr. Delange left her his house for a purpose, that by coming here, maybe she could find the key to unlock her past.

So it was foolish to hesitate now, here at the virtual doorstep, merely because a driveway filled her with a sudden need to shiver. Jamming the car in gear, she drove it down the long, winding tunnel of ancient oaks. Entwining overhead, heavy limbs blocked the sun, making it suddenly dark, and a good ten degrees cooler. As the breeze rustled through the branches, she thought she heard it whisper, "Betrayed."

She was imagining things, she told herself as she stubbornly drove forward. And no wonder, since she'd had the dream again last night, that hazy, recurring exercise in panic. Waking in the morning, she could only remember her terror, never the details, except for the single, whispered word, "Betrayed."

With great relief, she emerged from the trees into bright sunlight. The breeze shifted, bringing the cool, briny scent of Long Island Sound. She inhaled deeply, reassured, for it reinforced her image of a summer home, a quaint cottage on the beach. Smiling, she planned how she'd set up her easel on the porch. She'd discovered during her stint at the hospital that painting was something she did well.

Yet as the drive wound up a hill, her visions of a cozy cottage faded. To her right was what must once have been a huge expanse of lawn, before dandelions and goldenrod got the upper hand. Mentally calculating the amount of equipment and gardeners it would take to mow it, she was caught completely off guard as she rounded the curve and the house sprang into view.

Braking abruptly, she could only gape.

Poised on the rise was no simple cottage, but rather a mountain of a house, a showplace to rival Jay Gatsby's wildest dreams. Like Fitzgerald's hero, it, too wore an air of mystery, a lingering sadness rooted in the past. Four stories tall, with steep, gabled attics beneath the eaves, its weathered gray walls stretched in a horseshoe, with each wing facing the sea. Its host of windows must once have offered limitless vistas of sky and sea, but now each stood heavily draped or tightly shuttered. In the center, a large oak door discouraged entry, adding to the forlorn effect.

This was no summer place shut down for the season. Peeling paint and missing shingles spoke of a once proud home, abandoned to the elements and left to fend for itself. Sturdy construction helped it stand the test of time, but the days of joy and laughter had long since faded away.

Entranced, Julie drove up to it, drawn by the emotion that emanated from its walls. A family had laughed in that house, she felt certain. People had loved and dreamed there. More than she thought possible, she longed to have been part of it.

She was out of the car and tugging at a knob that wouldn't budge before realizing she had neither the key nor the legal right to go inside—not until the official meeting with the lawyers next week. She'd come to see the place, not take possession of it.

Yet it was with an intense possessiveness that she circled the house, here and there touching the weathered boards, taking in each minute detail. At the end of the right wing, a glint of metal caught her eye. Squeezing through a tangle of bushes, she came upon a hidden doorway.

She stood before it, hand on the brass knob. The brain has its reasons for choosing to forget, the doctors had warned, and a person often did more harm than good by forcing a memory. Too clearly, she could hear Gwen's warnings. Even if Delange had been a relative—a prospect her roommate found unlikely—why then had Julie forgotten him? Surely she wouldn't turn her back on a past that was pleasant. Having gotten the letter a mere two days ago, maybe she should wait to hear what the lawyer had to say about her mysterious benefactor before venturing into a situation that could prove a minefield to her hard-won peace of mind.

Walk through this door and she could well be opening her own Pandora's box.

Nonetheless, she turned the knob and the door squeaked open on rusty hinges, revealing a set of dark, narrow stairs. Heart pounding in her chest, she faced the stairway, torn by the same mixture of excitement and dread she'd known at the gate. Julie could sympathize with poor, silly Pandora as she gingerly took each step. Curiosity, and perhaps longing, drew her forward, even while logic decreed that she stop. After all, if she'd found that open door, then so too could some desperate vagrant.

Yet it wasn't the known threat that set her trembling; it was the *un*known that terrified her.

Something waited up there. She could feel it in the air, growing heavier with each step, every breath. An oppressive sadness, a sense of . . .

Betrayed.

She froze, wondering why that word from her nightmare continued to haunt her. Why here, why now, when everything else about this house seemed warm and welcoming?

Shaking off the negative feelings, she pushed on to the top step, where she emerged into a spacious loft. Instant warmth surrounded her. She felt as if she'd just come home.

She spun, taking in her surroundings. Sparsely furnished, the loft held a small table in the corner, a gilt-edged mirror to her right, a shelf with painting supplies, and a dozen mounted canvases stacked against the far wall. There was a second door, now standing closed, but more than enough light spilled into the room from two overhead skylights and a large bay window. Going over to sit on the richly upholstered seat lining the window, she found the three separate panes looked northward over the sound. A person could sit there and gaze at the water for hours, but stroking the plush cushions, Julie ached with the need to paint.

Restless, she crossed the room to the canvases. Lifting them up for inspection, she found one surface after another blank, waiting to be filled with color. Whimsically, she imagined William Delange learning of her talent, demanding that she must come here and paint in his house.

The fantasy dissolved when she looked down and saw the portrait.

It made her feel faint, the sight of that happy girl with features so like her own. Staring in helpless bewilderment, she denied that it could be her. The girl was young, barely twenty, her clothing from the early 1900s. It couldn't be Julie; she wouldn't be born for nearly another fifty years.

The girl stood at the edge of the sea, bare feet in the water, ankle-length skirt damp at the hem. In one hand she clasped an old-fashioned sun bonnet; the other hand reached for the cloud of golden hair blowing about her face. She was laughing, dancing, bursting with happiness. All around her, the artist had created a scene so vivid, Julie could almost smell brine, hear gulls screech overhead, feel the summer sun warm her heart.

Julie stared at the face in the painting, daunted by the resemblance—and by her response to it. Was the girl a relative, her grandmother perhaps? If so, shouldn't she feel a sense of belonging, some *deja vu*. It was more likely it was a chance resemblance. Having seen Julie on television, Mr. Delange had brought her here, hoping she'd take the girl's place in his life.

But then there could be other relatives, disinherited malcontents who would wish her ill. Gwen was right. Julie knew so little of her situation, its potential dangers. With a frisson of fear, she glanced up, startled to find troubled blue eyes staring back at her.

It was her reflection—the same sad stranger who gazed back at her from the mirror each morning.

Like a sleepwalker, she went to the gilt-framed mirror across the room, staring at the woman trapped within the glass. She had the same color hair and eyes as the girl in the portrait, but her features were far paler, the expression pained. Julie reached out as she neared, and her reflection stretched forward with undisguised yearning.

As her fingers brushed the glass, the fluttering in her chest picked up tempo. Was her mind playing tricks again, or did she actually hear a vague, distant chanting?

In dreamlike fashion, the room in the mirror wavered, grew blurry. Awash with a warm tingling, Julie watched the face in the glass slowly, subtly alter. The eyes began to sparkle; the lips wore the same youthful smile as the girl in the painting.

Jean shorts and blue cambric shirt gave way to the unflattering gray cotton shirtwaist of a turn-of-the-century British servant. Her shoulder-length hair had grown, reaching to her waist in a long, tight braid. Awed by the transformation, Julie tried to touch the image, but her arm refused to function. None of her other limbs would obey, nor any feature of her face. Her mind reeled with mounting alarm, but the girl in the mirror continued to smile with unrestrained joy.

Then, dramatically, the door swung open behind her. She had time to think of that desperate vagrant, to be frightened for her life, before she looked in the mirror and saw the man's face.

Hands on hips, he stared at her reflection, a small grin playing on his mouth. Sinfully handsome, was her gut reaction. Tall, dark, built like an athlete, he wore his wide-sleeved white shirt and dark slacks with a devil-may-care swagger, and with a splotch of green Julie realized was paint. Odd, that he'd be an artist. Eyeing her up and down, surveying her like some prize he'd just captured, he seemed more a pirate. It was easier to imagine him on the deck of some ship with his long, dark hair blowing unfettered in the breeze, rather than cooped up here, working in this studio.

"Why have you come?" he asked with European cadence, his expression half wary, half hopeful. "Can it be that you wish to be admired, after all? To be chased and wooed and whispered to in the night?"

The words were so soft, they seemed to come on the breeze— an invitation to lift off and fly away. Meeting his gaze in the mirror, Julie stared into eyes so green and deep she could well be drowning in the ocean's depths. Her mind began to stir—not with memories, but with emotions, conflicting ones—and an intense physical need for this man, so strong and compelling that she could not stop herself from leaning closer.

But it was his reflection she leaned into, the mirror that absorbed her touch, until with a warm tingling, she stood alone in the empty attic loft.

Disoriented, she glanced about her, finding the door tightly shut. The man, where had he gone? Desperate to see him again, she looked into the mirror as if it held the key to his whereabouts, but the glass merely showed that she was quite alone, tears glittering in her eyes. "Please," she heard herself whisper. She reached for the glass.

* * *

Victoria Howard stepped back from the mirror, confused. For an odd moment, the image in the glass seemed to change. The storage room had been as she wished it to be, well lighted by windows and uncluttered by all this dusty furniture—the ideal artist's studio.

She shook her head to clear it. Perhaps her mother was right and her daydreaming *was* getting the best of her.

"You don't belong here."

Victoria whirled, appalled to find her mother behind her. Olivia Howard should be her conscience, the way she always appeared when least convenient. An unimaginative woman, Mama followed the Puritan ethic to excess, forbidding such frivolous pursuits as drawing and painting. She would never condone her only child's daydreaming in front of a mirror.

"You were sent to dust the front bedrooms," her mother went on.

"I did the dusting."

Hands on her narrow hips, Olivia fixed her with a penetrating stare. Gray hair pulled tightly to her skull, she wore her bitterness openly, the lines of discontent etched so permanently into her face that many thought her sixty rather than her actual forty-three years. Mama had no need to don the severe black dress and starched white apron; there was no cause at all to impress an employer who'd yet to be in residence the ten years they'd lived here. But like a miser with his gold, she held tight to her anger, using the pose of servitude to fuel her resentment.

"You should be working," she said coldly, "not preening before a mirror, putting on airs. You'll come to no good end by thinking above your station, my girl."

How little her mother understood her. Victoria never came here to "put on airs." She wanted to escape, if even for a little while, from the feeling she'd soon suffocate. More and more lately, she felt as if she were trapped in a narrowing box from which she'd never break free.

Except here. Taking in each beloved inch of the attic, she refused to believe she was an intruder. From the moment she'd slipped inside to explore, this house had welcomed her. Her father might have deserted her, her bitter mother might be too busy

Barbara Benedict

to spare a smile, but alone in this attic, Victoria could pretend that she'd found a family, that she too had a home.

"I won't long remain his housekeeper if Mr. Delange finds I've let you wander free in his house." Now here was the heart of the matter; her precious job was what concerned Mama most. "Go home to the cottage he's so generously provided for us."

Glancing at the mirror, drawn by that strange pull, Victoria felt a spurt of rebellion. "The cottage is no home to me. It's more like a prison."

Olivia stiffened. "How dare you speak that way to me! You wouldn't if your father were here. Oh, if only the war hadn't taken him from me."

Something in Victoria snapped; she could no longer bear the lie. "Say what you want to everyone else, Mama, but we both know Papa was never coming back. He left us long before the war ever began. We weren't enough for him. He wanted to paint and travel . . . and live!"

Olivia's pose of martyrdom vanished. "You glorify that man," she said, the words dripping with venom. "He was selfish and wicked."

"Then forget him and stop pretending the past was so wonderful. If you ever hope to be happy, Mama, you've got to live in the present. And you've got to start letting me live, too."

Even as she uttered the words, Victoria knew her mistake. With a brief flicker in her cold, blue eyes, her mother struck her face. "I will forget you said that, provided you go home now and cook dinner. If not, you know the consequences of willful behavior."

And so Victoria did. As a child, she'd spent too many hours in an airless closet. At age eighteen, perhaps she could no longer be forced into one, but she could still be subjected to her mother's long, uncomfortable silences. It was her duty to reinforce how alone they were, Mama insisted, how she alone stood between Victoria and a lifetime of long, silent hours. All they had was each other, she maintained, and perhaps this house.

Too bad they viewed their ties to it so differently. Olivia might be content to clean and dust the house for another, but Victoria meant to one day claim it as her own.

Perhaps that was why, instead of creeping obediently back to the cottage, she took time to say goodbye to the house, strolling through the halls, running her hands lovingly down the balustrade of the grand staircase. Victoria liked to pretend she was the lady of the manor, her silk gown whispering as she glided toward the smiling gentleman on the landing below—a Delange, of course—unable to take his eyes off her face.

The loud chugging of a motor car broke into her reverie, causing her to flush with embarrassment. The last thing she wanted was the delivery man to catch her making a fool of herself.

But it was Tuesday, a good two days before Nick's delivery. Curious as to who it could be, she yanked open the front door, squinting against the sudden, bright sunlight. She watched the shiny new Ford approach, its polished black metal glinting, racing at her like some ancient royal messenger. Kicking up pebbles, it came to a halt at the foot of the steps.

A blond-haired gentleman stretched his long legs out onto the drive, pausing to gaze up appreciatively at her. Tall, fair, and agile, he was the American dream, the embodiment of youth and success, complete with good looks and likeable smile.

"Hello," he said tentatively, scanning the house. "This is the Delange place, is it not?"

Victoria nodded, suddenly wary. He seemed to have untoward interest in *her* house.

"Good, I thought so." He crossed in front of the car, standing before the steps. "It seems so different from the photos, I barely recognize it. Needs quite a bit of work. Can't imagine the last time the grass was cut."

Who was this man, that he could insult her house, or how they took care of it? "The groundskeeper retired earlier this year," she said stiffly, "though I can't see that it's any business of yours, Mr., er . . ."

"How remiss of me," he said, extending a hand as he climbed the steps. "Allow me to introduce myself. William Delange."

Abashed, she let her hand be engulfed in his, then pumped in a firm, friendly handshake. The Delange family should be in France, she thought desperately, all four of them kept safely on the other side of the ocean. What on earth was the oldest son doing here?

He clearly entertained the same question about her. "And you are?"

"Victoria Howard. The housekeeper's daughter."

Disappointment registered briefly in his eyes, but he recovered with a smile. "Then you're just the one to help me, Miss Howard. I need to inspect the house, but quite honestly, I can't imagine where I should begin."

"Inspect the house?"

He flashed another smile, one so bright and generous she could feel herself melt. When he explained that he meant to start a business in New York, that a good part of his job would be large-scale entertaining, she found herself agreeing it would be a crime not to make use of so grand a house, especially if it meant this handsome man—this Delange—would be within flirting distance. Too easily, she forgot her mother's warnings of what would become of her by dreaming above her station.

Victoria watched him as they toured the house, awed by both his poise and the scope of his planned renovations. He declared the dining room too dark, the parlor's draperies too old-fashioned, the study's Persian carpet a total disaster. She listened to his long list of improvements for the ballroom and the complete overhaul he planned for the foyer, but when he explained his extravagant plans for the kitchen, she had to ask, "Won't this take a great deal of money?"

He grinned. "My father maintains that you must spend money to make money." His gaze became distant. "I must soon show a profit. It's the least the old man will accept."

She tilted her head, surprised by his desperate tone, and more than a little curious about its cause. "Parents can expect too much sometimes," she said impulsively, thinking of her own mother.

"Father's a bit of a Tartar, I suppose, but then, it's my duty to impress him. One of his sons should follow in his footsteps. Lord knows, there's been disappointment enough with Robert."

"Robert?"

"My younger brother. I inherited Father's Yankee pragmatism, but Robert has my mother's French blood and lets himself be ruled by his passions. Between his exploits and volatile temper, he's forever landing in scrapes. I sometimes think Father wants me to set up here in the States so there's a place to send Robert when he indulges in one scandal too many."

Victoria sensed that he expected her to share his disapproval, but she wished this Robert would indeed be banished here. In her uneventful world, she'd never met such a rogue. "It sounds quite unfair," she said, feeling guilty for her interest. "It must be a strain, always having to be good. You could at least take turns at having fun."

William looked at her in surprise. "Fun is for children. Making a success of Delange Manufacturing is enjoyment enough for me."

She tried to conceal her disappointment. Suddenly he sounded too much like her mother.

"After all," he went on with a winning smile, "at my age, it is time to consider settling down. Time to find myself a wife."

He kept his gaze on her face, studying her as if she were under consideration for the position. This was her dream come true, she thought with a rush of excitement. Imagine a Delange pursuing her.

Her mother's voice rang out, calling her name, bringing her crashing back to earth. Victoria had the sudden urge to turn and run. Mama always found the worst ways to discourage the boys from "sniffing around" her daughter.

"I sent you home," Olivia attacked as she entered the room. "Oh," she said in angry surprise, noticing William. "Who is this boy, Victoria?"

"Allow me to introduce myself," William said smoothly. "William Delange III. I'm sorry if I've waylaid your daughter, but I needed someone to show me through the house."

Mrs. Howard looked from one to the other, her right brow raised.

William took a step forward, his smile polite, yet with a manner that left no doubt who was in charge. "I'm glad you're here, Mrs. Howard. I'll be moving in as soon as the necessary repairs are completed, so I need to consult with you. Have you a moment or two to spare?"

"Of course." A hand went up to smooth her hair, then down to straighten the unwrinkled apron. "In what manner might I be of service?"

Victoria stared in fascination. Her mother had dropped years off her age, preening like a girl with her new sense of importance. Then, as if to dispel that impression, Olivia turned primly to remind Victoria she must return to the cottage.

"Thanks for all your help, Miss Howard," William said, sparing a wink in Victoria's direction. "I hope I can rely upon it again in the future?"

Nodding, she left the kitchen, suddenly elated. Without offending Mama, William's wink managed to let Victoria know that he was sorry to say goodbye, and had every intention of seeing her again.

Heading toward the servant's entrance, still loathe to return to the cottage, she glanced at the back stairway and gave in to the urge to slip up to the attic. Mama would be busy with Mr. Delange; surely Victoria could take a few minutes to relish their brief flirtation.

For he *had* been flirting with her, she decided as she climbed the stairs. Rich, handsome William Delange passing time with Victoria Howard, the housekeeper's daughter. Recalling the seriousness of his expression as he spoke about finding a wife, she let her smile broaden. Victoria Delange. What a nice name. Oh yes, she'd quite enjoy being mistress of the manor.

Twirling before the mirror, she imagined herself in fine silks and jewels instead of the hated gray cotton. And her hair—she'd cut off the braid and bob it to be fashionable, just like the strange, exotic female she sometimes imagined in the mirror.

Reaching for the glass, she felt the same, sudden disorientation she had earlier. The glass surface was uncommonly warm, almost humanly so, and her fingers seemed to melt into it. She had the dizzying sense that with a bit more concentration, she could step into another world.

Frightened, she pulled her fingers away. As she did, she had the strangest sensation, as if part of her had taken flight.

Two

Julie stepped back from the mirror, rubbing her tingling arm as her vision snapped into focus. Jeans, shoulder-length hair—everything seemed back to normal.

Normal?

With building nausea she wondered if it were happening again, the strange voices in her head, the black-out episodes that led to her visit to Bellevue. Touching her face, Julie watched her reflection do likewise. That was good. It meant she had control of her actions now, not some imaginary girl in the mirror.

"You don't belong here," she called out, relieved to recognize the voice echoing across the room as her own, and not belonging to intimidating Olivia Howard.

It was a dream, she insisted, just the sort of thing her subconscious would concoct. Yet how real it had seemed, how immediate. She'd felt as if she were actually sharing Victoria's body, caught inside it, watching helplessly while the girl spoke for her, acted for her, making choices Julie could neither change nor correct.

All at once, she felt a strong need to warn Victoria. "Not William," she heard herself whisper, reaching again for the glass.

Three

Victoria preened before the mirror, well pleased with her image. Thanks to William, she had this beautiful blue muslin gown to wear, a matching ribbon for her hair. Her first party—was there ever a girl so lucky?

Of course, no one must know her true identity. William hadn't come out and said so, but she sensed he didn't want his friends and associates guessing that he'd developed such a close friendship with his housekeeper's daughter. It had been exciting these past few months, talking with him, helping him plan and execute his renovations; but thanks to Mama, she'd been ever aware of the difference in their positions.

Grinning, she thought of her mother's reaction should she learn her daughter had attended this housewarming celebration.

It was scandalous behavior, but Victoria enjoyed the subterfuge of sneaking out of the cottage, of climbing to the attic to don these clothes. Fleetingly, she'd wondered who the dress belonged to, but she'd rather die than ask William. Nothing must spoil this night. Somehow, with the help of these pretty clothes, she meant to show him she belonged in his world, that she could be witty and charming, the perfect candidate to be mistress for this house.

Strains of music drifted up to her. Lured by visions of twirling across the dance floor, she hurried down the inside attic steps. Reaching the winding staircase, she paused on a middle step.

People streamed in and out of the ballroom, an overwhelming cascade of color and sound and sophistication. With a rush of panic, she knew she was out of her depths. How childishly simple her gown seemed compared to the flashy, sequined creations these flappers wore. Small wonder that William, laughing with a bevy of such creatures, failed to notice she stood watching from the stairs. A man like that, surrounded by such beauty, interested in the hired help? Her mother was right; Victoria *did* dream too much.

"Intimidating, no?"

She looked down. There, at the bottom of the stairs, stood the incarnation of her every fantasy, smiling up at her with all the appreciation she'd ever craved. Green eyes twinkling with mischief, he watched her face for the slightest reaction. Too good to be true, with his long, dark auburn hair and striking good looks, this man was the epitome of every girl's dream—and every mother's nightmare.

"I never know what to do with myself at these affairs, either," he said with a grin. He spoke with a slight accent, sporting a devil-may-care attitude with continental flair. "I do not have the knack for all this inconsequential chatter. Could I convince you to dance?"

Giving her no time to refuse—if indeed she could have found the words—he led her into the ballroom. Swinging her into his arms, he swept her across the dance floor, his movements so smooth and fluid, she was soon lost in a glorious cloud of sensation.

Music blended with motion, his clean, fresh scent with the warm, solid feel of him. Part of her knew it was highly improper to dance with an utter stranger, yet another part recognized that this was where she belonged, here in his arms. She should be nervous, stumbling over his feet, yet she had never felt so at peace in her life.

With a wrenching, she felt him pull away. The tune had ended, she realized. Like Cinderella, she'd heard the stroke of midnight, and her fantasy must now come to an end.

But smiling like a true Prince Charming, he suggested that perhaps they could go for a stroll. Victoria found herself slipping her arm in his with all the trust in the world.

On their way to the French doors, he grabbed two glasses from a passing tray, handing her one as they paused outside at the patio balustrade.

"Champagne?" she asked, feeling deliciously naughty. "Oh, but I shouldn't, Mr.—"

"Please, you must call me Robert." He pronounced the name in the French manner, *Ro-bear.*

"I couldn't. It wouldn't be proper."

He stood before her, so close she caught a subtle whiff of cologne. "Couldn't, shouldn't. Is there anything you *are* permitted to do?"

"My mother has certain standards. If she were to hear—"

"I don't see why she must." He grinned down at her, green eyes sparkling. "We can let it be our little secret."

She looked away, trying not to smile. A conspiracy against her mother—how on earth was she to resist? "I must warn you, Mama can be quite formidable. There's nothing she despises more than what she considers my 'rebellions.' She will neither overlook nor forgive your encouraging them."

"Worry not, I can deal with your mother."

Perhaps he could, at that. Besides, it would take a far more experienced female than Victoria to resist what he offered. How often did such a handsome knight come to rescue her from the boredom of her life?

She looked at the glass, wanting to sip, fearing it would be tasting forbidden fruit. "You should know, I don't belong here," she blurted out, wanting him aware of her humble origins from the start. "I'm only the housekeeper's daughter."

With an impish grin, he raised his glass. "To a pair of rebels, then," he toasted. "I too came *sans* invitation, but I find now I am glad that I did."

He gazed at her so pointedly, she could not mistake his meaning. Flattered, yet flustered, she sipped her champagne, trying to regain her composure. "Really, Mr. . . . Robert, you shouldn't flirt so."

He looked genuinely shocked. "But isn't it every woman's wish to be admired? To be chased and wooed and whispered to in the night?"

A thrill went up her spine at the images his words inspired.

"Not all women are so frivolous," she told him stiffly, sounding too like her mother. "Some of us are more practical."

"A shame. I do believe I would enjoy very much wooing you."

He leaned closer, the veritable serpent tempting Eve, and for a breathless moment, she thought he would kiss her.

"Robert!" a male voice called out in the harsher, more conventional English. "What are you doing here, bothering Victoria?"

William approached, and despite his frown, she saw the family resemblance at once. Of course—Robert the rogue, his brother.

"Sorry." Robert shrugged, that very Gallic gesture, not one bit repentant. "I was keeping her company. She seemed terribly neglected."

"How considerate of you." His very stance scornful, William stepped between them to take Victoria's arm. "But now, if you'll excuse us . . ."

"You mean to protect her from me?"

"Those are your words, Robert, not mine."

Robert's expression turned sad, almost wistful. "We were enjoying ourselves, having fun. Where is the harm in that?"

William grunted. Looking over her shoulder as he dragged her off, Victoria was inclined to echo the sentiment. More than mere fun had been involved in the brief time she'd shared with Robert. A link had been forged between them, a need that should have been sealed with a kiss.

Whisking her off to dance, William held her at arm's length, his movements as stiff as his words. He approached the topic in a roundabout manner, but the message was plain enough. She was not to take Robert seriously.

"He's too volatile," he told her. "My brother sees love as a fleeting thing, pursued intensely one moment, forgotten in the next."

Though Victoria feared William was right, she couldn't help but wonder how it would feel to be chased and wooed by such a man.

William stopped dancing. With a frown, he pointed to his brother, who was now talking to a nasty-looking character across the room. The man was Red Stollenbach, William explained, a known bootlegger.

"See how Robert embraces danger? How he lives for the thrill? A sweet girl like you mustn't get caught up in his madness. In all, I think it's best that you leave now."

"But I just got here," she protested. "I've hardly met a soul and I want to dance."

"Yes, well . . ." Momentarily uneasy, he glanced around them, then with a shift of his shoulders became instantly resolute. "I'm sorry for that," he said in his take-charge tone as he led her from the room, "but I must insist. I've too many business obligations to look after you properly. There will be other parties, Victoria," he added with a forced smile. "Other opportunities for us to dance."

She was being dismissed. Was William ashamed of her, afraid someone would learn she was the hired help? Or was he merely angry at the attention she'd paid his brother? Either way, it seemed the end of her dreams of becoming the next Mrs. De-lange.

Yet when he stopped at the foot of the stairs, William stared at her so intently, she could not mistake his interest.

"You and I must talk," he said, taking her chin in his hand. "Meet me on the beach tomorrow at ten."

The words rang with promise, his expression declared that he'd like nothing more than to kiss her, yet Victoria found herself pulling away, forcing a smile before she turned up the stairs. What was wrong with her? Ordinarily, she enjoyed walking the beach with William, but tomorrow's outing loomed uninvitingly. It was Robert she wished she was meeting.

She went to the mirror, but for once, her reflection failed to soothe her. Something had happened to her tonight, something Victoria sensed would change her life forever. With his careless grin and mischievous twinkle, Robert had offered a glimpse of a world she'd never known existed.

All her life, she'd been taught to value stability and caution as the most admirable virtues, yet deep inside, where dreams sprouted, a doubt began to grow. She might cling to this house and the security William represented, but from this moment on, each time she gazed at him, she'd always be comparing him to his brother.

Sensing heartache ahead, she reached for the glass.

Four

With a jolt, Julie saw the jeans and shorter hair and wondered what had become of the blue dress. She ached with loss, felt cut in half. Dancing and flirting, she'd forgotten she and Victoria were separate entities; holding Robert, they'd fallen in love at the same time.

She reached toward the mirror with a sudden desperate need to see him, to know he was safe and well.

Inches away from the surface, reality intruded. Recoiling in alarm, she pulled back her hand. This Robert, surely he was the "pirate-artist" she'd glimpsed in the mirror earlier. Hadn't she decided he was a figment of her imagination? How could she yearn for a man who didn't exist?

Queasiness rolled through her gut. Was it all starting up again, that roller coaster ride into fantasy? The doctors always said she had a healthy imagination. Roughly translated, it usually meant they considered her a candidate for the psychiatric ward.

I won't go back to the hospital, she thought desperately, edging toward the stairs. She had no need for a future filled with uncertainty and danger. Maybe Gwen had a point. Julie might be better off selling her new house and following the suggestion of marrying Jeff, one of Gwen's umpteen cousins.

Turning toward the door, anxious to put distance between herself and the mirror, Julie thought of the house she shared with Gwen. Earlier, it had been a boring tract house, the suburban cliché, but it now seemed more a sanctuary, a haven she had to reach to keep her sanity intact.

Tomorrow she'd call the lawyer and make arrangements to put

this house on the market. That would put a stop to her overactive imagination.

Yet as she drove off and cast a quick, fearful glance backward, she found herself thinking about that mirror. A person couldn't just touch a piece of glass and melt into a different world.

Could she?

Refusing to give in to her qualms, Julie drove through the iron gate a week later. She'd been unable to resist a walk-through with the Realtor; she had to see her house before putting it up for sale. She should be all right, she insisted, as long as she avoided the attic.

Yet once again, she shivered as she passed through the tunnel of gnarled oaks. Perhaps it was because it reminded her of some fairy tale forest, the sort Hansel and Gretel might have wandered into.

You are no child, she told herself sternly, nor are you lost, and this mid-July day is too warm to be shivering. She'd come to close a chapter of her life, not open up scary stories of the past.

Odd though, how the meeting with the lawyer had confirmed so much of what she'd imagined. Two brothers *had* lived in the house in the 1920s—William, the business tycoon, and Robert, the artist—though the man hadn't mentioned Victoria Howard. Ninety-five-year-old William had died penniless, without known family, no doubt the reason for his eccentric bequest. The lawyer agreed that the man must have seen Julie's face in the media, and it struck some chord in his memory. Mere conjecture, of course, since senile old William hadn't shared his motives with anyone.

The lawyer also agreed that Julie should sell the place, since the upkeep would be astronomical with no provision in the will to support it. Gwen had been pleased with that decision, but not about today's visit to the house. But despite this, Julie had broken a lunch date with Gwen's cousin Jeff to meet with the Realtor.

Driving up to the house, Julie saw that the agent was already there, waiting by a glistening, late model minivan. Sondra Messina had been the lawyer's idea, the wisdom of which Julie already doubted. Introducing herself with a brittle smile, Ms. Messina grimly eyed Julie's rumpled shorts and tee shirt. Meticulously groomed in a red wool blazer, white silk blouse, and black linen skirt, the woman made Julie feel like a slug in comparison.

"Shall we?" Sondra said, brandishing a key as Julie neared. Her smile was much like her outfit—highly decorative, but meant to be removed at the end of the day.

Sondra slipped the key in the lock and the door slid open on oiled hinges. Stepping into the huge, empty foyer, Julie nodded obediently as the woman raved about the grace of the winding staircase and solid oak banister, the square footage of the rooms lining either side, but her mind reeled with recognition. In her imaginings, Victoria had stood on that staircase; Robert had led her across the dance floor of that ballroom.

Yet it was different now—quieter, emptier, filled only with dust. Nothing remained to indicate William's wealth, save for the scuffed marble tiles and a massive chandelier suspended from the ceiling two stories above. Clinking softly, its delicate crystals filled the foyer with a lilting tune.

A responsive chord was struck in her brain. All those bits of silver and glass seemed to spring to life, reflecting and refracting, filling the empty hallway with light. From a distant room came the strains of a waltz, the pattern of muffled laughter. Such a gay party atmosphere, yet she was completely divorced from it, as if she knew something bad was about to happen . . .

At a gust of wind, the door slammed shut behind her. Julie jumped, startled. She looked uneasily at Sondra. Had the woman seen that she was letting this house get to her again? That instead of exorcising her ghosts, she was dreaming up more?

But Sondra ignored her, clearly more concerned with the commission she'd earn from the sale of such a house. Brushing past, she led the way upstairs, marching down the hall, opening doors into one empty bedroom after another, continuing her litany of the house's attributes. The way she went on, one would think she was trying to sell the place to Julie.

Lost in her visions of profit, Sondra marched off down the

left wing. Annoyed, Julie went off on her own to explore the right.

As if pulled, she walked straight to the door at the end of the hall. Opening the door, she found a room filled with furniture, though it held the mustiness of a room long closed. She fumbled for a light switch, and finding none, crossed to the heavily draped windows. As she yanked the drapes aside, she smelled the dust on them; felt their worn velvet crumble in her hands.

Light spilled into the room, swimming with dust motes, lending it an eerie atmosphere. Julie could have stepped into another world, for here, in a house stripped of human pretensions, stood an oasis of early twentieth-century wealth. A plush Persian carpet stretched across the wide, oak floor; embroidered Irish linen runners lay across every night table and dresser. Two gold-handled hairbrushes sat on the cluttered vanity beside assorted pearl-inlaid combs and myriad vials of handcrafted crystal. On the far side stood a canopied mahogany bed, its four posts intricately carved. Its curtains had been drawn, the covers pulled down. Everything in the room seemed to be ready and waiting, as if anticipating the lady of the house would soon come home.

Julie couldn't understand why anyone would want to come home to this room. Though every comfort had been provided for, the effect somehow remained cold and cheerless. An unearthly hush shrouded the room; it seemed like a shrine. As Julie moved about, fingering invaluable ornaments, she could well be in a museum. She imagined a placard reading, "Room for a Rich Wife."

She saw it then, resting on a shelf with other books, yet standing out as if a beacon shone upon it. Its leather cover was a nondescript gray—black, when she dusted it—with the name *Victoria* embossed in tiny gold lettering at the bottom left corner.

She ran trembling fingers over the leather, realizing that this must be Victoria's diary. Letting curiosity get the best of her, she slipped her thumb inside. It fell open to the last pages, dated September 18, 1929.

Tomorrow, I must make a decision.
If I put it off much longer, the entire world will know what

*I've done. I wish I had the courage to face their wagging
tongues, but then, if I did, I'd have long since packed up my
brushes and run off to Paris to paint.*

*But as Mama continually harps, I am a female, with nei-
ther money nor father to support me, so where is my choice?
And in truth, wasn't my mind made up years ago, the first
day Mama and I came to this house?*

*I recall Mama staring at the imposing structure as if it
were some sacred church. It was the only lucky thing to ever
happen to her, she'd said in an awed voice. Not many housekeepers were guardians of so grand a house. And not many
housekeepers' daughters, I've since come to realize, have
the chance to become its mistress.*

*I was barely eighteen when I first met William. Such a
precarious age—so eager to get on with life, too impatient
to recognize vulnerability. The sound of his motor car coming up that long, lonely drive was a call to adventure and
I ran toward it gladly. Watching William alight from his
gleaming new Ford, I saw only the promising future he represented. As he stood before the house, every inch its lord
of the manor, I truly thought he was all I could ever possibly
want.*

Oh, if I but had that day to do over.

With trembling hands, Julie closed the diary, aching with Victoria's pain. Dear God, it was here, written in this book, everything she'd seen and felt when she touched the mirror.

Perhaps she *wasn't* losing her grip on reality.

If not, then what *was* happening to her? If Victoria was some
lost, unhappy spirit, haunting the house she loved so well, she
could be using Julie to relive her story. What better conduit, after
all, than a person with no past of her own?

No, Julie thought with a quick shudder; she had no wish to
experience anything supernatural, either. Looking about her, she
felt suddenly claustrophobic in this cold, cheerless room.

She glanced down at the diary, knowing she must read on,
certain she'd been drawn into this tale for a reason, but she
couldn't read here, not in this room that retained the essence of

Victoria's pain. Though she longed to learn what happened after the initial meeting with Robert, she was reluctant to read on here in William's house. At home, at least, there would be no ghosts, no mirrors.

Seeing Sondra in the doorway, Julie jumped.

"Oh, here you are," the woman said, stopping instantly as her gaze took in the room's contents. Fingering the gold and crystal, dollar signs gleaming in her eyes, she asked if the furnishings would be included in the sale of the house.

Julie felt a strange surge of possessiveness. She couldn't bear the thought of her house in this woman's hands. "Actually," she said abruptly, "I haven't yet reached a decision whether to sell or not."

Sondra barely batted a lash. "Oh? The lawyer implied your financial situation dictated an immediate sale. Of course, with the market as it is, we may have to haggle over the price, but I'm certain we can come up with a solution to make everyone happy."

Angry that the lawyer had been discussing her private affairs with this woman, Julie repeated stubbornly, "I'm still not sure I'm selling."

The smile stayed in place, as fixed as the lacquered hair, as Sondra took a business card from her purse and pushed it into Julie's hands. "Call me," she said, her words less a request and more a prediction. She could have said, "You don't belong here."

Julie followed her into the hall. "Er, Ms. Messina? The key?"

Sondra whirled, her stare accusing. "You're serious? You really think you can keep this place? That you can live here?"

"The key is mine. I'd like it, please."

The words, "You're crazy," hovered unspoken in the air, until, with a pitying smile, Sondra tossed the key, spun on a heel, and marched away.

Julie listened to the click of her heels as they descended the stairs, the sharp staccato echoing up from the foyer, and the slam of the door as she went out. How quiet it seemed when the mini-van drove off. How lonely.

She didn't know how it happened, but one moment she was standing alone in the hallway, and the next, she was up in the attic, staring into the mirror. Smiling at her reflection, she wondered if she'd meant all along to come up here. She couldn't help herself; she couldn't resist.

No more than she could stop from reaching out to touch the glass.

Five

Victoria stood before the mirror, imagining herself painting in this new loft that William had recently redesigned. It was so like the room she sometimes saw in the mirror, she had to look again and again to make certain she wasn't imagining it. Surely, the instant she dragged her gaze from the glass, she'd find it to be the same storage room it had always been.

Yet before she could look away, the door opened behind her. Staring into the glass, she saw Robert, lounging in the frame.

Her breath caught. She'd forgotten how classically handsome he was. "Why have you come?" he asked with European cadence. "Can it be you wish to be admired, after all? To be chased and wooed and whispered to in the night?"

She blushed, sensing he was teasing her. A man accustomed to beautiful, sophisticated women must find her naive in the extreme. "Please, forgive me," she said, turning from the mirror for the stairs.

"Wait." Taking three long strides, he reached for her, his hand warm and reassuring on her arm. "Where do you go now, my little Cinderella? First, you vanish at midnight and now, when I would return your glass slipper, off you run again."

She smiled; she couldn't stop herself, so infectious was his grin. "We both know I have no right to be here. My mother would lock me in chains if she knew I had trespassed on the hallowed Delange domain."

"Ah, she is quite the dragon, this mother."

Victoria pulled her arm away, feeling disloyal. "She means well. And it's thoughtless of me to be jeopardizing her position

here. Your brother could let her go, and then where would we
be?"

"William would be a fool." He said the words with disgust,
and with not a trace of the French accent. "Is that why you left
so early last night? Did my stuffy brother order you home?"

She shook her head, though in truth, wasn't that what William
had done? No, she told herself stubbornly, he meant only to protect her from Robert and his bootlegger friends. "Leaving was
my idea," she insisted. "I didn't belong at the party, any more
than I do in this attic."

"So you keep saying. But what, I can't help but wonder, brings
you up to my studio today?"

He spoke with the accent again, confusing her. "Why do you
do that?" she asked. "If you speak perfect English, why use an
accent?"

He shrugged. "Ah, you've guessed my guilty secret. The ladies
like a French flair, I've found, and I'm afraid I'm a notorious
flirt."

She thought of William's warning of how love was a game to
this man. Too naive to know the rules, she was in danger of losing
badly. She should go running for the safety William offered, but
she stood there in helpless fascination, letting herself be drawn
into this madness.

As if to encourage her, he grinned winningly. "But come,
you've changed the subject. Out with it. What brings you to hide
in our attic?"

"You'll only laugh."

"At you? Never."

Gazing into his eyes, feeling the link between them, she
wanted to believe him.

"Very well," she said, giving into the impulse to confide in
him. "If you must know, I come here to dream. To pretend this
house is mine, that I'm its mistress and no one can ever take it
away."

"It's so important to you? Four walls and a roof?"

"You Delanges have so much, you can probably never understand, but yes, it is *everything* to me. Here, I can dream of a

family, of parents who love me, of a future that holds promise. It seems possible in this house. It seems real."

She waited for him to laugh, but he nodded solemnly. Victoria exhaled, unaware she'd been holding her breath. She'd revealed so much of herself, more than she'd ever revealed to anyone.

Taking her hand, he squeezed it gently. "I must apologize for usurping your haven, but I needed the north light, you see. Without a studio to work in, I wouldn't come here, no matter what threats my father offered." He gestured toward the easel in front of the picture window. "I paint. Not commercially, which would make my parents happier, but with my own vision. I find I can create only what my heart can see."

Despite the casual air, she could see his work meant everything to him and his family's scorn hurt deeply. Moving closer to the sketch, she studied the scene, a lonely stretch of beach with a girl wading in the waves. She started when she recognized the features as her own.

Robert stepped behind her. Reaching for the sketch, he wadded it into a ball and with a low oath, flung it in the corner.

Surprised, she whirled to face him. "Why did you do that?"

He refused to meet her eyes. Jamming his hands in his pockets, he looked like a lost, lonely boy. "It was a preliminary exercise," he said in an offhand manner. "Mere dabbling. Far from what I hope to achieve."

"Dabbling? But it was so good."

"It is only begun." His intensity spoke of matters far more personal than a simple sketch. "When I'm finished," he added softly, "you shall know what I meant to portray."

Both his voice and gaze seemed to caress her. Watching him, waiting, she found it hard to draw breath. Surely he'd kiss her now.

Looking away, as if thinking better of it, he gazed out the bay window. "It's a gorgeous day. Would you like to go sailing?"

It was hard to keep up with him, harder still to resist the prospect of spending the day with such an exciting man. "Sailing? When?"

"Today. Right now. There's nothing quite so invigorating as the wide open freedom of the sea. Come, let me show it to you."

She longed to say yes, was on the verge of acquiescence, when her conscience reminded her of a prior commitment. It was ten; William would be waiting on the beach.

"I can't," she told Robert with regret. "Not today."

He studied her for a long moment, then shrugged. "Another time, perhaps," he said. But again, his breezy tone didn't fool her. He'd wanted to spend the day with her, as much as she wanted to be with him.

"I paint what my heart can see," he'd told her. Watching him go to his easel, already withdrawing from her, she longed to snatch the wadded sketch from the corner, to see what his heart was telling him.

She went to the stairs, hating that she had to go. Twice now, she and Robert had hovered on the brink of something wonderful, only to be yanked apart.

She wanted to think it was Fate conspiring against them, but it was far more likely a case of common sense. No good could come of giving her heart to such a self-professed rogue. No good at all.

Though late getting to the beach, she waited over an hour for William to finally make an appearance. Striding up, grasping her hands, he apologized briefly. "Business," he said, as if it explained all, and perhaps it did. Making money would always come first to this man; it was what drove him.

William went on to state that he must not tarry, that he was packed to leave town. With poorly suppressed excitement, he explained that this could be *the deal* to make his fortune. The venture would not only earn his father's respect and approval, it could earn him the funds to fix up the house properly for a wife and family. Squeezing her hands, he begged for her patience. With any luck at all, when he returned, he promised they would start talking seriously about the future.

Staring after him as he marched off, Victoria shook her head. He'd mentioned a wife and their shared future in the same breath; was it William's way of declaring himself?

Strange that she felt no excitement, no triumph. Marrying William would gain her the house. Wasn't that all she'd ever wanted?

Here, too, was a way to make Mama happy, ensuring that they need never leave.

Yet all Victoria could think about was that now, with William gone, she was free to go sailing.

Running over the sand, scrambling up the bluff, she raced to the attic. The pleasure on Robert's face when he saw her erased what few reservations she might still have entertained.

Nor could she regret her decision later as she stood on deck with the wind in her face, feeling free for the first time in her life. Watching Robert steer the boat, so at home on the waves, she sighed with envy.

"What is it?" he asked. "Already regretting that you came with me?"

"No!" she said, then with a blush, added far less emphatically, "I was thinking how lucky you are to just sail off on a whim like this. I could never be so impulsive."

"And why not?"

"I'm a girl. My life is governed by society's rules. I'm at an age where I'm expected to settle down, not indulge in frivolous pursuits."

"Frivolous?" He smiled mischievously. "That is your dragon of a mother talking. Stop being the dutiful daughter and tell the truth. If you were allowed but one silly pursuit, what would it be?"

"That's easy to answer." Smiling, she looked out over the sea. "I would leave this instant for Paris, so I could learn to paint. That's my dream. To be free to draw and paint whatever my heart desired."

"Ah, but why Paris?"

She shrugged. "I don't know. I suppose it just seems so romantic. I imagine any other city would do, as long as it's far away from my mother."

"Yes, there is that, but what I meant was, why travel all the way to Europe when you can study painting here, with me?"

Stunned, she turned to him. "Are you saying you'd teach me?"

His expression softened. "I'd try my best, though I have a feeling I'd be learning far more than I can teach."

"I don't understand."

"I look at you, at your freshness and zest for life, and I see how jaded I've let myself become. By working with you, perhaps I can recapture the passion I once felt in my own work. My life. Please say you'll come to the studio each morning. Promise that we can work together."

Victoria knew her mother would never approve—nor would William for that matter—but she could not bring herself to refuse. To see him, to be with Robert every day? Nodding, she seized this one, brief chance at happiness.

And throughout the following week, she was blissfully happy. Their mornings were devoted to lessons, the afternoons to jaunts, and in both, Robert proved the ideal tutor. There was more to art than applying dabs to a canvas, he insisted. His pupil must live, and that meant experiencing life outside the Delange gates. Driving his brother's Ford from Montauk Point to Manhattan, he took her touring Long Island, from the quaint whaling villages of the North Shore to the fishing towns on the Great South Bay.

One night, Victoria crept out of the cottage so he could take her to the speakeasies of Harlem to hear the jazz musicians. Plunged into the heart of the 1920s for the first time, she gaped like a child before a Christmas tree. Alcohol flowed as freely as the great Niagara Falls, politicians making a mockery of their own laws by sporting two or three glasses at a time. Celebrities, known before only as distant meteors, came and went like speeding trains, Robert playing the conductor by pointing them out. It was all the satin and fringe and flash she could ask for, pulsing with a life of its own. Watching it spin past their table, Victoria drank it all in as freely as she did the champagne.

Just as she felt she might get used to this lifestyle, that she might even try dancing the Charleston, they were approached by a garishly dressed woman, the sort her mother would call a floozy.

"This is Florinda." Robert introduced her as if she were a friend. "Here," he told the woman, slipping a few bills in her palm. "Use it for food this time, not booze."

Stuffing the money down the front of her dress, Florinda flashed a lopsided grin. "Thanks, luv. You're a prince. Now who wants the fortune? You or her?"

"Florinda won't take money without earning it," Robert explained to Victoria. "She says it's some Gypsy code of honor. Why not let her tell your fortune? I'm tired of hearing how I'll come to a bad end."

Florinda laughed. "That's your brother talking, Robbie. I've never read your fortune and you know it. You're too busy hiding from me, or maybe just from the truth." She turned to Victoria. "But this one, she doesn't know how to conceal her emotions. It's all here, in her eyes."

Uncomfortable under the woman's scrutiny, Victoria tried to look away, but Florinda took her face in her hands. "Inside, I see a lost soul," she said, her voice suddenly distant and vague. "A gentle spirit, trapped by time. She needs help finding where she belongs."

Uneasily, Victoria thought of the sad, exotic female she'd often imagined in the mirror.

"And that help will be offered for a fee." Robert chuckled. "Sorry Florinda, I can't afford it."

"One day soon, you'll think it well worth the cost," Florinda said cryptically. "You'll be back to ask for this Gypsy's help." Smiling saucily, she sauntered off with a swish of her orange skirts.

Unnerved, and completely drained, Victoria watched Robert stare after her. "Was she serious?" she asked him. "Was any of that real?"

"I don't know. She once . . ." He sat up abruptly, as if just coming to his senses. "I'm sorry. I can see she's upset you. Perhaps we should go."

Although he hadn't answered her, Victoria agreed to go home. It hit her that while it might be a narrow life she shared with Mama, at least she could understand it, predict what would happen. Who was this gentle spirit Florinda claimed to see inside her? The face in the mirror? But that was part of her hidden dreams, her secret longings. How naked she felt, how invaded, to think a complete stranger could see into her soul.

Feeling a need to be safe at home, she rose abruptly, but before they could leave, Robert was hailed from across the room. A blatantly important man sat at a front table, surrounded by half-empty bottles and six of the floozies Mama so scorned. Puffing on a cigar, barking orders to the waiters, he behaved like a sultan commanding his court. Victoria couldn't blame the women for acting obsequious. It couldn't be wise to say no to such a man.

With an apology, Robert excused himself to stroll to the table. Watching them exchange a few friendly words, Victoria recognized the man's florid face—Red Stollenbach, the bootlegger.

Uneasy that Robert could be on friendly terms with so undesirable a character, she remained quiet and pensive on the drive home. William might be stuffy and overly-concerned with making money, but at least with him, she encountered no Gypsies. Or gangsters. Perhaps there was something to be said for a life that plodded along as expected.

As if to prove otherwise, Robert braked the motor car before a dark, deserted stretch of beach. When she protested, saying it was late, he merely smiled and tugged her out onto the sand. "Here is yet another lesson about life outside the Delange gates," he explained as they strolled. "See the lights bobbing on the waves? Sweethearts come to this beach to watch them. Or so they say. With the stars overhead, the waves pounding the shore, I'm sure you can imagine what else they do here."

Imagining too well, she blessed the darkness for hiding her blush. "Are they boats?" she asked, hoping he wouldn't guess how the prospect of dallying on the beach tempted her.

He nodded. "They're booze runners. They land their cargo on Long Island to avoid the FBI patrols around Manhattan."

It was criminal activity, yet he sounded so unconcerned. "You know a lot about these bootleggers," she said, the words almost an accusation.

"Everyone knows. Prohibition is a joke, nobody takes it seriously. Not even my brother."

"Really? I can't imagine William strolling though a speakeasy, on a first-name basis with criminals."

"No? But he . . ." He stopped, shrugged, then forced a laugh. "My brother's a complex man, but yes, I suppose he'd hate to find himself in what he'd term a risky situation."

"I don't see how it's wrong to be cautious," she said stiffly, feeling suddenly disloyal to William. "We all want security."

This time Robert's laughter held a hard edge. "Perhaps, but I ask you, where is the thrill if we don't sometimes take chances? We have but one life, why not live it to its fullest? Why watch from the sidelines when it's far more exciting to get into the game, taking the pain with the joy and feeling each with equal intensity? To learn, we must immerse ourselves in experience. Security simply shouldn't enter into it."

In her heart she could see his point, could even agree with him. Yet where Robert had escaped early from his parents' influence, propriety had formed the foundations of Victoria's life. Convention provided the stays of her existence. Eventually choices would have to be made, and with a sense of foreboding, she feared their backgrounds would make all the difference.

As if recognizing this too, and not liking it, Robert changed the subject. "France is out there," he said dreamily. Standing with his hands in his pockets, his suit jacket blowing in the breeze, he stared out to sea. "Growing up in Paris, I dreamed of the day I could sail across the ocean to America. Even as a child, I knew there were so many places to see and experience. It's like an itch inside me, this need to see the world. Given the slightest provocation, I'd jump in my boat and sail away."

"You'd leave?" she blurted out, alarmed at the prospect. "Just like that, you'd be gone?"

He turned to her; she could feel his intensity radiating between them. "No, not now," he said in almost a whisper. "Not without you."

His arms encircled her, drawing her into his warmth As his lips lowered to hers, her entire body melted with pleasure. Here, at long last, was the promised kiss.

It was all she had dreamed of, and more. It started slow, touched by a trace of awe, the sweet surprise quickly deepening into passion until they were clinging to each other, touching each other, lost to all but the need to be joined as one.

Who knew what might have happened if she hadn't heard sudden laughter. Breaking away from Robert, struggling to straighten her clothing and regain her wits, she stared at the couple strolling past. Hugging and kissing, they were indulging in what Mama would call scandalous behavior, but it was nothing compared to what she'd just been doing with Robert. Blushing to the roots of her hair, she asked that he take her home.

"I'm sorry," he said softly, pulling her against him, cradling her head against his chest. "I never meant to frighten you. This one time, with you, I swore I would play the gentleman."

Lying against his chest, listening to his heart thump as madly as her own, Victoria knew it wasn't Robert who'd frightened her—it was herself. She'd been a new, wild creature kissing him. And given the slightest opportunity, she feared she'd become that creature again.

She told herself she felt only relief when Robert drove her home, yet as she lay in her lonely bed, she knew it was disappointment that kept her awake. And perhaps confusion. All her life she'd known what was expected of her, yet this thing she shared with Robert could never be part of it. Maybe she should stop seeing him, forget him entirely.

Could she?

She had her answer as she entered the loft the next day. Gazing at Robert, so absorbed in his painting, she felt an aching void in her heart at the thought of never seeing him again. It was impossible to imagine living a day without him. He was the color in her life, the excitement and brightness and hope.

He looked up, his handsome features breaking into a broad smile, as if he'd guessed she'd meant to avoid him and was delighted to see she'd reconsidered. As he did every morning, he took the canvas from the easel and put it down, facing the wall. He wanted no one seeing his work until it was finished, he'd told her. Only when it was done, he often reminded, would she know what he'd meant to portray.

He crossed to the bay window. "It's too lovely a day to spend indoors," he announced. "Let's walk on the beach instead. We can have a picnic."

Victoria thought of her mother, how it was becoming increasingly difficult to sneak off undetected. "But Mama——"

He turned with a grin. "Fear not, the dragon is off to town, stocking the lair for the master's return. You've no real reason to refuse me."

"Take chances," he might as well have said. "Live life to the fullest." Once again, it was impossible to say no.

Helping him set down their blanket in a secluded area, protected from the wind, she was glad he'd insisted. It *was* a beautiful summer day and as always, being with Robert made her happy, made her feel alive.

Walking along the shore, the waves lapping her bare feet, she told him about her parents, about the father who'd left them to go off and paint. His desertion had once made her sad, but smiling at Robert, she told him she'd come to learn that life had a way of offering other compensations. Staring at her face, intensely solemn, he said he would give anything to paint her as she looked in that moment.

They were interrupted by the raucous shouts of three young boys, chasing a large, very wet dog across their blanket. To her surprise, Robert laughed as the boys scampered off. William, she feared, would have stomped after them shouting indignantly, but Robert merely shook the sand from the blanket, insisting that no real damage had been done.

Sitting on the rearranged blanket, she watched him gaze down the beach at the departing trio. "I wish I had children," he said wistfully. "Imagine the laughter they could bring to that cold, cheerless house."

It made her uneasy, his appraisal of her house, but perhaps William's renovations *had* lent it more elegance than warmth. "You, a father?" she asked, the assessment making her again feel disloyal.

"How shocked you sound, my little skeptic." He sat beside her, pushing the hair from her face. "Someday I hope to be surrounded by a brood of little scamps, but not until I can devote all my time to them. I refuse to raise kids like my parents raised William and me."

Victoria was surprised by his bitterness.

"My father might as well have left us," he went on. "He and my mother were always flitting about Europe, and when they were at home, they set us in constant competition against each other. My father's expectations were near impossible to fulfill, so I gave up long ago trying to please him, but William has spent a lifetime toward that end. I've always felt bad for my big brother. I guess that's why I . . ."

The words trailed off. "Not that it matters," he said suddenly, as if shaking free of the sudden bleakness. "It's all in the past. Since coming here—no, since meeting you—it's like I've begun life anew. God, have you any idea how beautiful you are, with the sun on your face, the breeze blowing through your golden hair?"

Seeing the desire in his eyes, she felt a cold, hard stab of aware-ness. "Robert, please, you mustn't say such things."

He leaned toward her. "Why not, if they're true?"

"As you said yourself, you're a notorious flirt. I'd be a fool to take you seriously."

"Perhaps I've changed." His expression tightened. "Some-thing happened that night I met you. I've heard poets talk about seeing a face in a crowd, how with one single gaze, everything clicks into place and the world suddenly makes perfect sense. In the past, I'd always thought it sentimental nonsense. I didn't be-lieve in love at first sight."

"But now?"

He reached for her. "My first sight of you was a revelation. Tell me, there on the stairs, didn't you feel the shock of recog-nition, the inevitability of our coming together? Don't you feel it now?"

She nodded, unable to speak, unable to deny the truth. From the first, hadn't she known there was something between them, some link superseding logic and good sense? His grip tightened, desire flaring in his eyes, and she couldn't have broken away if her life depended on it. She wanted him to kiss her, needed him to, and it was her arms going up to encircle his neck that marked her decision to start what she knew she could never stop.

"Are you sure?" was all he said, like a man drowning and grasping for a lifeline.

"No. Yes. Oh, Robert . . ."

With a groan, he took her face in his hands, holding it like some precious gift as he lowered his lips to hers. For Victoria, the world and all its doubts vanished, becoming a softly cascad-ing collage of sensation.

Hazily, she was aware of being lowered to the blanket, but his warm mouth commanded her attention. How skillfully he used his lips, how masterfully he probed with his tongue, urging her to explore the sweet, melting magic of his mouth with her own.

His hands threaded through her hair, traveled down her neck and shoulders, her sides, stroking her everywhere. Over and over, he kept whispering how beautiful each part of her was, how perfect. Coming alive under the litany, she felt like a flower blossoming to life. Every inch of her seemed to expand, opening up to him, as if her body recognized that they were meant to come together.

Gently, he slid her dress and chemise from her shoulders, though she had no recollection of when he'd undone her buttons. She felt the sun's warmth on her bare breasts, and then his own warmth as his adept hands caressed them. Lost in the deepening enchantment he spun around her, she arched upward, offering her breasts to his lips, moaning deep in her throat at the sheer piercing pleasure of his intimate touch.

His hands eased down, stroking her, raising her skirt to find the secret, aching spot between her thighs. As he touched her there, caressed her, she thought she'd go mad with longing. "Please, Robert, please," she heard herself say, though she had no real knowledge of what she begged for.

Not until he entered her.

He did so slowly, gently, filling her completely. Smiling his reassurance, he watched her face, his own features concerned and loving. Clinging to him, she stared at his features, knowing she'd just found the part of her that had always been missing. Now, with Robert moving deeper inside her, at last she was whole.

He dipped down to kiss her with a drugging passion. In a sensual fog, she was aware of a small, burning pain, but Robert kept penetrating deeper, coaxing her to feel nothing but him. Wrapping her legs around his thighs she matched his movements, caught up in the deep, primitive rhythm.

"Yes," she heard herself cry out over and over, the words keeping time with their actions, building in power with every thrust. Up, up, she seemed to soar, arching ever closer toward him. Holding her, crooning in her ear, he stayed with her, her beautiful lover, taking her to the very summit of sensation, then crying out, even as she did, with glorious, shuddering release.

Clinging to each other, they floated back to earth together. For Victoria, the world shifted slowly into focus, though the edges remained soft and blurry. She heard the gentle lapping of the waves on the shore, the sweet, haunting music of the gulls overhead. Though a soft sea breeze brushed across her bare flesh, the sun was there to instantly warm her.

Holding Robert in her arms, she'd never felt more alive, never happier.

Yet even as she thought this, he rolled off to lie on his back beside her. "Ah Jeez," he said, and all she heard was regret. It came like a cold splash to the face.

She sat up stiffly, yanking her skirt over her knees, sliding on the chemise and jamming her arms into the sleeves of her dress. "Love is a fleeting thing to Robert," she could remember William warning. "Pursued intensely one moment, forgotten the next."

William, she thought with a spurt of guilt. What had come over her that she could so easily, so completely, disregard a lifetime of propriety and good sense? That she could forget her need for stability and risk losing the house only William could offer?

With a low oath, Robert rose to his feet, doing up his trousers. "Oh Victoria, I—"

"Don't say a word," she said, rising just as abruptly. "Not one single word. Let me at least pretend this was important to you."

"Important?" He took her by the arms. "Look at me, damn it. It was everything to me, but I swore this time I'd play the gentleman. For you, Victoria, only for you. At the least, you deserved satin sheets and champagne in crystal glassware, not some blanket in the bushes. Don't you see? I wanted your first time to be special."

It had been. That was the problem. He made it so hard to choose—William's security or Robert's magic.

Pulling her close, he kissed her gently. "I swear, my love, next time I shall make it special. Come to the loft tonight and let me show you."

She couldn't, she mustn't, yet when he looked at her with that pleading expression, she could not find the words to deny him. "Oh Robert, I don't—"

He touched her lips. "Whether you come or not, I shall be waiting."

It was all she could do to leave him, yet it was far too frightening to remain. Lord only knew what madness would have struck her had she spent two more minutes in his arms.

It was as well that she left when she did, for Mama waited at the cottage door, her lips pursed in ill-concealed fury as she asked point blank just what on earth Victoria thought she was doing.

She tried to bluff. "I can't imagine what you're talking about."

"Do you think no one has seen you sneaking off to be with that . . . that Lothario?"

Spurred by guilt, Victoria spoke more sharply than she'd intended. "How I spend my private time is my own concern."

Olivia blinked, clearly surprised by her daughter's retort, and not at all pleased. "Go on, sport your airs with me, the mother who's supported you all these years, but what about Mr. William? Have you forgotten he'll soon be home? I doubt he'll approve of your cavorting with his brother."

Mama was right. She *had* forgotten him, and he would not be pleased. She simply could not bear it if she'd risked all hopes of ever being mistress of his house.

"You've always been a willful child," Olivia went on, gathering steam, "but even you must see that no good can come of this. A cad like Robert will take advantage of your youth and innocence. He's only using you to while away his time until he goes back to France."

"You can't know that." Again she spoke sharply. Mama's words echoed her own doubts and fears too closely.

"Can't I? Look at them yourself. William is responsible, the steady and sane one. Robert is like your father, charming but undependable. My poor child, don't make my mistake. You can't trust a ne'er-do-well, a painter whose only fame is in breaking promises and breaking hearts."

Again she wanted to deny her mother's words, but they burrowed into her, haunting her all that day, and even that night as she stared at the lamp in the attic window. Hurrying up the back steps to the loft, she knew she was acting rashly, foolishly, but she was drawn by that light—no, to the man who had lit it—like a moth to the flame.

She found Robert waiting for her, sitting on a mattress covered by satin sheets. Beside him on the floor sat a bottle of champagne and two glasses. Approaching him, she couldn't mistake the joy on his face; it too nearly mirrored her own.

She'd come to talk, she insisted, she needed to know his intentions toward her, yet gazing at him, all she could think of was being held in his arms. Wordlessly, she dropped to her knees before him and raised her face for his kiss. Whispering her name like a chant, he sent all Mama's warnings skittering out of her brain.

He leaned over to extinguish the lamp, leaving the attic bathed in the silvery magic of moonlight. Slowly they undressed, revealing more and more of themselves to each other. How beautiful he looked in the white glow, as perfectly sculpted as a glistening marble statue of some Greek god. Dear God, she loved this man, and had loved him from the moment they'd met. As he lowered her to the mattress, their bare flesh caressed by the cool satin, she knew that nothing else existed, save this moment.

Time had stopped for them to love.

But all too soon, reality intruded. Lying in his arms afterward, knowing she must soon return to the cottage, she thought of her mother's warning. Victoria might love Robert with all her heart, but love didn't always cure life's ills. Only look at what had happened to her parents. "I shouldn't be here," she said, desperate not to repeat her mother's mistake. "It—it's wrong."

He rose up, leaning on an elbow to study her face in the moonlight. "Wrong? I've never felt so right in my life."

There was an odd note to his voice, but she plunged on. "This thing between us, it can't ever work," she said, voicing her doubts. "You have different needs. I must have the security you scoff at."

He frowned, suddenly angry. "I thought you wanted freedom and adventure. Whatever happened to running away to Paris to paint?"

"That was just a dream, as insubstantial as air. You know I've always dreamed of being mistress of this house."

"I can't give you this house, Victoria. It belongs to my brother."

The words hung between them, harsh and all too real. *Say something,* she pleaded silently. *Convince me that I won't need the security William offers—that I'll always have you.*

But Robert said nothing. Unable to bear the silence, she mumbled that she'd better go before her mother discovered her absence. He gave no teasing assurances that he could take care of the dragon, no indication that he wanted her to stay, save for a brief lift of his hand. Yet even as hope flared, he dashed it by dropping his arm, turning to relight the lamp.

She cried herself to sleep that night, swearing that she'd never again go to his studio. Yet when morning dawned, and she thought of facing the day without him, she found herself again trudging up to the attic. They had to talk, she decided; surely there must be some way to work things out.

Apparently not. Though Robert glanced up when she entered the room, there was no joyful smile. Scowling, he returned to his painting.

She went to her own easel, but for once, applying dabs of paint to her canvas held little appeal. She turned to watch Robert work instead.

He was in his element. Emotions played across his handsome face as he played God, bringing the scene he painted to life. She could see how important his art was to him in each smile and frown. Robert needed to be free; like her father, he'd be stifled by a wife and family. How selfish of her to try to chain him down, to ask him to change. In the end, she'd only make them both miserable. Wasn't her mother living proof of that?

Suddenly he looked up, his brush forgotten as he flashed a wistful smile. "I missed you," he said softly. Yet even as she began to hope, to rise to her feet to go to him, the door crashed open behind them. Seeing William in the door frame, she sank back to her seat.

"Your mother told me I'd find you here," he blurted out, looking from her to Robert. "She didn't, however, mention that you were painting."

Victoria could just imagine what Mama might have implied. "Robert's been giving me lessons," she said honestly enough, though carefully omitting the full scope of his teachings.

William studied his brother, then Victoria, and in that quick appraisal, his stance, his very attitude toward her seemed to alter. Striding over to stand behind her, he was suddenly more attentive, more possessive. "I do hope he hasn't turned your head or filled it with foolish notions," he said, placing a proprietary hand on her shoulder. "By now, you must be aware that half of what my brother says is mere flirtation."

"Foolish notions?" Robert asked stiffly. "Victoria is amazingly talented. Why don't you look at her work before judging it?"

"Hm, yes." William loosened his grip on her shoulder as he studied her half-finished seascape. "Darling, you should have told me you had this, er, interest. I could have helped you get professional lessons."

Darling? It took her aback, his use of so affectionate a term. Robert seemed likewise surprised. Far from pleased, he stood, clenching the handle of his brush. "I *am* a professional. I do occasionally get paid for my work."

"Work!" William snorted the word. "You dabble. You could have made a proper living out of it, but no, you scoffed when Father found you a position at his friend's advertising firm."

"There's a difference between selling your art and selling your soul."

Watching them, understanding both sides, Victoria knew each was partially right. If only William could be more daring, and Robert could prove more stable.

"It's useless, and downright rude to Victoria for us to be arguing over this," William pronounced. "You'll never change in any case. Come," he added, extending a hand to her. "We've a great deal to discuss. That business deal I spoke about? I do believe I've managed to pull it off."

"How wonderful for you," she said, genuinely happy for him.

"How wonderful for *us*." He pulled her to her feet, holding her a moment or two longer than necessary. Over his shoulder, she saw Robert watching them with a wary expression. His gaze pleaded with her not to leave with his brother.

This is William, logic insisted, who offered the future she'd always envisioned. Yet even as she let herself be tugged from the room, she gazed back at the furious Robert. She watched him fling the paint brush across the room, saw the stain, red and accusing on the floor, but the image that would remain imprinted in her mind forever was the pain she saw in his eyes. As if he'd said the word aloud, she knew he felt betrayed.

All that day, she tried to tell herself that she'd made the wise choice, the only choice, that she and Robert had been living a fantasy that could never last. William was the stable one, the brother with both the house and the money, as well as the ability for putting down roots. Eventually, excitement and adventure would call him and Robert would leave her.

So why, in all good sense, did she climb to his studio that night, once again drawn by the light in the attic window?

Busy cleaning his brushes, he looked up as she entered, his face set in deliberately impassive lines. "You're in the wrong part of the house," he said, his clipped tone slicing the quiet. "William resides in the other wing."

"I came to talk to you."

He pushed away from the shelves, leaving his brushes to fend for themselves as he crossed to the bay window. "Damn you, Victoria, you can't have it both ways. My brother by day, and me, worthless Robert, in the dark of night."

"It's not like that. You don't understand—"

"No?" He spoke to the window, refusing to face her. "Why didn't you warn me that you and William had an understanding? I felt damned stupid today when you walked off with him. I let me think you were different, but you're like all the others. Pretty Robert, such fun to play with, but in the end, women always choose my brother. Or at least his money."

She flinched, hurt, yet knowing there was a measure of truth in every word he uttered. "But I love you, Robert," she said, going over to him. "You've got to know that."

He whirled, so enraged he seemed ready to explode. "Do you

think that makes me feel better? I swear, Victoria, each time I think of you in his arms, I could kill you both."

"You can't mean that."

His knuckles gleamed where he clasped her wrist. "No? Hasn't William warned you that I have a beastly temper? That I'll stop at nothing to get what I want?"

"Robert, stop. You're hurting me."

With a low oath, he flung her arm away. "Just leave me alone, Victoria. You've got William, so you'll get this house. Why torture me?"

"I don't mean to." The words felt wrenched from her. "Oh Robert, I don't even know what I want anymore. Sometimes I think I must be two separate people. There's the tame, obedient girl Mama and William approve of; yet with you, I become this wild, free creature. The sensible me knows better than to come here, to start something I can't possibly finish; but then that other part takes over, coaxing me to follow my heart."

"Why not listen to that other part?"

"I wish I could, but all my life, my mother has kept me confined like a bird in a cage. I might know I can fly, but even when the cage door is flung open, I'm too scared to test my wings. I can't jump out into the unknown. Not without knowing that if I fall, someone will be there to catch me."

She held her breath as he studied her, waiting for his response. She'd bared her soul to him, giving him one last chance to convince her to stay. Everything rested on what he said next.

"If I had money, would you consider me then?" he asked, his eyes searching hers.

It would take very little for her to choose Robert, she realized. All she really wanted was a commitment, to know that he'd never leave her like her father had, feeling lost and forgotten and wondering what she did wrong. "Oh Robert, it's not the—"

"I could never amass a fortune like William," he went on, "but if I were to earn enough to buy a house and support us, would you then choose me over him?"

His gaze tugged at her, melted her, made her want to believe. "Yes," she heard herself say, finding it once again impossible to refuse him.

Something snapped into place in his eyes; the tension left his body. She'd pleased him. One simple word had made all the difference.

He took her hands in his. "Do you know what it means, your having faith in me? Can you keep trusting me, believing I can do the right thing?"

She nodded, almost afraid to hope. Was he talking about marriage, about being with her always?

"Of course, it won't be easy." All at once, his expression turned vague and distracted. "This is no small responsibility I'll be taking on. I'll need to think long and hard on this. Perhaps it's best that you left."

"You want me to leave?"

He gave her a sheepish grin. "No, it's far from what I want, but if you stay, I'll want to make love to you all night, and then where would we be?" His gaze delved into her, turning her warm and fluid. "I must do this right. Promise you'll trust me?"

"Yes. Oh Robert, yes." She flung herself in his arms, kissing him good night. In that moment, she'd have promised him anything.

But later, alone on her cot, she felt sick with longing. She wanted to be with him, needed the comfort of his arms. She found it easier to believe in Robert when he stood before her, smiling reassuringly.

And never had she been more in need of encouragement than early the next morning. Returning from church, she and Mama were putting their hats in the hall closet when they heard a knock at the cottage door. Mama was delighted to see William. Victoria was not.

She wanted to go to Robert, to learn his plans, but William's arrival put a stop to that. Seeing him only as an obstacle to be gotten rid of, she barely noticed his new suit, or the package he held in his hands.

"Come, sit here in the parlor with Victoria," Mama encouraged, fooling no one with her beaming smile. "I'll go fetch us some tea."

Victoria had to be nudged by her mother into the tiny receiving room, but she was far too restless to sit. She kept wondering what Robert was doing, what plans he might have dreamed up in her absence.

Not that William noticed. He didn't sit either, but went to the middle of the room. "I must say, I feel like a new man." He began to unwrap the plain brown paper from the package he carried. "Indeed, I feel positively free now that I need no longer act as watch dog. You can't imagine what difference it shall make in our relationship, Victoria, with Robert gone."

Her mind focused on the last word; an icy chill settled over her heart. "Gone?" was all she could manage.

Busy with his package, William failed to notice her pallor. "Yes, in his typically irresponsible fashion, my brother has up and left for Paris to paint. All he left behind was this, as a wedding present."

Aghast, Victoria stared at the painting he held up to her, the portrait of her on the beach that only Robert could have painted. Like in his earlier sketch, it was all there—her youthful longing, her love and hope—but it now stared back at her in cruel mockery.

"You'll know when I finish what I meant to portray," Robert had said, and so she did. He'd never have given his painting to William if he meant to return. In his "typically irresponsible fashion," Robert was saying goodbye.

A wedding gift, William said, yet it wasn't until he dropped to a knee that she realized which wedding he meant. With growing horror, she groped for the words to stop him, to prevent him from taking her down a path she couldn't bear to follow. But perhaps it was already too late.

Stall him, her brain protested. It was just a misunderstanding, there must be some way to make this right. It was easy enough to convince William she was confused, but a much harder prospect to get him to leave. Almost an hour later, he marched from the room, unhappily agreeing that she needed some time to think.

As he was going out, Mama entered with the tea tray, her sharp gaze taking in everything at once—Victoria's pallor, William's disappointment, the painting in the corner. "Are you out of your mind?" she rounded on Victoria the moment their guest was out of earshot.

"I didn't say no, Mama." Victoria tried to be firm but her voice began to waver. "I only asked for time to think."

"And how long before he discovers you're mooning after his brother? I warned you that ne'er-do-well would leave you, but did you listen? No, you must go on, making mistakes, making William angry. I swear, Victoria, if I lose my position over this, I shall *never* forgive you."

Covering her ears with her hands, Victoria ran off, ignoring her mother's shouts. She raced to the attic, praying that it was all some monstrous lie, a nightmare from which she'd soon awake.

Yet the moment she reached the loft, she saw the awful truth. All was gone—the easel, the paints, every last essence of Robert.

She stared at the blood-red paint stain on the floor, the stamp of his anger. Too passionate, William had called him. Had they argued, Robert stomping off to France in a fury? But William had also said that love was a fleeting thing to his brother. As she pictured Robert, mulling over the too large responsibility she represented, she thought it likely he'd decided to opt for excitement and adventure.

Turning, she saw her pale reflection. Two weeks ago, the same face had smiled back at her. That lucky girl hadn't known a man like Robert existed, hadn't dreamed a heart could hurt so. "Who will make me laugh?" she cried to the empty room. "Who will whisper to me in the night?"

Dropping to her knees before the mirror, she withered under the force of his betrayal. She'd wanted to trust him, believe in him, but Mama was right. In the end, all Victoria had left was herself. And this house.

She reached up to touch the glass and for a split second, joined in misery, Julie and Victoria became one.

Six

Blinking away the tears that blurred her vision, Julie stared at her tingling fingers, then the face in the mirror. "Oh, Robert," she said on a sob.

"Robert?" asked a familiar voice. "Am I interrupting something?"

Julie whirled, startled to find her roommate standing behind her. "Gwen, what are you doing here?"

"Looking for you. Why else would I be in this mausoleum?" Gwen took a step forward, her features a mixture of concern and exasperation. "You've been gone two days, Julie, during which you've had several angry calls from your boss, and a running litany from some Realtor who claims you've lost your mind. Watching you talk to a mirror, I'm inclined to agree with Ms. Messina. Poor Jeff won't like your crying over this Robert."

Jeff? It took Julie some moments to remember that he was Gwen's cousin. Practical, sensible Jeff, who wanted to marry her. Odd, but in many ways, he was a lot like William.

"Are you listening to me?" Gwen asked, suddenly at Julie's side. "I asked what you've been doing these past two days."

Julie kept blinking, glancing from the mirror to her friend. Two days? It was on the tip of her tongue to explain that she must have been living in the past, but even as dazed as she was, she knew how crazy that sounded.

"What's this?" Gwen stooped down, lifting up the black book. "A diary? Ah, Jules, have you been so engrossed in reading, you let yourself lose track of time again?"

Julie nodded, figuring it was easier than explaining the truth—

if she even knew what the truth was. Hard to believe she'd actually been inside Victoria's body, feeling her joy and pain; had she indeed been engrossed in the diary? For two full days? "It belongs to a woman who once lived in this house," she said haltingly. "Robert was her lover."

Raising a brow, Gwen tucked the diary in her purse. Julie wanted to protest, for the diary was hers, but she was tired and emotionally drained, and she feared if Gwen argued with her, she might cause an ugly scene. She'd get the diary later. "Let's just go," she said, leading Gwen to the stairs. "We can talk about this at home."

Over dinner, it was Gwen who did the talking. The Realtor was right, she felt; Julie must sell at once and break free of that financial nightmare. The house gave her the creeps, and no wonder, with all the tragedy it had known.

Gwen went on to explain that she'd been digging into the Delange family's past, learning that there had been an FBI investigation into bootlegging back in the twenties. Around the same time, William's young wife had been kidnapped and murdered. Well, actually, there had been a mysterious accident, after which the poor woman vanished—so foul play was strongly suspected. Since William's brother was known to be involved with gangsters, it was thought the wife must have stumbled upon his criminal activities. Some said he'd silenced the girl to save his own skin.

Chilled to the bone, Julie filled in the missing pieces. Poor Victoria must have decided to marry William. But why would Robert try to kill her?

To her dismay, Gwen took the diary to read in bed that night. Still wary of making a fuss, Julie waited until she left for work in the morning, but the moment Gwen pulled out of the driveway, Julie raced upstairs. She had five minutes to find the diary before she too had to leave for work.

Finding it on the bedstand, she reached with trembling fingers and opened it to the last page. She noticed the date, November 30, 1929.

As I dress for my wedding, I have the urge to run screaming from this house, for I know in my heart it is all one huge mistake. A trap, and one I have built around myself. Mama is right. I have little choice but to marry William quickly, no choice at all if my baby is to have a father.

Mama is delighted, for she sees herself as the dowager queen who shall now rule the castle. But as I watch William quickly and efficiently arrange every last detail of my future, I struggle to draw breath. I fear I'm trading happiness for security, letting him buy my body but not my heart. In his way, he probably loves me, and it will kill him to learn the truth—that no matter what Robert does, or wherever he goes, I shall love him to the grave.

The Greeks believe we poor mortals are locked inside our destinies, forced to run through our paces for the gods' amusement. This afternoon as I stood looking at the room, at the entire life William has designed for me, I could imagine I heard those immortals laughing. How neatly William has captured his little bird, how inevitable that I should return to my gilded cage.

Some might say I should be happy to have tasted freedom, to glimpse how it feels to soar through the air. Oh yes, I've had my glorious flight, but a taste is all this little bird shall ever know.

In five more minutes I must go down and say my vows, must face all those well-wishers with the semblance of a smile. But now, as I gaze at the stranger in the mirror, I ask her how on earth I shall bear it. How shall I ever get through the long, empty days ahead?

That was all. Scanning the remaining pages, Julie found no further entries. Disappointed, for Victoria's final words raised more questions than they'd answered, she turned from the room. As far as she could see, there was only one way to learn more. She had to go back to the house.

As she drove through the gate, the tunnel of oaks again reminded her of Hansel and Gretel. Their trek through the forest, she realized uneasily, had been just the start of their ordeal.

Her sense of foreboding built steadily as she climbed the stairs. She went straight to the mirror, her fingers hesitating mere inches away. What if what she learned now was too painful, too frightening?

It didn't change a thing. She *had* to know what had become of Victoria. No matter what happened, she had to see this through to the end.

Taking a deep breath, she touched the glass.

Seven

Victoria stepped back with a sad smile. One last time, she'd stolen to the loft to play pretend before the mirror, but from now on, she must put aside such childish nonsense. Too soon, she'd be a sedate, married woman and then nothing could help her escape reality.

Moving slowly down the back stairway, she was happy her stomach remained flat, even in this, her fourth month of pregnancy. Her mother was adamant that the child be kept secret until after the wedding, when they could tell William together. He'd understand, Mama insisted; by now, he must be accustomed to covering up his brother's mistakes.

That was exactly what Robert would consider this child—a mistake. A burden to his lifestyle. Reminding herself that she hadn't heard from him for over three months, she hardened her heart—too late now to yearn for what might have been. She should be thanking her lucky stars that he'd taken the decision out of her hands by running away.

If she'd had any doubts that he meant never to return, the sight of her portrait, hanging over the mantel in William's study, dispelled them. It helped her become resigned to this marriage, if not happy about it. Mama was right; it was the best possible solution for them all.

The wind was blowing hard as she hurried back to the cottage, and clouds covered the cold, November moon. At the cottage door, Mama fussed over her hair, straightened her dress, frantic that she look absolutely perfect for this most special of nights. Victoria hated the pretty pink silk creation William had presented. In her opinion, black bombazine would be far more appropriate. Someone should mourn the death of all her dreams.

Mama was in a festive mood, for tonight she went to the house not as a servant, but rather as a guest of honor. Bundling them both up in cloaks, she rushed Victoria out of the cottage. "Let's hurry," she said, shivering against the wind. "It's too dreadful a night to be out and about."

Still, Victoria would have delayed, preferring the chilly night air to the cold empty future awaiting her, but flashy automobiles already lined the driveway, dropping off guests. It was too late; her fate was signed, sealed and all but delivered.

The butler greeted them at the door with a curt nod to Mama, who'd assumed the airs of the Queen Mother, but he spared a sad, sympathetic smile for Victoria. The new staff felt sorry for her, she realized. They knew at a glance that she didn't belong here.

Laughter erupted from the ballroom, but she was bustled off to the parlor where Mama again fussed with her dress and hair. The moments sped by in a blur, tinged with an edge of panic. "I don't belong," she kept chanting in her brain.

And then it was time. The opening strains of the wedding march heralded the jaws of the trap ready to snap shut around her. As she stood beside William exchanging their vows, she thought him a stranger. He spoke quickly, with a manic, almost hysterical edge, as if he too knew they'd never be happy, yet was determined to prove his intuition wrong.

Then came the moment she'd dreaded, the announcement that made everything final. "Man and wife." To Victoria, it sounded like a death knell.

Afterward, standing on the dais to greet the well-wishers, she almost wished his parents could have made the journey from France. At least they'd be family, better than all these unfamiliar, unfriendly faces. Men came up to clap William on the back, women rushed over to kiss his cheek, while Victoria stood ignored at his side, numb with the knowledge that it was done. That now there would be no turning back.

She felt so detached, she nearly didn't notice the one face that didn't smile, a man at the back of the room gazing at her with a scowl. Indeed, even when recognition dawned, she was convinced she'd dreamed him up.

Heart pounding, she identified him. Robert.

And before she could draw another breath, he spun on a heel and quit the room.

Quaking inside and out, she watched him go, convinced his being here now was a slap in the face. No doubt he felt safe, that she could make no more demands on him if she was safely his brother's wife. Scrambling down from the dais—William too busy being congratulated to notice her departure—she heard the telltale slam of the oak door. How like him to come stir up all these unwanted emotions, and then turn around and leave without a word. Furious with him, she followed into the foyer, hearing the prisms of the chandelier clink together. Such a gay, party sound—she couldn't have felt more divorced from it.

Yanking open the door, she went into the night. The wind whipped her hair as she searched amid the sleek black cars in the driveway. She wanted to shout his name, but didn't dare make a scene. Besides, in this wind, she doubted Robert could hear her.

She saw him at the end of the house, making his way to the back, when a man stepped from the shadows to grab his arm. Robert shook free, and she realized they must be arguing, though she found it hard to hear them over the wind. She called out Robert's name.

She heard the other man say, "Get rid of her!" even as she recognized his face. With a gasp, she saw it was Red Stollenbach, the man William called a gangster.

Robert spun in her direction, his expression furious. "You little fool," he said sharply. "Don't you have the least sense? Go. Get back in the house. Isn't that where you said you belong?"

She wanted to protest, to scream and argue, but tears clogged her throat. After all this time, that was all he could say? Had she meant nothing to him at all?

Apparently not, for once again, he went marching off without looking back. Red Stollenbach, she noticed, had vanished.

She stood there for the longest time, nursing her anger, her only defense against the hurt. Clearly, the sole reason Robert had come was to concoct another illegal scheme with that gangster. How dare he snap at her, order her about.

When she turned and saw the light in the attic, she didn't think twice. She knew only that Robert must be there, and her anger needed an outlet.

She pushed open the studio door, letting it slam into the wall as she paused at the threshold, catching her breath. Robert stood before the bay window, his posture stiff and rigid. He had to have heard her graceless entrance but he didn't turn around. "What are you doing here?" she bit out. "Why did you come back?"

"When I make a promise, I keep it," he said, his own anger vibrating in every syllable. "Too bad you couldn't do the same."

"What are you talking about? What promise?"

He turned to face her, his eyes boring into her. "So much for your faith in me. What did it take? A week, two maybe, to betray that trust? To decide that William and his money was a better proposition after all?"

His attack surprised her; she floundered for a response. "What did you expect me to do? You left no word, no hope."

"I left my promise. Damn it, Victoria, you let me hope I'd actually found someone who had faith in me, someone who believed I was worth waiting for. I sold my soul for you. Maybe I don't have a fortune, but I made money enough to keep you safe and secure. I could have freed you from your gilded cage, if only you'd had an ounce more faith in me."

She steeled herself against his words, forcing herself to remember the portrait he'd given William as a wedding present. "I had no choice but to marry your brother," she argued. "At least he offered me a home."

"A home?" He was more than angry; he seemed ready to kill. "For this damned house, you betrayed me?"

"There was more than just you and me to consider." Without thinking, she rested her hands on her abdomen.

"A child? Dear God, is it . . ." His gaze hardened. "Oh, but of course it's mine. William is too much the gentleman, and far too practical, to sire an unwanted child."

Unwanted? Mama had said he'd call their baby a mistake and once more he'd proved her right. "Don't fret," she said, lifting her chin defiantly. "Your brother will raise the baby as his own." Sheer bravado, since she had no guarantee of this.

His features clouded with renewed fury. "You'd give William my baby, too? You'd lie to our child, deprive him of the truth?"

It took all her willpower not to give way to tears. "And what truth would I tell?" she lashed out, wanting to hurt him as much as he hurt her. "That his father consorted with criminals, that the only money he could earn to support us was from bootlegging?"

"Damn you, I could kill you for that."

Instinctively, she backed away from the rage she saw in his eyes. Slamming his right fist into his left hand, he turned and strode to the door.

"Robert, wait, where are you going?"

"Anywhere to escape you," he flung over his shoulder, "before you goad me into something I'll later regret."

"Go then," she cried, the words wrenched from her. "I have William. I don't need you."

He stormed through the storage rooms to the inside stairs, his every footfall an accusation. Trembling violently, she wondered how he could act as if he'd been the one wronged. What had he meant by saying he'd sold his soul for her?

"Good riddance!"

Startled, Victoria found her mother at the door, glancing back toward Robert's retreating figure. "I'm happy to see that you've at last come to your senses," Mama said primly. "It's time you sent that one packing."

Senses? Now that he was gone, Victoria could see that she hadn't acted sensibly at all. Bitter words were all they'd exchanged. Robert had spoken about working hard for a life for them, she now realized, but she'd given him no time, no room for explanations.

"William has been looking for you." Grinning like the Cheshire Cat, Mama stood with her arms folded, guarding the door. "You should be getting back to the party. It's not every day a girl gets married."

"I have to go after Robert."

Mama stood blocking the door, all color draining from her face. "You mean to sacrifice a future with William for that criminal? I despair of you, Victoria. Are you like all his other women, willing to let him get away with murder?"

Murder? She tried to dismiss the word as more of her mother's exaggerations, but Robert *had* been with Stollenbach, and he *had* threatened to kill her. Lord knew, he'd been livid enough to do something foolish.

Yet it wasn't for herself that she feared most. She remembered him talking about sailing away, recalled her mother saying it was a dreadful night to be out and about. Surely he wouldn't try to sail off in this weather?

Pushing past her mother, she was suddenly desperate to reach him.

Mama's nails sunk like talons into her wrists. "Have you lost your mind? Think what you're doing. William will toss us out on the streets."

"That's all you care about?" Victoria cried, jerking away. "Living in this house is more important to you than anyone living in it? Even me?"

Her mother stared back with such utter coldness, she realized the woman had never cared about her, had never loved her at all.

Breaking free, racing through the storage rooms to the inside stairs, she heard her mother shriek behind her, "You little fool, didn't you hear him? He wants to kill you."

Not Robert, Victoria prayed as she reached the second floor and raced down the hall. If she couldn't believe he still cared about her, life would not be worth living.

Reaching the winding staircase, she was about to descend when she was grabbed from behind. Cold hands encircled her throat. Struggling wildly, she broke free of her unknown assailant, only to lose her balance.

It happened so quickly. One moment, she was hurtling through the air, tumbling down the stairs step after bruising step, and the next, she lay in a broken heap at the bottom.

Every inch of her throbbed in terrible agony, and it was all she could do to hold onto consciousness. She heard shouts and hurried footsteps, then William's horrified, "How did this happen?"

She couldn't speak. Even her jaw seemed broken. Just before her entire world went black, she heard someone answer, "Robert!"

Eight

Julie woke slowly, aware of incredible pain, and two voices talking beside her. It took some moments to recognize them. Olivia Howard and William Delange.

Olivia crossed to the foot of the bed, tightening the covers. "My poor Victoria," she said. "How disquieting, the way her eyes open, yet show no other sign of life. Nor is the doctor encouraging. He says it's hard to assess the full extent of her injuries if her mind refuses to waken."

Julie froze. She was in that cold, awful room William had designed for Victoria, and while she could hear and see, she was unable to move her arms and limbs. How on earth was she to get upstairs to the mirror?

"Is it amnesia?" William asked from the other side of the bed. "It was a terrible accident. Perhaps she prefers not to remember it."

"If it *was* an accident." Olivia paused, facing William with grim determination. "Forgive me, but it must be said. Your brother was there, and he's known to be ruled by his passions."

No, not Robert, Julie thought. Like Victoria, she couldn't bear it if he'd been the one who pushed her. Uneasily, she remembered his anger, recalled hearing his name. Had Victoria seen him shove her and that was why her mind snapped?

"I think he tried to kill her because she was carrying his child," Olivia went on. "She lost it in the fall. That's why there was so much blood."

William looked as if she'd just punched him. "A baby?"

Julie shared his shock, feeling as if she'd taken one in the gut.

The baby, that tiny, precious replica of Robert—must she lose that, too?

In a haze of pain, she heard William say that he'd get even with his brother. The FBI had been asking questions. A word in the right ear and Robert could become the target of their investigation. Mrs. Howard was not to worry; Robert wouldn't bother Victoria ever again.

Julie wanted to protest as he marched from the room, but she remained mute and helpless inside Victoria's catatonic body. Choosing not to watch Olivia's self-satisfied smile, she closed her eyes and drifted into a troubled sleep.

It was dark when she next woke, and at first she thought she was deep in her recurring nightmare. Alone and vulnerable, she lay prone on the bed, watching a form break away from the shadows to creep toward her. As if he had whispered the word, *betrayed,* she recognized Robert.

A sliver of moonlight sliced across his face, lending his features a satanic glint as he relentlessly approached her. In her mind, she could hear Olivia hiss, "He's come to finish what he started." She braced herself for the pillow over her face, the knife at her throat, knowing she could do nothing to stop him. It broke her heart, seeing his tight, tortured creatures. If only she could speak, explain. There must be some way to reach him.

Yet she couldn't speak, and he kept coming at her, extending his hands as he reached the bed. "Robert, no!" she called out in her mind, even as his hand went to her brow, his fingers gently tracing the lines of her face. "Oh Victoria," he whispered fiercely, "what have I done?"

She felt awful for doubting him; she was no better than Victoria for ever thinking he could hurt her. She wanted to hold him, to tell him that all that mattered was that he was here now, but she couldn't get her lips to move. Aching with frustration, with longing, she felt hot, salty tears slide down her face.

His fingers stopped on her cheek, his entire body seemed to stiffen. "Florinda was right," he said, half in awe, half in triumph. "You *are* still in there." Leaning down, he gently kissed her tears.

With a heavy sigh, he sat beside her on the bed, taking her limp hand in his own. "Me and my beastly temper," he said softly, his voice cracking. "The past few months have been torture, dreaming of you, longing for you—then to come here and find you marrying my brother? I think for a moment I went a little insane. Why else would I stand there hurling accusations when all I truly wanted was to take you in my arms?"

He reached down for her, pulling her up to hold her tight against his chest. "My sweet, lovely Victoria," he crooned, rocking her gently. "I can never replace our child, but I can see that you're safe."

Standing, he slipped his arm under her, lifting her body up against him. "I've got to get you away," he whispered in her ear. "I know how you feel about this house, but it's no longer safe here."

Silently, he carried her into the hallway, setting her mind buzzing with questions. Where was he taking her, and why was the house unsafe? She didn't doubt his need for haste; indeed, she could feel the danger like a net closing in around them.

"Stop!"

Olivia appeared like a specter in their path, her gray hair loose and wild around her shoulders. The lamp she held cast strange, menacing shadows across her face.

Robert ignored her, pushing past her to the attic stairs.

"I'll summon your brother," Olivia called out behind them. "He'll put a stop to this."

Muttering a low oath, Robert quickened his pace. He was taking her to the attic studio, Julie realized, though she couldn't guess why. She thought he wanted to get far away from here.

"You certainly took your time," a woman said as they entered the loft. "I told you I am in too much of a hurry to dally on this errand of mercy."

"You're a regular pearl, Florinda. Where do you want her?"

Hands on hips, the woman surveyed the room, pointing to the mirror. "There. Yes, I can feel the vibrations." As Florinda turned to her, Julie recognized the Gypsy they'd met in the speakeasy.

Bewildered, Julie wondered what they meant to do. It seemed she'd have to wait to find out, for no sooner had Robert set her on the floor than William barged into the studio. "What in God's name do you think you're doing? Unhand Victoria at once!"

He looked boyish in his rumpled pajamas, his hair poking up at odd angles. There was nothing charming, though, about the gun he brandished. "Get away from her," he said, waving the weapon at his brother.

Robert stepped back, glaring at him. "Damn it William, if you have any conscience left, you'll go now and leave her alone."

"Alone? Let me remind you, this is *my* house and that is *my* wife. Victoria belongs to me."

"You talk as if she's a piece of property. Do you think you can steal Victoria back and display her over your mantel like you do my painting?"

"You gave me that painting," William said, affronted. "You said it was a wedding present."

"I meant for our wedding. Victoria's and mine."

A misunderstanding, Julie thought. All that heartache for nothing.

"Shoot if you must," Robert said, "but I'm taking her away from here, far away where she can be happy. Where she will be safe."

"You must be out of your mind to think I'll let her go off with the man who tried to kill her."

Robert shook his head sadly. "You're my brother and I love you, but I'm not taking the blame for you this time. That woman is my life. I'll die before I let you harm one more hair on her head."

"Me?" The gun drooped. "You can't possibly think *I* pushed her?"

"But if it wasn't you . . ." Robert paused, clearly puzzled. "Then it must have been Stollenbach. He went crazy when Victoria saw him here at the house. The way he's panicking over this federal investigation, he must have decided to get rid of her."

William shook his head. "Red wouldn't hurt her. We're business partners. He'd never touch my wife."

"Don't be naive. The man's in the business of hurting people—he'll kill anyone who gets in his way. I warned you not to get mixed up with the likes of him."

"You're one to talk."

"I worked for you, not Stollenbach. I only ran booze to help you out of a bind, but I'm done now. I want no more part of it."

So William was the real bootlegger, Julie thought. Thinking back, she realized that Robert must have known all along. He could have told her, using the information to gain advantage, but instead he'd kept his peace.

"You can't quit," William said on a desperate note. "With the market crashing and banks failing every day, I need the extra income. What will I say to Father if another business venture fails?"

Robert shrugged. "You'll blame me, like you always have."

Julie remembered Robert talking about how hard it was for William to please their father. He'd cut himself off abruptly, but she knew now what he'd been about to say. Long ago, he'd fallen into the habit of shielding William. It was easy enough; everyone expected him to fail anyway. No wonder it had been so important that she, at least, believed in him.

Only she'd let him down. She'd betrayed him.

"Don't get greedy," Robert told his brother sadly. "If you take the money Stollenbach offers, you'll only get deeper under his thumb. Eventually, he'll ask you to make a choice—Victoria's life or your own."

"He has no need to kill her," William blustered. "She's no threat to anyone if she can't speak."

Hunkering down before Julie, Robert gently shifted the hair from her face. "Maybe she can't move her lips, but she hears every word we utter. She's in there somewhere, William, and I won't rest until we save her. Remember when we were boys, and we found that injured bird? As much as we loved it, when it came time, we happily let it take flight?"

"You were happy. I was sad. I missed it when it was gone."

Robert sighed. "You'll probably miss Victoria, too, but would you rob her of the chance to be free?"

William lowered his hand, the gun all but forgotten. "What have you planned?"

"Ask Florinda." Robert nodded at the woman, now standing beside the mirror.

William looked appalled. "That—that Gypsy?"

"I shall send her into the future." Florinda drew herself up, now almost regal. "Time, it is a fluid thing," she said eerily. "There are conduits, doorways, through which some lucky souls can slip."

"A door through time?" William scoffed. "Come now, Robert, surely you're not falling for this. For how much is she fleecing you?"

"My payment will be only this mirror." Florinda's dark eyes flashed fire. "I am no charlatan. I would try this for no one else but Robbie."

Robert smiled at her. "My brother's a born skeptic—never even believed in Santa Claus." Sobering, he turned to William. "I know it sounds far-fetched, but I keep thinking, *what if?* If there's the slightest chance to save Victoria, to help her walk and laugh again, I've got to take it."

"This is absurd. I shall take her to the very best doctors, see she has the finest care possible."

"And the moment she can talk, Stollenbach will be waiting. If we send her into the future, she can have better doctors, more opportunity to mend and heal."

William looked from Robert to Julie, his features clouding. "You mean to go with her, don't you?"

"I'm not certain you can slip through," Florinda interrupted. "Some make the journey, many do not."

William raised the gun, pointing it at his brother's chest. "It's all academic. If I can't have her, neither will you."

Robert stood, his expression grim. "We're no longer boys, and this isn't some toy we're fighting over. Damn you, William, if you let Victoria go, I'll take the blame for everything, even the bootlegging."

William hesitated. Julie could see he was tempted. "And you won't go with her?"

Robert held up his hands in a gesture of surrender. "As long as you're still alive, you have my word, we will not be together."

William gave a little laugh. "I have you beat, then, for we both know you always keep your word. You're a romantic fool, Robert, and too damned noble."

"I love her."

The ensuing silence emphasized the power of those simple words. Once again, Julie could feel moisture on her cheeks.

William stiffened. "She's mine, Robert. If this works, and she appears in the future, I'll be waiting and watching for her. I'm stubborn enough to live to a ripe old age. I'll have her yet."

"Yeah, but you may be too old to care." Robert grinned, showing a spark of his former mischief. "Besides, she'll still be a young woman. What would she see in a decrepit old man?"

"She may not want me, but she'll always want this house."

All humor faded from Robert's features. "I suppose you're right. You'll let us try then? You won't do anything to prevent her escape?"

Even as William nodded, Julie heard a loud, "No!" from the doorway. Olivia Howard stood there, looking half wild in her fury. "She is my child, and I say she will not leave this house."

Robert moved closer to Victoria. "She must. Her life is in danger."

"I heard," Olivia interrupted, "But she's safe enough as long as she stays where she is and does what she's told. Isn't that right, Victoria?" She marched across the room to Julie. "I've sacrificed half my life for you—you who've been nothing but a burden since the day you were born. Did you think I'd let you prove as useless as your father, running off and leaving me behind to pick up the pieces? Did you truly think that now, when I'm this close to my just reward, I would ever let you leave me?"

Seeing the cold, unreasoning hatred in Olivia's gaze, Julie felt the shock of recognition. Red Stollenbach hadn't made the attempt on Victoria's life. It was this insanely bitter woman, who'd rather see her daughter dead than lose her position in this house.

No wonder Victoria had withdrawn from reality.

Julie felt as if she could never be warm again. With great relief, she watched William step up to lead Olivia away. "Come along, Mrs. Howard, you and I need to talk."

Olivia turned with a smile, not seeing the gun in his hands. "No need to fret, Mr. William. I shall stay to nurse Victoria, to take care of you both."

William turned to his brother, nodding. Both knew the truth, Julie realized; both now found it imperative to get Victoria away from her mother. "Let's go downstairs," William told Olivia, steering her by the elbow. "You can fix me something to eat."

As he glanced back, Robert mouthed the words, "Thank you."

William shook his head. "Just remember," he reminded his brother, "you gave your word."

"We must hurry," Florinda said the minute William closed the door behind him. "Danger gathers around us. Quick, lift her closer to the glass."

Julie struggled helplessly, desperate to find some way to stop this. She no longer wished to return to her own time, not if it meant she'd never see Robert again.

Taking Julie's hands, Florinda began to chant as she raised them to the mirror. *No!* Julie screamed silently, but her lips would not move and no one could hear.

"She's fighting me, Robbie," Florinda said, stopping her intonations. "Your woman, she doesn't want to leave you. Come, take her hands and help me."

Julie felt his warmth, heard his soft voice in her ear. "Ah sweetheart, don't cling to this life. It's time, little bird, to leave your cage."

The tingling began in Julie's fingertips, spread throughout her until her vision swam. Through it all, Robert whispered in her ear. "Have faith in me. If there's any way possible, I will come after you, just as soon as I am able. God, Victoria, don't you know by now how much I love you?"

The words echoed, tumbling all around her as she floated away. She tried to reach out, struggling not to lose him, but Robert grew dimmer and less distinct until he faded completely before her eyes.

Time speeded up, her life playing before her in super-fast motion, her past catching up with her until she was back in the attic before the mirror, her memory whole and intact. "My God," she said, gazing with wonder at the face she now recognized. "I *am* Victoria!"

"Yeah, and I'm the Queen of England."

She whirled, finding Gwen behind her. As always, she felt the quick jolt of nausea, but this time, she had no doubts about her sanity. At long last, she knew who she was. "Oh Gwen, I remember everything. William, my mother . . ." It was hard not to shudder at that memory.

"I read the diary, too. Your Victoria writes well. Even I got sucked into her story, but not to the point of taking on her identity. Don't you see? You're so desperate to have a past, you've dreamed this up. Jules, honey, you've been gone another two days, and when I come here to get you, I find you staring dreamily into that old mirror again. At the risk of being cruel, are these the actions of a well-balanced woman?"

Julie looked at the mirror, unable to stop the smile. William must have gotten it back from Florinda. His leaving her the house, the portrait left in the studio, proved it had all happened. "I know it sounds crazy, but I was there, Gwen. I felt it all."

Yet even as she said it, she wondered if she'd actually relived her life. Or had she stood here before the mirror, watching as the veil of amnesia lifted an inch at a time, her trauma fading as she realized it was her mother—and not Robert—who tried to kill her?

Robert.

He was there, inside the mirror, and she had to go to him. She was whole now, ready to trust and believe; surely it would make a difference. All she had to do was reach out and touch the glass.

"Damn it, Julie. Enough!"

In slow motion, she watched Gwen's high-heeled shoe come hurtling though the air. Though Julie reached for it, it went sailing past, hitting the mirror and splintering the glass into a hundred pieces. Julie felt as if her heart shattered with it.

"I had to," Gwen said defensively. "C'mon Julie, someone has to bring you to your senses."

Looking at her roommate, Julie felt nothing but loathing. How like her mother Gwen was, ordering her around under the premise that it was for Julie's own good, urging her to marry a cousin who could well be another William. Even in her new life, she'd been repeating the same pattern. Indeed, the only thing missing was Robert.

She choked down a sob, trying to absorb the loss, not wanting Gwen to guess how devastated she felt. Though she could still feel his warmth, the comfort his arms had given her, the sensation was fading. One thoughtless act, and Gwen had made certain she'd never feel it again.

Julie stooped down, reaching for a piece of the glass. For an insane, desperate moment, she considered taking each piece and gluing them together, but deep down, she understood that it was much too late. Robert was gone, as far away as the moon.

At Gwen's prodding, she left the attic; but as she did, she made plans to move out of the house they shared. She didn't need someone like Gwen running her life. Smiling sadly, she thought of Robert's last words. He had done his part, setting her free from her cage.

Wasn't it time she learned to fly?

Months later, Julie closed the oak door of the house and locked it. Tomorrow the new owners would be sending in contractors to change the very personality of the place. Surprisingly, she found she wouldn't miss it, except for the studio. But then, she'd spent many an hour there, painting the seascapes that would soon grace the walls of a Manhattan gallery.

Smiling, she knew Robert would have been proud. She hadn't just flown when she left her cage; she'd soared.

She had an apartment in the city now, and a job at the same gallery to supplement the income from her painting. Her days were full with her new friends, but not a night went by that she didn't long for Robert.

Taking the path down the bluff, she strolled along the beach, visiting the places she'd once laughed with him. She often thought about his last words, how he'd promised to come after her if he were able. It seemed impossible, with the mirror broken, yet he'd asked her to have faith in him and this time she would. After all, he'd given his promise and she knew he always kept his word.

Her friends all thought she was crazy, choosing a solitary existence, but there could be no other man for her. No matter how long it took, even if it stretched into a second lifetime, she would wait for her Robert.

She sighed. Others might say it was her imagination, her longings getting the best of her, but sometimes she almost sensed he was near, as if he waited behind some curtain of time to come to her. "Robert," she'd whisper, as if his name were a talisman that could somehow summon him.

At first, when she saw the easel down the beach, she thought it a trick of light—all that dark auburn hair blowing in the breeze a mere product of her yearnings. She nearly turned away, unable to bear the memories the man stirred, until she saw the splotch of red paint on his shirt.

Heart crashing against her ribcage, she shaded her eyes from the sun. She blinked and the image remained, the face—that dear, familiar face—turning to her as if she'd called him. She took a step forward, then another, until she was running through the sand. "Robert," she whispered again, her voice increasing in pitch as she ran. "Oh dear God, Robert!"

He glanced up, surprised, before his features slowly broke into a dazzling smile. Flinging down his brush, he took the remaining steps to greet her, holding his arms open as she ran into them. With a joyful laugh, he spun her around, both of them talking and laughing at once. She touched his face in silent awe until, with a sense of inevitable rightness, he leaned down to kiss her.

"Ah Victoria," he said when he could bring himself to pull away. "It seems such a miracle to see you, to hold you at last. I'd begun to despair that I'd ever find you."

"I know. After Gwen broke the mirror, I thought I'd lost you forever. What happened? How did you get here?"

"I'm not sure. I came through the mirror in a shop in Harlem. Since Florinda had died years earlier, I had no way of knowing where, when, or even *if* you'd come through. After arranging for the mirror to be delivered to the house, I went out looking for you. I've been searching ever since."

"I came through two years ago but I wouldn't have known you if you'd found me: I had amnesia until a few months ago."

He shook his head, bemused. "It's like a hand was guiding us. I came through the day after William died, as if the mirror knew I must keep my promise not to be with you as long as he was alive."

Florinda had said time was a fluid thing, but perhaps it just moved under its own special laws. Gazing at Robert, as beautiful as the instant she'd met him, she realized that their coming together *had* been inevitable.

She smiled up at him. "I don't care how it happened. All that matters is that you found me. Just like you said you would."

"Chasing around got me nowhere, so I decided to wait here." He glanced up the bluff. "I knew you'd always come back to this house."

Hating to hear his bitterness, she placed her hands on his shoulders and met his gaze squarely. "I've sold the house. I've learned that I don't need it to be happy. My home is wherever you are."

Taking her face in his hands, he kissed her again, long and hard. "My absolutely beautiful Victoria," he said after a time, "does this mean you will marry me and give me lots of beautiful children?"

"I'd say that depends." She was so happy, she couldn't resist teasing him. "You said yourself, a woman should be courted first."

He grinned, leaning down to kiss her again. "In that case, my frivolous Miss Howard, prepare yourself to be chased and wooed and whispered to every night."

About the Author

A native New Yorker, Barbara Benedict now lives in Southern California with her family. The move, she says with a grin, was one way of getting to see America. Fascinated by history, she has written several historical romances, two regencies, and one time travel romance, *A Taste of Heaven* (published by Zebra Books). Barbara is also the author of *Destiny,* a historical romance set in ancient Greece (also published by Zebra Books). Barbara's newest historical romance, *Always,* will be published in October 1995. Barbara loves hearing from readers and you can write to her c/o Zebra Books. Please include a self-addressed stamped envelope if you wish a response.

Lion's Pride

Janice Bennett

One

Fog, a gray haze against the darkness of the night, drifted low and thick across the rippling waters of Inlet Bay. Jessica Howard scooped up an armful of the voluminous skirts of her Elizabethan costume and waded calf-deep through the cold wavelets. Behind her on the beach, the annual Non-Discovery Day bonfire flared high into the sky, the laughter and shouts of the celebrants sending an ache of loneliness through her heart.

She could sit here on the jagged rocks—but someone might see her and drag her back, insisting she not be alone. Why did her family's friends think she needed noise and activity all the time? That prescription hadn't helped so far during the four long months since the head-on car crash which had killed her parents and brother. It wouldn't help now. She stirred the rippling water with her toe, watching the fiery orange and russet reflection blend into the deep green blackness around the rocks. She'd played her part today, as she did every July 23. True, she hadn't joined the strolling musicians with her lute as she usually did, or even taken her turn with a spinning wheel at her cousin Monica's craft booth. Nor had she marched in the parade along with the other members of the precision spread-your-cloak-in-the-mud drill team. But she had washed and sliced endless flats of strawberries for the booth supporting the homeless shelter.

It took a town as tiny as Inlet Bay to come up with anything as ludicrous—and as much fun—as the annual celebration of Non-Discovery Day. The event commemorated the approximate date in 1603 when Sir Roger Allendale, the Elizabethan explorer/pirate, sailed his ship, the *Lion's Pride*, right past their tiny harbor without discovering it. The day-long festivities had attracted an incredible crowd this year; they must have driven in from as far away as San Francisco and Monterey Bay. It looked like most of them were still here, too, to join in the huge bonfire on the beach. When this reached its height, everyone, in time-honored tradition, would troop down to the rocky water line and yell: "Over here, Roger!"

Roger. Sir Roger Allendale. Jessica reached into the non-authentic pocket she had made for her gown and drew out her crumpled sketch of the famous explorer. She didn't need the erratic, flickering bonfire light to envision every strong line of his face, every thickly curling wave of his red-blond mane and beard. She knew them by heart. Almost, she knew *him* by heart. She had dreamed of him, imagined what such a man must be like.

She refolded and replaced the sketch, then forged on through the shallow waters, avoiding rocks, closing her ears to the sounds of celebration. The light from the flames danced across the surface of the bay, setting highlights in the craggy recesses, reflecting off—Jessica peered into the murky darkness. Something had glimmered down there, half-buried in the sand. Broken glass?

Cautiously she reached for it, her fingers encountering the smooth sides of a small bottle wedged among the rocks. She drew it out and examined it, fascinated by the way it glowed purple in the wavering light. No soft drink container, this. She'd seen enough antiques to recognize the air-bubbled glass for a historic artifact. It might even date back to the Spanish occupation of the area. A seal—lead, perhaps?—was fastened about the narrow neck. Carrying her treasure, she splashed her way to the dilapidated dory moored at the end of the ramshackle pier.

She climbed in and sat, cradling the bottle in her lap as she stared out across the bay toward the invisible horizon. Here she was, twenty-two, a degree in botany behind her, a comfortable inheritance so she could go to graduate school and then take time finding exactly the right job. She had everything—especially a vast emptiness in her life, filled only by dreams and memories.

Behind her on the beach, the celebrants began their annual march to the water's edge to holler for Sir Roger's attention.

Normally she'd be with them, shouting for her explorer as loudly as anyone else. Perhaps she should—

An eerie glow shimmered just beyond the rocky land spit that formed the mouth of the bay. She blinked, but it didn't vanish. Instead, it brightened, taking on distinct shape, solidifying. A high-masted ship . . . no, an ancient galleon . . . .

In a mixture of wonder and growing delight, she watched as the vessel took on form and substance. A ghost ship, come to fulfill the demands of the crowd on the beach, perhaps? Or to fulfill the longings of her heart?

A wave of dizziness washed over her and a ringing grew in her ears until it blotted out the laughing and shouting from the beach. She clutched the bottle as her vision blurred. The world spun crazily about her, and as she started to rise, the rough timbers of the dory spiraled up to greet her.

TWO

Hands, grabbing her arms, roused Jessica. A wave of dizziness—not the first, she remembered hazily—swept over her, then receded, leaving her nauseous and shaken. The gentle roar of the ocean filled her ears, and the salt air— She gagged as the pungent odors of sweat and onions assailed her. The hands that gripped her tightened their hold.

"Easy, lass." A rough voice sounded near her ear, and a finger trailed along the line of her cheek. "Now, what would you be doing here?"

Jessica opened her eyes, then blinked at the brightness that surrounded her. No trace remained of the heavy July fog that had blotted out the stars and moon during the bonfire. No trace of night, either. She must have slept for a long time. The morning sun rode high in the sky, its warmth caressing her back.

She caught at the splintery gunwale of the fishing dory in which she lay and stared up into the grinning, dirty face that hovered so close to her own. Greasy brown hair hung lank over a narrow forehead and broad nose. The skin showed innumerable pockmarks, and the mouth boasted three missing teeth that she could see. As for the breath—she recoiled.

"Strong his arm and keen his scent is," she murmured, quoting from her much-loved *Pirates of Penzance*. She shook her head, trying to clear her fogged brain. She had to give him full credit for the authenticity of his Elizabethan seaman's costume. Her own gown she had reproduced carefully in modern, easy-care polyester blends. Neat. Easy to clean. His looked much more realistic, complete with grime and tears—and the smell of long-dead fish, ocean salt, and a variety of bodily odors too pungent to be real. "He's a pirate now, indeed," she pronounced more clearly, finishing the song's line.

"Nay, sweeting. It's in Her Majesty's service we are." He grinned at her, once more displaying his incredibly realistic dental decay.

Other details began to occur to her. The man knelt on sand, beside her dory, which now rested on the beach. The last she could remember was clambering into it, where it rocked in the shallow waters of Inlet Bay, tethered to the dilapidated pier. How—?

She pulled a hand free and wiped the back across her gritty eyes. "I must have fallen asleep." She dragged herself to a sitting position. "Did you bring the dory ashore?"

"Found you here, I did. Never thought to get me hands on a treasure like you." He pulled her to her feet and his gaze hungrily devoured her. "Buss me, sweeting, there's a love." He leaned closer to take the demanded kiss.

"In your dreams." She leaned into his embrace only to bring her forearm down on his, breaking his hold on her and knocking him aside.

He staggered back, eyeing her with startled disapproval. "Now, there's no call to go—"

"Dickon!" a man's deep voice called from up the beach. "What is that you've found?"

Another wave of dizziness washed over Jessica, leaving her weak and disoriented, her memory not functioning. Who—She forced her eyes open once more as the man—presumably Dickon—half-lifted her from the ancient rowboat to the sand.

The dinghy must have come loose while she slept. She blinked blurring eyes at the rope, which trailed back from the high tide mark, tangled in drying kelp. No plastic garbage, at least, she noted with vague satisfaction. No—

She straightened, barely aware of the man who tugged at her arm. No pier.

She ran a shaky hand through the jumble of her dark brown curls. No *pier?* It couldn't have collapsed over night—even though that possibility was a standing joke in the little town of

Inlet Bay. Her gaze strayed up the beach. No traces of last night's Non-Discovery Day bonfire, either.

Three men stood on the sand, near where there should have been the remnants of the burned driftwood. She narrowed her gaze, trying to focus on them. Their costumes looked as authentic as that of the man at her side.

Uncertain, her gaze darted about the beach, looking for something familiar to help anchor her reeling world. The line of Monterey pines, which broke off from the forested area and separated the sand dunes from the street leading to the town, wasn't there. If it weren't impossible, she'd swear even the dunes had changed shape.

That explained it. Her dory must have come untied and drifted along the coast during the night, and she'd slept right through it. Yet the shape of the narrow, treed ridge of the peninsula, the spit jutting out into the ocean, even the location of the rocks, were right for Inlet Bay. She'd grown up playing on them, knew each and every one . . .

She took a step, only to have her knees buckle beneath her. Dickon seized his opportunity. He slipped an arm about her waist and half-carried, half-propelled her the short distance to another dory, much larger and in better condition than hers, which lay half in the lapping waves, half on the wet sand.

Through her dizziness, the men's voices sounded, rough and laughing. The words washed over her, making little impression as her world continued to reel. One—Dickon, she thought—said something that he accompanied with a ribald laugh.

"The master'll 'ave aught to say about that," one of the others warned. The hand that gripped her eased its hold.

"Master?" She dragged herself from the fog that still engulfed her and raised her gaze. "Where are you taking me?" For the first time, she realized they headed straight out into the bay, not along the coastline.

"The ship," one of the men announced. "We wouldn't camp ashore."

A ship? She peered over her shoulders and stared in disbelief at the vessel—*a galleon*—anchored within the line of jutting rocks.

It had been damaged, she realized as she studied it. One of its three masts—the mizzen—had been broken in two. The top half had crashed across the railing, breaking it, and hung into the water, supported by the splintered remains. Just like . . .

Memory flooded back of the glowing shape she'd seen just before she'd lost consciousness. No ghost ship, but a reproduction, complete with costumed crew, come for the Non-Discovery Day celebrations. Yet she hadn't heard of anyone building a replica of the *Lion's Pride,* or any other vessel of the Elizabethan era.

Curious, she watched as the men's long, powerful oar strokes drew them closer to the ship's side. She'd never seen anything like it, except for in pictures. It was smaller than she'd expected, perhaps a hundred feet long, not large and heavy like the Spanish galleons depicted more often in books. Those were designed to carry the treasures from the New World back to swell the coffers of King Phillip; this was the lighter English galleon that enabled Elizabeth's pirates to loot and harass their enemies at sea.

The ship creaked as it swayed in the water, bobbing with the gentle waves. It didn't really look like a reproduction—unless they'd deliberately given it that weather-worn appearance. If they'd painted the rich brown hull at any recent date, then they'd gone back and given it a good sandblasting, as well. Still, much of the red and gold trim remained.

She caught a glimpse of the gilded lion's head attached to the bowsprit, the figurehead of Sir Roger Allendale's *Lion's Pride.* And there was the name, emblazoned in worn gilt across the stern. She could almost believe this was his vessel. It certainly looked as if it had endured the passage through the freezing Strait of Magellan and the incredible storms below South America.

And as for the damage. . . . An acrid smell reached her, stronger even than the saltiness of the bay. Smoke? Perhaps a fire could explain the damage, the fallen mast.

The dory drew up against the side, where a rope ladder dangled. One of her companions stood, his hand still on her arm, as he thrust her toward the ladder. "Carry you up, shall I?"

"No, thanks." She caught the rope and, with an uneasy glance at the four waiting men, started climbing.

The fibers bit into her hands. She'd never encountered any this coarse before. The builders seemed to have stuck to as many period details as they could manage. She dragged herself up, hand over hand, wincing as the sharp tufts bit into her bare feet. The smell of pitch and tar surrounded her, almost overwhelming the gunpowder. For that was what it was, she realized. Not fire. There'd been an explosion here.

Voices reached her, harsh with strange accents. They seemed to be going to a lot of trouble for a recreation. It left her with an unsettled feeling creeping up from the pit of her stomach.

Hands grabbed her as she reached the top of the ladder, dragging her up the last few feet and swinging her over the rail. As she straightened, she stared into the stubbled, begrimed face of a slightly built dark-haired man. Blood—a great deal of it—crusted on his torn, Elizabethan shirt.

From behind her, the man she had first encountered on the beach said: "Don't you be touching her. The master'll have something to say to that, he will." He swung easily to her side, took hold of her arm with an air of wary respect, and urged her forward.

Jessica remained where she stood, her gaze transferring from the sailor to the ship itself. Everywhere signs of battle met her horrified gaze. Two men lay on the main deck, their low moans mingling with the creaking of the timbers. Others knelt over them, their filthy, torn garments waving in the breeze. One man bandaged the arm of another. A pile of dirty stained rags lay at their side.

A wretch of nausea assailed her stomach at the putrid odors, at the total lack of hygiene. No one would go this far to recreate the atmosphere of a period—would they? Actually endangering their own well-being? These were real injuries. She had no doubts about that. While the gore could have been faked, those smells told their own tale.

Her companion escorted her through the wreckage that showed hasty signs of being cleared to the center of the deck, where three men stood, all in those authentic costumes. Or were they costumes? She cast another uneasy glance about the ship as a horrible possibility occurred to her. But that was ludicrous.

She couldn't have been transported through time, back to 1603 and the real *Lion's Pride*. Besides, Sir Roger Allendale never had ventured into Inlet Bay. That was the whole point of Non-Discovery Day.

"Captain," her companion said.

One of the men turned to her, and Jessica's heart shot up through her throat, then plummeted to the depths of her stomach. She stared into the most striking countenance she had ever seen. A mane of red-gold hair waved back from a high forehead, falling to the man's shoulders. Hawk-like blue eyes regarded her from beneath bushy brows that met above the craggy nose. A neatly trimmed beard of deeper red lined his strong chin.

Hearty laughter filled his face. "And what treasure is this you have brought me? A delicacy lost by the Spanish, perhaps?"

Jessica opened her mouth, but could not command her voice. Every line of that face remained etched in her memory. She had seen it so often. Replicas of it from one of his portraits had flown on innumerable banners yesterday. And she carried his image with her, even now, folded in her pocket.

Yet it couldn't be him . . . could it?

She had never imagined how his brilliant blue eyes could flash with so much humor, how his very presence could rob her of breath, how so much power and enthusiasm could be contained in one body. She'd seen only an image. Now she saw the man come to life, in the flesh.

"Oh, no. I'm not buying into this," she said through gritted teeth—yet she knew she was. She drew in a deep, ragged breath. She actually thought of him as Sir Roger. Yet that was impossible. It had to be.

A slight frown creased the man's forehead. "There is no need, madam. We will carry you gladly, if that is your need." He swept her a bow. "I am Roger Allendale, and I am entirely at your service." He straightened, his eyes glinting as his gaze traveled over her. "Allow me to welcome you aboard the *Lion's Pride.*"

She felt herself grinning like an imbecile. "Thank you. It's a nice ship. I—I've never been on one quite like it, before." And what other inanities would she blurt out? she wondered. She shook her head. "Sorry, I—I seem to be a little dazed by all this."

"It is no wonder—" he began, only to be interrupted by a word from one of his men.

As he turned to the sailor, Jessica closed her eyes. Get a grip, she silently ordered herself. Yet the huskiness of his voice sent a shivering thrill through her, leaving a quivering heap of Jell-O where her brain should have been. He was so much more than she had ever imagined. So strong and daring, a man so charismatic that he could hold a crew of men together over the long, dangerous voyage, one who could command in battle and storm, one who would be obeyed without question.

Her last doubts had faded, she realized with a touch of rising hysteria. It couldn't be—yet the very power of the man made the impossible seem credible. Her gaze slid past him, across the deck of the battle-scarred ship, then toward the shoreline no longer familiar yet hauntingly reminiscent in its contours. She had sailed this bay too often not to know its rocky outline by heart. Yet what had happened to the trees, the road, the shift of sand dunes—unless this really was Sir Roger, and somehow, incredibly, she had been transported back through time?

Three

As if by the mere acceptance of this fact, her reeling world settled and her dizziness faded. For the first time since waking up in that dory to find the sailor bending over her, her mind and senses functioned with their normal clarity. In fact, she'd be in complete control of herself—if it weren't for her overwhelming awareness of this man.

Sir Roger turned back to her. "If you will excuse me but a moment, and await me over there?" He nodded toward the bow of the ship. "I have a somewhat pressing matter here that demands my attention, and I fear it cannot be delayed." With a polite bow he turned from her.

Her gaze followed him, resting on the broad expanse of his shoulders in their deep green doublet. His hands . . .

His hands drew a begrimed, blood-stained knife from its scabbard at his belt. Jessica blinked, then for the first time saw that he stood before a raised plank, on which lay a man. Blood smeared this poor sailor's doublet and hose, both of which showed numerous gashes. He groaned, his head tossing against the wood, and one of the men who aided Sir Roger grabbed the victim by the shoulders while the other gripped his ankles.

Sir Roger steadied himself for a moment, then slowly he raised the filthy knife, reaching for a ragged tear in the man's hose, which was covered in smears of crusted blood. The poor sailor must have been given so much to drink to knock him out, he didn't have the faintest idea what was about to hit him.

"You can't!" Jessica cried. "What do you think you're doing?"

He turned to look at her. "What must be done." An edge of steel sounded in the words.

"But that thing's filthy! Can't you boil some water?" She encountered his uncomprehending stare. "You've got to sterilize that knife!" she tried again.

"Madam," he said, his tone as patient as if he explained to a child, "I need only remove a ball that has lodged itself against the bone. And it is best if it be done quickly."

"It is best if it be done with a clean knife!" She lunged for his hand, but he moved it out of her reach. Frustrated, she spun about to find that most of the men on deck had stopped their activities and stared at her, unmoving. No help there. She turned to the two who held down the injured sailor. "Stop this maniac. You can't let him do this—this butcher job."

"Good lack!" Sir Roger breathed, and his countenance turned thunderous. "Who are you to come aboard my ship and give orders?"

"Who are you," she countered, "to do anything as stupid and dangerous as to operate with a germ-ridden knife?"

"Germ-ridden? Phah! What nonsense is this?"

Her teeth clenched. "I can put up with a lot, but that's one thing I cannot and will not allow. I want that thing sterilized. Now."

For a long minute he stared at her, then his brow cleared and he burst out laughing. "A female, to order the running of my vessel? Come, lass, I'll show you how such a shrew should be treated."

He cast the knife on the deck, and before she realized what he was about, he caught her hands behind her in one of his massive ones and dragged her against himself for a resounding kiss. As his mouth came down upon hers, self-defense training took over. She wrenched one wrist free and, grasping the fingers of his other hand, peeled them from the nape of her neck. In one move she jerked downward, twisting his arm behind his back and up toward his shoulder blades, buckling him over.

"I'll thank you to keep your hands to yourself," she snapped. Yet part of her had wanted to melt against him. She thrust that thought aside. "You might even try taking a bath and brushing your teeth if you want a woman to welcome you."

"Stand back!" he shouted.

His men, who had started toward them, stopped. Jessica eyed them warily, unsure what to do next, or what form Sir Roger's retaliation would take.

He shifted against her hold. "A veritable hellcat, a lioness," he breathed, his tone half marveling, half suppressed fury.

Or was that suppressed laughter? Deciding to risk it, she released him and stepped back, her uneasy gaze resting on him as he straightened, rubbing his hand.

He faced her, returning her regard, his eyes gleaming with amused appreciation. "I cry pardon," he said with mock humbleness.

"Do you really?" She eased herself a step farther away, not fooled for a moment by his tone.

"Indeed, I do. It seems we have somewhat to learn of one another." He studied her a moment longer, then nodded as if coming to a decision. "Very well, I'm willing to be taught. You may have your way, and let us see what comes of it." He raised his head and looked about at his men, who remained frozen, their stances wary. "Dickon, Edmund, is there no one about to boil water for the lady?"

Murmurs rose from the men. "Women!" Dickon muttered, but went to do the bidding.

Sir Roger remained before her, arms akimbo, his gaze resting on her. "Well, lady? What will you with this water when you have it?"

"Clean the knife. Boil it for at least ten minutes."

His eyebrows rose. "And what purpose in that? Have I taken a witch aboard my vessel?"

"Nothing so—" She broke off before she could add "useful." In his time, a witch was considered evil. "Nothing like that. It's—" She thought fast. "It's a Chinese idea. Just humor me, all right?" She didn't feel up to explaining germs to him. She had a sneaky feeling the idea of something so small he couldn't see it causing illness would only make him laugh. "Before much longer, everyone will be boiling surgical instru-

ments in water and keeping their hands—and themselves—
clean."

"Chinese." His eyes narrowed, his expression arrested. The
look he directed at her held a wealth of speculation and appraisal.
"Chinese. I have heard they know much of medicine in the East.
Do you share that knowledge, then?"

"Some," she admitted, though her knowledge was purely bo-
tanical in nature. Still, at this time, what other kind of medicine
would he mean—except for folk charms? Then, as inspiration
struck, she added: "My father was a doctor, studying the ways
of the East." That sounded safe. There would be no way he could
check on her story, and it might explain some of her strange
ways. Unless she wanted to be burned for a witch on the spot,
she could hardly tell him she came from the future.

From a safe, very distant future. Her home. The modern world,
where germs and basic hygiene were common knowledge. Would
she ever see it again?

She turned away, lost, disoriented once more, hugging herself
against the fear that rose within her. What was she doing here?
And more importantly, how could she ever get home?

"Lady." His deep, rumbling voice gentled as he moved toward
her, and his hand closed on her shoulder. "You have nothing to
fear from me or mine."

She turned to face him, fighting back the panic that threatened
to overcome her. She stared into his face and saw no threat
there—except the threat to her heart. How easy it would be to
trust a man like this, to share in his wild adventures. But this
was a man's world, where a woman was expected to wait quietly
at home, never to have any excitement or fun. *Not* her world.

Abruptly he stepped away, turning his back to her. "Is there
aught else you would have us do for our injured?"

She swallowed, glad to have a practical focus for her rampag-
ing thoughts. "Wash—wash as many cloths as possible," she
said, and was pleased by how calm her voice sounded. "It doesn't
look like you have anything clean at all on this ship."

He stooped and picked up the knife, then presented the hilt to
her. The smiling eyes that regarded her held a disturbing glow.

"Will you see it done to your satisfaction? Or will you trust my men to do it to your instructions?"

She inclined her head, and a smile tugged at her lips. It was too easy to respond to him. "You know them better than I do. It's pretty simple, though. Think they can be trusted to do it right?"

His eyes danced. "They would pay with their lives if they disobeyed an order, madam."

Somehow, she didn't doubt it. Another sign of how barbaric this time could be. Definitely, this was not where she belonged.

He raised a hand, gesturing to the stocky, brown-haired man who had held the injured sailor's feet. "Edmund, see this done."

"Scrub the knife 'til it's clean, then drop it in water that's already at a full boil," Jessica said quickly. "Ten full minutes. Then wrap it in a clean cloth."

The look Edmund directed at Sir Roger spoke volumes, but he held his tongue. Carrying the knife, he strode toward the companionway.

"Have you other comments to make concerning the running of my ship?" Sir Roger inquired. A note of challenge lurked just beneath the surface of his bantering tone. "The set of the sails, perhaps? Or the distribution of cargo in the hold?"

Jessica shook her head, meeting his gaze with direct candor. "Only your health hazards. Though on second thought, I'd probably rather not know. This place looks like one big hygienic nightmare."

His eyes gleamed as he turned to check on the injured sailor. He spoke in a low voice to the man who stood waiting at the sailor's head, then with a sweeping bow to Jessica, he excused himself and strode to where the other injured men had already received treatment. Jessica watched his progress as he moved on from them to examine the damage done to the mast. He seemed to be everywhere, moving with the grace of a restless animal across the swaying ship.

She crossed to the rail and leaned her back against it, her gaze following him as he strode from one group of his men to another. Occasionally one of the sailors cast her a surreptitious glance, then returned at once to his work. The mizzenmast, it seemed, would be taken down. Already, tools appeared and a work party assembled.

At last, Edmund emerged from the companionway bearing a cloth before him in his hands as if he carried a sacred vessel. He strode over to Sir Roger who, with a nod of his leonine head, directed him to Jessica. The man approached her, eyeing her with uncertainty, then lifted back the cloth to reveal the scrubbed and polished knife within.

"Does it meet with your approval now?" Sir Roger asked.

"It does," Jessica admitted. "*You* don't. Go scrub your hands—and with soap."

His eyes narrowed, but the humor remained. He turned on his heel and strode down the companionway.

Edmund stared at her and fell back a pace. "No one orders the master about," he said, his tone wondering.

Jessica raised her eyebrows. "It's about time someone did, then. A man should never get his own way all the time. It's not good for him."

Edmund opened his mouth, closed it again without speaking, then bore the knife away to the patient's side. Sir Roger returned, bowed before her, and presented his hands for her inspection. "Do you intend to oversee the removal of the ball, as well?" he demanded.

An involuntary shudder set her shaking. "Don't you have a ship's doctor?"

"Lady," he said, his eyes once more glinting with humor, "you have seen him awaiting the removal of a ball from his own limb."

Jessica turned away. "Don't let the knife get dirty before you use it," she said without looking over her shoulder.

She stood at the rail, studiously watching the bay, the waves washing up the sand, until Sir Roger's voice called for an ointment. Then curiosity overcame her squeamishness and she joined them as he smeared an evil-smelling salve over the wound and bandaged it. Edmund and his assistant bore the ship's doctor away, still on his plank.

Sir Roger picked up the bloodied knife. "What would you have me do with it now?" he asked, still amused.

"Clean it, I should think," she said.

He wiped it on some dirtied rags and returned it to the sheath that hung from his waist. "Now then," he said. "You must forgive me for dealing with those pressing matters before giving you my undivided attention." He fixed her with a long, appraising look. "How do you come to be so far from anywhere, and how may I be of service to you?"

Jessica froze. How could she possibly explain herself? How *did* she get here—and more importantly, how could she get home?

The glint in his eyes faded, and his expression, for the first time since she'd met him, turned somber. "I have told you, you have naught to fear while aboard my vessel, either from me or my men. And rest assured, I am yours to command. The voyage to England is long, but not unduly hard. Drake has encompassed it already. The worst is behind us. We have only to make the repairs to the ship, then we will be off." Once more, his eyes twinkled. "Our hold is already heavy with Spanish treasure."

"I—" She broke off, at a loss. Was she stuck here, in the past? But why should she be? Surely this must be nothing more than a brief visitation. She would return to her dory this night and go back to sleep, then wake up in the morning in her own era and discover no time had passed. This would be a memory, a dream, nothing more. All she had to do was feed him some plausible tale, enjoy the company of this man she'd made into her personal hero, then slip away. That had to work. To believe anything else would be to go mad. Now, for a story . . .

"My name is Jessica Howard. I—I told you. I've been with my father in China." That was her story, she reflected ruefully, and she was stuck with it. "Our boat went aground on a reef, and we were taken on by a Spanish vessel that brought us to Mexico." Heavens, what did they call it at that time, New Spain? He made no comment, though. "My father died," she plowed on, "and I thought it best to escape. I've been working my way along the coast, trying to find a way out of this mess."

Some lingering skepticism in his expression warned her he wasn't completely buying her story. She braced herself.

All he said was: "You have found help," and awarded her another sweeping bow. "As I have said, my ship and I are at your disposal. Do you care to return to shore for the nonce? After a few weeks at sea, you will long for the solid ground, I promise you."

"What happened to your ship?" As far as she knew, Sir Roger and the *Lion's Pride* never entered Inlet Bay. But something had certainly occurred to damage the galleon.

"We encountered two Spanish vessels a little to the south, in the bay of Monte Rey. One we plundered, which is why we now ride so low. Then the other came upon us and gave chase. It managed to get off a lucky chain shot—two cannonballs, chained together," he added at her puzzled look. "We drove them off, but pursuit won't be far behind, I fear."

A man, the one called Edmund, approached to stand a respectful distance from them. Aware of him at once, Sir Roger turned. "Have all been tended?" he asked.

"They are as comfortable as possible. We are ready to join the other party ashore."

A broad grin spread across Sir Roger's face. "Let us be off at once. Lady?"

Jessica started forward, curious to see more of the area as it was so long ago, wondering what she might recognize, or if any traces of her own time remained for her to find. Sir Roger offered his arm, his elbow extended. After a moment she placed her fingers on it and allowed him to lead her to the rail where several men already descended the rope ladder.

"With your permission, Lady?" A sparkling challenge lit his eyes. Without waiting for her answer, he caught her up in his arms, tossing her lightly over his shoulder.

She caught her breath, fighting against the wealth of sensation that swept through her. She didn't feel outrage at all. In fact, the desire that filled her was no way to feel about a man who would have been dead somewhere around three hundred and fifty years before she would even be born! And one who most likely would vanish from her life in only a few short hours. If he didn't . . .

She balanced herself with her hands about his neck. "I could climb down on my own," she said, speaking softly into his ears. Yet she hoped he wouldn't take her at her word.

"Lady," he murmured with a chuckle, "I do not doubt it for

a moment. Nor do I doubt that I carry you but by your sufferance."

She worked out his meaning. "You got that one right." Then she clung to him as he eased them both over the rail.

"Had you objected—" he gripped the rope with one hand and began lowering them to the dory that rocked gently at the ship's side, "—I feel I should even now be once more doubled over with my arm twisted behind me."

"Nope. You'd be flat on your stomach on the deck. With my knee on your neck," she added as he set her on her feet in the stern.

"Lady." He raised her fingers to his lips for a lingering kiss. "That is a challenge I find difficult to resist."

He released her, and she sank onto the bench and clung to the gunwale. Did that mean he might try to take her in his arms again? If he did, her instincts were likely to produce a very different response than fighting.

She looked up, and over the heads of his men he met her gaze with a look of predatory enjoyment. Hot blood rushed to her cheeks, setting her tingling all over. Quickly, she turned to the shore, away from him. In his eyes she saw a very tempting danger—tantalizing, irresistible . . . and terrifying.

Two men rowed the boat with practiced ease. Jessica forced her mind away from Roger, back into composure. Yet how could she keep him from her thoughts when his deep voice rumbled behind her, answering questions, issuing instructions to his men?

At last, the bow struck the sand, and the men jumped out into the knee-high water, grasping the sides of the little boat and dragging it forward, beaching it. Sir Roger waded through the shallow wavelets near the rocks where she had found that odd bottle—was it only last night, or was it truly nearly four hundred years in the future?

"Lady?" he asked again.

"Isn't a woman allowed to do anything under her own power?" she demanded. Yet the temptation proved too much. She held out her arms, and he scooped her up once more, this time cradling her before him. She held herself stiffly, as much away from him as possible, uncomfortably aware of his men about them. Still, she had to struggle against the urge to wrap her arms about his neck and bury her face in that golden-red beard. The smell of salt and sweat that clung to him helped.

The men set forth at once for a stand of trees a little way up the beach. Sir Roger set her on her feet on the damp sand and stepped back, amusement in his eyes. "Your pardon, Lady. There is work that awaits. Do you care to watch?"

She cared to do anything that involved being in his company. He didn't need to know that, though. She gave what she hoped to be a casual shrug. "Sounds like it's the only game in town. Might as well."

His brow creased. "I doubt they will make a game of it."

She grinned. "Don't worry, I'll live." She set forth after his men, leaving him to follow.

The sounds of sawing, axe blows, and creaking wood reached her, followed by a splintering crash. She crested the dune and reached the forested area to find the men standing about a newly felled tree. One squared the base with an axe while others stripped the bark and branches from the straight trunk. The new mast.

Another tree also lay on its side, already cleaned. Two men with saws hewed planks to replace the damaged ones on the ship's side. Sir Roger inspected the work, nodding approval and giving a word of encouragement and praise. He was going to be very busy.

She wished she could spend what little time she might have in his company, but he had to repair his ship—and leave no clues to his presence. She found the prospect of Non-Discovery Day never coming into being daunting. Where would the little town of Inlet Bay be without it?

She might as well wander, look about while she had a chance. Just to be on the safe side, she selected a short, stout branch and peeled away the tufts of needles. Sir Roger might assure her his men would leave her alone, but sailors who had been long at sea might need a reminder. Her self-defense class had covered the basics of stick fighting.

The branch in her hand gave her confidence. She moved away, hiking across the yielding sand and over the grassy dunes, making for the more densely forested area to the south. Not much farther and she'd reach the area where the pier would be built.

Now, though, the bay spread out before her, devoid of any so-called improvements. Only the rocks interrupted the water's cresting swells as they raced toward the seaweed-strewn sand. The cries of gulls reached her, a sound so achingly familiar it tugged at her heart.

Pine needles crunched under an incautious booted foot, and smiling, she turned to greet Sir Roger. Instead, three strange men stood before her, black-haired, bearded, swords in their hands, dressed in the steel breastplates and helmets of the type she associated with Spaniards of the era. Spaniards . . .

A scream tore from her throat as the first of the men sprang toward her. She jumped aside, at the same time bringing her branch down on the man's outstretched arm. Before he could recover, she'd brought it back across an exposed area of his neck. He dropped to his knees, gasping for air, and she spun to face the next as a deep shout, accompanied by the crashing of a body forcing itself through the undergrowth, sounded from within the trees.

Jessica stood ready, tensed, watching the Spaniard nearest her, but both men now turned to meet Sir Roger as he charged onto the dune, his sword free in his hand. He joined blades with the nearest opponent, and Jessica, swallowing her panic, took advantage of the distraction he caused to strike the other man's sword hand.

A yelp of surprise and pain escaped the man as the blade dropped to the sand. To the accompanying clang of steel striking steel, he dove after it. Before his numbed hand could close over the hilt, Jessica caught him in the throat with her branch.

Which left Sir Roger's man. Trembling, she turned toward them to find that neither swordsman had so much as a glance to spare for her. The back of the Spaniard's knee remained vulnerable, she noted, with only the leather straps of his greaves binding it. She waited until a deep lunge left him open, and she struck hard. His supporting leg buckled, and with a cry he dropped to the sand. Sir Roger brought the hilt of his sword against the man's temple, completing the job.

He stepped back and glared at Jessica. "Do you doubt my ability to deal with a Spanish dog?" he demanded. "There was no need—"

"You may get your chance, yet," she broke in, "unless we get them tied up." Already, the first man she'd felled stirred, and a groan issued from his throat. "Where did they come from?" she added as Sir Roger knocked the hapless Spaniard once more into unconsciousness.

"An advance party, most likely. That ship that escaped us knew they'd done us damage. They must have sent these men to spy us out, find where we have put to for repairs. Pursuit must be closer than I realized." He fell silent, brooding, then raised his head and gave a mighty shout. "I wonder," he added as if to himself, "how long they'll wait for these three to return before it occurs to them something has gone amiss."

Jessica hugged herself, fighting off a chill of reaction and nerves. "I wonder if there're any more wandering about."

"What, Lady, fear from you?" The quizzical smile lit his eyes. "They thought you an easy prize, and in faith, you should have been. How could they know they faced a lioness?"

She shook her head, fighting to keep control of herself. "It— it's a martial art I learned—in China." Suddenly, she was glad she'd made up that story.

He raised his eyebrows. "Never could I have dreamed I might seek instruction in the art of fighting from a female. But it seems you have some valuable skill."

"My father thought it essential for a woman to be able to protect herself," she said, for once with perfect truth.

The sounds reached them of several men running as best they could through the soft sand. Jessica moved away, averting her face, leaving Sir Roger standing amid the three fallen Spaniards. As his men crested the dune, shouts of surprise and amazement broke from them. In short order, they bore their captives away.

It was over, she—and Roger—were safe. Her hands began to shake, and the branch fell from her clenched fingers.

"Lady." Roger reached her in three long strides and possessed himself of her chilled hand. "There is naught to distress you, now."

"I—I know. It's just—" She broke off, fighting back an overwhelming desire to burst into tears. "I—I've just never had to use those techniques before. I've done them in practice, but I've never actually *hurt* anyone. It was *awful*." She blinked away the moisture that tried to fill her eyes.

"Softly now, Lioness." He raised her hand to his lips, kissing her fingers, then turned it over to press a kiss into her palm.

Her breath caught in her throat and the strain of the moment before faded beneath a welter of new sensations, so compelling as to render insignificant anything she had ever experienced before. She had loved him as a dream hero most of her life, and now here he was, in person, standing so close he filled her every sense, her very being, with the vitality of his presence.

Slowly he brought his other hand to her cheek, touching her with one finger, then smoothing the hair from her eyes, his expression one of awed discovery. Her heart twisted within her. Here, with this man from another time, she had found her match, her life. He embodied every dream, every longing in which she had ever indulged. She wanted him. Yet she didn't belong in his world. She didn't belong with him.

Four

Shouts from down the beach carried through the cool, crisp air, shattering their cocoon of solitude. Roger traced the line of her jaw, then stepped back, away from her.

"If our Spanish friends are coming to themselves once again, I would like to speak with them. Will you come back with me, Lioness?"

"No need. I—"

"Think you there might not be others? In truth, you could shame a man in battle, but it takes only one mischance to be bested. Nay, Lioness. I have work to be done, and I dare not spare the men from their repairs to guard you."

"I can guard myself," she muttered, but beneath her breath. When he turned to lead the way back through the trees, his steps sure and steady even on the yielding sand, she followed. No point in occupying his mind with worry about her. He had to leave here, as soon as possible, and without leaving any trace of his presence. As a loyal adherent of Non-Discovery Day, she had to assure that.

She sat on the gnarled trunk of a driftwood tree and watched, from some distance away, while Roger, the man Edmund, and several others faced their Spanish prisoners. It did not seem to be going well, though one of the Spaniards spoke at some length. Probably cursing Roger for his pains. Her sense of unease grew, though the English crew made no move to force information from their prisoners by violence. Yet in the end, she never doubted Roger would learn what he wanted. Her respect for him grew.

She closed her eyes, reliving the sensations he had created

within her by the tenderness of his touch. What a fool she was. What a complete fool. Yet he had held her heart since the first time she had seen his portrait.

He rose abruptly from where he had rested on one knee, directed a smiling word to Edmund, and the Spaniards cringed. Ignoring them, he turned on his heel and strode over to join Jessica. With a sigh, he settled on the end of her log and stretched out his long legs.

"Learn anything?" She shaded her eyes from the sun so she could study his face.

"We will. Do your Chinese know any secrets for obtaining information from people?"

She shook her head, smiling. "Undoubtedly. But I never learned any of them."

"Did you not?" His eyes widened in mock startlement. "Lioness, you amaze me. Well, we shall have to rely upon our own methods." He rose. "Is there aught you require?"

More of your company, she wanted to say, but kept that to herself. "I'm doing just fine," she assured him.

"Then you will excuse me?" For a long moment his gaze lingered on her. His lips twitched into a lopsided smile; he gave her a brief nod, then he strode down the beach toward where the plank makers sawed another board. Beyond them, the new mast neared completion.

Jessica fought the temptation to trail after him. She liked watching his decisive movements, and his cheering voice thrilled her. But she'd only be in the way; his crew had much to accomplish, and possibly little time.

She glanced back at the prisoners, to see one of Roger's men toying with a dagger. The Spaniards, no blame to them, appeared ill at ease. Was that his method? To wear them down with thought of what might happen if they failed to provide information? Anticipation of pain could do far more damage than bullying and shouting. Yet what effect would such tactics have upon men who lived under the shadow of the Holy Inquisition?

A crash, followed by a splash that set the swells of the bay roiling, brought her attention back to the *Lion's Pride*. The old mast now floated free of the ship. Half a dozen men, under the direction of Roger himself, rolled the new one to the water's edge. It was rough and coarse, but serviceable. With the block and tackle already in position, it would not take long to raise and fasten it securely in place.

She became aware of a gnawing hunger that must have been growing on her for some time. The sun, she noted, had crested its zenith, and now made its steady and rapid descent into the familiar bank of fog that crept inward from the ocean. It was well into the afternoon, and she'd had nothing to eat since last night, she realized. Earlier, she'd felt too disoriented to think of anything so mundane as food. Now, it took precedence in her mind. Darn, she should have asked Roger about it when she had the chance.

She began to consider whom to approach about this all important matter, when one of the sailors sidled up to her with wary deference, bearing a small but ungainly bundle. This he thrust at her with a muttered word she couldn't catch, and beat a hasty retreat. Were they afraid of her? That possibility amused her— and gave her a measure of courage. Did they think her a witch? Or was it their captain's protection of her of which they went in awe?

She opened the cloth wrappings to find a slab of bread, a chunk of cheese, and a small flask. She uncorked the latter and sniffed: wine. She wouldn't have to go begging, after all. Lunch, it seemed, was served. She tackled it with considerable relish.

Roger still worked; did the man never rest? His energy seemed boundless. He checked the replacement of the damaged planks, turned to shout a warning to the crew handling the new mast, then strode over to speak a word to the prisoners' guards. How could one small galleon contain him?

Tangy dampness surrounded her, and she breathed deeply of the cool ocean fog. It would make the labors of the men easier— though it would also make the keeping of a watch at night more difficult. With the moon and stars blocked from sight, a Spanish ship could slip silently into the bay—if it dared negotiate the rocks, which also would be veiled. She shivered.

The blanketing grayness settled over the mast, which now rose above the deck. New yard arms extended from the scraped trunk, and two sailors labored to attach the rigging. Would they be able to raise the sail before night? If not, the *Lion's Pride* would be a hapless victim for any ship that guessed—or knew—their whereabouts.

Fog. A blessing, a menace. It foreshadowed the coming of night—and how much more? There had been heavy mist last night, as she sat in the dory and saw the glimmering ghost ship sail toward her across the ages. Now here the fog came again. Did it signal the nearness of her return to her own time? Would the *Lion's Pride,* like Brigadoon, vanish into the mist, leaving her once more in her own familiar setting with only the memory of a magical occurrence?

At last, Roger returned to escort her back to the ship for dinner. While the oarsmen drew them out to the waiting vessel, she sat silently at his side, experiencing an unaccustomed contentment in his company. They pulled up to the side of the ship and he stood, bracing himself, and held out his hands to her.

"Lioness?" he asked softly. "Will you accept my aid again?"

"I really don't—" She broke off. Who was she trying to kid? She longed to feel his arms about her, holding her tight to his shoulder. "Yes, please," she said simply.

A slow smile lit his eyes, setting them aglow with a possessive warmth. He scooped her up, fitting her comfortably over his shoulder, then cradled her there. As he mounted the first rope rung, her hand stole about his back.

He swung her over the rail, then set her gently on her feet, releasing her slowly, as if with reluctance. Her gaze met his, and heat flooded through her at the intensity she encountered. Behind them a man coughed, and she looked away, suddenly aware of his crew.

"Thank you." It took an effort to keep her voice calm. Sedately, she took the arm he offered to lead her across the deck and down the companionway.

A wicked gleam flickered in his eyes. "Would you care to see how the patients go on?" he inquired. "I cannot but feel certain you must have some advice to offer about their care."

She inclined her head. "No, I'll leave that in the hands of your men. As long," she added quickly, "as the dressings are changed, and more salve applied." And she could only hope there was nothing disgusting in that salve.

"You may be assured we know that much about tending wounds." He stopped before a cabin door and opened it, then bowed her inside. "This will be your apartment for the duration of the voyage. I am only sorry it is so plain and free of such amenities as a lady must desire—but perhaps after the privations you have endured, it will not seem so poor and contemptible."

She wouldn't be needing the cabin—she couldn't *really* be stranded in this time—but the impulse to offer it had been kind. "Whose is it?" She looked up at him, uncertain. "Yours?"

"No. Master Edmund's. He is only too happy to turn it over to you. My own man will wait upon you. An able enough creature, though I doubt he has such accomplishments as are necessary to please you."

"I—thank you," she faltered. "But I don't need anyone to wait on me. I'm used to doing all that for myself. In fact—" She broke off, not sure how to go on. "I've slept so long outdoors, it'll feel—confining, to be inside again."

His steady gaze rested on her, assessing. "I feel certain you will accustom yourself quickly enough."

Jessica moved into the cabin, repressing a shiver. If her suspicions were right, and the ship vanished in the fog with her on board, what would become of her? Would she remain in 1603? Or would she find herself floundering in the cold waters of the bay, with the solid wooden hull fading into nothingness around her? She didn't want to find out the hard way.

She straightened and met his look with one of determination—and a touch of defiance. "This one last night I'll spend on solid ground. After that—" After that, if she were still in his time, she'd have no choice but to accept the cabin and sail with him. But it wouldn't—it *couldn't*—come to that.

Traveling through time was impossible. This whole thing had to be a magical illusion, a brief interlude into another dimension. The sort of thing you woke up from the next morning, wondering if it had all been a dream.

Roger took her hand, and his spell wrapped about her. Whatever might happen from this point on, at least she was with him now.

"I am sorry to disappoint you, Lioness," he said, the challenging glint once more in his eyes. "I fear I cannot permit you to stay ashore. It isn't safe. If another party of Spaniards came upon you in your sleep, I doubt you could save yourself. And if they came in force, even a guard of my men might not be sufficient to protect you."

She shook her head. "I'll be better off away from your ship. It—it isn't safe for me here." How could she possibly explain that he, his vessel and all his crew were going to vanish from her life while she slept? Staying aboard the *Lion's Pride* seemed by far the more dangerous course to her.

"Another 'Chinese' idea?" His expression hardened. "Is it the thought of my men that disturbs you? Rest you easy on that score. The cabin may be bolted. See? Though I assure you, no one will try to enter. No one would dare. And not only for fear of me. Word of your prowess at protecting yourself has got about."

"I—no, I'm sure they're all perfect gentlemen." Only the mildest sarcasm tinged her words. His men were the least of her worries. She had other fears, ones of which she could never speak to him. Like the fact that the longer she remained in his company, the less she wanted to go home, back to her own life where she belonged.

Staying here, in the past, with Roger—She fought the desire that welled within her to do just that. Even if it were possible, no woman who would shortly ring in the twenty-first century had any business mucking about in a world that had only just welcomed in the seventeenth. She'd never fit in.

She studied the set lines of his face for a long moment. To argue with him would avail her nothing; she knew stubbornness when she saw it. She would feign acquiescence, then make her own arrangements for slipping back to shore. What he didn't know wouldn't hurt him. Or her. Only her wistful heart.

Five

Roger's smile broadened as she made no further protest. "My man—Josiah is his name—will bring you water to wash, and a comb for your hair, and anything else we can discover that you might find useful. We will dine in an hour, if that will give you enough time?"

A short laugh escaped her. "I don't exactly have anything to change into. That will be more than long enough."

He carried her fingers to his lips, then bowed himself out, leaving her to eye the small cabin with considerable curiosity. Roger might call it plain, but she detected a quiet beauty about the dark oak paneling and the gleaming bronze fittings. An intricately carved chest and wardrobe stood against an inner wall. She flung the latter open only to find someone had emptied it. The same with the chest.

Poor Master Edmund could have kept them, and with her blessings. She certainly didn't need anyplace to store her nonexistent belongings. But if she were wrong, and she *were* trapped in this time, she'd have to set about getting a few things. Like a tooth brush, a pair of shoes, a change of underwear—heavens, they didn't have any yet, not at this time. No way was she staying.

She repeated that sentiment, with vehemence, a moment later as she eyed the netted contraption suspended between two hooks on opposite walls. No bunks, no mattresses, just a hammock and blanket. A *hammock,* for crying out loud. Her heart screamed for coiled innersprings.

A knock sounded without, interrupting her determinations to somehow make it to the shore, to sleep where the very floorboards didn't sway beneath her unsteady feet. Before she could respond, the door inched open and a tall, gaunt figure dressed in sober hose, shirt, and leather jerkin entered, his arms laden with a variety of garments.

"Madam." He inclined his head in a deferential manner, but his curious gaze burned questions into her. "My master bids me bring you these few offerings—his best velvet doublet, a matching cloak, and the finest of linen shirts. I have some aptitude with a needle and can fashion for you a gown, if you will permit. Not a fine one, I fear, but one that should, with your tolerance, suffice. And now," he laid his armload across the top of the chair, and from underneath a pewter ewer emerged, which he clasped in one hand, "you will wish to tidy yourself, for my master dines in as much state as circumstances allow."

"He does?" Jessica blinked, at last dragging her gaze from the beautiful materials of Roger's garments and turning back to Josiah.

Except for the man's clothing, which appeared more like that of the sailors, he could have passed for a gentleman's gentleman of any era. And his more proper setting should be a palatial country mansion, not a small galleon thousands of miles from its home port. She couldn't help but wonder if he had brushed out with meticulous care the hairs and wrinkles from Roger's velvet doublet before dinner, even while the storms off Tierra del Fuego had tossed the valiant little ship. She'd bet he had. *And* admonished his master to hold up the hem of his cloak so it wasn't sullied in the water that washed over the side of the ship.

When Josiah at last escorted her to a cabin three doors down, she entered to find two men present. She almost didn't recognize them, they had changed so much. Instead of their worn and faded garments of the day, they had decked themselves out in velvet doublets, slashed to allow the fine linen beneath to be puffed through. Their hosen were complete with knotted ribbon garters above the knee, and starched ruffs showed at their hands and necks. Then the brown-haired one stepped forward and smiled, and she recognized Master Edmund.

"It will be pleasant to have the company of a lady at our dinners." He bowed before her.

She detected a touch of constraint in his manner. Embarrassment? she wondered. They probably felt they had to watch their language and stories before her. Better she should watch hers. She fought back a sudden grin and tried to look properly shy. "Thank you for letting me use your cabin. I'm sorry to have put you to so much trouble."

"Nay, lady, it is no trouble." He flushed. "Indeed, it is an honor—a pleasure—a—"

"In fact, you love being put out?" she suggested.

He blinked, momentarily at a loss. "Never consider it so. It is a pleasure, an honor—"

"You said that." His companion, a fair-haired gentleman in his early twenties whom Jessica had seen earlier giving orders on deck, poured her wine in an exquisitely colored glass. "Spanish," he assured her, with a hint of mischief lighting his gray eyes. "Alicante, in fact. An excellent vintage."

"Thank you." She returned a grateful smile, then succumbed to a touch of mischievousness. "I had forgotten what it was like to be among civilized people."

She sipped the heady wine and looked about the cabin while the two men returned to a low-voiced review of the day's doings. It was even more beautiful than the cabin to which she'd been shown, she decided, admiring the paned glass of the lanterns that hung suspended by chains from the beams. Embroidered tapestries hung on the walls, and the bench beneath the porthole boasted a needlework cushion. Roger had spared no expense in the outfitting of his ship—and no wonder, considering this must be more his home than any manor house in England.

"Forgive us." Master Edmund came to stand by her side. "Ship's business, but we should not have let it intrude upon you. You must tell us of your adventures. Is it true you have lived for some time in China?"

"I—" She broke off, grinning feebly. She'd been afraid that story would return to haunt her.

Roger strode in, saving her from having to fabricate elusive details, awing her with his elegance of both attire and manner. He bowed low over her hand, carrying her fingers to his lips; the simple touch set her pulse racing. The glow of his regard warmed her.

"Lioness, forgive me for being late." He accepted a glass of wine from Edmund.

"My own fault," she assured him. "I took up too much of your man's time."

He shook his head in mock sorrow. "You have quite eclipsed me. He can think of nothing but the fashioning of a gown for you. I left him going through my things once again."

"Sorry about that." She offered him an apologetic grin. "I *did* tell him not to. If anything you particularly like goes missing, I'll try to rescue it."

An answering gleam lit his eyes. "He well knows the limits of my patience, although for you he dares to stretch them."

He drew out a chair for her at the table, and the other two men, who had been standing discreetly to one side, joined them. Roger spoke a joking word to Edmund, then poured them all more wine. His seemingly innocent remark set the two young men off on a laughing argument of apparent long standing. Roger leaned back in his chair, his gaze brushing over them, then coming to rest on Jessica.

She met it steadily, savoring it, until Edmund recalled his attention. Toying with her glass, she continued to watch him, allowing her nerves to unwind and giving herself over to the pleasurable sensations of her surroundings. No rough fighting ship, this; it could have been some modern millionaire's yacht. And for the ease and grace of Roger's manners, they might be anchored off the coast of Monte Carlo rather than in enemy seas far from their homeland.

The food, which Josiah himself served a few minutes later, proved amazingly delectable. There was fish, of course, served in a silver dish and cooked in a creamy herb sauce, and accompanied by potatoes and a dried fruit compote. She couldn't help but wonder what the rest of the men on board ate. Probably not much different fare. Roger presented her with a gilt-trimmed silver bowl, filled with perfumed water, and after a moment she realized it was for rinsing her fingers.

Josiah offered a variety of wines to her, but she drank only sparingly. She couldn't allow a muddled brain to affect her thinking. Already her daydreams about Roger had become longings. But this wasn't her reality. If she didn't want to wind up swimming home, she'd better get off the ship before she fell asleep.

At last, Edmund rose and bowed to her. "Pray excuse me. I must return to my duties."

The other man stood also. "With your permission?"

Roger waved them away, and the two man departed. For a long moment he sat in silence, his gaze resting on Jessica. "You will be glad to see England once more," he said.

His deep voice rolled over her, and her senses quickened. "I . . . hardly remember it. It's more like something I read about in a book."

A slight frown creased his brow. He led her to the cushion-lined bench beneath the porthole, and she sat at his side, her pulse fluttering as if she were a teenager hoping he'd ask her to dance. Darkness had already descended outside the porthole, and the heavy fog hid any lingering traces of the late sunset. Here, in this little room lit only by glowing lamps, they might have been alone together, in a private world all their own. All that was needed for atmosphere would be a radio playing some guitar love ballads softly in the background. The gentle lapping of the waves against the hull did well enough.

He refilled her glass. "You have family awaiting your return?"

Oh, no. Here came the personal inquisition. She braced herself. "Not that I ever heard of. I think my mother had a brother, but he died."

His frown deepened. "Where did your father intend to take you? What were his plans for when he returned?"

"He wanted to teach what he'd learned. In London." That sounded safe.

"But now you are alone."

"Yes." Her voice echoed with hollowness. Her parents and brother really were dead. But why did that have to be the one truth in the whole of her ridiculous story?

He laid his hand over hers. "Never fear, Lioness. I will take you to my sister until we decide what is best. She will consider it a treat."

Jessica tilted her head to one side and studied his face. "What is she like?" She couldn't remember ever hearing anything about his family.

"Much like you," he said after a moment. "She is always laughing, and I have never known anything to unsettle her."

"She sounds more like you." She smiled, finding comfort in his presence. He set her at ease, as if they had spent the better part of their lives together rather than a single day. As if they belonged with one another.

That thought brought dangerous longings to Jessica, dreams of long-term relationships.

She stiffened. Long-term? Like until she fell asleep tonight? The urge to stay awake, to stay with him always, overwhelmed her. Yet even if by some miracle her wish were granted, what sort of future could they possibly have together? They needed something in common to make it work, mutual goals, mutual ways of viewing the world. Their worlds could hardly be less alike, and as for the difference in their backgrounds—!

"Still worried?"

His deep voice startled her out of her frantic reverie. She shook her head, fighting back a wistful smile. "I'm just tired. It—it's been a *very* long day." He'd never believe just how long.

He took hold of her chin with one hand, trailing a finger along her throat, and lifted her face to look up into his. For a long while he studied her, a slight frown in his eyes. "There is naught to fear, Lioness, either for the future or for now. I will see you safe home to England, as I promised. We should be well away tomorrow, long before the Spanish venture after us."

Spanish. . . . That brought her back to the problems of the moment. "Did those men talk?" she asked quickly.

Humor glinted in his eyes. "That they did. No, never fear. They've taken no serious harm. While they were sent to find our position, others were sent south, back to the bay at Monte Rey, to fetch supplies to repair their vessel. We've set a watch, of course, but there is little chance of their overtaking us, unless a ship had already set forth in pursuit before the messengers reached it. The chances of that are slim, but we have prepared ourselves."

She nodded. A ship under his command would always be ready, she felt certain. A yawn threatened, which she failed to stifle.

He stood at once. "I keep you up too late, and after all you have gone through. You must wish to retire." He took her hand, raising her to her feet. "I will bid you a good night."

She lingered, fighting another yawn, struggling to keep her eyes open a little longer. She should retire at once, for he would most likely seek his own cabin once she was gone. She had to stay awake until he, and all his men, fell asleep, so she could sneak ashore. And what of the sailors standing watch? She'd need to be alert and stealthy, not stumbling about for lack of sleep.

This would be the last time she ever saw Sir Roger Allendale face to face. She couldn't bear to leave him, her hero, the figure about whom she'd woven all her romantic daydreams. Yet she had to. Longing filled her, and she touched his golden-red beard, then stood on tiptoe to steal one last kiss. Before he could react—before she could surrender to the craving to melt into his arms, to feel them about her one last time—she pulled away and darted out.

She was a fool, she freely admitted, as she slammed the door to her own quarters behind her. But at least she retained enough sense not to join him in *his* cabin. The possibilities of sharing a hammock with him, though, held a certain challenge she found intriguing.

She went to the bench beneath her own portal and stared out into the fog. She was on the ocean side. Where did his cabin lie? Facing the shore? If so, and he sat up sleepless, gazing out into the night as did she, he'd catch her at her escape. And that, as much as she might like to see him again, she could not have.

She remained where she sat until she caught herself nodding off, succumbing to her exhaustion and the lateness of the hour. She rose and splashed water over her face until she felt more herself, then set about unfastening her dress. She was going to have to swim for it, and the heavy fabric of the Elizabethan costume would drag her down—or bell out about her, attracting any glance that might otherwise pass over her. She rolled it into a ball and, still wearing her shift, eased herself to the door.

The bolt grated as she drew it back, and she caught her breath, freezing where she stood, waiting for some door to bang wide and a head to emerge into the narrow confines of the corridor and demand to know what was toward. But as seconds dragged by into a minute, then another, she began to relax. It must have sounded overly loud to her tensed nerves.

She slid open the door and stepped without. What time was it, anyway? she wondered. With so much fog, there would be no way she could tell from the position of the moon.

All about her lay in stillness. The only sounds that reached her were the normal creakings of chain and wood as the ship rode low at anchor. Everyone—except the watch—must have fallen asleep long ago. Good.

Behind which door did Roger lie? A temptation assailed her, so strong it almost overpowered her, to find him, to join him in his hammock, to bury her face against his chest and rub her forehead in his thickly curling hair. Hair, she reminded herself sternly, that smelled of pitch and salt and fish. With that unappealing thought, she started up the steps.

The night could hardly be darker if it had been moonless and starless. No glimmer of light slipped through the thick curtain of fog. And no lantern showed on the ship to reflect back. She moved each foot with care, expecting at any moment to collide with some stray rope or tool left abandoned on the deck from the day's labors.

A shape—more a deeper shadow in the murky darkness— moved at the bow of the ship. Jessica froze, allowing her eyes to adjust to the night. The watchman moved along the rail, his gaze steadily trained out to sea, down the coast. Apparently, they did not expect any attack over land. Just as well for her. A Spanish raiding party didn't fit in anywhere with her plans for the rest of the night.

She remained where she stood, in the shadows of the stern castle, waiting, her gaze following the watchman. Sure enough, another shadow moved toward the first—the guards passing at the rail. She could only hope there wouldn't be others.

They exchanged a word, their voices carrying unnaturally loudly in the muffling stillness of the fog-enshrouded night.

Great. She could count on any sound she made reaching them. She'd just have to make sure any chance noises sounded natural.

She'd practiced a few gull calls in her time, she reflected. What she really needed, though, was a ship's cat to take the blame. "Silent be, Again the cat." The lyrics drifted through her mind while she sought the tune. Something like: "Carefully on tiptoe stealing, dum de dum dum dum dum dum, Ev'ry step with caution feeling. . . ."

Except that was from the *H.M.S. Pinafore.* What she needed was something from the *Pirates of Penzance.* Much more suitable. With the jaunty refrain of "With cat-like tread, Upon our prey we steal," running through her mind, she crept toward the side of the ship opposite the guards. She ended with "A fly's footfall Would be distinctly heard" as her toe collided with a coil of rope.

Well, had she found her piratic "skeletonic keys" or "centre-bit?" She'd always wondered what that last was, but never wanted to ruin her speculations by looking it up. No, this was better by far. Her hands felt out the shape of the rope ladder. And by the greatest good luck, it was still tied to the rail. She could thank heaven for that; her brother—damn, she missed Phil—had always told her she made a lousy boy scout in the knot-tying department.

Next step, get it down to the water. She huddled low against the side, peering back over her shoulder. Neither watchman was in sight. She gathered the rope in her hands, then ducked down once more as one of the watchmen strode into view, heading for another tour of the bow.

There should be a little bit of time when she couldn't see them—and presumably they couldn't see her, either. She waited until the men's pacing carried them once more from view, then went into action. So quietly that the lapping of the wavelets covered the sound, she let the ladder over the side.

So far, so good. But her Elizabethan costume was heavy. She dragged off her shift, used it to tie her costume securely so that it hung about her neck, and eased herself over the rail.

The ropes rubbed against the wood, but the creaking of the anchor chain drowned out the tell-tale sound. Still safe. Her heart beat in her throat, so loud it seemed impossible no one else could hear it. She descended the first rung, then another, gaining confidence as she went. At last, raising her costume over her head with one hand, she lowered herself into the chill waters of the bay.

The current caught her, pulling her a little to the south. If she drifted too far that way, one of the guards might see her from the stern. She headed slightly north to counter it, striking out with a one-armed side stroke. She'd always been a strong swimmer; growing up by the bay, she'd had little chance to be otherwise. Still, her muscles began to feel the strain long before her elbow struck sand.

She looked up, calculating her position, then angled toward the rocks, crawling now through the shallow wavelets, keeping low, not wanting her body to stand out like a pale beacon. She reached the point where trees grew low over the rocks and made a dash for it. For a long moment she huddled just beneath the cover of the underbrush, shivering as the night air caressed her wet skin.

She needed a towel, but her dress would have to do. She went to work with it as best she could, and wished she'd been wearing fast-drying nylon underwear instead of good old comfortable cotton. Her brother had been right in his teasing; she'd make a rotten boy scout. She couldn't even keep to their motto, "Be Prepared." But who could ever be prepared to go time traveling? In disgust she removed bra and undies, both drenched, then donned her lightweight shift. Well, she'd made it to shore; she was safe.

She gazed out to the *Lion's Pride,* bobbing gently at anchor not so very far away in the bay. No, it was an eternity away. She shivered, hugging herself against the cold. Yet it was less the fog-damp air that chilled her than the emptiness of her own heart.

"Over here, Roger," she whispered into the darkness, then turned, blinking back the moisture that filled her eyes, to make her stumbling way deeper into shelter.

Six

Jessica stopped at last in the middle of a stand of pine trees and looked about, not sure what to do. There was nowhere to go, no town of Inlet Bay where she could seek warmth, shelter, or a strong cup of coffee. She fought the urge to return to the ship, to crawl into the hammock and huddle in a warm blanket. No, that was a sure way to get drenched when she was drawn back to her own time.

But what if she were wrong? Should—*could*—she forget her past and start over—with Roger? Yet such a life was unknown, terrifying. And she would never fit in. Roger might laugh at her unconventional ways now, but what if she went with him back to England? She'd be branded a witch for sure. No, she'd done what was right—though the choice probably wasn't hers. She belonged in her own world.

With determined busyness, she hung her underwear over branches—probably to get wetter from the fog rather than dry. Still, it seemed the best course. That accomplished, she gathered a bed of pine needles, then drew her costume over her like a blanket.

Roughing it, she decided a moment later, was over-rated. The sharp needles pricked right through her shift, the ground—in spite of its supposed cushioning—was hard and unyielding to her hip bones and shoulders, and every little rock and pebble made its presence felt in no uncertain terms. She should have brought the hammock and blanket with her. Or would they vanish along with the ship, along with all traces of the *Lion's Pride?*

She could just imagine getting dumped unceremoniously on the ground when she and her bedding parted times.

She huddled beneath her dress, trying to keep her thoughts from Roger, from dreams of being held gently in his arms, of resting her forehead against his broad shoulder, of—damn, there she went again. She rolled over, winced as a twig caught her on the cheek, and concentrated instead on willing herself to sleep.

She must have drifted off at last, for an aching stiffness brought her fully awake. The fog remained, but no longer as a pale shroud against the blackness of night. It glowed with the coming of dawn. She sat up, hugging her gown about her. Morning. She breathed deeply of the sharp, tangy sea breeze, and memory flooded back.

Roger—Sensations of tremendous loss washed over her, and she closed her eyes, trying to shut out the ache. Roger . . .

Torn by her turmoil of emotions, she threw the costume aside and thrust her way through the underbrush, knowing only that she had to see the empty bay to assure herself her impossible—wonderful—dream had truly ended. She broke from the covering pines, her bare feet torn by the rocks. Grasping a tree trunk for support, she stared through the heavy mist to the gray, white-capped waters below. And the great dark ship that rode at anchor just within the mouth of the bay.

Shock hit her, and she sank to her knees, clutching at a boulder for support. The *Lion's Pride* was still there. Which meant *she* was still there, still in 1603, not in her own time.

Irrationally, her first reaction was outrage that she had spent an incredibly cold and uncomfortable night on the pine needles and rocks for nothing, when she might have been warm and rocking cozily in a hammock. Or even sharing Roger's.

She shivered with hysterical laughter. All that had buoyed her before, all that had given her courage to face this weird and awesome experience, had been the certainty that she must return home when next she slept, as easily and mysteriously as she had arrived here. But now that hope had been taken from her. *Home* had been taken from her. She was here . . . to stay. Alone, cut off from everything she knew, all that was familiar, all that she loved.

Except Roger. Now she would see him again. And again and again, every day, during the long voyage back to England.

Yet making a man her anchor in this new world was risky. She would have to make her own identity, become a person others would seek for herself. She was a botanist, she knew a great deal about herbal remedies. She would make her own way. And she could still see Roger.

How wrong they all were, the thought drifted through her mind. Roger *did* discover Inlet Bay. He stopped here to make his repairs. Yet she was glad the people of her town never knew the truth. She could think of no celebration which was as much non-sensical fun as Non-Discovery Day. She would have that memory always—and the knowledge of the truth to make it doubly ironic and enjoyable.

She returned, chilled and shivering, to where she had slept and pulled on her costume, taking time to smooth the skirts and fluff out her little neck ruff. Good heavens, was she going to have to get used to wearing one of these all the time? They made her itch. It was a pity Queen Elizabeth—

Jessica frowned as she ran her fingers through her tangled hair. Queen Elizabeth had died a few months ago, and James I of Scotland had come to the throne. She bet Roger and his crew didn't know that, yet. She'd better not be the one to tell them.

With a last shake of her skirts to remove the lingering pine needles, she headed through the underbrush once more, then slowed as she neared the rise overlooking the beach. If she went down there, she could be seen from the *Lion's Pride.* How could she explain to Roger why she'd disobeyed his direct orders and stolen away from the ship? Maybe he'd just chalk it up to her general refusal to do as she was told. Or maybe she could convince him she woke early and went for a swim.

Trying to concoct a plausible story, she turned her face to the morning wind and climbed along the line of trees that led to the ridge of the peninsula. As long as she kept amongst the pines, no one should be able to see her. She shivered. What if Roger had already risen and knocked on her door, only to find her gone? He'd probably search the whole ship for her, wasting time that would be better spent finishing the repairs and getting the *Lion's*

Pride away from where the Spaniards would undoubtedly soon come looking for them. She paused at the top to catch her breath and looked down the far side, away from the bay.

And saw another galleon approaching from the south.

She stared at it in dawning horror. This vessel had been built along the same basic lines as the *Lion's Pride,* but there the resemblance ended. This was a heavier ship, one designed for ferrying the plundered wealth of the new world home to the old. A *Spanish* galleon.

Jessica drew in a steadying breath. The galleon hugged the shoreline, moving with surprising speed for its bulk. The stiff morning breeze filled its sails as it angled along the curve of coast, toward the point of the peninsula. Once around that, it would sweep into Inlet Bay, trapping its quarry.

She ran the short distance to the other side of the ridge and peered down at Roger's ship. She could make out the shapes of two figures climbing in the rigging, attaching the sail. They couldn't possibly see over the line of trees—they couldn't know about the Spanish ship that crept silently and steadily up on them.

Jessica shouted and waved her arms, but could detect no response from the sailors. She was too far away for them to hear; and the same southwesterly breeze that drove the galleon onward carried her words away, inland, where they did no one any good. She wiped back her tangled hair, then headed to the opposite side to check on the Spaniards' progress. They came on all too fast for her liking.

She had to reach Roger, warn him. She raced down the ridge to the beach to where her ancient dory lay beached amid the seaweed and driftwood. With every ounce of her strength, she dragged it over the damp sand until the wavelets slapped against the stern, then farther, feeling the cold waters sucking at her feet, billowing about her ankles, then her calves and knees as buoyancy took over and the little craft floated. She pulled it farther, to where her added weight wouldn't mire it on the bottom, then gathered her drenched skirts about her waist. Balancing the dory as best she could, she clambered in.

Only one oar remained in the leaky boat. That didn't really matter, she reflected. She was rotten at rowing, anyway. She much preferred kayaking. She'd just treat this like a canoe. She struck savagely at the water, fighting the onshore breeze, then swung the oar to the other side and repeated the sweeping stroke. She barely seemed to inch forward.

Would she be able to reach Roger with her warning in time? In her frantic mind, she envisioned the Spanish galleon putting on a burst of speed, rounding the peninsula, and settling itself with its cannon aimed at the *Lion's Pride*. She couldn't let that happen.

She shouted once more, but again no one so much as glanced in her direction. She might as well save her breath for the paddling. It would be a sprint—and this was one race she desperately needed to win.

She gasped for air, her lungs burning, her arms aching with her efforts. But she was nearer—perhaps half the distance from the shore to the ship. Without letting up her efforts, she raised her voice in another shout.

This time one of the sailors raised his head and looked in her direction. He must have said something to his companion, for the other man looked up also. Then both returned to their work.

Jessica's heart sank, and a scream of frustration welled within her. Didn't they care? Wasn't it obvious that something was amiss? Did they think she had gone rowing—or rather, paddling—in the early morning fog just for the *fun* of it? Why couldn't they catch on?

Closer. She had to get closer. She had to make herself heard— *understood*—before she collapsed with exhaustion. She had to reach Roger.

The thought of him drove her onward. Once she reached him— once she told him—she could leave everything in his capable hands. He knew how to fight the Spanish, his crew had a great deal of experience. As long as that other galleon didn't take him by surprise, he'd be able to handle them. He had to.

She blinked back the blur in her eyes and saw the *Lion's Pride* had drawn closer. She shouted again, her voice going hoarse, but this time an answering cry came back. They'd heard her! Men moved about on the deck, and she yelled once more, but this time it came out more like a croak.

Then several men gathered about the rope ladder and one—Roger, she realized with a lift in her heart—began a careful descent. She pulled harder with her single oar, hope and elation renewing her energy. The dinghy drew nearer and nearer, then somehow she had reached him where he hung on the bottom rung and he caught the bow, pulling her in, securing her.

She threw her paddle into the bottom of the dory and rose unsteadily. Roger stepped into her boat, setting it swaying, and in one staggering step she fell into his arms, too winded to do more than gasp the word: "Spanish."

"My heart." He spoke the words softly as he gathered her tightly against himself.

She tilted back her head, her warning uppermost in her mind, only to have his mouth descend on hers with a passion that sent her senses reeling. For a long moment she simply clung to him, memorizing the feel of his lips, the prickliness of his mustache and beard. The scent of the ocean surrounded him, combined with a touch of herbs. He must have bathed in the chill bay waters, she realized. For her. His freshly washed red-gold mane dripped onto his clean shirt.

With an effort she wrenched free, and her hands gripped his shoulders as she looked up into his face. "The Spanish," she gasped. "Over—over there." She nodded with her head toward the jutting land spit of the peninsula. "Sailing. Fast."

Roger's head jerked back. "Spanish!" he shouted, and his men took up the cry.

He hadn't doubted her, nor wasted a moment with needless questions. He simply reached for her to scoop her up to his shoulder, but Jessica waved him toward the ladder instead. "Go—go ahead. I'll follow." When she'd caught her breath.

He stooped to drop a kiss on her forehead. Already calling directions to his men, he scrambled up the ladder and swung easily onto his ship. The next moment he paced across the deck with leonine restlessness, roaring out encouragement and orders.

Jessica sank onto the dory's seat and fought back the craven urge to burst into tears. She'd made it. She'd warned him. She'd been in time.

Above her, the sailors leapt to their positions. The heavy anchor chain creaked as three men set themselves to the winch to crank it up. Jessica pulled herself together and, ignoring the protest of her aching arm muscles, dragged herself up the ladder.

As she crawled onto the deck, exhausted, a shout rose from the sailors. She raised her head to peer across the deck, toward the ocean beyond. And there it came, just beyond the rocky tip of the land spit, the heavy Spanish galleon under full sail.

Seven

Jessica drew back, seeking a place where she would get in no one's way. The last thing she wanted was Roger to be distracted by fears for her safety. The idea that she might be of help, she dismissed at once. Being able to defend herself against a mugger was one thing. Sea battles, where the primary weapon would be cannon, was a field in which she had absolutely no training whatsoever.

She settled near the door to the stern castle where she could see the Spanish ship maneuvering into position. Roger shouted an order, and the sails dropped into place, flapping wildly in the breeze. The next moment they billowed and filled, and the *Lion's Pride* surged forward through the churning water to meet its foe.

Roger strode into view, his gaze locked on the enemy, his sword raised in one hand. Every inch the commander, he paced along the deck, calling some joke to his men. His deep laughter floated back to her, and Jessica caught her breath. Tension filled the air, but she sensed eager anticipation instead of nerves or fear.

A puff of smoke billowed from the side of the Spanish ship, followed at once by a reverberating, ear-shattering boom. Water exploded about thirty yards in front of the *Lion's Pride,* shooting high into the air. A cannonball.

The next landed closer, and Jessica's heart pounded in her chest. The *Lion's Pride* couldn't be sunk here, she reminded herself. Roger made it back to England to receive the honors and acclaim of his king and country. If he hadn't, he never would have become famous. Only Inlet Bay would remember him—not as their revered non-discoverer, but as the failed mariner whose ship lay rotted and buried beneath their waters.

Roger made it home.

Unless her presence here in the past changed everything.

No, she couldn't let herself think that way. The enemy galleon moved slowly, no match for the lighter, quicker English vessel. And no commander could be the match of Roger.

As the *Lion's Pride* drew nearer, Jessica could see more details of the Spanish ship and its crew. Men dressed in heavy, glinting breastplates lined its rail, each holding ropes secured to the yardarms. A boarding party, she realized, noting their axes designed to dig into the side of a ship and hold. Then the English cannon fired, and a portion of railing vanished from the enemy galleon.

Roger leapt down from the steps behind her and caught her in his free arm. "Lock yourself in your cabin, my heart, and don't come out until this is over."

"Roger—" She touched his cheek.

He stooped and kissed her soundly. "There'll be a battle aboard one ship or the other, fondling. I would we had been under full sail at the start, then you would have seen how sweet is my *Lion* to maneuver. We may yet gain the speed we need in time."

She caught his hand. "Is there anything I can do? Anything I can help with?"

"Your cabin," he repeated. Taking her firmly by the arm, he guided her through the door of the companionway.

She turned back, gripping his hand. "I can't stay hidden away where I can't see what's happening! If you're fighting, I want to be there. If I could just find some weapon—"

The timbers shuddered about them, and a rousing shout, a mingling of Spanish and English cries, sounded from above. "Grappling hooks," he announced. "Go, my heart. The real battle is about to begin." He touched her cheek, then strode out, shouting orders as he went.

She darted after him, only to stop in her tracks at sight of the deck. Men swarmed everywhere, cutlasses and swords swinging, the morning sun reflecting off the chased breastplates and helmets of the Spanish. Even if she could find a spare blade, she could never wield it with the efficiency these men displayed.

Roger—Her gaze sought his powerful figure through the me-
lee. There. Already he'd reached the far side of the ship where a
Spaniard lunged toward him with his sword. Roger swirled the
cloak he clasped in his free hand, entangling the blade, dragging
it aside.

Her heart leapt to her throat. Without conscious thought she
started forward, only to be knocked aside by the fighters. She
dodged another, staggered backward as the ship swayed, and
landed against the rail. And she spotted her perfect weapon.

She grasped the belaying pin, weighing it in her hand, and her
panic faded into relief-tinged determination. This she could
swing to good effect, even better than the branch she'd used yesterday. "Much better," she muttered, suddenly not feeling quite
so helpless.

Once more she started forward, trying to gain Roger's side. It
proved no easy task, for the simple gripping of the belaying pin
did not make her immune from chance slashes of the flashing
swords. She moved with care, but when one Spaniard retreated
toward her, she stood her ground, waiting, her lower lip caught
between her teeth. As he neared, she brought her club against the
side of his head with all her might.

He crumpled at her feet. For a long moment she stared at him,
both appalled and elated by what she had done, then she raised
her gaze to meet the wide-eyed incredulity of the English sailor
her victim had been fighting. She managed a shaky, half-apolo-
getic grin. "Sorry, did you need him for something?"

"No." The Englishman shook his head. Before he could say
anything more, another Spaniard bore down on him.

Jessica looked about once more for Roger.

There. They'd come nearer to each other, she'd reach him in
minutes. She started forward, keeping a wary watch out as she
moved. So many Spaniards swarmed over the deck; did they keep
coming?

She spared a glance toward the other galleon, and froze as she
saw one lone Spaniard standing at the edge of its deck, a pistol
raised in his hand. Jessica traced the direction of his aim, and
found it pointed directly at—

"Roger!" She screamed his name as she dove forward, knocking him to the deck in a flying tackle as the explosion rang out.

"God's—" Roger broke off his oath as he rolled aside, grasping his upper arm. Blood seeped through his fingers.

Jessica sank back, shaken. "It—it would have struck you in the chest—"

"Not when I have my Lioness to guard me." His breath escaped in a deep laugh as he threw himself into a roll, out of the way of a Spaniard's lunge.

Jessica scrambled to her knees and swung her belaying pin, knocking the man's cutlass away. With the return stroke she brought it back against the Spaniard's knee. The man cried out, and collapsed.

"Roger—?" She looked about and spotted him, his arm dripping crimson, already closing with another swordsman. He raised his weapon in the briefest of salutes to her.

About them, she realized, the clamor seemed to have lessened. A number of men, both Spanish and English, lay sprawled on the deck. Two of Roger's crew freed the great grappling hooks, disengaging the enemy galleon. First one, then another of the Spaniards jumped for the other deck, swinging on the ropes they had used such a short while ago to board the *Lion's Pride*.

"Loose the cannon!" shouted Roger. He strode toward the middle of the deck, holding a filthy rag to staunch his bleeding.

Once more, a cannon shuddered with its explosion, sending a ball flying toward the masts of the other vessel. Its retreat quickened, and the Spanish ship eased away. Jessica drew back as the Englishmen went to work, disarming the remaining enemy, reloading the weapons, preparing for another onslaught.

It didn't come. The other galleon turned tail. After one last shuddering explosion of a cannon, Roger signaled for a halt.

He staggered forward and called for Edmund. "Let it be. They'll not be in condition—or heart—to give us chase this day or the next. We'll set the prisoners and wounded ashore, and be off for England. Our holds are too laden for pursuit, and now we bear a more important treasure I would not carry into greater risk." His gaze settled on Jessica as he said this last. He drew a steadying breath. "I have a ball lodged in my arm. See to the worst of the injured, Edmund, then remove it for me."

Jessica hurried forward and clasped his good arm. "Sit down and rest. You're losing a lot of blood."

"It would be more if not for you, my Lioness. Never think I don't know it." He touched her cheek. "But now I have much to tend." He kissed her fingers, then strode over to where several of his men gathered the prisoners.

She looked for Edmund and spotted him among the wounded. She went to his side, and for some time aided him in the application of ointments and the bandaging of wounds for English and Spanish alike. When they had tended the last man, Edmund turned his purposeful step toward Roger.

"Will you be more comfortable here, or would you rather go below?" he asked.

"Here, where I can keep an eye on preparations to sail." Roger tore back his blood-drenched sleeve, revealing the nasty wound.

One of his men handed him a bottle, and he took a long drink, then another. Behind him, others laid planks between barrels to form a makeshift operating table. Edmund drew his dirty knife, and Jessica opened her mouth to protest.

Before she could speak, Roger glanced up from the bottle he drained. "What, have you boiled water already and scoured your weapon?"

"Boiled—" Edmund regarded him with suspicion.

"Boil it, man." His voice held only the slightest slur from the wine he had consumed for a sedative, and his eyes glinted with laughter. "Ten minutes, was it not, my Lioness?"

The warmth of his gaze enveloped Jessica. She stared back, bereft of speech as her heart turned over. He accepted her ideas, adapted himself to her seeming whims. She loved him . . . had always loved him . . . yet this world of his remained unknown, alien both to her and to every modern idea with which she'd been raised. And she was stuck here. Somehow the fact she'd had no choice, that this time had been forced upon her, made it all the more terrifying.

But Roger, dear Roger, made it easier.

While Edmund saw to the knife and his hands, Jessica ordered the bringing of a flask of brandy. This, though, she did not present to Roger to drink. Instead she clutched it to her, standing back while Edmund approached his patient. Roger remained motionless on the boards, not drunk enough to be immune to pain, yet betraying almost no sign of it. The operation was over literally in seconds, the ball located and neatly scooped out.

Then Jessica poured the brandy over the wound, and a howl of rage broke from Roger. He sprang upright, sputtering in protest, then grew silent as he glared at her. "Another Chinese idea?" he demanded between gritted teeth.

"That's me, just full of surprises." Gently, she pressed him down against the planks.

"I shudder to think what you have in store for me next." He lay back and closed his eyes.

"So do I," she murmured.

One of the crew nudged her arm, then pressed a small bottle into her hand. Herbal salve by the smell, and almost empty. As she took it, she noted the odd lead seal that fastened about its neck, and it struck a chord in her memory. She'd seen one like it before . . . on that ancient bottle she'd found wedged into the rocks that night of the Non-Discovery Day bonfire.

That bottle. Had it been not her longings, but a bottle, that brought her back through time to Roger's side? Had all this been for some purpose, so she could play out this strange episode in history, to save Sir Roger Allendale from being struck in the chest by that Spaniard's shot—or from death by infection from a germ-ridden knife?

Her fingers tightened on the cool glass, and a wave of dizziness shot through her, leaving her disoriented. It *had* been the bottle, she realized. The fog, her sleeping—none of that had mattered. She'd needed the bottle. And now— Her awareness of her surroundings wavered as the bottle's hold on her strengthened. "It's going to take me home again," she breathed. Home, where she *should* be, where everything was familiar and safe. . . .

"What?" Roger's bleary eyes opened. "What can? What are you talking about?"

"This bottle." She struggled through the mists that surrounded her, bringing him back into focus. "I can go back where I belong."

He dragged himself into a sitting position. "I've told you I'll take you safely home to England."

"That's not where I come from. My world—" She fought against the rising dizziness. "There's no way you can take me *there,* where I belong. But this bottle—*it* can." She looked up at Roger. "I *can* go home."

"No." He pulled himself to his feet and stood over her, swaying slightly as he cupped her face. "I'm not letting you go anywhere. You are mine," he added with sudden ferocity. "My lioness, my pride—my wife."

He held her with his uninjured arm, and her senses filled with the salty freshness of his long hair, the herbal scent that clung to his shirt. At home, only loneliness awaited her. Here she had Roger. But she didn't belong in his time. She had her own future.

She pulled away from him, squeezing the bottle between her trembling hands. For a long moment she clutched it as the mists swirled about her and wave after wave of dizziness washed over her. The galleon, its crew—Roger—all shimmered before her, fading, vanishing from her life.

She could barely see through the hovering darkness of approaching unconsciousness. In moments all would go black, then she'd wake up and find herself in her own time, in her own place. This would all be gone, she'd be home with nothing but memories . . .

"No!" The denial tore from her throat. She spun about and flung the bottle from her, as hard as she could, over the railing. It sailed high in an arc, glinting in the sun, then vanished beneath the darkness of the waves. During the course of the next few hundred years it would wash toward the shore, at last coming to settle among the rocks for her to pick up. But now—

She turned back, steady once more, sure for the first time, and found herself enveloped in Roger's warm embrace. "I can *make* myself fit in. I want my own future, the one *I* choose. And I choose you." She snuggled even closer against his shoulder. "And don't you dare ever tell anyone where you found me. You never discovered Inlet Bay."

About the Author

Janice Bennett holds two B.A. degrees and an M.A. from the University of California. She is the author of seventeen books, including numerous award-winning Regency and time travel romances. Her next book is entitled *Amethyst Moon* and will be released by Pinnacle in August 1995. She lives with her husband, son, computer, horse, dogs, cats, rabbits, goldfish, birds, and any other animals currently in need of a home.

Summertime Blues

Amy J. Fetzer

To Dawn Bingham,
who hates being called a dependent spouse *as much as I do.*
Thanks for being there, girl friend.

One

Kayla was naked.

Blissfully bare and brazen; her arms swinging, flip-flops slapping, and Froot Loop earrings bouncing with everything else she owned as she strode toward the river for a dip in the skinny.

She smiled at her last thought. Her entire childhood was broken up with weeks of grounding for her wild behavior: three days for wearing her busty friend's bra, stuffing the cups, and then on a dare, visiting the ice cream man in all her bosomy glory; five days for painting a mural on the garage door; two weeks for piercing her ear with a darning needle and a potato; a month once for shaving a track in her head just to see if her skull was lumpy. Heck, Mom didn't like this cut either, she thought, plowing her fingers through her neatly cropped hair and fluffing it in the breeze. Looks like something from *Fern Gulley,* her dad had commented with a teasing smile. Pixie hair.

Yet, it didn't do a thing to relieve the discomfort of the heat, and she couldn't wait to dive into the rushing waters of the Red River. Wet and cold, yeah momma.

With her great-great grandma's cabin fading in the distance, her towel slung over her shoulder and grazing her bare buttocks, Kayla Fairchild ignored the touch of man in the rotting tree stumps littering the path and relished her surroundings, inhaling fresh clean air.

She needed this solitude. Her sky-rocketing one-of-a-kind

jewelry business had exterminated any form of a social life, along
with the ability to carry on a conversation about anything but
product marketing, lapidaries, design symmetry, and silver
smelting. Heck, her last two dates ended with a weak handshake
and a "when you can find the time to join the human race," sort
of dig, warning her that she was close to becoming a, yes, dreaded
workaholic yuppie. The thought of conforming like everyone
else her age made her cringe. Leisure time was long overdue,
and creatively, she was brain dead for fresh ideas and forced to
hire two artists to help complete her designs. Her latest, the kicky
Froot Loop earrings made of colored Australian crystal dusted
with sugar-like opal chips, were her hottest seller with her
younger buyers.

And they border on crass commercialism, a voice pestered.

Yeah, well, I'll fix that. A vacation full of free expression will
help, she thought with a wry grin and quickened her pace.

Her next step met wood, and Kayla stopped, staring immediately down at her feet. I've gone off the path, she realized, glancing briefly at her sparse surroundings, then kicking away the
decomposing leaves and dirt. Wood slats? And they'd been here
awhile, the edges hidden somewhere beneath the dirt and the
base of a dry tree stump. Kayla bent to examine the boards, a
strange, almost magnetic pull gripping the souls of her feet. Just
as she realized she still stood on the planks, the rotting slats
splintered instantly beneath her slight weight. She lurched forward, her torso slamming against the tree stump, her hands clawing wildly for something to keep her from falling further. She
caught an exposed root, the crackling vein sifting a few inches
through her fingers before she tightened her grip. The abrupt
halt nearly tore her arms from the sockets.

Her lungs worked violently. Three-quarters of her body dangled in the pit, into nothingness. She tried to hitch her leg over
the edge, but the opening was too narrow and prodding the air
with her foot only met more air.

Like trying to climb out of a fish bowl.

Kayla froze, sudden and frightened, feeling a tugging, not at
her legs but on her entire body. *But nothing's touching me.* Confused, she twisted her head, trying to see below into the darkness,

eyes scanning. Her fingers slipped on her anchor and she was too afraid that if she worked hand over hand, she'd fall. She called out for help, her voice echoing back to her, sounding slurred and pitifully weak. A tingling raced up her legs from her toes, itching her skin, and she resisted the urge to wiggle. Then, as if a giant pair of cold hands gripped her waist, she was yanked, the dying underbrush instantly disintegrating in her fists.

Kayla fell backwards, her shoulder thumping against the broken wood as she dropped into nothing.

She screamed and no one heard.

She swiped the air and touched nothing.

Then she hit bottom, the jolt driving up her legs, rattling her fillings and knocking air from her lungs. She crumpled beneath the impact, sinking to a bed of dry branches and rocks.

Dazed, Kayla remained still, feeling as if she'd been kicked in the solar plexus and willing herself to take a slow breath. Her chest expanded, nostrils sucking in dust and cobwebs.

I'm alive, she thought, swiping at her face, the pin-pricking driving over her skin like a swarm of ants. She cringed, slapping wildly at her skin. The violent motion sent pain spiking through her shoulder and she winced, attempting to sit up, moaning and rubbing, finding no cuts but the beginning of one heck of a bruise. Lucky fool. She tilted her face toward the sunlit hole, light bending enough to shine only a thin white slice across her face. A mix of relief and dizziness swept over her. The cut in the earth wasn't as far up as she imagined, though she'd no idea of how she could climb even that height. Her towel dangled annoyingly from a jagged piece of wood like a flag of surrender.

Never, she thought, climbing slowly to her feet. Nausea churned, souring her mouth, her body unreasonably lethargic and she bent over, hands braced on her knees until the awful sensation left. She needed to retch, but instead brushed at the dirt and leaves sticking to her naked skin. Of all the dumb luck. Kayla glanced above as if the hole might have conveniently grown a set of steps, then squinted to the area directly beyond her, reaching out for something solid. Nothing. Bravely, she took a step, feeling the ground with her pointed toes, her imagination producing a twenty-foot drop.

"Okay, God? Give me a little help here," she said, testing the sound of her voice and its bounce off the interior. Far too hollow for the pit to be very narrow, she thought, turning slowly and groping in the opposite direction. Her hands swiped the air, churning dust motes in the faint dagger of light as she inched forward. Her fingertips grazed the wall, hard and glass-like cool, and in the dark she searched for a protruding rock or root to grasp. This had to be the cleanest well in existence, she thought, her hands frantically skimming the perimeter; smooth and hard-packed, like cleanly buffed porcelain.

A bubble.

She squatted, sliding her hands down the surface toward her feet. It sloped smoothly to the floor beneath her, and she palmed the ground for something to dig foot hold gouges in the wall. Her search yielded nothing. There were sticks and rocks before— but now . . . not even a decent chunk of wood.

Weird. She straightened. Didn't wells have a narrow bored hole that drew the water from the earth? And this one was close to the river, so why was it dry? Why was it even here? A dry start, maybe?

Hardly matters, Kayla reasoned, since scaling a slick wall was impossible. Unless a nifty ladder happened to fall in after her. Tilting her face toward the opening, she frowned. Where the heck was her towel? She would have heard it drop if it had fallen. Her brows drew tighter. Flickering shadows of trees she swore weren't close enough to shade before, now hid the light. Maybe I just didn't notice, she thought and cupped her hands around her mouth. Shouting seemed the next logical step.

"Help! Anybody out there?"

There wasn't. It was why she chose to spend her vacation in the drafty old cabin. Total isolation to recover the clever imagination she'd lost. Privacy enough that she could strut to the river naked, she reminded, with a reproaching smirk, then called out uselessly. There wasn't another soul for a good fifty miles, and until someone realized she was missing—hope instantly dissipated, for it would be two weeks before her uncle Seth returned to retrieve her from the *gall-derned wilderness*.

She plopped to the ground, sitting Indian-style, elbows

propped on her knees and her chin in her palms. She tried desperately not to panic.

The picture of the cellular phone she'd left on the kitchen table burst into her mind. She hadn't thought to bring it. It wasn't as if she could order pizza way out here, anyway. But you could have called 911, she reminded, then smirked. *Naked woman rescued from abandoned well; film at eleven,* she imagined the lead story of the evening news. Dad would just love that. It wasn't bad enough that she made the newspaper's "Believe It Or Not" column when she dropped an earring down a flushing toilet and nearly got her arm sucked off trying to catch it.

Yet, she didn't think another handsome rescue volunteer was going to happen along anytime soon. No hero for you, girl friend.

"Well, God, if you wanted me to see that life is dull and too short to spend it alone, you made your point."

Kayla often conversed with God, especially when she was confused or frightened. And she was both. Though she considered her conversation partner as more of a friend who never contradicted or interrupted, the sound of her own voice and the small prospect that someone might actually be listening, comforted her. Aside from the fact that if she said something she shouldn't, she figured she'd be struck dead by a flaming lightning bolt anyway.

"And now that I've graciously conceded that skinny-dipping is hazardous to my health, do you think you could zap that cellular phone down here?"

Silence, terrifying and empty, the impact of her situation hitting like a cold slap.

"No?"

A scratchiness worked in her throat and she blinked back useless tears.

"Then how about a rope?"

The solitude was unnerving and in between her quiz with a higher being, Kayla shouted for help in the off chance that someone might be hiking by.

"How 'bout a Diet Coke, maybe?"

Please, God, Kayla prayed, tilting her tear-streaked face toward the light. I didn't quit swearing to die like this.

Promenade, Texas
1878

His head lolled, his Stetson tipped low on his brow, shielding the sun. A tiny sound pierced his nap, and Benjamin Tate stirred, blinking, swearing he was dreaming when the faint muffled noise came again.

He scrubbed his hand over his face, then shifted the horse off the road, his gaze searching for the source.

The further he meandered up the hillside, the clearer he heard what resembled a one-sided conversation.

"I know that time I blew up Dad's compost heap wasn't the swiftest thing I've done, but it stunk to high heaven and was right below my bedroom window. And well . . . you understand, don't you?"

Blew up a what? Ben wondered as his horse abruptly stopped.

"How 'bout a little mercy, Big Kahoona." A pause and then, "I can't believe you intend for my fate to be discovered as a pile of bones and a darling little pair of earrings."

Tipping his hat back, Ben looked down at the freshly dug well.

"Hey, God, you listening?" Feminine, demanding.

"Doubtful . . . but I am," Ben answered politely.

"Thank God!" Relieved, grateful.

"No. Ben."

Kayla smiled. Comedian.

Ben dismounted, pushing his horse back from the crumbling edge before he peered into the black void. "How the hell, beg pardon, did you get down there?"

"Oh gee, I fell." Sarcastic, impatient.

Ben smirked. Ask a stupid question, he thought.

"Ahh, Ben. There are crawly things down here, if you catch my drift." Almost childish and frightened.

Ben grinned. "Have you out in two shakes." He went to his horse, unlashing a small keel of rope and making a loop as he returned to her prison.

"It's about twenty-five feet down," she said, skeptical.

"Naw, just slip your foot into the knot and let me do the rest, little lady."

Little Lady? Great. Her hero was a condescending chauvinist. That wasn't nice, she scolded. After all, she would have been a skeleton before anyone else found her. The rope grazed her head and she grasped it, hiking her leg to slip her foot into the loop. She stilled, glancing up to the slice of light.

"Ahh, excuse me?"

Ben's brows scrunched. "Ma'am?"

"Are you wearing a shirt?"

Ben looked down at his chest to see if he was, in fact, wearing one, then shook his head at his own gullibility.

"Yes, I am."

"You sure? Took you long enough to answer."

"Is there a reason you needed to know?" he said, irritated.

"Drop it down to me."

"What?"

"I said, drop it down. Please," she added and Ben's frown softened. God, she even sounded pretty. Stripping off his shirt, he deposited it into the well and Kayla watched it sail down, the pale blue fabric draping over her head. Quickly she slipped it on, cringing as pain darted through her shoulder, slowing her movements as she hastily buttoned the garment. The scent of man and bayberry and sweat made her feel safe again. You big baby.

Wiggling her foot into the loop, she hollered, "Ready!" The slack tightened and she was surprised by how fast he hoisted her from the cavern.

The closer he drew her, the clearer Kayla could hear him breathe, no groans from exertion, just deep even breathing. And when Kayla emerged from the well, she saw why. He was huge, his arms and shoulders were like skin-covered boulders.

She was light as a child, Ben thought and when he saw the thatch of bright auburn hair, he gave a mighty heave and the woman popped from the earth and into his arms. She fell softly against him and he swept her safely away from the edge.

Kayla gripped thick damp muscles and stared into the face of her rescuer. His eyes were crystal blue, thickly lashed, and holding a gentle warmth she'd never seen in a man. She would dream for weeks about those eyes, she decided right then, yet for all his bulk he looked incredibly boyish, his smile shy, dark hair waving down over one eye. His beige cowboy hat sat tipped back on his crown, enhancing the quality. She smiled, then briefly looked to the sky and mouthed *thank you* to the heavens. His low chuckle sanded deliciously beneath her skin.

She met his gaze. "Hi, hero." He still held her close, and she was in no hurry to let go. Talk about cute.

Ben's gaze toured her face, from the unfashionably cropped auburn hair to the wide green eyes dominating her small face. She looked like a fairy or a wood nymph. Hell, he'd almost expected her to squeak when she talked.

"Thanks for fishing me out."

He touched the brim of his hat, bringing it down to shade his eyes. "Happy to 'blige, ma'am." Deep and husky, and melting through her like warm syrup.

"I'm Kayla," she said, easing out of his arms.

His gaze dropped immediately to the shirt, his shirt, haphazardly buttoned, which was about three off and exposing a bare shoulder, the curve toward her breast, and an abundance of leg.

"You're naked!" he hissed as if someone would hear.

"I was headed for a swim when—" She waved at the hole in the ground.

"You were going to swim . . . in the *altogether?*" He choked off the last word.

Another judge and jury appalled at her behavior. "No, in the *all nothing*," she goaded his Church Lady sensibilities.

He hooked his thumbs in his belt loops. "Most folks wait 'til they get to the water before stripping."

"I'm not most folks," she said, folding her arms. She winced, sucking in air through clenched teeth and rubbing her shoulder.

He stepped closer, sympathy shaping his handsome face. "You're hurt."

Kayla took a step back, her eyes widening. "It—it's fine," she stammered, her gaze glued to his hips, or rather the gun holstered there, and Ben glanced between her frightened face and his pistol.

"Benjamin Tate," he introduced softly as if gentling a frightened child.

"Are you the sheriff or with the Rangers or something?" she asked, her voice rising with her panic. He shook his head and she blasted back with, "Then why the hel-heck are you wearing *that*, Benjamin Tate?" and pointed to the gun.

"So I don't get killed." Good God, she looked ready to run for the hills.

"By whom?"

Ben shrugged, sweat-slick muscles flexing as he bent to retrieve his rope. "Gee," he mocked, winding the line. "Indians—"

"Aren't any—"

"— Desperados,"

"Oh get real—" she said, rolling her eyes.

"Rustlers," he listed, then leaned closer and added with a quick grin, "How 'bout forest fairies popping out of Joe Anderson's well?"

Her expression faltered. "Anderson? I'm afraid you're wrong. This is my family's land." She twisted to gesture at the cabin on the hill and stilled, her hand lowering slowly to her side. She couldn't see the cabin as clearly as before. The tree line was heavier. In fact, the wide cleared path was only a bit of trampled terrain now.

But how—? Her gaze darted to her surroundings, frantic and jumpy.

The area was denser. She was sure of it. And greener. Green with grass and bushes and leaves. Trees shadowed them now and it was definitely cooler, she realized, the fruity scent of wild berries filling the air and her senses. She spun about, facing the river. The water's edge was uneven, clustered with boulders and bushes and it looked narrower—no, it *was* narrower than before. *Before what,* a voice pestered. Her gaze jerked to the well and she inhaled sharply. The broken wood was missing, the earth around it rich, dark bottomland, not dry and trampled. And the tree stump was gone! Slowly, she bent to look inside for the towel she knew she wouldn't find and realized the well wasn't as deep as before, the bottom churned with overturned rocks and a discarded pick ax.

That wasn't there before.

"Joe's homesteading here, on *McFarrel* land," Ben stressed, and Kayla's gaze sharpened on him, searching his face for the lie.

"Which McFarrel?" Her voice trembled.

"Don't know." Ben shrugged. "Never lived on it, just owned it. No, wait," he said, a memory, blooming. "Kaitlin McFarrel did awhile back, maybe five years, but left. Once in a while someone shows up to see if the place is still standing, but never stays." A pause and then softly, "You alright? You're lookin' a might peaked."

Peaked? Fried chicken lips! Schizophrenic was more like it.

"Do you want to sit down?"

Kayla shook her head, not knowing if she was answering him or not. Okay, okay, get a grip, Kayla. There is a logical, sane, *very* sane reason for this. But Kaitlin KcFarrel was her great-great grandmother. And she was dead.

Nearly a hundred years dead.

Oh, shi-shoelaces! This can't be happening, she thought, staggering back, the soft cool earth giving beneath her feet. She flailed.

"Whoa, hold on," Ben said as he caught her, pulling her clear, and she wrapped her arms around his neck, clinging to the stranger.

"What's happened to the land? To me?" she mumbled to his chest.

"Land's got holes and you keep trying to dive in," he answered, and she made a strained sound.

Ben tried to be dispassionate, he swore he was, but she felt so delicate and fragile, trembling too damn hard for such a little start, and finally, he gave up, sagging with resignation, his arms sliding slowly around her. She felt wonderful pressed warmly against him, like a part of him he'd lost and just found.

Kayla willed herself not to panic, not to scream. She'd return to the cabin and this would all be explained. *Yeah, right. If you're so sure, then why can't you let go of this man's neck?*

Because he feels strong and safe and unbelievably *normal*, she thought, and his concern for a naked nut he pulled from a shallow well touched her.

Slowly she leaned back enough to look him in the eye.

What was different about him? He wore boots, black button fly jeans, and a simple leather belt. Nothing unusual there, except the jeans fit him looser than a man with such an exceptional body might wear. Benjamin Tate was harmless, she decided. *Yet he wears a pistol like I wear perfume.*

Ben stared into lush green eyes and thought instantly of passion and love and childhood freedom. He wanted to kiss her, to see if his imagination could be matched, and bent closer, shifting his hands. His fingers grazed bare skin and he groaned softly.

"God almighty, please tell me you've got clothes around here somewhere," he rasped, suddenly lowering his arms and hunching his big shoulders.

Kayla stepped back, her insides shivering, and she wanted desperately for Ben to hold her again. He didn't.

He stared at his boot toes for a moment, then glanced up from beneath his hat. "You look like her." His smile was barely there.

Ice cold gripped Kayla's spine. "Who?"

"Kaitlin," he answered softly, studying her face. "Just a little, 'round the eyes."

Kayla swallowed, licking her lips. How could he have known what Kaitlin looked like? "You must be mistaken."

Ben shook his head, slowly, and she knew he wasn't.

The past minutes replayed in her mind like a video in rewind. The newness of the land, the shallowness of the well. And, oh, jeez—the sensations she experienced just before she fell in. The grip, the pull. Into where?

"I—I have to, uh, have to go," she muttered, not feeling her feet move around the open well.

"Can I escort you to the door?" Ben offered, recognizing fear when he saw it.

"No, no thanks. Bye."

The cabin. She had to get to the cabin. Everything would be okay once she was inside.

"You sure, Kayla?"

Her name on his lips made her twist to look at him. He's a

good man, she thought, his tender tone mirroring the gentle concern she saw in his eyes.

"I'll be fine, hero."

Just then the breeze caught the shirt, billowing it briefly and offering him an unobstructed view of one curving buttock and a bit of slim hip. He wanted to see the rest, he thought, his eyes widening when he glimpsed a tiny winged creature painted high on her hip.

Well I'll be.

A tattoo.

His gaze jerked to hers. But she was off in a dead run up the hill.

"Hey! My shirt!"

"I'll get it back to you!" she called, not stopping.

Wonderful, Ben thought, throwing up his arms and turning back to his horse.

How was he supposed to explain riding into town, shirtless, without compromising her by revealing how he'd lost it.

He wouldn't, he decided after a moment and followed the path she'd taken.

Two

Kayla pushed open the door, already knowing what she'd find. Nothing was the same.

The grocery sacks and her compact CD player were gone. The cellular phone was gone. Heck, the counter wasn't even there!

A hulking black monstrosity replaced the efficient gas stove, a braided rag rug instead of the lush sculptured carpet.

Replaced, yet here. Kayla knew she was not in her time, her world. The fall down the well had changed that. She swallowed, moving slowly across the room and tripping on the rough boards. She caught the edge of the kitchen table, then pulled back a chair and dropped into the seat. She rubbed her palm across the rough unfamiliar wood, her gaze darting to the pump over a dry sink, the stove housing neatly stacked with pots and wooden spoons, to the hutch and cupboard filled with blue and white dishes and cups.

Kaitlin's place, she thought with a quick, hard chill. It was a woman's home, with doilies and curtains and easy access to dish rags. She twisted in the seat to look at the living room. The parlor, she silently corrected: a sofa, rocker and a foot stool, neatly arranged with oil lamps perched on two adjacent tables. She noticed framed pictures resting on the mantel and she couldn't move fast enough, snatching one off the narrow ledge. It was old, a daguerrotype, shades of brown and nearly white of a man; a man who looked amazingly like her father and she knew instantly that she'd seen this photo when she was a child. Great-great grandpa. And if this photo was here, where was he? Where was Kaitlin? God, Kayla thought, what events would be twisted if she ran into her great-great grandmother now?

Replacing the photograph, Kayla inspected the room, searching hopelessly for her suitcases. She strode quickly into the bedroom, yet knew she wouldn't find them, no matter how hard she looked. Now what do I wear? Spotting an armoire, she flew across the room, flipping the catch and opening it wide. Sighing with relief, she inspected the simply sturdy clothing. Like vintage costumes, she thought. This is Kaitlin's room, Kaitlin's things . . . *and I'm in Kaitlin's time.* No doubt remained. Nor a way back.

Muscles squeezed in her chest, dizzying her with heartache. Mom. Dad. Uncle Seth.

I can't think about that or I'll go mad. Maybe this is a dream and she was here temporarily? Perhaps the impact of hitting the bottom of the well had done something to her? Regardless, she was here, in these surroundings, and she had to make the best of it 'til she discovered a doorway out of this time warp.

And dressing enough to meet whatever was coming next was her first priority.

Stripping off Ben's shirt and rummaging through the dresser for *proper* underclothing, Kayla found what she needed. She dressed, perspiring through the chemise and long-sleeved blouse, and by the time she managed the stockings, long, dark skirt, and heeled boots that were a bit too snug, droplets were rolling down her back and between her breasts.

Turning back her sleeves, she stilled when she heard heavy footsteps. God, I'm going to be attacked by Indians or tossed out by my great-great grandmother, she thought, walking quickly into the main room.

Ben stood on the threshold, eyeing her up and down.

"Hi, hero." He filled out those jeans nicely for a man his age.

Tipping his hat back, he leaned against the frame. "Clothes suit you," he said with an easy grin, and Kayla melted right there on the spot.

"Are you saying I look better with them on or off?"

He flushed a little, but maintained the sweet smile. Damn, but she was bold.

"Least ways *all* the citizens of Promenade won't be shocked," he commented dryly.

Promenade. Now if she could only get the date out of him
without looking like a complete idiot.

"This place looks good, considering," he called as she disappeared into the bedroom, returning with his shirt.

She smiled her thanks, handing it over. "Considering what?"

"That it's been locked up since '73."

God, he was a big man, Kayla thought, watching the incredible
flex of muscle as he slipped on the shirt. "Twenty-two years?"

"No," he said carefully, frowning. "Five."

Bingo, Kayla thought. It was 1878. 1878!

"You're looking peaked again, Kayla."

Oh, it's nothing, she wanted to say. I've just discovered I've
fallen one hundred sixteen years back in time. How's your day
been?

"I'm tired, I guess," she said lamely, then gestured inside as
she moved into the kitchen. She opened cabinets and peeked in
a pantry off to the left and found the shelves filled with jars of
vegetables, sacks of corn meal, and a couple of hams hanging
from the ceiling. At least I won't starve, she thought, then considered food-poisoning if she ate that stuff.

Yet a quick glance of the cabin sent her mind in a different
direction. An open book lay face down on the small table in the
parlor. The stove was spotless, the pans stacked as if freshly
washed. A straw hat hung from a wall hook, a long coat and scarf
beside it. A basket lined with fabric lay discarded beneath the
coat. It was eerie, as if someone had just closed the door and left,
and when she saw the tapestry bag overflowing with white lace
and linen, Kayla knew the tatting was the beginnings of the table
cloth her mother prized most amongst all her heirlooms.

With Ben in the room, she had a hard time thinking clearly,
but knew she couldn't live without money, and she needed to get
to town to find a job.

Promenade was mostly open land, far from what it was a hundred years ago, and her insides suddenly jumped with excitement. She was going to see Promenade in its glory.

"Can you give me a ride to town?"

Ben smiled, a flash of straight white teeth. "Bored out here already?" He straightened, gesturing politely for her to proceed him.

"And the adventure continues," she muttered dryly as she swept out the door.

A hour later, from her position atop Ben's horse, she saw the town—active, bigger than she imagined, and intimidating. Tucked close to Ben, feeling his warmth and protection, Kayla hated to admit she needed him. A woman alone in 1878 was vulnerable. Mostly to the whims of men.

"You can quit hiding," Ben said a bit too loudly and Kayla twisted on his lap, frowning. He stared at her for an incredibly intense moment, then inclined his head to the side. She looked in the direction, her eyes widening as a small boy slipped from the tree line and walked quietly beside them.

"How'd ye know?"

"You clomp like a wild boar, Asa."

"You aren't going to tell, are you, Mister Tate?"

"No." The kid smiled. "You are." Asa's grin evaporated and Kayla couldn't help but laugh at that crestfallen pout.

She hadn't noticed that they'd come upon a school 'til Ben stopped the horse. Sliding from the saddle, he helped her down, then gave Asa a meaningful glance and a nod. The kid sulked toward the teacher standing on the top step trying to herd children back inside.

"I sent word to your home, Asa," the teacher said. "You've been very disrespectful."

He's been playing hookey, Kayla thought as she and Ben neared.

"Why are you having classes in the summer?" Kayla asked. Poor kids, they look as if they were heading into the gas chamber.

"They've missed far too much school this year," Ben told her.

"But it's vacation time—time for swimming, games, being a child," she said vehemently and obviously too loud, for the children cheered agreement, and it took the teacher considerable effort to regain control. A few scattered back outside to play an instant longer and the rest refused to go inside, complaining of the heat. The teacher, a slim man in dark austere clothing, pursed his lips, his frustration showing in his mussed hair and loose tie.

"Can't you have class outside, at least?"

"Christopher, Polly, and Michael, come in and take your seats!" he shouted, then sent Kayla a how-dare-you-interfere glare. "Madam, I have a difficult enough time maintaining order to teach these—these—" he looked at his students as if they were fungus, *"children.* Outside would be impossible."

He acted as if he were doing the world a favor rather than his job.

"That all depends on how you teach."

"Kayla," Ben said, a warning in his tone.

"What, Ben? What?" came her impatient demand.

"Last winter was hard. The snow was so bad they couldn't get here."

"But all summer?" Kayla remembered being grounded for being herself and spending her eleventh summer in summer school while her friends went wild at Camp Oom pah-pah or some such place. The memory clouded her judgment.

"They need to make up for time lost," Ben said.

"I know that, but how much are they going to absorb when—"

"The children are nearly an entire year behind," he interrupted. "And they *need* an education!" He was in her face now. "They are nothing without it!"

"Okay, okay, jeez, calm down." Good God, he was just a little bit too anal about all this.

"Andrew! Ellie! Aaron! Come back this instant!" the teacher shouted and was ignored.

"They will attend school, Kayla, so don't even think to start trouble!"

"Ben, I said all right!"

Ben stepped back, his anger settling as quick as it came, and she eyed him for an instant. But the children, well, with the adults talking, they were being kids, making noise, wrestling in the dirt, running, teasing each other—energy out of control. Then a pair of six-year-old boys playing tag made a wild dash for base and caught the teacher about the legs. The man lost his footing and tumbled down the steps, landing on his rump. The kids froze, terrified of retribution and itching to laugh.

Kayla's lips twitched. The teacher looked like Barney Fife.

"Do you see what I must work with?" the teacher snapped, scrambling to his feet. "It's impossible to teach such, such ill-bred, rude, disgrac—" words died when a child beaned him in the head with a dirt clod. *"That* is *it!"* he ground between clenched teeth and innocent giggles snuck past pinched lips. "If you think *you* can teach this pack of . . . heathens," he shouted, "then you do it!" Throwing down his pointer, he stalked to the buggy, climbed in, and snapped the reins. He was lost in a cloud of dust—and when it finally dissipated, Kayla realized half the town had witnessed the scene. Parents curried their children close, glaring at the stranger as Ben folded his big arms, looking intimidating and furious.

"Happy?"

She sputtered an excuse that would fall short of anything he had in mind and couldn't begin to imagine what he was thinking. "You could always ask him back?" she offered, wincing at the mess she'd made.

"He's quit three times in the last month."

"Well, then, that proves he didn't really want to do it," she rushed to say.

"And you think *you* can do better?" he growled down at her.

She looked from the children to the school, then back to Ben. "Is that a bet, Mister Tate?" she challenged, and his eyes narrowed, his gaze snapping over her, pausing briefly at her hip.

"Damn, if you aren't a hellion, Kayla Fairchild. Comin' in here and stirrin' up trouble."

"Perhaps that's why I'm here." His scowl deepened with confusion and she reached up to smooth the wrinkles. "Trust me."

When his expression remained darkly unapproachable, she sighed disappointedly and stepped back, her gaze shifting beyond him to the block of angry parents. Running her fingers through her hair, then tugging at her shirtsleeves, she rolled her thinking back one hundred sixteen years and approached the town folk of Promenade.

* * *

She was the new schoolteacher. *School marm.* How antiquated, she thought as she rang the bell and yawned. She'd risen early, scouting the area and planning the day's event. This was going to be the summer camp she'd missed and the kids would love it. She was sure of it. But as they clomped dispiritedly into the classroom, Kayla had second thoughts.

They slugged to their benches, poking each other and stirring up foul moods and she imagined they were all punished for their behavior yesterday.

Poor dears. It wasn't their fault. They had the summertime itch, as her mom used to call it. She clapped her hands once sharply and the noise died, a dozen sad little faces looking up at her. She made each child stand and say his or her name. Kayla had an excellent memory; it got her out of trouble, because no matter how much she screwed around, her grades were always good.

"I'm going to make a deal with you," she said to the group. "School will be different, fun, I promise, but you," she pointed a finger, sweeping her arm back and forth to encompass the entire lot, "must do as I say."

"What kind of fun?" a boy of about ten asked.

Aaron, she recalled. "Experiments and hikes and perhaps . . ." she eyed them once, then whispered as if giving away a secret, "swimming lessons."

They oohed and aahhed over the possibility, faces beaming.

"But—!" Quiet and impatient kids shifted in their seats. "I expect good behavior, and for the older children to help watch out for the younger ones. If we have but one incident," she warned with an effective glare, "then I'm afraid I'll have no choice except to take our studies back into this school. Agreed?"

Affirmation came sporadically and Kayla wasn't satisfied.

"Agreed?" she stressed, and they answered in unison. "Good. Leave your books and take your lunch pails," she said and exited the classroom, a dozen children following her in single file like ducklings.

Her step suddenly faltered, her smile drooping.

Ben stood on the edge of the school yard, his stance like a judgmental sovereign, his face creased in a deep scowl. He'd been the only opposition last night when the townfolk had met and discussed her taking over the teaching position she helped vacate. He demanded she be tested since she'd no credentials—and there wasn't a question she couldn't answer. In fact, when she delved into the subject of teaching the children about plants and agriculture, she was a shoe-in with the farmers and ranchers.

But Ben still wasn't satisfied, storming out of the town hall, and she half-expected him to be her watchdog today. But as she and her students walked the path toward the clearing she'd found, he remained on the outskirts, daring her to fail. A little pain bit into her heart. Couldn't he have even a shred of confidence in her, she thought, then reasoned that he didn't know she possessed one hundred sixteen years of experience.

"Want to join us?" she called and his expression softened even as he slowly shook his head. "See you at two then." Question lingered in her words and she hoped he caught her meaning.

Three

The small group surrounded the foot-high mud mountain, their teacher kneeling and pouring a liquid into an opening fashioned in the top of the mound.

"Move back," Kayla said, looking skeptically at the lump of dirt and clay. Nothing happened and the children glanced at her for explanation. "Well that's odd. I'm certain . . ." She leaned over the mound and white foam shot her in the face. She sputtered, laughing at herself, scraping the goop from her view and flicking it at the giggling children.

"Miss Fairchild!" Ben called, storming across the clearing and halting beside the group. "Miss Fairchild." Quick silence accented his words.

With the sereneness of Mother Teresa, Kayla looked up at him, white froth sliding down her forehead and dripping off her nose. "Yes, Mister Tate?"

"Is this your idea of teaching? They could have been hurt by that!" He jabbed a finger at the mound.

"It's harmless, Ben, just a baking soda and hydrogen peroxide explosion."

"A what!"

Kayla refused the bait of his disapproval, again. She knew the children were learning. Why couldn't he just give her the benefit of the doubt? A total skeptic to her methods, he was always near, spying, though she sensed his presence with uncanny clarity. His doubt wounded her, for when they weren't arguing over her lack of conformity, they were recognizing the powerful attraction they shared.

She was sure of it.

"Ellie, tell Mister Tate what you've learned today."

The eight-year-old stood and recited, "For every action there is an equal and opposite reaction."

Kayla nodded approvingly at Ellie, giving her a wink. "And Andrew, what does this experiment represent?"

"This is the earth's surface, Mister Tate." His hands hovered over the mud mountain. "The core of the earth is liquid, and when it heats up, it swells, 'cause heat expands things. Anyway, there isn't any more room in there, so the hot core has to go somewhere and moves upward. It breaks the earth's crust and releases the core, or the lava. That's a volcano." Andrew nodded to the mud mound now caving in from the dampness.

Kayla applauded, whistling, pumping her fist like Arsenio. "Home team wins! Give that man," she pointed to Andrew, "an A for effort, explanation, and articulation!"

The children laughed at her antics, expecting the unexpected from her, yet when she looked up at Ben, he was glaring down at her like a black thunder cloud.

"Come on, Ben, be reasonable." she said softly, climbing to her feet.

"You, ma'am, are beyond reason," he growled.

"Learning doesn't have to be boring or painful, you know."

Ben didn't know what to say. He was drowning in those liquid green eyes and he didn't have a fit retort. God, he always felt disarmed and ignorant around her, and he didn't like it one damn bit. "Goodbye, Miss Fairchild," he uttered before turning away, and Kayla watched him leave, hurt twisting in her chest.

Why did that goodbye feel so final?

Kayla sighed, used her shirt sleeve to wipe her face, then plastered on a smile as she faced her students. Fanbelts and fruitcake. How was she going to survive here when her only opposition was the one man she wanted in her life?

Benjamin Tate slammed his mallet against the glowing horseshoe, the force bouncing the massive hammer back toward his shoulder. He repeated the measure over and over, then shoved the shoe into a water pail, the contact sending steam spiraling upward and heating the already stifling livery. Throwing the tongs aside, he crossed to the doors, pushing them open, pausing a moment to enjoy the breeze cooling his skin. Turning back inside, he stilled when he heard a familiar voice. His head jerked to the left.

Kayla. His heart jumped in his chest at the sight of her, reed slim and brimming with energy. She was instructing her students, out-of-doors as usual, and it seemed she'd cajoled the grocer into joining her lesson.

Children raised their hands excitedly, one girl offering up two apples to her question. How the hell could she be teaching a decent class when they were out shopping?

Aproned in leather, Ben strode across the street, stopping just close enough to hear her ask, "Now, Andrew, if you have fifty cattle to feed and each cow consumes a sack and a half a week, how much would you tell Mister Finkle you needed."

Ben's gaze slid to Andrew, a tall lad of about twelve. "Seventy-five sacks," he said proudly, then frowned. " 'Cept cattle don't eat that much and 'sides, they graze on open land."

"I stand corrected, sir, but you're right. And the proper pronunciation is *except* and *be*sides."

Ben listened as the children, each holding a penny, figured out exactly how many pieces of rock candy they could purchase. And as Kayla herded the children inside, her gaze scoured the area for stragglers.

Then she saw him. And his heart slammed against the wall of his chest. God almighty. She took his breath away.

"Hi, hero," she said and her soft voice blended with his blood. He maintained his frown and her smile instantly fell. "You've come to argue with me again, haven't you?" Flat, disappointed, and he felt it like a spear to his chest.

"You can't tell me this is proper learning." He gestured toward the mercantile. "Taking them shopping?"

"It's a daily used skill, Benjamin Tate. Practical. We wouldn't want the merchants to cheat them, or them to short-change the grocer, would we?" Something shifted in his unyielding gaze, the sadness striking a weak spot in her. "These are future farmers and ranchers and mothers and teachers here. And they're getting more than the basics. Ask any one of them."

"They need to be in a classroom, Kayla."

She stepped off the porch, and that's when he noticed she wore trousers—denim trousers.

Damn. Made her look more enticing than she already did.

"Were you taught to blacksmith in a schoolroom?"

"No, but—"

"Do you think the ranchers learned to corral cattle inside a building?"

"You're being petty."

"No, Ben, you are." She gazed up into his handsome face, wondering how she'd lost him, when she never really had him. He was in her heart, Kayla realized, and if she wasn't the sport for the local gossips, she'd kiss the big ox right here and now. "It's been nearly two weeks and you've not so much as given an inch with my ways. Why?"

The wind ruffled her hair, green eyes waiting for a response. "What about book learning, Kayla?"

He might have asked her to come to bed with him, so intimate was his tone. "We go over it in the morning class and take an outing in the afternoon." Was she answering him or drooling?

"It isn't enough. They're nothing without—"

"Have dinner with me tonight," she whispered disarmingly and his brows rose. "At my place," she added with a feline grin.

Ben felt unhinged, powerless. "I don't, ah, think I—"

She arched a brow. "Scared of me, Benjamin Tate?"

"Scared of me being *alone* with you, hellion." His low voice suddenly crackled with intimacy.

"I'm a big girl," she said for his ears alone. "And I promise not to rip your clothes off."

He choked and sputtered, eyes wide. "Kayla Fairchild, you are—"

"Outrageous? Irresistible?" Her gaze swept him provocatively. "Inspired?"

He took a step closer. "God, I want to hold you," he rasped, his heart in his eyes.

The children rushed out of the store, laughing and waving tiny bags of booty as they surrounded Kayla and Ben.

"I have to go," she murmured apologetically. "I promised them a swim."

"In what?" He made a show of looking her up and down, remembering how he'd found her.

"The river," she replied tartly, turning on her heels. His gaze dropped to her hips and the luscious package shifting inside those jeans. "And Ben?" she tossed over her shoulder.

He brought his gaze to her face. "Yeah, hellion?"

"Bring a horse for me to buy, I'm tired of walking."

Kayla fidgeted nervously over the simple meal, which wasn't a normal thing for her, since she lived alone and usually dined out or popped something in the microwave. But here she had to cook, real slave-over-the-stove cooking: beef from Andrew's father, corn from the pantry, mashed potatoes, gravy, and biscuits. And Kayla never worked so hard in her life. This, she thought as she fought with another potato lump, is not my element.

"Nice dress, Kayla."

Kayla yelped, nearly left her skin as she spun about, flinging potatoes across the room. She looked first at Ben, clean shaven and neatly dressed in jeans and a blue shirt, then to the glob clinging to the wall.

"Rats and radishes," she muttered, marching over to the splatter and wiping it with the edge of her apron.

He stared at the toes of his boots, his hat in his hands. But his quaking shoulders gave him away.

"You can laugh, Ben, I'm not that sensitive."

He did, deeply, politely. "Sorry. God, you ought to see yourself, hellion."

Kayla bent forward to look in the mirror hanging near the coat rack and smiled. Aside from the fact that she looked like a wilted flower, she had flour in her hair and a clump of some unidentifiable matter sticking to her cheek like a wart.

"I guess this proves my talents don't lie in the kitchen," she said, fluffing her hair and sending up a puff of white dust.

"And where do they lie?"

He was close, wiping a potato chunk from her skin and Kayla's body jumped to life. She wished he'd kiss her. And quickly.

"That's a very suggestive remark, Mister Tate."

"I know." He bent closer, his gaze shifting to her mouth.

Please, her mind screamed, the heat inside her steaming out of control. Her gaze toured his features, chiseled and rugged, and she noticed a scar along his brow. He stared at her, his emotions unmasked in his blues eyes, adoring her, wanting her, and it was Kayla's turn to feel powerless.

"Ben," she breathed, laying a hand to his chest. His heart thudded wildly beneath her palm, the steady pump humming up her arm and into her body. He leaned down, his broad hand slipping to her waist, nudging her gently closer. Her body brushed against his and he made a sound, half pained, half needy.

"I gotta taste you, Kayla."

"Hurry, hero."

He did, gently, tenderly, but the fire in her wouldn't be patient and her hands slid up his chest, circling his neck, her slim body pressing firmly to his. It was like opening a flood gate. His kiss turned hungry, savage and crazed with want, and Kayla's exotic response tore him in two. Her fingers sank into his hair, pressing him closer and he indulged, savored, his arms winding tightly around her and lifting her off the floor.

Kayla clung. Never in her life . . . never in her dreams had she felt such electricity in a man. He was sensual and reserved, gentle and powerful. And Kayla wanted to stay with him. Wanted to love him. It would be so easy. And as his mouth trailed her cheek, down her throat, she gripped his shoulders, leaning back to give him better access. *Oh, my, my.* He whispered her name over and over, his lips seeking hers again and again and Kayla's insides melted and puddled and left her with nothing to feel but the glories of Ben.

"God almighty," he murmured against her lips, "I wanted to do that the instant I laid eyes on you." He let her feet touch ground again, and the swelling evidence of their stolen moment pressed warmly against her.

"No kidding." She kissed him leisurely, palming the strength in his massive shoulders.

"Obvious, was I?"

"I'm a woman, Ben, not a tree stump."

He chuckled, deep and short, his hands roaming her spine. "God, I'll say." He clutched her, recalling the past days when he'd watched her without being seen; Kayla teaching her students and learning to ride a horse; Kayla walking through the streets like the Pied Piper, her pupils following her, singing and doing some cute little dance as they went off on a new adventure. His forest fairy, a woman full-grown with the heart of a child.

"Who are you, Kayla Fairchild?" He nuzzled the spot below her ear.

"I'm an artist," she blurted.

"Hmm?" He met her gaze, loving the soft jade green of her eyes.

"An artist." She gestured sluggishly to the sketches on the table, the ink and graphite neatly arranged.

He straightened, his gaze shifting and his brows drawing together as he went to the table. Kayla sighed to the heavens, licking her unsatisfied lips. Ought to learn to keep my mouth shut, she thought as she entered the kitchen to finish preparing their dinner.

Bracing his palms on the table, Ben studied the sketches, flipping one, then another. "These are incredible," he said, awed.

"Thanks. It's hard to get them down on paper, they move too fast."

"But you've captured them so perfectly." He chuckled. "Like this one of Andrew. God, he looks so . . . adult."

"He is, Ben." In this time, she thought. "He enjoys school more than the others, absorbs everything so quickly and remembers word for word. Good grief, he reads faster than I do."

When Ben didn't comment, she twisted to look at him. He hovered over the papers, his expression so disappointed, she set aside the spoon and crossed the room.

"They're learning, Ben, I swear." She picked up a paper she'd been grading. "This is David's. Look, he's only six." She handed it to him.

"I know." He gave it a quick perusal. "And it's good, Kayla, real good."

He handed back the paper and Kayla frowned, studying Ben as he flipped another sketch. His skin suddenly flushed red, and she glanced down. It was him, hovering over the forge, slamming that massive hammer on a shoe. She even managed to get the sparks flying from the blow. And he was embarrassed.

She reached past him, turning over another page; Ben atop his horse the day she met him, Ben watching her teach, his arms braced on the fence rail outside the Andersons' meadow.

"You knew I was there?" he asked cautiously, not looking at her.

"I always know where you are, Ben."

His gaze flew to hers.

"Don't you feel it? This connection we have?" She traveled back in time for a reason. She was sure of it. Yet whether it was to find the love of her life or not, she couldn't know, but she was definitely here for Ben. To love him? Or leave him?

She inhaled deeply and smelled something burning. Kayla sniffed. "Oh, no!"

She tore out of his arms and flew into the kitchen, grabbing a dish cloth and opening the oven door. "My biscuits!" she cried. "Oh, sugarfoot!"

"Sugar what?"

"Foot! Foot! Foot!" she cursed, removing the pan and dropping it in the dry sink with a disgusted frown.

She made a face at the pile of smoking black blobs, then checked the remainder of the meal, relieved it had survived her bumbling. In minutes she laid everything on the table, gesturing for him to sit. He hadn't moved from the spot near the little side table where her sketches lay.

"Not hungry?"

His gaze traveled with unspeakable slowness over her body.

"I'm not on the menu, Ben." *Liar. You want to be dessert, you tart.*

He blinked, then smiled and sauntered across the room—really sauntered, she thought. Those had to be the sexiest rocking hips she ever had the pleasure of seeing.

He pulled out a chair, grinning maddeningly as he dropped into it. "Feed me, woman, I'm starving."

Kayla laughed to herself. If any other man had said that, she'd have beaned him in the head with her biscuits.

They dined in silence, but the energy filtering across the rough-made table was enough to start a forest fire, she thought, draining her tea and pouring more. She considered, for all of two seconds, telling him where she'd really come from—then decided it wasn't wise just yet. But she wasn't leaving, of that she was certain. She'd checked the half-dug well every morning and night and it was still the same; never as deep as when she'd first fallen inside.

"When did you get that tattoo?" he asked as she rose to clear the table.

Kayla glanced back over her shoulder. He must have seen it when she was wearing nothing but his shirt. "It was in my college days, when I was young and stupid and drunk."

"College?"

"Yup." Uh-oh, did women go to college in 1878? She couldn't remember. "Art school," she fudged, pumping water into the tub. He came up behind her as she scraped the plates—well, only hers, really, the man left nothing behind. God, the grocery bills he must have to feed all that muscle, she thought, casting a side glance in his direction. She wanted to kiss him, again.

"I own a jewelry store." He looked at her sharply and she knew she couldn't lie to him. "I make all the pieces myself . . . well, now with two other jewelers, but I design them all."

"Like these?" he asked skeptically, flicking her Froot Loop earrings.

"Yeah. Sad, aren't they?"

"New, they look like candy, as if you could eat them."

If you only knew, she thought, scrubbing the dishes. He dried and put away, yet not a word passed between them as they worked.

"My turn for a question." She toweled a dish and slapped the dish rag over her shoulder as she faced him.

"I'd rather kiss you," he said, leaning closer. She pushed him back, shoving a just-washed pot at his chest. He made a face, drying it, then turned away to set the Dutch oven on a shelf in the pantry. Pausing on the threshold, he folded his arms, bracing his shoulder against the door frame.

"When were you going to tell me you couldn't read?"

His face went molten, with rage or embarrassment she didn't know, but when he straightened, snatching up his hat as he stalked to the door, Kayla flew to him, blocking his path.

"Talk to me, Ben."

He didn't, his expression blank, a muscle working in his jaw. He wouldn't even look at her.

"This is why you were so adamant about the children's book learning. Wasn't it?"

No answer.

"Wasn't it?"

His gaze collided with hers. "Yes, damn it! Yes!" A pause and then very softly, dejectedly, "God, how did you know?"

"David's paper, you were reading it upside down."

He flushed deeper, crushing his hat in his fists, his gaze clinging to the floor, and she stepped closer, ducking to look beneath his bowed head. He wouldn't meet her gaze and she tipped his head back, staring into blue eyes filled with shame.

"I'll teach you."

"No."

Four

"Why not?"

"I'm too old, Kayla."

"That's a crutch, one you've been leaning on for years, apparently."

His gaze snapped to hers, a dark brow arching menacingly, though lingering guilt tainted the black look.

"You can't read," she said without mercy. "But you *can* learn."

"Mind your own business, damn it."

He brushed past her, storming toward the door.

"You are my business, Benjamin Tate, and if you walk out on me now, you'll prove nothing except that *you* let the opportunity pass . . . again."

He kept going.

"Jeez Louise! You've already wasted years! And the only thing stopping you now is your own fool stubbornness!"

He stalled, hesitant. "Kayla." Tortured, shamed, and she softened.

"I adore the man you are, Ben."

Silence, unyielding.

"The fact that you can't read never stopped me from wanting you near, wanting to kiss you. And it won't change. But think of all the wonderful adventures you can have in books and articles and—how the heck did you run a business without reading?" she redirected suddenly.

He glanced at her, working his hat into a crimped disaster. "I use symbols." His broad shoulders moved restlessly. "And numbers have never been a problem."

"Then you can teach me, 'cause I can't balance my checkbook."

He frowned, feeling as if she was mocking him. "Check what?"

"My accounts," she fudged, hating the half truth. Soon, she thought. And I'll tell him everything.

She moved slowly toward him and Ben watched her, his heart thundering in his throat and his hopes swelling. He'd always been too embarrassed to ask for help. He knew it was childish and uselessly prideful, but he just couldn't emasculate himself enough to say the words. His lack of knowledge always made him feel inferior, trapped, and yet here was his forest fairy, a slender speck of a woman possessing the consternation of an ox and the excitement of fireworks—ready to help, prepared to fight *him* for his chance to learn. And she didn't think any less of him.

God was smiling on him the day he pulled her from the well, he thought, staring into her determined green eyes.

"Do you want to learn?"

"Yes." Passionate, greedy for the knowledge.

"Well then, come on." She grabbed his hand, tugging him toward the table.

"Now?"

She looked back over her shoulder. "You have a shoeless horse that needs your attention, or perhaps a woman?"

He smiled crookedly, yanking her into his arms. "Hellion," he murmured huskily. "You're about all a man can take."

"Conjunction junction, what's your function?" Kayla sang, her arms rotating like a locomotive's wheels, and Ben roared with laughter. She was full of antics and a half-dozen silly songs to help him remember, and he admitted her methods made learning sentence structure easier. Watching her jean-covered bottom wiggle didn't hurt either.

"Enough, enough." Ben swiped at a happy tear, his shoulders shaking.

Kayla stilled, looking affronted. "Don't like my dance, Ben?"

His gaze glossed over her with undisguised interest. "I like it just fine, woman, now let's see if I can do it."

"Of course you can." Kayla beamed, dropping into the chair opposite him, and he smiled one of his shy heart-stopping smiles that left her breathless. She was proud of him. With his eagerness and intelligence, he grasped the fundamentals in less than a week and progressed rapidly to writing.

And he refused to be daunted.

He was like a sponge, absorbing, memorizing, repeating, writing. Even the town folk noticed the difference in him, commenting that the quiet blacksmith was never seen without a book tucked under his arm. He made conversation where before he'd refrained from socializing too closely, from joining his township and really living.

"Kayla?" She blinked, realizing he was waiting for her to continue with the lesson, his pencil poised over paper. She recited a sentence and he wrote it, the scent of roasting turkey making her mouth water.

"I'm hungry," Kayla said.

"Not yet." He held up a finger, his pencil moving swiftly across the paper. It was another moment before he was satisfied with his work and handed it over. Ben studied her expression, her eyes moving rapidly across the page, then his gaze dropped to the shirt opened at the collar, the curving swell of skin hinting at her breasts, bare beneath the worn fabric. He swallowed. For weeks he'd been the gentleman, concentrating on his work, but to sit near her every evening breathing in her perfume, her excitement, without touching her was driving him mad with want.

"Perfect!" She rose and came around the edge of the table, laying the paper in front of him. "You don't need so much space here," she said, pointing, hovering over his shoulder. "And now conjugate cannot and would not."

Ben stared at her profile, then twisted in the chair, pulling her onto his lap.

"This is not conjugating, Ben," she warned even as she ducked closer. It had been so long since he'd held her.

"I can't, she can't," his arms circled her, "he can't, we can't—"

"We shouldn't."

"But we will." He kissed her, warmly, slowly, enticing her to join him. And she leapt to the challenge, not stopping him as his hand rode her thigh to her hip, slipping beneath her shirt. He enfolded her breast and she moaned, curling her body around him and he deepened the kiss, a seduction of deliberate slowness, fanning the desire he'd kept harnessed for the past weeks.

Softly he thumbed her nipple and she clung tighter, wanting his mouth there, and when he flipped open the buttons of her shirt, anticipation swept her.

"Tell me to stop, Kayla," he breathed against the flesh of her throat.

"I can't." She shrugged the shirt off her shoulder, baring herself to him, and Ben ducked lower, his lips closing over her pebble-round nipple. Her body liquified against him, a tingling radiating outward, rushing through her body as he laved at her breast. She wanted more and her hands rubbed over his broad chest, sweeping down to the hardness bulging his trousers. She shaped him, fingertips gliding, and he groaned, his embrace tightening.

"Oh God, Kayla, quit."

"But I want you, Ben. It's been so long since we touched."

"I didn't come here to get you into bed."

"I know, but I feel like I'm going crazy."

"I won't compromise you."

"I don't care about—"

Her thoughts ended as his hand moved to the buttons of her jeans, flipping them easily. She lifted her gaze to his.

"Let me please you," he whispered as his hand slid smoothly beneath the baggy fabric to cup her softness. "Let me give you this, Kayla." It was a tender plea and before she could respond, he parted her, sinking a finger inside.

Her breath shuddered through her like warm rain.

"Oh, Ben," she moaned and he stoked her, watching her body undulate in glorious waves. She stretched on his lap, lithe and slim, her back arching as he took her nipple into his mouth, his rough tongue sanding erotically over her damp flesh. Kayla struggled for air. He introduced a second finger, his thumb circling the bead of her sex, and she palmed his arm from shoulder to wrist, urging him deeper, faster. Her hips rocked, her mouth searing over his.

"Ben." His name sounded desperate, a warning, and he felt her climax as if he wore her skin, the hot ragged shudder, the tight feminine muscles squeezing and clenching. A sweet eruption, and he held her snugly as she rode the currents of her passion. It was a tremendous thing to see, abandoned, lush, and he wanted desperately to be inside her, stroking her body with his. But he couldn't. He couldn't compromise her, couldn't risk destroying her reputation. Not when he was damned unworthy of this tiny woman. Not when she'd given him a new life.

After a moment she lifted her head, meeting his gaze. She smiled, shyly, for the first time since he'd known her, and he ached to see her passion ruffled and feline sexy in his bed.

"That was so incredible." Her fingertips whispered over his lips. "But what about you?"

"I have all I need, hellion."

Kayla stared into his soulful blue eyes and knew he wouldn't "compromise" her, no matter what it cost him.

"Besides," he said dropping a kiss to her forehead. "I think your turkey's burning."

Kayla scrambled off his lap and flew into the kitchen, hitching up her jeans as she opened the oven.

"Oh sugarfoot!"

Her hands shifted frantically between fastening her breeches and removing the turkey before it was ruined, and Ben came up behind her, grasping the seat of her jeans as she removed the nearly scorched turkey.

She dropped it on the stovetop, hissing another one of her colorful curses. "I'll never learn to cook in this thing!"

Ben jerked on the jeans, drawing her back against him and burying his face in the curve of her throat. "Never learn?" he murmured. "Anybody can, hellion, didn't you know that?"

Kayla tucked the bread and vegetables in her basket, then strode to the door of the mercantile. "Miss Fairchild," Mister

Finkle called, and she glanced over her shoulder, her hand holding open the door as he came around the counter. "Your change," he said, dropping it into her palm.

"Saw Ben yesterday, headin' out to the McFarrel place, after supper," a man commented from somewhere outside and she stilled.

"In the evening? Alone?" another asked.

"Yup, with a book tucked under his arm and a hell of a spring in his step."

"Hell, Clarence, you'd be happy too, ifin you was beddin' the prettiest girl in town."

The color drained from Kayla's face and she looked at Mister Finkle. He stared at the countertop, his polishing rag moving in slow circles. But she knew he heard. His flushing cheeks said more than she wanted to know. She glanced around the store; the other customers refused to meet her gaze, suddenly interested in examining merchandise.

Oh no.

They all thought she was sleeping with Ben. Which to them, explained his late unchaperoned visits to her home, or rather Kaitlin's, and his surprisingly good mood lately. It was small-minded and petty, she told herself, insisting she didn't care, and as she left the store, sweeping past the embarrassed group of men, Kayla wondered what this rumor would cost her.

Two days later she discovered the price.

"Mrs. Doherty, I can't believe a free-thinking woman like yourself would fall prey to gossip."

Jenna Doherty stared at Kayla, sympathy in her round, dark eyes. But before she could speak her piece, her strapping ox of a husband stepped in front of her.

"I knew your kind of teachin' would lead to somethin' like this."

"Like what, Mister Doherty? Like your son learning? Aaron is bright and intelligent. One of my hardest-working students."

"Not anymore," Doherty snarled, grabbing Aaron's arm and

leading him from the school. Kayla sent a pleading look to his
wife, but she simply offered an apologetic smile, trailing her
husband.

Kayla couldn't let it go and followed.

This was the fifth student pulled from her class on the basis
of a rumor, and she was without recourse. The children's upset
over not going to school should have told them she'd done her
job, no matter what they assumed.

And it *was* assuming.

For inasmuch as she wanted to lie naked in Ben's arms, in her
heart she knew now that it would mean more than making love—
it would be a commitment, leaving everything she knew behind
to stay in 1878.

And now she was no longer welcome.

The rumors and the repercussions reached Ben's livery, ironi-
cally delivered by an unsuspecting man passing through and
seeking to make conversation with the blacksmith while Ben
repaired his wagon's wheel. That man lay unconscious on the
hay-dusted livery floor while the blacksmith rode toward the
schoolhouse, furious and impatient to smash something else.
Sawing back on the reins, he slid from the horse's back in the
yard as Andrew's parents carted him away, three members of the
school board following the boy. Kayla stood on the front step,
her slim body stiff, her hands clenched at her sides, and the steam
went out of him at the sight of her.

She looked as if she'd been betrayed.

"Why didn't you just tell them why?"

It was a moment before she looked at him, her attention glued
to Andrew as the boy sulked away behind his parents.

"Do you really think they'd believe me—a woman with no
family, no past, a newcomer? These are more your people than
mine, Ben." Her voice lowered a fraction. "I couldn't embarrass
you like that."

"But it's *my* fault."

"No." She watched the dust cloud dissipate, marking Andrew's departure from her life. "I'm the one who wasn't thinking in 1878," she said more to herself as he mounted the steps, stopping in front of her.

"What do you mean by that?"

Kayla swallowed, gazing into his crystal blue eyes. *Tell him. Tell him,* a part of her shouted, but she felt cheated by the townspeople and couldn't handle his rejection, too.

"I hadn't considered how this would look to the town folk, Ben. And now I'll never get my job back."

"You've been fired?" he shouted, outraged.

She nodded, then moved around him and headed toward the cabin—Kaitlin's cabin.

Ben caught her elbow, and something inside him broke loose when she lifted desolate eyes to him. "I'll make it right, Kayla."

"How?" she cried, fighting tears. "I'm branded a whore! What mother would let me near their sons and daughters now?"

"A married woman."

She blinked, staring up at him as if he'd completely lost his mind.

Suddenly he pulled her into his arms. "Marry me, Kayla."

"Do you think that will fix everything?" she shot back, thumping his shoulders, trying to push free. He wouldn't let her, and she cursed his warm blue eyes and sheltering embrace.

"If it doesn't, we'll leave and start somewhere else."

"Oh Ben," she moaned, sagging against his strength. "This is your home. I can't let you do that."

"Do what? Be happy? Let me have the chance to love you like I've been dreaming?"

"It's just gratitude for teaching you to read," she mumbled and he stiffened.

"Damn it, Kayla!" he hissed. "You know that isn't true!" When she didn't respond, he tipped her head back and searched her features. Her tears cut him in half and he felt her slipping away from him. "Don't you?" Suddenly he kissed her, deeply, impatiently, and she responded with the same energetic excitement as before, clawing at his wide shoulders and sinking her fingers in his hair. His hat tumbled to the ground, and he deepened his assault on her senses.

"Stay with me, hellion." His breath fanned her lips.

"I don't know," she said between kisses.

"Tell me you don't care for me and I'll leave and you can go . . . wherever."

"I don't care for you."

He looked stunned.

"I love you," she added before he could remark, and Ben grinned, wide and bright, then crushed her mouth beneath his.

"You'll marry me, then?"

Her gaze faltered. "Let me think about it."

He started to protest, then thought better of it. There was a part of her that was unreachable and he was desperate to touch it, yet Ben feared if he pushed too hard, he'd lose her forever— like a bubble, once popped, never retrieved. And instead of insisting, he kissed her, his movements unhurried, his emotions uncapped and spilling over into the seduction of her mouth.

"Think all you want, hellion," he said against her lips. "I love you and there isn't a power strong enough that'll keep me from you."

Abruptly he released her, loving her dazed look as he turned away and mounted his horse.

"Where are you going?"

"To educate a few narrow minds," he said with a smile, and before she could stop him, his horse lurched into a gallop.

Kayla watched him leave, absorbing the gallant sight. Her knight errant off to champion her virtue. For what little good it would do. Sighing, she left her horse tied outside the school and walked toward the cabin, kicking dirt clods and pebbles and thinking.

Marry me.

If she married Ben it meant never looking for a way back home.

What would her parents do? God, the pain they'd feel. And what about her business, her house, her friends? And if Kaitlin came back, what then? What would happen to her in the future, if she met her great-great grandmother now? And Ben, was it fair to marry him when he truly knew nothing about her, simply to save a reputation she cared nothing about, except what it would cost him? She loved him, God knew she did, but it was all happening too fast. The decision would change her life forever, in her time and his.

She walked aimlessly, her limbs growing heavier with every step. Her head pounded furiously and Kayla knew she needed to get out of the heat. Should have taken the bonnet, she thought, tossing a few yards of skirt over her arm for easier walking.

She licked her lips, nausea churning up to her throat, and she glanced around to get her bearings, recognizing the cabin in the distance and gravitating toward the relief from the heat. She misstepped, the unexpected stumble sending her lurching forward, her hands flying out in front to catch herself. But they met air and she flailed for purchase as the opening of the dry well came rushing toward her face. Kayla dropped into nothing, screaming Ben's name.

Ben paused in his tirade at several parents gathered outside the mercantile, a chill running up his body from his toes. It was as if his heart missed an entire heart beat—cruelly ripped from his chest.

He stared off toward the hills.

Kayla.

Kayla landed with a thump on the bottom, her shoulder smacking the ground like the first time. Time. *Oh, no! NO!*

Catching her breath and scrambling to her knees, she searched the ground for the pick axe, for the differences, yet even as she felt the barren ground, she looked up, inhaling sharply. She was over twenty feet down. Her towel hung from the broken wood. She was back. And she was naked.

"Ben!" she wailed, a tortured howl of loss and devastation. "No! I didn't want to come back!"

"Kayla?"

She choked on a sob. "Uncle Seth?"

A figure crossed the blade of light.

"Jesus Christ, Kayla, you okay?"

"I'm fine," she sniffled. "Get me out, please."

"Sure, darlin'." He moved away and Kayla sank to the ground in a defeated heap, sobbing hopelessly. Ben. He was gone. Dead. She knew it even as she prayed for it not to be true. Why, Lord? Why did you give him to me, only to take him away?

A rope dropped before her line of vision and she lifted her gaze to the light, hesitant to touch the rescue line, dispirited and wanting to stay in the dark hole forever.

Oh Ben, her heart cried. *I'm sorry.*

What would he think? Would he believe she abandoned him? Would he feel guilt over the cause?

"Kayla girl?"

"Drop down your shirt, Uncle Seth," she said in a dreary voice and he did without question. Covering herself, Kayla swiped at her eyes with the sleeve cuff, then sighed. She fashioned a loop for her foot, allowing her uncle to pull her out of the well.

"I swear, Kayla, you do the derndest things," he commented after he assured himself she was fine. "Skinny dippin'. Yer maw'll have a fit."

Let it ride, she told herself, accepting her uncle's comforting arm across her shoulder. And when she entered the cabin, it hit again that she was back in her time. The cabin was just as she'd left it—modern, mechanized, untouched—her suitcases, CD player, even the food was still in the grocer's sacks. Uncle Seth said he'd forgotten to turn on the gas for the stove and returned, only hours after he'd left her there, to do it.

Hours. In 1994.

Weeks in 1878.

Oh, God.

She would never see him again. Never.

Fresh heart-stabbing pain lanced through her chest. She wanted to stay *there,* wanted to love him and have babies and teach in a one-room school! And the sudden loneliness tore through her chest, coupling with the agony that Ben thought she'd left him.

Five

One Year Later

"I'll be in early to finish those last Victorian pieces, all right?"

Kayla offered a smile to her assistant as she pulled the key from the shop lock. Her newest romantic designs were selling so well, customers were putting in orders for work not yet completed.

"We're on schedule, Zack. Take a breather." She gave him a push when he was about to argue. "Go home. See your girlfriend. Have a good night," she added, testing the door before she turned in the opposite direction, walking down the old town area of Promenade. Her steps took her before the blacksmith's shop, her heart clenching every time she saw the familiar framework and tack. It was a bookstore now, rustic and quaint, each old horse stall holding a different genre collection.

The store was brightly lit tonight, which was unusual, since all the shops along the strip shut down about six. She peered in the window, the sound of children laughing catching her in the chest with the force of a blow. Briefly she closed her eyes, trying to pull back the memories that seemed too much like a long forgotten time, like childhood. Watered, faint. So vague now, she'd reasoned that it must have been no more than an unconscious dream. *Some imagination, girl friend.*

Another burst of giggles drew her attention inside, beyond the glass, and her gaze searched for the source. Pushing open the door she followed the sound. A bizarre tingling ran through her blood stream as she saw the group of children clustered around a man bent over a stack of books. An author signing, she realized, the tingling scaring her as much as it kept her riveted to the floor. She strained to see his face. The children laughed at something he said and he finally straightened, handing over a copy of his book to a boy of about thirteen.

Kayla swallowed tightly, waiting, yet not knowing for what. He looked up sharply, his gaze frantically searching the area, sliding past her, then abruptly jerking back and colliding with hers. She couldn't breathe, her heart spinning in her chest. Feelings of warmth and tenderness, of being loved and denied the precious emotion swam through her, and she rode the wave of sensations, excited and scared and hopeless all at once.

And she could tell by the look on his face he felt it, too. Who was he? His gaze swept over her, pausing, before coming back to meet hers. Then he smiled, crooked, boyish, and she gripped the wood post of a stall, gazing into blue eyes that had looked at her a hundred times. Eyes that would take an eternity to forget.

The children drifted away and Kayla forced herself to move closer.

He's not Ben, she told herself. That was a dream and this man . . . he's slimmer and sandy-haired, but—

"I'm Thane Brooks," he said, his deep voice caressed her senses.

"Kayla Fairchild," she managed and his gaze intensified, scrutinizing her. Nervously, she turned her attention to his books, thumbing through an edition. "These are wonderful," she said without hesitation. They were children's stories, short, funny tales with a moral woven into the plot, and the publisher's note said they were a modern continuation on a series written over a hundred years prior—maintaining the same style and pace.

"Thanks. It's a new profession, actually."

She frowned, confused, and she looked at him. The moment stretched before he spoke again.

"I didn't know I could write until about a year ago." He shrugged, flushing at his own success. "Sort of just came on me, like an obsession. Turned thirty and boo, I *had* to write."

Hell, Thane thought as she turned her attention to the book. He'd had trouble for the past year explaining to his friends and family why he'd quit training horses to write kids' books. But the dreams, the sense of seeing someone else's life through his own eyes drove him. And he never had an inkling as to why—until this moment. It was her. He'd seen this slim woman before, naked but for a man's shirt; standing on a porch in front of a one-room schoolhouse wearing a long skirt and white blouse; defiant in the middle of a dusty street—and looking up at him! Couldn't be, he thought, blinking and shaking his head, yet without thought or reason, he reached behind himself and grasped a frail copy of an old book.

"This is a first edition," he spoke softly as if gentling a frightened colt, and Kayla's eyes flashed, locking with his as he slid the book across the table.

Without breaking eye contact, he opened it to the first page.

"And it . . ." He swallowed tightly, disjointed memories flooding his mind, "belongs to you," he finished, not knowing where the knowledge had come from, yet deadly certain of its authenticity.

Kayla dragged her gaze from his and read the opening dedication.

To Kayla,
The forest fairy
My heart will never forget

Ohh Ben, she thought, covering her mouth with trembling fingers. He'd become a writer! She could hardly believe it was real, yet her own sketch of Ben graced the facing page!

But how did Thane know? Cautiously she met his gaze and they stared.

People milled around them.

Somewhere a book fell to the floor.

The bell over the shop door chimed.

And a current, intimate and aware, channeled between them, blooming vibrant with recognition.

"Hey, hellion," he whispered and Kayla gasped, her knees folding.

Thane caught her, pulling her close, and he knew beyond doubt that he'd loved this woman, in another time, another life. And she'd—

"You left me," he accused in a tortured voice.

"Then I *was* there!" she choked on a sob, her trembling fingers running over his features, circling his eyes. "It wasn't a dream!"

"No, hellion, because I lived it, too."

"Oh, this is crazy!"

"Is it?" he said, arching a tawny brow, his hand riding familiarly over her tattooed hip.

"You know!" she gasped, experiencing the rushing heat of his touch.

"What is it, anyway?" he said with bashful curiosity. "A bird or a butterfly?"

"As a matter of fact—" Kayla blushed, realizing how intimately she was speaking to a man she literally just met. "It's a fairy."

"Now, why doesn't that surprise me," he drawled with a crooked grin.

"I don't know, hero," she whispered, breathless with wonder. "But after today, nothing should."

Epilogue

"Somebody wants to say good night."

Thane looked up from his computer screen at the sound of her voice, a smile wreathing his face as he relaxed back into his chair. Kayla stood in the doorway, their son cuddled in her arms.

"Da. Da," the baby crooned sleepily, his chubby arms reaching, and Kayla crossed the room, letting Ryan fall into his father's protective embrace. The child immediately wiggled into a comfortable position, jammed his thumb in his mouth, and stared mesmerized at the screen.

"How's it going?" Kayla asked, nodding to the computer.

"This isn't as easy as I first imagined," he replied, kissing the top of his son's head and meeting her gaze. "How about you? You didn't even go into the store today, did you?"

"Rats. And here I thought you'd notice all that peace and quiet."

"Him?" He nodded to Ryan, his expression surprised. "In the store? Oh, you really got a lot of work done, right?"

"No." In fact she had done nothing but chase Ryan, snatching jewelry and dangerous equipment from his lightning fast little hands. "Now ask me if I care." She stroked his baby-soft curls, then looked at Thane. "Sometimes I wonder why we hired a nanny, since I can't bear to be apart from either of you," she confessed, almost guiltily.

Thane smiled tenderly, urging her to the arm of the chair. They hadn't been apart for more than a day since that evening in the bookstore. And he couldn't get enough of loving Kayla. He held her, his arm wrapped around her slim waist, their son warm and innocent between them.

"I still can't get over how real it all was," she said after a quiet moment, and Thane knew without asking what she meant.

"Does it matter?" They hadn't spoken much about the memories they shared for some time, both agreeing to build a life in the present and not on the past. "Reality doesn't always have to be something tangible, Kayla. . . . Then again?" His hand worked up her back, cupping her nape and drawing her closer. "God, I love you, hellion," he moaned deeply, his emotions suddenly on the surface.

"Oh, Thane, I love you," she nearly sobbed, sinking into his kiss. Promenade and Benjamin Tate would always be a part of their lives, Kayla knew, for those moments in time brought them together. So they could begin again.

But Kayla didn't want to think of that just now, her body screaming for the release his hungry kiss promised. She plowed her fingers into his tawny hair, loving the softness sifting against her skin. She adored him. Needed him. He was kind and patient and generous with his love and she wanted to be naked and wild with him in their bed. His kiss deepened, their bodies yearning for more, and just as his hand shifted to cup her breast, Ryan squirmed, his head bumping their chins. Kayla and Thane broke apart and looked down.

"Story, Da? Story?" the eighteen-month-old peeped, then popped his thumb in his mouth, looking from one parent to the other.

"Sure, pal," Thane said softly, storing his work and flipping off the computer. He kissed his wife, whispering his love and how much he would show her, later. Kayla watched her husband leave the room, their child smiling and waving to her over his daddy's shoulder. She waved back, blowing him a kiss.

A half-hour later she found them snuggled in her great-great grandmother's rocker, asleep. The book, *Summertime Blues,* Ben's first story about a child's mischievous antics while attending summer school, lay discarded on the floor. Kayla leaned against the door frame, watching them sleep, her heart singing with almost excruciating joy. Thank you, she mouthed to the heavens, just in case she forgot, then looked back to her family. She found Thane smiling at her, his amusement and love for her shimmering in the tiny nursery.

It left her breathless, shaken. Always had.

And Kayla knew a love that was boundless, far stronger than the barriers of time.

About the Author

Amy J. Fetzer lives in San Clemente, California with her husband Robert and their two sons, Nickolas and Zackary. The author of three novels and two novellas published by Zebra Books, Amy's next novel scheduled for publication in 1996 is the long-awaited time travel sequel to her first book, *My Timeswept Heart,* featuring the adventurous and charming Continental Marine, Ramsey O'Keefe. You can write to Amy at: P.O. Box 274, San Clemente, CA 92674.

Leap of Faith

Katharine Kincaid

"Next on the course at the Rolex competition being held this beautiful afternoon at the Kentucky Horse Park is Lexington's own Casey O'Donovan, riding her seventeen-hand thorough-bred, Flight-time . . ."

As Casey heard her name crackle over the loudspeaker, she couldn't stop her hands from tightening nervously on the reins, causing Flight-time to toss his head in protest and prance beneath her. *Breathe,* she ordered herself. *Relax. Everything's going to be all right.*

She concentrated on taking deep, slow breaths, a technique she had learned to help overcome the paralyzing nervousness that usually swept her before a major competition. She refused to think about the fact that today was the biggest competition of all, a contest whose outcome would decide whether or not she'd be able to compete in the next Olympics.

Winning the three-day Rolex would guarantee her a place on the United States Equestrian Team, but at this point, she would happily settle for a clean, safe round in the upcoming cross-country phase and a placing in the top ten riders overall. She stood fifth in dressage and knew she would be hard to beat in the stadium jumping; the cross-country was her weakest event—the one she feared the most. In it, she must guide her horse over a series of widely spaced, impossible-looking jumps, each with its own special challenge, within a prescribed period of time.

Flight-time was a talented jumper, but still a bit young and green, and the tricky turns and twists of the course required him to have total trust in his rider. If Casey had doubts or was hesitant in any way, Flight-time would pick up on it and refuse a jump or jump badly.

Don't think about the Shutterbug, Casey counseled herself as she waited for the starting signal. The Shutterbug was the jump that terrified her the most. At the top of a short, steep hill, it was a round, brush-covered hoop resembling the shutter of a camera—hence, its name. The Shutterbug gave the illusion of jumping into space, for horse and rider must jump through the hoop without being able to see where they were landing and then race down the other side of the steep hill.

Earlier, Casey had walked the course and studied the jump from all angles. It was less technically difficult than many of the others, but for some mysterious reason, the Shutterbug made her break into a sweat just thinking about it.

Fighting back a new surge of dread, Casey straightened in the saddle and listened to the announcer giving some of her history and family background.

"Casey comes from a long line of renowned equestrians, beginning with her great-great grandmother, the first Casey O'Donovan, a stunt rider who performed death-defying feats in turn-of-the-century Wild West shows . . ."

Lily. Lily must have told them all that. Lily was Casey's indispensable groom who accompanied her to all the shows and also handled the paperwork and publicity. Without Lily, Casey didn't know how she would manage. Unfortunately, her friend had an annoying fascination for Casey's family history and never bypassed an opportunity to tell the world about it. She was also responsible for Casey's less-than-flattering nickname: The Iron Maiden.

Casey didn't think she was as cold and unfeeling as the name implied; she simply refused to be sidetracked from her ambitions by intimate relationships with the opposite sex. As a head-in-the-clouds romantic, Lily blamed Casey's singleminded dedication to her sport on her genes. The first Casey O'Donovan had thrilled audiences by jumping a blindfolded horse through a ring of fire—and then shocked her adoring public by bearing an illegitimate child, Casey's great grandfather. As the first girl in several generations of male descendants, and also because she had red hair, Casey had been named for her. But she had *not,* apparently, inherited her predecessor's courage and wild, brave spirit.

If the signal didn't come soon, Casey feared she might be sick to her stomach right in front of the television cameras. Suddenly, the crack of the pistol sounded, and Flight-time was off and running—tearing down the beaten track toward the first jump.

Mustering her frayed concentration, Casey settled down to ride. As Flight-time gathered himself beneath her, she took her forward position and squeezed with both legs. They cleared the jump easily and pounded toward the next one. The jumps had colorful names: the Bourbon Barrels, the Kentucky Ramp, the Jenney Lane Crossing. Flight-time was having no problems, and Casey began to relax. As they flew over the Log Cabins, she experienced that heady burst of exhilaration that made all the long days of training, aching muscles, dog-tiredness—and yes, loneliness and celibacy—worthwhile. She was one with her horse, flying over each obstacle, galloping the long path to the next one, and using the time between jumps to focus her energy.

At the Lexington Bank, a series of tight turns made the triple jump a real challenge. Then came the Water Ford, where splashing water temporarily blinded Casey, and she lost a few precious moments by not turning fast enough to seek the next obstacle.

The Shutterbug was coming up soon—Fence Number Nineteen. Casey's nervousness caused Flight-time to stumble coming out of Fence Number Eighteen, but he gamely raced up the steep incline toward the jump that so terrified his rider.

Casey's concern for the horse gave her the determination to urge him onward as Flight-time hurtled up the hill. When he reached the top, she could feel him push off the ground, then leap through the small opening of the brush-covered hoop. She stayed with him through the moment of lift-off and felt the weightlessness of flying through the air. On the downward arc, sudden panic swamped her, and she inadvertently closed her eyes and squeezed the reins in a near death-grip.

She knew it was a mistake the moment she did it. Flight-time abruptly lost momentum. Casey had the sensation of pitching forward and plunging head first into a wall of blackness. A roaring sound filled her head. Then there was . . . nothing. Nothing at all.

When Casey awoke, she was lying flat on her back, and the world was still spinning crazily. She didn't know where she was or what she had been doing only moments before. Turning her head slightly, she saw a man running toward her. He was dressed like . . . like a cowboy, which struck her as ridiculously incongruous in view of . . . of what, exactly?

Upon reaching her, he dropped to his knees and leaned over her—affording a close-up, almost nose-to-nose view of very blue eyes and a tanned face handsome enough to merit a double take. Only Casey felt too weak, dizzy, and confused to make the effort. She could only stare up into that incredibly handsome face with its blue, blue eyes, straight nose, slash of a mouth, and deeply indented chin.

The man had coal-black hair beneath a white cowboy hat, and curly black hair on his chest. A tuft of it was poking through the front of his red shirt, which was unfastened halfway down to his navel. His shoulders were so wide that he all but blocked out the sun shining brightly overhead. Casey had never seen him before in her life, and thus could not understand the scowl on his face. Surely, it had nothing to do with her! But when he spoke, he seemed angry, his ire centered on her.

"What in hell happened? Are you all right? Damn it all, if you break your neck now, I'll never forgive you. Casey, say something. . . . Speak to me."

Casey. The name sounded familiar. What on earth was her last name? Casey wondered.

"Who . . . who am I?" she managed to get out. "Wh . . . where am I?"

"Come on, honey. Concentrate. You're Casey O'Donovan, and this is . . . this is . . . hell, I don't know. It's some little godforsaken burg between Philadelphia and Boston."

Casey O'Donovan. Philadelphia and Boston. The first sounded right, but the second alarmed her. What was she doing in some little town between Philadelphia and Boston?

"Can you sit up?" the man demanded. "Here, take my hand."

Casey moved tentatively. Nothing seemed to be broken. She

had probably just had the wind knocked out of her. She finally grabbed his hand and discovered that it was warm, strong, and firm—and his touch made her nerve endings tingle. As he attempted to pull her upright, an explosion went off in her brain. She bit her lip, but a groan still escaped her.

Immediately, he drew back, his black brows knitting together in a frown. "Maybe you shouldn't get up yet, after all. Where does it hurt? Can you tell me?"

Closing her eyes, Casey lay still a moment. "I think I'm all right. I'm just dizzy, and my head aches. Just how did I wind up on the ground?"

She opened her eyes to see that his frown had grown more pronounced. The scorching blue gaze relentlessly searched her face. "You mean you honestly can't remember? You were jumping the hoop. Pegasus cleared it all right, but when he landed, you went flying. I didn't see the whole thing. The crowd got in the way."

Nothing he said made a lick of sense. "What hoop?"

"That one." He jerked his head to the right, and moving slightly, she saw it—a huge flaming hoop. A circle of fire. No one in her right mind would get within ten feet of it.

"I . . . I jumped through that?"

"You and Pegasus." He grinned, and the effect was dazzling, causing a queer little leap in the pit of her stomach. "Pegasus does all the work. You just hang on . . . except this time you didn't."

It was on the tip of her tongue to point out that no one just "hangs on" going over a jump. There was a great deal more to it, but she was still too confused to argue. She sighed. If only she could roll over and sleep, then wake up to discover that this was all a dream.

"Come on," he said. "I'd better get you to the wagon and send someone for a sawbones. You don't look well."

She didn't feel well, so she allowed him to scoop her into his arms and cradle her as if she were an infant. From this new vantage point, she had a much better view of her surroundings—and what she saw shocked her. Spectators lined a large grassy field hemmed in by heavy ropes. The onlookers were all dressed in period costumes from some bygone era—the women in long skirts, high-necked, frilly blouses, and ribbon-bedecked hats, the men in dapper suits, vests, and bowler hats.

Leading a beautiful white horse, a man was coming toward them. Saddled and bridled, the horse nickered when he saw her and started to prance. "Whoa, Pegasus! Easy boy. Easy now," the man pleaded, trying to calm the restive animal.

"Pegasus, behave!" Casey automatically snapped, and the big horse quieted, as if accustomed to obeying her voice. Casey pondered that mystery as she was borne out of the arena to the cheers of the crowd gathered around it.

"Wave. Smile at them," her blue-eyed rescuer urged. "Let them know you're all right."

But I'm not all right, Casey wanted to argue. Instead, she merely did as he said. It seemed easier that way. She waved and smiled, then closed her eyes and laid her aching head against his shoulder as he threaded his way through the throng of noisy people.

"Here we are," the man said, and Casey raised her head to see where he had taken her.

They had arrived at a large wooden wagon, painted bright yellow, with a picture emblazoned on its side. The picture depicted a red-headed young woman jumping a blindfolded white horse through a ring of fire. Beneath the picture, it said: *CASEY O'DONOVAN, HORSEWOMAN EXTRAORDINAIRE.*

Casey knew she didn't have long hair like the young woman in the picture, even if the name *was* the same. She reached up to check on her short pixie-cut and could hardly believe it when she encountered two long braids neatly coiled and pinned in place at the back of her neck. She hadn't had braids since . . . since . . . she couldn't remember exactly when. Indeed, she couldn't remember much at all. Her entire past seemed to have been wiped out, leaving a big throbbing hole in her befuddled brain.

As the blue-eyed man went around the back of the wagon and kicked open the door, Casey anxiously examined her clothing. She was dressed like the girl painted on the wagon, too—in a long split skirt of soft, supple white leather, matching fringed leather vest over a blue blouse, and . . . and cowgirl boots! Yet she had never dressed like this in her entire life. She *knew* in her heart it wasn't her style.

"In we go," the man said, mounting a small step placed at the back of the wagon.

The inside was dark and shadowy, especially when the door swung shut behind them. The man carefully deposited Casey on a narrow bunk, then sat down beside her so that she had to scoot over or her hip would be pressed into his. "Now, I want you to lie here and rest a few minutes while I go see if this town has a doctor."

Suddenly terrified of being left alone, Casey clutched at his arm. "Don't go, please! I . . . I don't want to be . . . to be abandoned in this strange place!"

"Casey, be reasonable. I'm not exactly abandoning you, and this is hardly a strange place. You've been living in this wagon for over five years."

"I . . . I have?" Casey squinted at her surroundings. She wasn't a very good housekeeper, it appeared, for clothing, boots, cowgirl hats, and other personal items lay scattered throughout the wagon, covering the narrow bunk, the table, and two wooden chairs.

More items were spilling out of half-open cupboards and drawers. Despite the general messiness, the interior of the wagon appeared quite adequate to take care of all of a person's most basic needs—with the exception of certain embarrassing bodily functions suddenly uppermost in her mind.

"Where's the . . . uh . . . ladies' room?" she croaked.

"The what?"

"The . . . you know."

"I do?" The blue-eyed giant looked momentarily perplexed, then grinned in a slow, infuriating fashion. "If you're talking about the necessary, it's right behind that curtain there . . ." he jerked his head in the direction of a curtain. "Where it's always been."

"And just how do you know where it's always been?" Casey challenged, irritated by his knowing smirk.

The smirk broadened. "I've been here before, Casey. Don't

tell me you've forgotten all the delightful hours we've spent together inside this wagon?"

She couldn't tell if he was joking or not. She certainly had no memory of any delightful hours spent inside a wagon with this wickedly handsome man. Just what had they been doing for all those hours? As if he knew what she was thinking, he smugly nodded.

"Is it all coming back to you now, sweetheart? All those times you let me in during the dead of night after everyone else had gone to bed?"

"I never let you in during the dead of night!" Casey snapped upright in indignation, only to fall back on the pillows in real pain. Whenever she moved too fast, her head felt as if it might split open.

"Easy . . . easy, now, sweetheart." The teasing look in his eyes gave way to genuine concern. "Lie quietly now, and I'll be back shortly. Shall I send in Madeline and Jube?"

"I don't know any Madeline or Jube."

"Yes, you do, sweetheart. Damn, you really *don't* remember, do you?"

"Did you think I was fooling all this time?" Casey rubbed her aching forehead. "Please don't send in anybody. I don't think I can stand another encounter with strangers who claim they know me."

"All right," he said. "I'll tell everyone to stay out, but I'll be back as soon as I can with a doctor. Just promise me you won't move or go anywhere."

"I promise. All I want to do is close my eyes and rest a few moments." *After I use whatever's behind that curtain,* she added silently.

"Good idea." Before she could even register what he was about, he bent down and brushed a kiss across her forehead. "See you shortly," he whispered.

Then he was gone—leaving Casey alone to grapple helplessly with her confusion and rising panic. Why didn't she know the man? Why couldn't she remember anything? Fighting waves of dizziness and nausea, she got up and made her way to the curtain, pulled it back, and discovered a . . . a large pot with handles and a lid. No running water. No toilet paper. No scented soap to wash her hands. No sink, for that matter.

It was worse than the outdoor latrines she usually encountered at . . . at . . . *where, damn it?* She used the pot for its intended purpose, then staggered back to the bunk and collapsed upon it—holding her throbbing head in both hands. Never had she known such a terrible headache! If she had ever experienced one like this before, she would *not* have forgotten it. Closing her eyes, she tried to shut out the agony by imagining herself floating on an inner tube in a quiet green pond. The image helped somewhat, dulling the sharp edges of the intense throbbing in her head.

All too soon, the noise of people climbing into the wagon shattered her new-found serenity.

"Here she is, Doc, just like I said. No apparent injuries except a headache—and claiming she doesn't know who she is."

I don't know who I am, Casey thought angrily. *I only know what Mr. Blue Eyes told me.*

A tall, lean man with a bushy brown beard bent over her, and Casey caught a whiff of stale tobacco that made her wrinkle her nose in distaste.

"Miss O'Donovan?" Tobacco Breath said. "How many fingers do you see?" He held up three in front of her eyes.

"Eighty-nine," she snapped. "Give or take a few."

Tobacco Breath frowned, and Blue Eyes laughed. "She's still feisty as a bull terrier, Doc. That nasty spill didn't change her personality any."

"Is that true, Miss O'Donovan? Are you always this contrary?" Tobacco Breath gave her another blast of bad air.

"I don't know. Ask him. He seems to know everything." She pointed to Blue Eyes. "All I know is that a dozen war drums are beating all at once inside my head, and I can't even remember my own name."

Tobacco Breath peeled back her left eyelid and peered at her eyeball. "Perfectly understandable considering the fall you suffered. Let me examine you, Miss O'Donovan. Then I'll give you my best opinion as to what's wrong with you."

Casey lay still and allowed the man to do what he wanted. He tapped here and probed there, flexed her arms and legs, and searched her head. He removed several tools of his trade from a black leather satchel and earnestly listened to her heart and checked her respiration. No one said anything for several moments, until he had completed his examination.

"Well, Miss O'Donovan. It appears you have a mild concussion, easily cured by a few day's bed-rest. As for your headache, I can give you a powder to relieve it. I find no other injuries, but I do advise you to eat well over the next few days and get plenty of sleep. Sleep is a wonderful restorative after a severe trauma such as you have suffered."

"What about my memory? How soon can I expect its return?"

"Oh, I wouldn't worry about that if I were you. If you do as I just told you, it should return in no time."

"How soon can she go back to work?" Blue Eyes demanded.

"Oh, not for a while—five or six days, at least."

"Five or six days!" Blue Eyes exploded. "Will she be well enough to attend the wedding next Saturday after the afternoon performance?"

"Next Saturday? Well, let's see now . . ." Tobacco Breath stroked his bushy brown beard. "Today's Monday, so that's five days away. Why, yes, I think so. She should be fully recovered by then—assuming her memory returns, of course."

Casey was annoyed that they were discussing her as if she were absent—or a moron. "I haven't any intention of returning to work," she informed them both. "Not if work means jumping through a flaming hoop on horseback."

They both looked at her with surprise. "But that's what you do, Casey," Blue Eyes explained. "You're the main attraction of our show. In every little town we visit, people come from miles around just to see Casey O'Donovan perform her dare-devil tricks in person. Without *you,* the show would go broke in less than a month."

Casey lay still, digesting that for a moment. "What kind of show *is* this?" she asked in a small voice that betrayed her uncertainty.

"A Wild West Show. You know—as in Buffalo Bill's Wild West Show. Except we haven't got Buffalo Bill, Annie Oakley,

Sitting Bull, or any of the other big names in the business. All we've got is *you*, Casey O'Donovan, Equestrian Extraordinaire."

"Oh . . ." Casey felt an unwelcome weight settle on her shoulders. "I'm it, am I?"

"Well, the rest of us do our best to entertain the crowds, but you're the star attraction."

"And you'll be back to jumping through flaming hoops in no time," Tobacco Breath assured her. "I attended the show two days ago, Miss O'Donovan, and let me tell you, you were a sensation."

"Thank you," Casey said, wishing she could recall the performance as well as he could.

Tobacco Breath tipped his hat to her. "Good day, Miss O'Donovan." To Blue Eyes, he whispered: "If there should be any worsening of her condition, don't hesitate to summon me."

Casey wondered what worse there could be. The headache and loss of memory were bad enough.

Blue Eyes showed the doctor out of the wagon, but returned almost immediately. "Shall I fix you some tea to wash down that headache powder? Once your headache is gone, maybe you can get some rest like the doctor ordered."

"Wait a minute. What about this wedding you mentioned for next Saturday? Who's getting married? I take it I know—or *knew*—the bride and groom."

Blue Eyes folded his arms and sat down on the bunk beside her, stretching his long legs out in front of him in a thoroughly indolent fashion. "Yes, I suppose you could say that. The bride is a beautiful red-head named Casey O'Donovan, and the groom is . . . well, it's . . . me."

"You! But I don't even know your name! I only just met you this very afternoon. We can't *possibly* be getting married on Saturday!" Casey edged as far away from him on the bunk as she could get.

He leaned over her, seized her hands, and imprisoned them against his broad chest. Beneath the taut fabric of his shirt, she could feel his heart pumping strongly, echoing the sudden racing of her own heart. "Oh, come on, Casey. . . . You must be able to recall *some*thing. Can't you?" he wheedled.

She stared at him in horror. "No. Nothing. I haven't the slightest idea what your name is."

"You just want me to have to say it," he accused. "The whole damn thing, don't you? I know what you're up to."

"I'm not up to anything, least of all marrying a man I don't even know."

"All right, you win. It's Oliver Percival McClaren. There. Are you satisfied?"

"Oliver Percival McClaren? That's your name?"

It didn't fit. In fact, it was ludicrous.

His handsome face bore a pained expression. "My parents christened me with that impossible name, yes, but my friends, thank God, call me Mac," he said stiffly.

She couldn't help it. She burst out laughing. But her laughter ended in a hiccup as his expression darkened ominously. "I shouldn't have let you pry that secret out of me a second time. Mac is all anyone in the show knows me by, and if you tell them my real name, I'll turn you over my knee, Casey, concussion or no concussion."

"I'd never tell anyone your real name if you didn't want me to," she responded with a suppressed giggle. "I don't know why you're so ashamed of it. Really, it's not that bad."

"Then why did you laugh?" He was still holding her hands, and his thumbs were making tiny circles on the sensitive skin of her wrists.

"I . . . I don't know." She was suddenly flustered. Her wrists—indeed, her whole body—felt very hot. "I guess I shouldn't have."

"No, you shouldn't," he agreed. "After all, you're going to become *Mrs.* Oliver Percival McClaren next Saturday."

Her throat seemed to constrict. She could neither breathe nor swallow. "Oh, I really don't think . . . I mean, I can't possibly. . . . Well, how can I marry a man I can't remember?"

The pressure of his thumbs increased, burning the delicate skin of her wrists. "I'll make you remember me, Casey. I certainly won't allow you to use a mere bump on the head as an excuse for not marrying me—not after I've had to beg for two years to finally gain your consent."

"I've known you for two years?" she repeated, dumbfounded.

"Longer than that. You've known me for four years. It took me two years just to get your attention."

"I don't believe this."

"I don't believe you can't remember. It's got to come back to you, sweetheart. And I'm going to do everything in my power to make sure it does."

"What can you possibly do?" Casey immediately regretted the question, for he began to lean closer.

"This," he whispered just before his lips pressed down upon hers.

Casey wanted to resist. She thought it only proper that she refuse to allow him to kiss her, considering that their acquaintance was remarkably short—at least, for her. Yet somehow she couldn't muster the proper indignation. The kiss felt so right. So warm and comforting. He was careful to keep it from becoming demanding, but at the same time, knew exactly how to make her feel all warm and buttery inside.

Very gently, he took her in his arms which meant that he had to lie down beside her on the bunk. Narrow though it was, there was just enough room for him—provided they nestled close together. Then he proceeded to feather tender little kisses across her brow, along her cheekbones, and lastly down the length of her nose, ending at the very tip. And she let him do it because she couldn't find the strength to say no. He was a wonderful kisser. His kisses were very, very gentle with just the right amount of ardor.

"My goodness," she murmured on a sigh.

Touching his forehead to hers, he grinned. "Miss O'Donovan, you always have been unable to resist my kisses. Why, on any number of occasions, a mere kiss or two has caused you to come perilously close to losing your virginity. The fact that we cannot keep our hands off each other should be a good indication that we were *meant* to be husband and wife."

"We . . . we can't keep our hands off each other?" She was beginning to sound like a mindless parrot. She had a sudden mental image of him touching her intimately, and her whole body flushed. Their bodies were mere inches apart. An inch or two closer, and she would be able to feel him all down her entire length, breast to chest, belly to belly, and. . . . Lord, she mustn't dare think about it!

"No, sweetheart, we can't," he purred, stroking her back, then cupping her bottom in his two hands and drawing her closer.

With his hot hard arousal pressed against the juncture of her thighs, he resumed kissing her, and this time, the kiss was deep and searching, involving not just her lips but her tongue and her whole mouth. She drowned in the taste and feel of him. A strange lassitude came over her, and she felt herself sinking into a whirlpool of delicious sensation. It happened so quickly that she hardly knew what had hit her. The impact was as stunning as being thrown from a horse.

She could have gone on kissing Mac forever had he not pulled away with a long sigh of regret. "Damn, we shouldn't be doing this. You need rest and nourishment. I'm sorry, Casey. . . . But do you remember anything now? Did the kissing help?"

"Yes . . . no. I don't know. It did seem to stir something to life in me, but I'm not sure it was my memories."

She was sorry when he rolled off the bunk and stood up. At the exact same time, her own behavior shocked and mortified her. What sort of woman was she—to allow a perfect stranger to take such liberties? Try as she might, she could not recall kissing *anyone* like she had just kissed Mac.

"I guess it's too soon to expect miracles," he said with a disappointed shrug. "Well, now I'm going to feed you, and then you're going to get a good night's sleep. By tomorrow, you'll probably be good as new."

"Probably," she agreed, though privately, she doubted it.

"Rest," he ordered. "I'll wake you when supper's ready."

She nodded, her eyelids already feeling heavy. Her lassitude had turned into fatigue—or perhaps exhaustion was a better word for it. The strength seemed to have drained from her body, and she could no more have risen and helped him than she could have tap-danced her way to the moon.

She let herself drift off and was barely aware of Mac bustling in and out of the wagon, people knocking on the door, voices discussing her. Mac handled it all, keeping visitors from coming into the wagon and gawking at her, patiently answering questions, then sending the well-wishers away again.

Thank God for Mac. She couldn't deal with anything else today. It was a tremendous relief to allow him to take charge—and amazingly, no one seemed to question his right to do so, though a woman did loudly demand reassurance that she wasn't dying. She almost sat up and told her not to worry, but it would have taken too much effort. Besides, Mac didn't seem to need her help.

"You can see her tomorrow, Jube," she heard him say clearly, just before she drifted off again.

He woke her with a hand on her shoulder. "Come on, sleepyhead. Open your mouth, so I can spoon in some soup."

She noticed that it had grown quite dark. A single glowing lamp hung down from the ceiling, casting weird shadows on her scattered belongings. Mac plumped a couple of pillows behind her and made her sit up, then began feeding her a hot savory liquid that tasted of chicken. She didn't mind being waited upon, because she felt too weak even to lift a spoon.

"Thank you," she murmured between unladylike slurps. "This is delicious."

"Chicken soup will cure whatever ails a body. A couple bowls of this, and you'll be doing handsprings."

She'd be happy if she could just get out of bed. Even the wonderful soup couldn't keep her awake.

"I don't know why I'm so tired," she apologized, shaking her head when he offered her some bread.

"Delayed reaction. Your body's protesting its ill treatment. . . . Well, that should be enough soup." He took away the bowl and spoon, and returned with a heavy quilt. "Time to get tucked in for the night."

Spreading the quilt over her, he made a great fuss over making certain she was comfortable, and she was grateful. Tonight, she needed coddling. "You certainly are nice to me, Mac. I'm not sure I deserve it."

"You don't," he agreed with a grin. "And as soon as you're better, I'll make you pay for it."

"How?" Despite her exhaustion, she was intrigued. Indeed, everything about Mac intrigued her.

He smiled smugly. "We'll see. If you need anything during the night, just call. I'm going to bed down right outside your door."

"Where—on the ground?"

"Not all of us are fortunate enough to have a comfortable wagon in which to sleep. Some of us bed down under the stars every night. Others have tents. I only put mine up if it looks like rain."

"What does everyone do in the winter?"

"Go where it's warm. Or if we can't get any bookings down South, we perform in the big cities where lodging is adequate, and there's enough space indoors to perform. January and February are slow months. Sometimes, we split up and live off our earnings until the weather allows us to start up again."

"I've been doing this for five years?"

"Five years as the star of the show. Before that, you were a rag-tag kid trying to learn the business, which took you quite a few years. That's all I'm going to tell you for now. If you still can't remember by tomorrow, you can ask me some more then. Goodnight, sweetheart."

He dropped a light kiss on her hair, then took down the lamp and departed the wagon, leaving Casey alone in the dark. She didn't mind—not as along as Mac stayed right outside the door as he promised. And somehow she knew he would. She lay still thinking about him for several moments, but the need for sleep soon overwhelmed her, and she succumbed to oblivion with a grateful sigh.

When next she awoke, she did so with a strange expectancy, certain that when she opened her eyes, she would be back in familiar surroundings, awakening to a morning like a hundred other mornings. The sun would be peaking through her Venetian blinds, illuminating a painting of galloping horses that hung on the wall opposite her bed. Her peach-colored bedspread would be sliding off the foot of the bed onto the lime-green carpet. Sheba, her tawny-orange cat would be curled up on one side, and George, her Scottish terrier, on the other.

She could stretch out her hand and find the phone on the bed-side table, plus a pile of showbills listing classes in shows she planned to attend. Her radio clock would be set to awaken her with music from her favorite station. Since it wasn't yet playing, she still had time for a luxurious stretch and maybe even another brief snooze before she had to get up. She loved waking up earlier than necessary; it made her feel as if she had a jump on the day.

Opening one eye, she searched for the painting. It wasn't there. Neither were her dog, cat, phone, or radio clock. Ditto the peach bedspread and lime-green carpet. Bitter disappointment flooded her. She was still lying on a narrow bunk in a cramped wooden wagon, surrounded by someone else's belongings. The only bright spot in this otherwise dismal scene was that she could now recall jumping through the Shutterbug, blacking out, and then awakening to this new reality.

A headache still hovered on the fringes of her consciousness, and when she tried to recall other details of her past life, the faint throbbing became more prominent, warning her not to try re-membering too much too soon. Sighing mournfully, Casey stud-ied the beamed ceiling of the wagon and thought about her present circumstances. She wasn't sure exactly what had hap-pened to her, but there was nothing to be gained by indulging in despair.

"I must take charge of this situation," she said aloud, and just hearing the words gave her a burst of confidence. Whoever she was—or had been in some other life—she wasn't the sort of person to lie in bed bemoaning her fate.

Gingerly, she sat up. When nothing untoward happened, she jumped off the bunk, used the necessary, slapped some water on her face and hands from a basin Mac had thoughtfully provided, then headed for the nearest overcrowded cupboard. There had to be some clues in this wagon about the woman known as Casey O'Donovan. At least, she could find out more about her without having to ask Mac.

The cupboard yielded little of interest, but an overstuffed drawer contained a bunch of clippings from newspapers around the country—each of them describing the Wild West Show in general and Casey O'Donovan's equestrian exploits in particular.

According to the newspapers, not only did she regularly jump Pegasus through flaming hoops, but she had also jumped him over a team of mules, a pyramid of live cowboys, a spring wagon, and an outhouse. . . . But Casey couldn't remember any of it. And the newspapers were dated long before she was born—or thought she was born.

Apparently, she had been traveling around the country performing in a Wild West Show exactly as Mac had said, for the last five years. The most recent clipping was dated July 6, 1898. It referred to her as "the toast of Pittsburg, Casey O'Donovan, the red-headed darling with the cast-iron nerves."

Was she really *this* Casey O'Donovan? Or could she possibly be another Casey altogether? . . . She seemed to remember something about an Iron Maiden. And then she remembered something else: Her great-great grandmother had been named Casey O'Donovan!

While Casey was puzzling over this amazing piece of information, the door to the wagon opened. Bearing a tray with a napkin-covered plate and a cup of something that smelled enticingly like coffee, Mac entered the wagon.

"Up early, are we? That's my girl. I knew you wouldn't let a little thing like a spill from your horse keep you down for long."

She started to rise. "Mac, I was looking through the wagon, and I found these clip—"

He never gave her a chance to finish. Swiftly setting down the tray on the tiny table, he crossed the wagon in two strides and pulled her into his arms. Her dazed senses barely had time to register the fact that he was even more handsome this morning than she remembered from last night. He was all gleaming black hair, dazzling blue eyes, and pearly-white teeth flashing in the wagon's gloom . . . and he smelled of soap and coffee.

Claiming her mouth in a sweet, sensuous kiss, he tasted of coffee, and his kiss was as heady as drinking some strong, hot brew liberally laced with rum and sugar.

Casey pushed him away in mingled wonder and panic. "Mac, stop that! I'll never get to the bottom of this mystery if you keep turning my brain to mush."

"Did you say mush? Why, that's what I brought you for breakfast. Scrambled eggs and mush. Sit down and eat before it gets cold."

Suddenly realizing that she was ravenously hungry, Casey decided she could eat first and argue later. She sat and ate, consuming every last bite with relish and savoring every sip of the coffee. When she had finished, she again tried to open a conversation on the subject that most interested her.

"Mac, about these clippings. The person they're describing is really my great-great . . ."

He didn't seem to be listening. Instead, he was gazing at her with a look of intensity that made her toes curl. "Do you know you look adorable with your hair all mussed and your clothes wrinkled? I swear. I don't know how you do it, Casey. Any other woman who had just rolled out of bed wearing yesterday's garments would look like a hag, but not you. You look like an angel."

He was straddling a chair turned around backward. With one elbow propped on the ladder back, he looked appealingly masculine and boyish. He was also squeaky clean.

"I could use a bath," she sniffed. "And I need to find a hair brush and some clean clothes."

"I'll bring you a bucket of hot water. Not enough for a bath, but you can make a good job of washing with it."

"I'd appreciate that."

"Well, I'd appreciate it if you stopped acting so formal, sweetheart. It's me—Mac. Remember? The man you love. The one you're going to marry on Saturday."

She wished he hadn't reminded her. "Yes, I *know* who you are, but I still don't remember you. And I . . . I do recall some of my past. I woke up this morning expecting to find myself in a different time and place altogether."

"I hope *I* was there." Cocking his head, he studied her with a slightly worried expression.

"You weren't," she said gently. "You couldn't have been, for my past is . . . is . . . sometime in the future."

He stared at her a full minute without speaking. "I don't understand. I don't follow you, Casey."

Casey glanced down at the dirty dishes to avoid the intensity of his blue-eyed gaze. "I . . . I don't understand exactly either.

But what I remembered this morning is that my great-great grandmother was named Casey O'Donovan."

"You never told me that. But I guess it's nice you finally remembered it."

"No, you still don't understand. The . . . the woman you think you love must . . . must be my great-great grandmother. I'm . . . I'm the *future* Casey O'Donovan."

Mac was out of his chair so fast that it tipped over. He pulled her roughly to her feet and clasped her so tightly to his broad chest that the breath was squeezed from her lungs. "Damn it, Casey! I was hoping you were better, but now I think you've gotten worse. I'll get that doctor back here fast. Don't you worry about anything, sweetheart. Ole Mac will move heaven and earth to make sure you recover."

"Mac! Mac, stop it!" Casey had to pound on his shoulder to get his attention. "I'm all right. I'm just fine. Really, I am."

"No, you're not," he disputed. He continued holding her in a bear hug, his breath hot on her ear. "Oh, God, Casey, if you don't get better, I don't know what I'll do!" he muttered fiercely.

Her heart somersaulted. He really seemed to care about her. She wondered if her great-great grandmother had known what a lucky woman she was—assuming, of course, that the first Casey O'Donovan and the woman Mac loved were one and the same. They must be. But how and why had she managed to wind up in her shoes? Her boots, rather.

"Mac, please listen to me," Casey pleaded, again pushing him away, though she would have preferred reveling in his exciting embrace. "I have to tell you something."

"What?" he growled.

"How I got here."

As he held her lightly, his arms loosely entwined about her waist, she told him the whole story—or as much of it as she knew. She couldn't go into details because the details still eluded her. All she really recalled was that she had been jumping a frightening obstacle called the Shutterbug when she somehow fell off her horse or blacked out. And she lived in a place where there were telephones, radio clocks, and lime-green carpeting. . . . Oh, yes, the room had also had a television and a VCR.

Mac had never heard of such wonders, and he found her story incredible. "Casey, honey, I think you dreamed all this. You cracked your head a good one, lost your memory, and are trying to come up with some way of explaining who you are. The plain truth is that you're the girl who's supposed to marry me next Saturday. I love you, and you love me, and if this is just another ploy to delay the wedding again, you can forget it. It won't work. This time, you promised to go through with it, and I'm holding you to that promise."

Casey was uncertain how to argue with him. Her tale did seem unbelievable. She thought of something else that greatly confused her. "If it's true that we love each other, why would I keep trying to put off this wedding?"

He heaved a sigh of exasperation. "That's what I want to know. What are you so afraid of? Marriage is what people do when they fall in love."

"I . . . I can't answer these questions. Until I can—and I regain my memory—I don't see how we can get married."

"Well, we *are* marrying, and that's final. I mean it, Casey. I've waited long enough. If you don't marry me come Saturday, I'm . . . I'm leaving the show. And leaving you."

He dropped his arms from around her waist and stepped back, the very image of wounded pride. She saw that she had bruised his male ego with her doubts and hesitations—or else her great-great grandmother had.

"Mac," she said placatingly, holding out a hand to him. "Give me a chance, will you? Help me regain my memory. Go out with me and show me around. Let me talk to people. Maybe it will all come back to me then."

He glowered at her another minute, then capitulated. "Oh, all right." He took her hand and pulled her into the circle of his arms again. "But I still think you'd remember everything much faster if you just let me make love to you the way I'm itching to do."

The reference to lovemaking made her insides quake. It also made her think of another thing she had wondered about. "Mac, am . . . am I really still a virgin? Be honest, now. We haven't actually gone to bed together yet, have we?"

"No," he informed her, his tone laden with disappointment.

"We haven't, more's the pity. If we had, I assure you that you wouldn't have forgotten it. And we sure as hell wouldn't be arguing about whether or not we should get married. You'd have no doubts."

What supreme arrogance! Casey thought. The trouble was: She doubted she could have forgotten it, too, or that they'd be arguing now. She was beginning to feel at home in Mac's arms. Since she regarded home as a place she never wanted to leave, the notion was downright scary—but also exhilarating. Had she ever felt such a sense of security and . . . and rightness with a man?

Reluctantly, he released her. "Go comb your hair while I get that wash water. If we're going visiting, we have to hurry. The show must go on whether or not you perform, Casey. That means that the rest of us have a lot to do before this afternoon. We're adding some new numbers to replace your act, and we have to practice. I've got to work with Pegasus."

"You're going to jump him through the burning hoop in my place?"

He shook his head. "No. He'd never do it for me. But I'm hoping he'll perform some of his other tricks—bowing, playing dead, and so on. If you feel up to it, you can give me some tips for working with him."

"But I don't remember working with him! Never mind," she sighed. "I . . . I'll do the best I can, Mac."

"That's good enough for me. See what you can find to wear, sweetheart, and I'll be back shortly with the water."

Casey was at first utterly baffled by the garments she found in the wagon. Other than her cowgirl costumes, they were all of the long-skirted, high-necked, ruffles and lace variety she had seen on the spectators the day before. Even the simplest blouses and skirts were made fussy with bits of ribbon or other decoration that appealed to Casey's feminine side but seemed impractical for everyday use. And the undergarments were even worse! Did women really wear such hot cumbersome things beneath their clothing? It was a wonder they could move and breathe.

She finally found a slightly plain green skirt and light jacket to wear for the outing, then had to choose from among odd-looking high-heeled footgear and long stockings. She had a hard time braiding her hair and pinning it up, but otherwise managed to look decent in a reasonable amount of time. Mac gave a low whistle of admiration when he saw her and proudly held her hand as he took her around the show grounds and introduced her to people she supposedly already knew.

All of them seemed happy to see her up and about, and a few embraced her and thumped her enthusiastically on the back. She surmised that Madeline and Jube were good friends. One was a tall brunette, the other a petite blonde. Both were cowgirls who did a singing duet on horseback, were captured and borne off by painted Indians, and then rescued by cowboys in white hats, one of whom was Mac, the main hero.

The girls knew how to ride, but seemed afraid of their own horses, and Casey found herself standing in the middle of a practice ring giving advice she did not know she knew. She watched all the rehearsals for the acts involving horses, and her suggestions demonstrated a thorough knowledge of horse-training and handling—but she could not recall ever having done this before, even though it was obvious she had been working with horses all her life.

Beaming each time she said something, Mac rarely left her side for a moment. Funny, charming, kind, and solicitous, he proved to be everything she could wish for in a companion. He was also far too handsome for her peace of mind. Whenever they had a moment alone together, he stole a kiss or a sly caress, exclaiming: "Damn! I just can't resist you in green, sweetheart. It matches your eyes. Maybe you should have worn some other color. You'd look good in pink, blue, red, or black, too—but you'd look best of all without *any* clothes."

Casey went weak in the knees more than once in response to his outrageous comments, and so the day passed, with only the horses themselves striking a chord of recognition in her. Besides Pegasus, there were three others she was training. Two were youngsters and not very far along. They all seemed to know her, however, and she felt as if she could slip so easily into the role of the Casey everyone claimed she was. . . . Could that *other* Casey be a figment of her imagination?

The show proceeded without a hitch, though there was loud hissing and booing when it was announced that Casey would not appear. Mac gave a wonderful performance as the heroic lawman who rescued Madeline and Jube from the Indians. When he rode into the arena at the show's end on Pegasus, the crowd cheered. Pegasus bowed on cue, but refused to kneel or lie down when asked, and Mac had to pretend that he hadn't wanted the horse to do those things in the first place.

Watching from the sidelines, Casey knew exactly what Mac had done wrong and then had to ask herself how that was possible if she wasn't *this* Casey O'Donovan, the one Mac wanted to marry.

Supper that evening was a family affair, with everyone gathered around a communal kettle for stew and cornbread. Casey sat quietly on the end of a big log, afraid to participate in the conversation because despite what everyone said, these people were still strangers to her, and she didn't know what to say to them.

Nor did they seem to know what to say to her in view of the fact that she couldn't remember their shared experiences. Madeline, Jube, and the show manager, Hank Wilson, did their best to draw her out, but when she responded inanely, they all exchanged glances and gazed at her pityingly.

Only Mac seemed undaunted by the challenge of her lost memory. "Jube, tell her about the time we had to perform in the mud after ten straight days of rain, and the horses kept slipping and sliding all over the place, and we all got so muddy we could hardly stay on them. Maybe it'll help her remember it."

Jube dutifully related the incident, and then everyone leaned forward and stared at Casey, until she shrugged her shoulders and sadly admitted, "No, I'm afraid I don't recall that."

Soon, they were off on some other story. It grew disheartening, and Casey's head began to ache again. Finally, everyone said goodnight and wandered off in the direction of tents, wagons, or bedrolls, leaving Casey and Mac alone together beside the embers of the dying fire.

"You're tired, aren't you?" Mac moved closer to Casey on the log and slid his arm around her waist.

"A little," she admitted. "But I still want to ask you a few things, Mac."

"What? Didn't we dredge up *any* old memories or remind you of things in your past?"

"No," she sighed. "But thanks for trying. You've talked about a lot of things tonight, but somehow managed to skip the most important ones. Tell me more about . . . about me, Mac. Or about the woman you *think* I am."

"The woman you *are*," he corrected. "All right. What do you want to know?"

"How I came to be working in a Wild West Show, for starters."

"All I can tell you is what you yourself told me."

"Then tell me."

"You were orphaned at the age of thirteen, at which time you ran away to join Major Cannaby's Wild West Show."

"He allowed me to join at the tender age of thirteen?"

"Well, you lied about your age, and since you showed no fear of trying anything on horseback, Major Cannaby let you stay. He wouldn't allow you to perform for the first year or two, but you helped take care of the horses and learned everything you could about them. He finally let you have a few bit parts, and as your horsemanship improved, you graduated to the level of a minor star. That's when you really became creative. By the time I came along, you were a big star, and you looked down your nose at me for not being able to ride as well as you."

"That wasn't very nice of me, especially since you ride extremely well."

"I do now, but I didn't then. I was an impulsive young hothead, a city boy looking for adventure, and the Wild West Show offered me a chance to travel and see the world. I thought it would be exciting—a way to put off becoming an adult and assuming responsibility. I could drive a horse and ride one, but I couldn't do anything fancy. You had to teach me, and at first, you resented it."

"What happened to the man who taught me—Major Cannaby?"

"He died a year and a half ago. That's when Hank Wilson took over. The Major's death was a terrible blow to you, Casey. Are you sure you can't remember that?"

Casey sadly shook her head. "No, I'm sorry. I can't remember him at all."

Mac was quiet for a long moment. "That's real strange, Casey," he said at last. "Because you were always fiercely loyal to the major and to the show itself. That's one of the reasons it took you so long to agree to marry me; you didn't want to divide your loyalties. There wasn't room in your life for anything or anyone but the show and the horses. They meant everything to you."

"Not, surely, more than you!" She elbowed him playfully in the side, but he surprised her by remaining sober as a fence post.

"This . . . the show and all . . . is all make-believe, Casey. It's fun, and it's challenging, but it's just playing. The real West isn't anything like we portray, and what we're doing can't go on forever. One day, we'll have to find *real* lives to live. Real problems and challenges, not just make-believe ones. I've been saving my money for that day, and when it comes, I'll be ready. You don't have to worry that I won't be able to take care of you, Casey."

He was so earnest that she didn't dare poke fun at him. If anything, she was deeply touched. She sensed that this was of vital importance to him, something they had perhaps disagreed about in the past.

"Did I—do I—share your opinions?" she ventured timidly.

He grinned. "You didn't at first, but when you agreed to the wedding on Saturday, I took it as a change of heart. I promised you we wouldn't leave the show until you're good and ready, and I mean to keep that promise. But sooner or later, we'll have to get on with our lives, Casey. We'll have to find a corner of the world to call our own."

"That doesn't sound so unreasonable." She wondered what had prompted her great-great grandmother's resistance to Mac's plans.

"I'm glad you think so." He pulled her closer and commenced nuzzling her ear. "Ah, Casey, it's going to be so good for us.

Even aside from our mutual passion, it's obvious we were made for each other. I'm not as good with horses as you are, but I feel the same affection for 'em. I also like little people; don't you like little people?"

She leaned back to look at him. "Little people? You mean children?"

"Of course, children. Did you think I meant midgets? We had a midget in the show once. Called him Shorty. He claimed that when he sat on a horse, he felt as big as the next man."

"What happened to him? Why isn't he with the show now? I didn't meet any midgets named Shorty today."

"He left to join a circus. They were going to let him ride elephants. From the back of an elephant, he found he could look down on everybody, even the tallest men around, even men on horseback."

Casey burst out laughing. She didn't know why. The story wasn't the funniest she had ever heard, but somehow it tickled her. Everything Mac said had a way of delighting her—touching her heart in new, surprising ways.

"Yes, I like little people," she assured him. "Children *and* midgets."

"That's good," Mac whispered, licking her ear. "Because I intend that we should have a few."

"Children or midgets?"

"Whatever the good Lord gives us. As long as you're their mother, I'll love each and every one."

He turned her toward him on the log and began kissing her in earnest. In no time at all, she was floating—weightless as a feather and free as the wind. She didn't care who she was as long as Mac was kissing her. The kissing led to heavy breathing and heart palpitations. Before it could lead to anything else, Mac gently set her away from him.

"Bedtime, sweetheart. You're supposed to be getting lots of rest, and instead, you've had a long, hard day. No wonder you still can't remember everything."

She came back to earth with a thump. "You're right. And tomorrow's Wednesday, and after that, there's only two more days until Saturday. I have to get my memory back before Saturday,

Mac, or there's just no possible way we can marry. You do realize that, don't you? I mean, I don't deny that we're attracted to each other, and we seem to share the same interests, but . . . but . . . I just *can't* marry you under these circumstances! It wouldn't be fair to either of us."

"You've got an odd sense of fairness, Casey. I don't happen to think it's fair to keep me dangling any longer. I want you so much I'm in agony. And you want me—don't you?"

Did she? Oh, yes, she wanted him all right! She wished he had never stopped kissing her. But *marriage.* . . . It was such a big step, especially when she had only known him for slightly over twenty-four hours.

"Please, Mac. Don't pressure me any more tonight. I'm trying to remember. Really, I am."

He squeezed her hand apologetically. "I know you are, honey. Forgive me. I'm sorry. Come on. To bed with you now."

She allowed him to escort her to the wagon. And she allowed him to kiss her again. He kept it brief and affectionate, but she still felt the flare of blazing need, a physical attraction so instantaneous and powerful that it rocked her to the core. And she knew he felt it, too. It was too dark to see his face, but desire emanated from him like the scent from a full-blooming rose. She could practically smell it vibrating in the air between them.

"Goodnight, Mac."

" 'Night," Casey. Let's do something special tomorrow. Go on a picnic or something."

"But what about the show?"

"No shows on Wednesdays. We take Wednesdays off."

"I'd like a picnic."

"Then that's what we'll do. It'll be restful for you."

Casey doubted that anything involving Mac would be restful, but already she was looking forward to it. "Tomorrow then."

His hand came up to caress her cheek. "Tomorrow," he murmured longingly. Then he turned and strolled away whistling, filling the air with the sweet, plaintive sound.

As Casey entered the wagon, she couldn't wait for tomorrow to come. She didn't even bother lighting the lamp, but made her way to the bunk and collapsed upon it still fully clothed. What did a girl wear on a picnic, she wondered. Something green, because Mac liked her in green. She would have to wake up early in order to search the wagon for an appropriate outfit, something to knock him over.

She fell asleep smiling, brimming with anticipation . . . and suddenly, she was back in the world of phones and radio clocks, televisions and VCRs. She remembered how hard she had been working to become a member of the United States Equestrian Team representing her country at the Olympics. She relived the many hours spent on horseback, mastering the fine points of dressage, the intricacies of cross-country, and the challenges of stadium jumping.

Never before had she had time for men and picnics. She didn't have time for them now. She had to get back to her own world—that distant world of jet planes, microwave ovens, and computers. She didn't belong in a bygone era where women wore petticoats and long skirts, and horses were still the only means of trans-portation. . . . What was she doing in the past, living her great-great grandmother's life? And how on earth was she going to get back to her own life?

"Mac?"

"What, sweetheart?"

Casey was sitting on a quilt spread beside a stream in the shade of a beautiful old oak tree. She still didn't know the name of the nearest town—or even what state they were in. Nor did she care. The site of their picnic was a bucolic setting, pretty as a picture, and she was enjoying every minute of their time together.

They had eaten fried chicken and fresh peach pie. Mac was lying down dozing with his head in her lap, and she was leaning against the oak tree watching the bees buzzing in the clover and listening to the stream gurgle over the rocks.

"This has been one of the most beautiful days of my entire life," she told him.

Without opening his eyes, he smiled at her up-side-down.

"That's not saying much since you can't remember very many days of your life."

"Oh, but I can," she disputed.

"Casey! You mean it?" He rolled over, opened one bright blue eye, and gave her a right-side-up grin. "You've regained your memory?"

She nodded. "Yes, and exactly as I've told you before, my name *is* Casey O'Donovan, but I'm *not* the Casey you know." She proceeded to tell him more of the details of her past life, all that had come back to her the night before in her dreams.

"I still don't believe it," he said flatly, when she had finished. "You couldn't possibly have jumped through a brush-covered hoop and landed in the past, somehow taking the place of your great-great grandmother."

"I know it sounds incredible, but it's the only possible explanation for how I got here. Somehow, I went through a . . . a time warp, or something. And maybe my great-great grandmother took *my* place."

"That's absurd." He sat up. "You're making up this whole thing just so you don't have to marry me on Saturday."

"I'm not, Mac. Honest, I'm not. The world I came from is far, far different from this one. Why, we can fly now. We can get in big machines called airplanes, and go from one end of the country to the other in a matter of hours."

"So can pigs fly," he scoffed. "Do you take me for a fool, Casey?"

Sadly, she realized she could never explain her world to him. The things she took for granted he would consider too farfetched. Tears gathered in her eyes, and she swallowed against the sudden lump in her throat. She didn't want to hurt Mac; she wanted him to *understand,* but he couldn't. She didn't understand it herself.

"Hey," he said. "Don't cry."

He gathered her into his arms. "We've got a problem, Casey. That's all it is. But we can work it out. You're all mixed up in your head, and somehow we have to *un*mix you. What do you say we get married anyway and work it out together?"

"Oh, Mac!" she sniffled, glad he wasn't angry anymore. "You're the most wonderful man in the world! I don't deserve you. Really, I don't. I mean, my great-great grandmother doesn't deserve you—wherever she is. Probably jumping the Bandbox on the Rolex course in Kentucky right about now."

"You don't make a bit of sense; you know that?" He toppled her backward on the quilt. "Just say you'll marry me, Casey, and I don't care if you're as dumb as a mushroom. I'll love you 'til the day I die."

"A mushroom!" she squeaked indignantly.

"Our children can all be little mushroom-heads. Just say you love me, and you'll marry me on Saturday. That's all I care about."

"Mac, I . . . I have to think about this some more. My great-great grandmother never did marry—though she did have a child out of wedlock who turned out to be my great grandfather."

Dear God! Could this be why I was sent back to the past—in order to right this wrong and marry the father of my great grandfather, who surely had to be Mac?

The thought struck with blinding clarity, and she wanted desperately to discuss it with Mac—except that he thought her outlandish claims were all a result of falling off a horse on her head.

"You don't have any illegitimate children that I know of, Casey. But you damn well might if you don't marry me this Saturday," he threatened. "Do you even have a wedding gown for the event?"

The question caught Casey off-guard. "A wedding gown? I . . . I have no idea. There might be one somewhere in the wagon. I'll have to look for it."

"Don't bother. I have a better idea. Tomorrow, I'll take you shopping for one. We'll pick it out together."

"Oh, Mac, I really don't know if we should—"

"Of course, we should. You're already committed to this, Casey. It's too late to back out now. Eventually, you *will* remember, but in the meantime, you just have to trust me—and your own feelings. We've waited long enough, sweetheart. Too damn long, if you ask me. Besides, I've made all the arrangements."

Mac could be very persuasive, especially when Casey was already half-persuaded. She finally agreed to go shopping with him the next day, but that night, after he had kissed her goodnight and reluctantly departed, she again searched the wagon. If she could find a wedding gown, it would be proof that her great-great grandmother had at least *intended* to marry Mac. It would corroborate everything he had thusfar told her. Obviously, something had happened to prevent the marriage, in which case her theory made a weird sort of sense. She *was* supposed to right the wrongs of the past.

Casey searched high and low, but discovered nothing resembling a wedding gown or bridal veil. Ready to admit defeat, she sank down on the edge of the bunk—and felt something hard and lumpy beneath the mattress. It turned out to be even better than a wedding gown; it was a red, leather-bound journal, in which the first Casey O'Donovan had recorded her thoughts, dreams, and ambitions—and every detail of her relationship with Mac.

Casey stayed up most of the night reading, and what she read opened her eyes to her great-great grandmother's dilemma. The first Casey had fallen in love with Mac at first sight, but had fought her desires every step of the way thereafter. She hadn't wanted to live a conventional life—or to quit riding and performing death-defying feats. In an age where men controlled women's lives from the cradle to the grave, the first Casey O'Donovan had found freedom, adventure, financial independence, and the right to be her own person in the Wild West Show.

When Mac came along, the first Casey could not decide if she should sacrifice everything for love. Mac had sworn he didn't want to change her, that he loved her the way she was, but the first Casey had had grave doubts.

"Isn't change inevitable in marriage?" read one entry in the journal. *"Just look what happened to my friend, Zoe! As soon as she became pregnant, her charming but frequently drunken husband, whisked her out of the show and shut her up in a dreary little farm house. In a fit of temper, he beat her, and she lost her baby and her will to live. . . . Couldn't a similar terrible thing happen to me? People aren't always what they seem, and life has a way of bringing out the worst, along with the best, in us."*

Casey turned the pages with growing empathy and horror. She, too, had friends—supposedly fine, stable people—whose marriages had ended in disaster. So she knew just how her great-great grandmother must have felt. The first Casey hadn't wanted to lose her one chance at love, but she had put off making a decision until Mac issued an ultimatum: Marry him or he would leave the show when it reached his hometown of Boston.

Casey recalled Mac telling her that they were performing in some little town between Philadelphia and Boston. Was that where they were headed now—Boston?

"Mac is tired of traipsing all over the country," she continued reading. *"He wants to go out to the real West, settle down, and raise horses and cattle. . . . I think I could live with that, but what if he changes his mind and doesn't really do it? It will be too late for me; I will already have made my commitment."*

In a rush to see what her great-great grandmother had finally decided, Casey turned to the last entry in the journal. *"Well, I've done it—agreed to marry Mac a week from Saturday. Can I really go through with it? What will happen if I do? Worse yet, what will happen if I don't? Oh, I'm so confused! Why does love demand such difficult choices? I'll probably change my mind at the very last moment. If I do, Mac will surely leave, and that will be the end of it for both of us . . ."*

Stuffing the journal back under the mattress, Casey wrestled with the idea of marrying Mac because that's what her great-great grandmother *should* have done. The first Casey had endured painful notoriety while trying to raise a child alone in the atmosphere of a Wild West Show. It was a well-known fact in Casey's family history that her great grandfather had been ostracized from polite and proper society. Never living long in one place, he had grown up half-wild, as crazy over horses as his mother, and had passed that legacy down to her own grandfather who had bequeathed it to her father who had put Casey herself up on a horse when she was barely three years old.

All of the O'Donovan men had been horse-crazy. All had sired a single child—male, until Casey came along—and they had all been unable to maintain stable, long-term relationships with their wives. Either divorced or separated and always on the move, the O'Donovan men had died young and tragically, driving fast cars or riding hot horses. Casey's own mother had described the lot of them as having "cursed, unsettled lives."

Fearing the taint of that curse, Casey's mother had begged Casey not to pursue the dangerous sport of three-day eventing, in which she, too, would always be traveling. But Casey had ignored her mother's pleas and followed her dream, regretting nothing except not having spent more time with either of her estranged parents before they died.

In the midst of her reminiscing, Casey suddenly realized that she was the last of her bloodline; if she herself never married, there would be no one left on earth descended from the legendary Casey O'Donovan.

"But I know how you feel," Casey whispered to the ghost of her great-great grandmother, just in case it was hovering nearby. "I know just how you feel. People don't understand what it takes to be a success, do they? You'd be interested to know that things haven't changed much in all the years since you were alive. Women are still expected to sacrifice their careers for the sake of love. Many of them do it gladly. That's why I myself haven't let a man get too close to me. I don't want that conflict in my life. . . . I don't know if I'll ever want it. Besides, I don't have time to fall in love or nurture a relationship."

Casey wondered if she was going insane—talking to a dead ancestor. Maybe she was insane thinking she was lying in her great-great grandmother's wagon, debating whether or not to marry her great-great grandfather. Maybe she was actually lying in a hospital trussed up in a straight-jacket and imagining this whole thing . . . or maybe she was dreaming it.

But she didn't think so. Mac was too real. Somehow she had traveled back to the past. Her sojourn might be temporary or it might be permanent, but whatever it was, she had to decide what was the right thing to do now. And her heart was telling her to go ahead and marry Mac. After all, he was a wonderful man, and . . . and she loved him!

Yes, she might as well admit it. Irrational and illogical though it was, *she loved him.* He made her feel things no other man before him had ever made her feel. She *needed* him, *wanted* him. He made her laugh and aroused a deep tenderness. Here, in the past, she need not deny her most basic instincts. She felt no loyalty to the Wild West Show—and competing in the Olympics wasn't even a remote possibility. Here, she could indulge her femininity and simply enjoy being a woman in love with a handsome, sexy, kind, funny, solicitous man.

She fell asleep saying "I do," and dreaming of the wedding gown she and Mac were going to buy.

The next morning, Mac arrived bright and early to take her shopping. Casey was delighted to see him, but couldn't resist scolding him for not telling her about all the arguments and conflicts they had had in the past.

"You might have told me you coerced me into agreeing to marry you this Saturday by threatening to leave the show when we hit Boston," she said primly on the buggy ride down Main Street of the little town where the show was playing.

Mac managed to look charming and guilty at the exact same time. "So your memory of here and now *is* returning in its entirety."

"No, but' I found a journal in the wagon last night while I was looking for a wedding gown. It told me everything I wanted to know about you and me."

Mac raised an eyebrow. "It did? I never knew you kept a journal."

Casey let that comment pass. "So are we actually going to find the Real West one day? Or have you changed your mind and now plan to lock me up in a dull little house in Boston?"

Mac gathered the lines in one hand and took her hand in the other. "Casey, honey, I'm not like the fellow who married your friend, Zoe. I'd never lock you up anywhere. I know very well that you're a free, untamed spirit, and if I locked you up, that spirit would wither and die. Then you wouldn't be the Casey I love anymore."

Casey couldn't say another word. Emotions swamped her. Blinking back tears, she smiled tremulously and clung to Mac's hand as if her very life depended upon him. In a way, it did. In this strange new world, he gave her definition, confidence, and security, so that she didn't *want* to be anyone else except the woman he loved.

The rest of the outing proved magical. In a little shop along Main Street, they found a lovely white shirtwaist featuring Valenciennes lace at the throat, sleeves, and hem. Never having worn anything so frilly and feminine, Casey was enchanted. She also loved the white slippers and veil they bought to go with it, though Mac complained that he preferred her in green.

"Well, you aren't marrying a frog, you know," she reminded him.

"If you were a frog, I'd still marry you in a minute," he teased. "And we'd make sweet music together forever after on our own little lily pad."

The shop clerk laughed at their foolishness, and Casey laughed, too. She could not recall ever having laughed so much in one afternoon. Never had she herself been so witty or felt so happy and beautiful as she did with Mac. They had lunch at a hotel featuring a large front porch with brass railings. When Casey exclaimed over the luxury of the place, Mac confided that he had already reserved a room there for the weekend. They would spend their wedding night in the hotel.

At the thought of her wedding night, Casey blushed. Heat flooded her cheeks. She blushed even harder when Mac whispered: "I can't wait, sweetheart."

Beneath the tabletop, his hand found her knee and squeezed it. Casey was sure all the other guests in the hotel could see what he was doing and were watching her reaction. "Mac, stop that!"

He smiled innocently and only removed his hand when she kicked him in the shins. They had to hurry to get back in time for the show that afternoon. Casey watched proudly from the sidelines as Mac rescued Madeline and Jube from the Indians, then blew her a kiss. The audience cheered, but their mood turned hostile as the show drew to a close.

"Where's Casey?" someone shouted. "We want Casey!"

"I paid good money to see Casey O'Donovan jump a horse through a flaming hoop, and if we ain't gonna see it, I want mah money back!" demanded another.

There were hoots and catcalls. Mac explained that Casey wasn't yet able to perform, but would be back in the show as soon as possible. The crowd insisted upon knowing when. Mac looked over at Casey. To keep from being recognized, she was wearing a big straw bonnet with a gauzy veil that partially concealed her face. Lifting the veil, she mouthed Saturday, and Mac scowled, his face a mask of disapproval.

"Miss O'Donovan should be well enough recovered from her recent accident to resume performing on Saturday," he reluctantly announced. "The show is scheduled for four o'clock. We hope to see all of you there."

The cheers were deafening as Mac bowed and rode out of the arena. A moment later, Madeline and Jube descended upon Casey. "You sure you'll be all right to ride again come Saturday?" Madeline tossed a long brown braid over one shoulder.

"You don't seem to be entirely yourself yet, Casey, " Jube protested. Her blond hair made a charming frame for her heart-shaped face, but her blue eyes were worried. "Maybe you better wait at least 'til after the weddin', honey."

"I'll be fine," Casey protested. "If I'm well enough to get married, I should be well enough to perform. You'll have to excuse me now, I promised to meet Mac at my wagon right after the show."

"Wait a minute, Casey." Madeline touched her sleeve. "You think you'll feel up to helpin' me and Jube tomorrow with our ridin'? We didn't do as good tonight as we should have. That's probably why everyone was so upset about you not performin'. We gotta do better tomorrow night. Friday's crowd is always a big one—and Saturday's the biggest of all."

"I'd be glad to help. As I said, I feel perfectly fine."

The two watched Casey worriedly as she hurried away to meet Mac. No sooner had she arrived at the wagon and removed her hat, when Mac burst through the door. "Saturday's too soon for you to go back to work, Casey. I never should have promised that."

"Hush," she said. "Hush . . ."

To forestall any further debate, she threw her arms around him and kissed him soundly. Sighing, he clasped her to him. "Damn it, Casey, when you kiss me like that, I can't remember what we were arguing about. All I can think of is making you mine and becoming yours as soon as possible."

He resumed kissing her, and somewhere in the middle of the fifth or sixth kiss, Casey had a disturbing thought. When she married Mac on Saturday, he wouldn't actually belong to her alone. He thought he was marrying the *first* Casey O'Donovan, and he wouldn't even admit to the possibility that she had once existed in another time and place. Under the circumstances, jealousy seemed ridiculous, but she couldn't stop herself from feeling it.

Later that night, after dinner, she tried to reintroduce the subject, but Mac became angry. "Casey, if you keep talking about living in some other world, I won't let you perform on Saturday. I don't care if the crowd starts throwing rotten vegetables at the rest of us—I don't want you riding and jumping if you're still ill and confused."

"But I'm not ill or confused. I've never felt better in my life, Mac."

"Nevertheless, you're going to bed early tonight," Mac announced with infuriating high-handedness. "What with the show and the preparations for the wedding, tomorrow will be even busier than today, and you need your rest. So good night, Miss O'Donovan." He gave her a brotherly peck on the cheek and started to leave the wagon.

"Mac!" she nearly screamed in frustration.

"What is it now?" He gave her a silk and steel look that melted her irritation in five seconds.

"Mac, are you positive it's *me* you love—and not . . . not—"

"There's no one else, Casey. Don't even say it. Don't think it. *You* are the one I love, and *you* are the woman I'm going to marry on Saturday."

"But Mac—"

"No, Casey." He touched a finger to her lips. "I won't listen to any more foolishness. Put it all out of your mind, and just hold on to the truth. You're Casey O'Donovan, soon to be Mrs. Oliver Percival McClaren, or Mrs. Mac, as I envision everyone calling you."

"Mrs. Mac?"

He nodded solemnly, then kissed the tip of her nose. "Quit worrying, sweetheart. Everything's gonna be just fine."

Swept with doubts and a feeling of dark premonition, Casey could only nod. Mac left her then, and Casey readied herself for bed. Praying she wouldn't dream that night, she lay down to sleep, but no sooner had she closed her eyes when she was riding Flight-time toward the Shutterbug again. Her heart was thundering in her ears, and she was so scared she could hardly breathe.

Why am I so afraid of this jump? It's not so hard. I can do it. This jump is easier than most.

All night long she tried to reassure herself, tried to jump the obstacle and get it over with, or else slow the horse and go around it . . . but she kept reliving that same moment, over and over. She was galloping toward the jump, signaling Flight-time for the take-off, feeling him gather himself and make the big leap . . . and then . . . and then . . .

Casey awoke drenched in perspiration and shivering uncontrollably. It was morning, and someone was banging on the door. "Honey? You awake? Madeline and Jube are out here with breakfast. Come join us. The coffee's hot."

Casey had to drag herself out of bed. After she washed and dressed, she felt better, except for a slight headache and a lingering sense of terror. An uneasy feeling remained with her through most of the day. One part of her calmly went about helping Madeline and Jube with their riding, coaching Mac and Pegasus, and going into town with Mac to make certain that the lady who was baking their wedding cake hadn't forgotten about the wedding . . . but another part of her hung back.

On the way home from town, as Mac was clucking the horse into a fast trot so they wouldn't be late for the show, Casey's fears got the best of her. "Oh, Mac!" she wailed. "Are you sure we're doing the right thing getting married tomorrow? Maybe we should call it off and get married next week, instead. Or next month. Or better yet, next year."

Mac took one look at her face—which was probably as white as the frosting on the wedding cake—and pulled the horse to a stop. "Don't turn coward on me now, Casey," he said in a low soothing voice. "This is definitely the right thing for both of us. You mustn't be afraid."

"But . . . but marriage is forever! It's making vows we may not be able to keep. It's a lifetime commitment. It's promising to love each other no matter what happens. I may not be strong enough, Mac. This could be a terrible mistake. What if we're setting ourselves up for a lifetime of misery?"

As she sat beside him on the seat of the cart in the early afternoon sunshine, she gripped her hands together so tightly in her lap that her knuckles turned white. Mac placed his strong brown hand over her clenched fingers. "Honey, listen. Marriage isn't much different from jumping your horse blindfolded through a ring of fire. You can't ever know if you'll land smoothly or fall on your head instead. Either way, it's a leap of faith."

Casey thought about that for a moment and decided he was right. All she really needed was courage, determination to succeed, a sense of adventure, and a willingness to commit to the unknown— the same things she needed when she jumped, nothing new or different.

"Aren't you ever afraid?" she asked. "Just a little?"

"Of course, I am. Hell, I'm so scared I might wet my pants right in the middle of the ceremony!"

Feeling better already, Casey started to laugh. "Thank God, we only have one more night to worry about it!"

"We're not going to worry tonight. We're going to celebrate. I've planned a special prenuptial dinner for all of our friends after the show. Didn't you smell chicken baking at Mrs. Barlow's?"

Mrs. Barlow was the lady in charge of the wedding cake. "Yes, but I assumed she was just making supper for her family."

"She's making a feast for tonight," he informed her. "This very minute, her husband's roasting a pig to go with the chicken. And I've got whiskey and champagne, too. Since we're going to the hotel tomorrow night after the wedding, I thought we should have a party with our friends tonight. . . . So you see, you won't have time to worry or be nervous on this last night before the wedding. We'll be too busy celebrating."

She thought she must be marrying the sweetest, most wonderful, most thoughtful man in the world. "I love you, Mac! I don't know how you know me so well, but it seems you do. A party tonight will be perfect—exactly what I need."

He reached up and chucked her under the chin. "You've got a lot of other needs I intend to satisfy, too, Casey O'Donovan. Ole Mac is going to take good care of you; I promise you that."

The party was a huge success, and everyone ate and drank too much, got rowdy, and made innumerable silly toasts. Along about midnight, Mac broke it up. "Hey, everyone! Casey's still recovering from her fall. Since she plans to perform tomorrow, she needs her sleep."

"Mac, you can't send everyone away so abruptly," Casey protested. "Madeline and Jube, don't go yet. Hank, please stay awhile longer."

Actually, Casey was hoping the party would go on all night. That way, she wouldn't have to sleep alone in the wagon . . . and have more bad dreams.

"Mac's right, honey. The party's over. We *all* need our rest before a Saturday performance." Madeline hugged Casey and whispered in her ear. "Be happy, honey. Mac will make you a fine husband. Time you settled down anyway, and he's the right one for you."

Jube said nearly the same thing. "You lucky girl. I'd give my right arm to find a man who looks at me the way Mac does you."

When everyone had gone, Casey started cleaning up the mess from the party, although there wasn't much to do. Madeline and Jube had already done most of it. Mac kicked dirt over the fire, then took Casey's arm to escort her to the wagon. When they arrived at her door, he accompanied her inside, calmly lit a lamp, hung it on the peg over the narrow bunk, and began to take off his shirt.

"What are you doing?" Casey asked, dry-mouthed, as she stared at the fascinating expanse of hairy chest revealed in the lantern light.

"Getting ready for bed. Why don't you get ready, too? I'll just turn my back while you change out of your clothes."

"You're not sleeping here tonight! . . . I mean, the wedding isn't until tomorrow."

He gave her one of his devastating grins and casually kicked off his boots. "Surely, you didn't think I was going to leave you alone tonight to toss and turn and have doubts about tomorrow. As you've already noted, I know you very well, Casey, and I'm not taking any chances you'll change your mind at the last moment."

Oh, he knew her very well, indeed!

"But where will you sleep? And . . . and . . ." *How will we keep our hands off each other all night long?*

As if he'd heard her thoughts, his grin widened. When he spoke, his voice was as smooth as the fine brandy Casey had tasted for the first time that very evening. "Will it really make such a big difference if we wait until *after* the vows are spoken to sleep together, Casey? I'll wait if you want, but it's going to be damn hard for both of us, and I don't see what difference it makes in the long run. You need me tonight. I can see by your expression that you need me to hold you all night long and keep all the doubts and fears away."

He was right. He was so damnably right! And of course, they both knew what would happen if he stayed in her wagon tonight.

"I should make you leave," she croaked in a voice gone hoarse with a devastating surge of desire. "And I shouldn't marry you tomorrow. No matter what you say, Mac, I'm not the woman you love. I *know* who I am and where I came from, and I'm not the Casey you think I am."

His grin disappeared, and he regarded her soberly for several long breathless moments. "Casey, if what you're saying is really true, if you really are the great-great granddaughter of the woman I love, and you've somehow been sent back to the past to correct her mistakes, then you might as well let me make love to you tonight, or you yourself might never be born. As I see it, you've got two choices. Sleep with me tonight, then marry me tomorrow and give any child we've conceived a proper name, or toss me out on my ear and doom your own self to non-existence."

Casey considered this. "Maybe I've had too much brandy," she finally said. "But you're beginning to make sense."

His hands paused at the front fastenings of his Levis. "So which is it to be, Casey? Do I go or stay? Do we love each other tonight, or do we take a chance on waiting? Who knows how much time you've got left in my world? One or both of us could die in our sleep tonight—or be transported elsewhere, and *then* where would you be?"

Casey thought of her dark premonitions, her feeling of impending doom, and realized that she did not want to lose this one chance of giving Mac the love she had bottled up inside her. What if it *was* the only chance she would ever have to let him know how she felt about him?

"Stay," she said, and opened her arms to him.

He crossed the distance between them in two short strides. Then he was hugging her tightly and muttering: "You won't be sorry, Casey. Not about tonight, and not about tomorrow. I swear it. You won't be sorry."

He began to kiss her. Kisses rained down upon her face, eyes, and hair. He kissed her until she was breathless, her head spinning. Then he freed her breasts from her bodice and lavished kisses upon them. Her nipples puckered as if they meant to kiss him in return, but all she could do was moan and surrender to the pleasure he was giving her.

After several long moments of tantalizing love play, he divested her of her clothing, tore off his, blew out the lamp, and carried her down with him onto the narrow little bunk. Casey clung to him instinctively, not sure of what to do next, but more than willing to try anything he might have in mind.

Their naked bodies writhed and entwined as they sought to learn the tastes and textures of each other. Mac was all hard muscle, leathery scent, and pure aroused male. Casey could not get enough of him. She reveled in her explorations of his body and drowned in sensation as he in turn explored hers.

"Oh, Casey," he muttered. "You're so beautiful. So damn beautiful, and sweet and tender."

She thought they complemented each other perfectly, hard against soft, fitting together like two pieces of a puzzle. She no longer had any doubts that she had made the right choice. All her life, she had been heading toward this moment; she was destined for this love, this passion, this exquisite giving and taking. She saw now that she had been searching for Mac for a long time. So very long. He was the missing part of herself that she hadn't even known was missing until just this moment—when he came inside her, filling her completely, driving . . . driving . . . carrying her toward an explosion of ecstasy.

She swooned in his arms, and the next thing she knew, it was dawn, and he was dressed and leaving. Before he slipped out of the wagon, he pressed a kiss to her temple. "Just remember, sweetheart. Today will be the happiest, most momentous day of our lives. Tonight when we lie together, we'll be man and wife."

She tried to pull him down on top of her, but he laughed softly and resisted. "I have to go, wanton. There's so much to do. I'm sorry, but I'll make it up to you tonight."

Blowing her a kiss, he departed.

The day passed quickly. There was so much for her to do, too. Casey never had another moment alone with Mac until the crowds were gathering behind the ropes of the main arena. Even then, they had time only for a brief embrace. Casey had to don her costume and ride Pegasus well before it was time for her act. To her immense relief, she discovered that she and the horse were so attuned to each other that it seemed as if she had been riding him forever. She was sure she would have no problems with her performance.

Neither did the thought of the wedding hold any fear for her. Her fears had miraculously disappeared. The preacher waved from the sidelines, and Casey waved back enthusiastically. Mac had been right. Their night of loving had banished all her doubts and hesitations. She was a new person, more than ready for this next stage of her life to begin.

Midway through the show, Mac joined her in the tent where everyone changed costumes and mounted their horses before riding into the arena. "Do you feel all right? Will you be able to perform? If not, we can still call it off."

He sounded anxious, probably due to the size of the audience. People had come from miles around to witness her performance.

They had refused to buy tickets until reassured that Casey was going to jump through the ring of fire.

"I feel great. Is Hank setting up the hoop? I'm first on after the intermission, aren't I?"

Mac nodded. "It's almost time. I go out first. Then you ride out after me. I fasten the blindfold on Pegasus and light the fire on the hoop. Then you jump it. That's all there is to it. You've done it a hundred times, Casey."

She wondered if he was trying to convince her, or himself. His dark brows had a worried slant, but she wasn't afraid. She had already popped Pegasus over a few small obstacles and had no doubt she was riding a horse who liked jumping. He wouldn't balk at the flaming hoop—he couldn't even see it.

Long before the intermission ended, people began stamping and hollering her name. "Casey! Casey! We want Casey!"

"I'd better get out there and calm them down," Mac said. "I didn't think I'd be nervous, but now I just wish it were over, and all we had to think about was the wedding."

"Go on," Casey urged, giving Mac a push in the direction of the arena.

He grinned, blew her a kiss, and walked away. She listened to him calm the crowd, assuring them that she was coming, and building their excitement.

Then it was time for her grand entrance. She rode out into the arena to the sound of wild applause. Pegasus galloped the perimeter as if he knew he was the real star.

As Mac stood by with the torch and blindfold, Casey reined in the big white horse and turned him to face the jump. Mac stuck the torch into the ground and tied the blindfold over the horse's eyes, then stepped back with a flourish. He picked up the torch and touched it to the brush tied to the big iron hoop which hung suspended from a scaffold. The flames leapt and crackled.

And that was when Casey noticed something: From this angle, the obstacle looked exactly like . . . the Shutterbug.

Her heart slammed against her rib cage. Fear washed over her in waves. She couldn't move or breathe. She knew that if she jumped it, something terrible would happen . . . just like the last time.

"Casey? What is it? What's wrong?" Mac's voice sounded unnaturally loud in the hush that had fallen over the crowd. Casey could feel everyone's eyes on her. They were all waiting . . . waiting. Mac hurried over to her, the lit torch still in his hand. "Casey?" He lifted the torch so its light nearly blinded her.

"Mac, I can't do it! I . . . I want to get off." She started to swing her leg over the saddle, but the crowd erupted into protests and pandemonium.

"Jump!" people shouted. "Jump! Jump!"

They had been waiting all afternoon—indeed, all week—for this moment, and they weren't about to be cheated. "Jump, Casey!" they screamed.

"Don't be afraid," Mac said, reaching up to grab her hand. His was the only sane voice she could hear, the only one she could trust. "In all those times that you've done this, you've only fallen once. You won't fall this time, Casey. You can do it. Forget about the crowd. Don't dwell on your fear. Just think about us . . . and about the wedding after the show. One little jump is all you have to do—just to prove to yourself that you can still do it. After today, it'll be easy . . . and as soon as you're done, you can go put on that pretty gown we bought yesterday."

He no longer looked worried, and his confidence proved infectious. Casey suddenly remembered her own father picking her up after a nasty spill, setting her back on the horse, and saying almost the exact same things to her: "You can do it. Don't dwell on your fear. One little jump is all you have to do—just to prove to yourself that you can do it."

She had to trust her own abilities. Had to believe that whoever had been watching over her thusfar was still watching over her now. She was here to marry Mac, wasn't she? She had been sent back to the past to do what her great-great grandmother should have done when she had the chance. That meant that everything would be all right. After the show, she and Mac would marry and live happily ever after. It was time to make that leap of faith. . . .

She settled back into the saddle, and bent down and kissed Mac on the lips while the crowd roared its approval. Then, as he stepped back, she signaled Pegasus for a canter. The big horse took off, galloping in a straight line toward the jump. Casey aimed him for the center of the flaming hoop, waited for the proper moment, then leaned forward and squeezed hard against his sides.

Pegasus soared. So did Casey's heart. It was so easy. So effortless and exhilarating. She felt herself flying through the air . . . but on the descent, blackness also descended, falling like a big heavy shroud over her consciousness. *Oh, no! It's happening again . . .*

And it did. She tumbled and fell, spiraling downward through a long dark tunnel, at the end of which was . . . nothing. Nothing at all.

Once again, Casey awoke to find herself lying flat on her back and gazing up at the brilliant blue sky. Turning her head, she saw the Shutterbug, and not far away, crowds of people standing behind a safety cordon. Television cameras and camcorders were trained on her, and she could hear the wail of a siren in the distance.

She reached up to unbuckle her helmet, which felt very hot and confining, then sighed and simply lay there, waiting for help. Tears burned in her eyes, momentarily blurring her vision. Mac was lost to her. She would never see him again. Never feel his kisses, hear his laughter, or have the chance to marry him. It was over. She had lost her one opportunity for love. In her present life, with the way things were going—the way they had always gone—she would never have another. There might be other men, but not another Mac. And she didn't want anyone else anyway.

Suddenly, a man was leaning over her—an exceptionally handsome man with very black hair and very blue eyes. Casey gaped. He looked exactly like Mac—except he was wearing modern-day English riding clothes: tall black boots, skin-tight breeches, a creme-colored turtleneck. . . . A badge pinned to his shirt identified him as a Rolex official.

"Don't move," he warned in an all too familiar voice. "I believe you lost consciousness for a few moments. Do you know where you are? Can you tell me your name?"

"I'm Casey O'Donovan, and I'm at the Kentucky Horse Park in Lexington. I'm competing—or trying to compete—in the Rolex. I know who I am; what I want to know is who *you* are."

The blue-eyed man grinned, that same heart-stopping grin that Casey remembered so well. "Well, my parents gave me the impossible name of Reginald Octavius McIlvane, but my friends, thank God, call me Mac."

And that was when Casey knew exactly what had happened to her, and why. It was all very clear to her, but she didn't have much time to ponder it because medics arrived at that moment and began making a big fuss.

"I'm not hurt. I'm fine," she protested when a stretcher was set down beside her, and she realized that they intended to lift her onto it.

She scrambled to her feet. "Really. This isn't necessary. Someone just bring me my horse, and I can get back on and—"

"No, Miss O'Donovan." Mac grabbed her arm. "I'm sorry, but you can't remount and continue, not after a fall like that. You really should be examined by a—"

"Flight-time? Is Flight-time okay?" Casey strained to see where they had taken her horse and finally spotted the big Thoroughbred in the center of some other Rolex officials. A man in a pale blue coat was bending down to check Flight-time's legs.

"I think he survived without a scratch," Mac soothed. "When they caught him, he wasn't even limping—just trying to run back to the barn. However, it's *you* I'm worried about."

"Oh, thank heaven he's all right . . . and so am I." Casey waved the medics away. "You don't have to bother about me; I'm a big girl now, and I can get back to the barn all by myself."

The medics started to protest, until Mac intervened. "I'll go with her," he said. "Just to make sure."

He nodded to the medics, who looked disappointed that this wasn't a matter of life and death, then he walked over to retrieve Casey's horse.

"Miss O'Donovan and I will take him back to the stable," he told the veterinarian.

"Fine with me. Doesn't seem to be a thing wrong with him," the veterinarian responded.

"Thanks, Mac," one of the other men said. "Uh, oh. . . . Here comes the next rider. We'd better get off the course."

Mac returned to Casey with Flight-time in tow. "Shall we go?"

She nodded, and as they left the scene of the jump, the crowd applauded. Casey waved for the television cameras, but shook her head when one of the reporters headed in her direction. "Later!" she called out. "You can have an interview later. Right now, I just want to take care of my horse."

And be alone with Mac.

As they returned to the stabling area, Casey couldn't find much to say. She hardly knew where to begin. Fortunately, Mac did all the talking—telling her how much he admired her horsemanship, how skilled and talented she was, what a wonderful horse Flight-time was. He told her that he had long wanted to make her acquaintance. Having read about her, followed her career, and watched her compete on any number of occasions, he had wanted to walk up to her and introduce himself. But he hadn't, for he feared intruding upon her during the stress of competition. Plus, he had heard she had a reputation for rebuffing men she didn't know. In fact, it was said she was a regular dragon. The Iron Maiden, they called her.

"Is that true?" he asked with a twinkle in his eye. "Are you the Iron Maiden—your heart, body, and emotions all encased behind heavy metal? Now that I've met you, you seem quite friendly and open. Gentle as a lamb, actually."

"Oh, I can be friendly, gentle, and open when I want to be," she agreed with a laugh. *When I finally meet the right man.*

"What do you do when you're not officiating or attending horse shows?" she dared to ask, not that it mattered *what* he did. He was Mac, and that was *all* that mattered.

He grinned and ran a free hand through his tousled black hair. "I'm an attorney, with aspirations to one day be a three-day-eventer like yourself, and perhaps even compete in the Olympics. But of course, as a rider, I'm nowhere in your league, Miss O'Donovan. I could learn a lot from you."

This was Casey's cue to tell the young man that she had no time to teach newcomers; her own career demanded all her concentration. But she found herself smiling like a fool and offering to give him all the help he might possibly need. By the time they arrived at the stable, where Casey's groom, Lily, and her trainer, Gus, were anxiously awaiting her arrival, Casey had agreed to meet Mac for dinner.

Handing Flight-time over to Lily, Mac winked at Casey. "See you later." He walked away whistling.

"You look none the worse for your fall, Casey. But are you sure you should be walking around?" Holding on to Flight-time, Lily was staring after Mac's departing figure. "And who is that drop-dead gorgeous man? Is he really going to see you later? Or is he just another victim of wishful thinking?"

"His name is Mac, and yes, he's going to see me later. Actually, he's taking me to dinner."

"He is?" Lily's jaw dropped. "You mean the Iron Maiden actually accepted a date for tonight—when she has to compete again tomorrow? I can't believe you accepted a date, period."

Casey nodded, then turned to hide her smile against Flight-time's glossy neck. "You bet I accepted a date," she whispered, more to herself than to Lily.

Behind her, Lily said to Gus: "She doesn't look like she's hurt, but we better keep a close eye on her and have a doctor examine her anyway. Could be she got kicked in the head. She certainly isn't behaving like her usual self."

No, I'm not, Casey had to admit. But then she *wasn't* her usual self. She was an altogether different person—and she owed it all to her great-great grandmother. Somehow, her namesake had known that Mac was in her future and that Casey would never have given him the time of day, much less allow him to get close enough to propose to her. And so, the first Casey had intervened. Obviously, she didn't want her great-great granddaughter to make the same mistakes she had made.

And then another astounding thought occurred to Casey: Maybe this was a second chance for her great-great grandmother, as well! Maybe when one generation messed up, another was given a chance to. . . . But no, that idea was just too incredible. She mustn't get carried away making all sorts of foolish deductions. She and Mac couldn't possibly be the same Casey and Mac who . . .

"So what are you going to wear tonight?" Lily inquired as she unsaddled Flight-time.

"I don't know," Casey answered dreamily, but as she forced herself to focus on the question, she *did* know. "Whatever it is, it has to be green."

The Keeper of Time

Joan Overfield

Author's Note

The Dr. Faraday mentioned in this book is an actual historical figure, and is widely regarded as "the father of electricity." If you're ever in London, be sure to visit the Royal Institution on Albemarle Street and view his laboratory.

—Joan Overfield

This story is dedicated to the victims of the Fairchild AFB shooting, June 20, 1994. You are not forgotten.

One

THE KEEPER OF TIME
ELIZABETH TIPPLETON. PROP.
ESTAB. 1851

The hand-painted sign on the old bowed window was scarcely legible, the blue and gold lettering all but obliterated by the ravages of age and the layer of gritty soot coating the thick panes. Gillian Brooke stood in front of the tiny shop entranced as much by the sign, as by the odd assortment of watches and other timepieces that comprised the jumbled window display.

Finally, she thought, her lips curving in a rueful smile as she studied the tangled clutter, *an antique shop I might be able to afford.* After spending the afternoon peering into the expensive and elegant shops lining the twisting streets off Picadilly, she was beginning to think she'd have to go home with nothing but a plastic bobby helmet as a souvenir. Holding her purse closer, she pushed her way through the throng of Saturday shoppers and other tourists, and opened the shop's door.

The brass bell hanging above the door announced her arrival with a rusty-sounding tinkle, and Gillian waited for the clerk to make his or her appearance. She wondered if it would be one of those supercilious men with an exaggerated upper-crust accent, or a bored teenager with a ring through her nose and not the faintest idea what sort of merchandise the shop carried. She'd been waited on by both since arriving in England ten days earlier, and she'd quickly learned to expect just about anything.

As she waited with mounting impatience Gillian glanced around, her eyes adjusting to the gloom that seemed to permeate every corner of the shop. There were no overhead lights, and had it not been for the art deco lamp featuring a naked sylph holding a glowing white bulb above her head, she'd have thought the shop's owner had neglected to pay the electric bill. The same way he'd apparently neglected to clean, she mused, grimacing at the dust that lay on every surface.

She shifted from one foot to the other, uneasiness replacing her impatience as the multitude of clocks about her loudly ticked off the passing minutes, and no one emerged from the back room to help her. Finally she could wait no longer, and nervously cleared her throat.

"Hello?" she called out, her voice echoing eerily in the empty shop. "Is anyone here?"

The ticking of the clocks was her only answer, and after a few minutes she tried again. "Hello? Are you open?"

More silence, and now she was beginning to grow genuinely alarmed wondering if she'd just walked in on a burglary—or something worse. She began backing toward the door, recalling she'd seen several bobbies patrolling on Picadilly. She'd just go back and tell them about the abandoned shop, and—

"Just a minute, just a minute," a voice sounding as old and dusty as the shop itself called out in obvious irritation. "Give a lady a chance, can't you?" A few seconds later an elderly woman with a shock of white hair and a pair of gold-rimmed spectacles perched on her nose emerged from behind the tattered curtain. She walked up to the counter, faded green eyes snapping with impatience as she glared at Gillian.

"Well?" she demanded querulously. "You weren't shy about interrupting my break, were you? I'm here, now. What is it you want?"

"I'm sorry," Gillian began, and then halted abruptly. Reminding herself that it was she who should be receiving the apology, she gave the clerk a cool look.

"I'm sorry," she repeated, but this time with a note of haughty disdain in her voice. "But when I came in and no one answered me, I thought the shop was deserted."

The elderly shopkeeper surprised her by giving her a roguish wink. "Only looks that way," she said, tapping the side of her nose. "Keeps out the tourists and the other riff-raff. I've one of a kind merchandise here, and can't be bothered to have just anyone and their dog pawing over it."

Gillian glanced at the items piled haphazardly about and managed a polite smile. "Yes," she said, deciding it was time to beat a strategic retreat, "I can see that you do."

"What is it you're after?" The woman asked, not seeming to notice her sarcasm. "I'm busy, and can't stand about all day chatting. Time doesn't keep itself, you know. Do you want to see a watch?"

Gillian frowned at her, puzzled by the odd choice of words. "Pardon?"

"A watch," the elderly lady repeated irritably. "Do you want a watch?"

"Oh." A light flush touched Gillian's cheeks. "Actually . . ."

"You'll be wanting something new and digital, I shouldn't wonder," the woman grumbled, rummaging through a box behind the counter. "You're an American, aren't you, and it's all shiny and high-tech for the lot of you. High-tech, now there's a word," she shook her head in disgust. "Folks thinking themselves too busy to correctly pronounce a word. No wonder time is in such a muddle."

As it happened, Gillian shared the shopkeeper's dislike for that particular word. It had been one of her ex-husband's favorites, and he'd used it so frequently there were times she could have screamed. "Actually," she said coolly, "I'm rather fond of old things. That *is* why I came in here."

"Old things." The shopkeeper gave a disgruntled snort. "Older than what? Older than last year, do you mean?"

"Older, as in Victorian," Gillian said between clenched teeth, wondering why she didn't just turn around and leave.

That seemed to catch the woman's attention, and she gave Gillian a wary look. "Victorian?" she repeated, her white eyebrows meeting in a scowl. "Are you certain?"

"Of course I'm certain!" Gillian exclaimed in annoyance. "Why?"

The clipped demand made Gillian frown. "Why am I certain?"

"Why do you want to see something from then?" the other woman asked, abandoning her search to study Gillian intently. "Why not something from the Regency or another period? Why Victorian?"

"I—I don't know," Gillian stammered, too taken aback by the question to do anything but answer honestly. "I've always liked the period, and felt as if that's where I really belong. My ex-husband used to say I was born about a hundred fifty years too late," she added with a weak laugh, hoping she didn't sound as foolish as she felt.

"Did he now?" she gave her a considering frown. "And what did you say?"

"That he was probably right," she admitted, remembering how her answer had angered Doug. Yet at the time it had felt like the truth. It *still* felt like the truth, she thought, bemused by the admission.

To her relief, the shopkeeper didn't seem alarmed by her confession. "It's possible, I suppose," she said, looking thoughtful. "Don't care what anybody says, this time business isn't as exact as we'd like, and it would explain why the shop let you in. Thought the blasted thing was broken again. Last week it let one of those green-haired punkers in, and I had the devil's own time getting him out again." She scratched her nose and shot Gillian a quick smile.

"Well, what part of the Victorian period do you belong in?" she asked briskly. "Old girl was on the throne for quite a while," you know."

By now Gillian had given up any attempt to make sense of the woman's rambling conversation. "Something from the first part of her reign when Albert was still alive," she said, hoping the woman wouldn't have anything to show her so she could leave. "The year your shop opened would be nice."

"Eh?" she looked puzzled.

"1851," Gillian reminded her. "That's what the sign in your window says."

"Oh that," the woman shrugged. "I'm not certain when this place opened, to be honest. Not that it matters, I suppose. Time's relative, isn't it? A minute, a millennia—over in the blink of an eye."

"According to Einstein it was," Gillian muttered, unaware she had spoken aloud.

The woman's expression darkened. "Einstein!" She spat out the name with indignation. "Pah! A presumptuous schoolboy, that's what he was! Him with his theories and formulas . . . we had a good laugh over that, I can tell you. Well," she rubbed her palms together and gave Gillian a bright smile, "if it's 1851 where you belong, I suppose I might have something that would interest you," she reached beneath the counter again and extracted an old, dust-covered cigar box.

Gillian eyed it dubiously, certain it held nothing that could be of possible interest to her. "I'm afraid I couldn't afford a real antique," she began, not wishing to hurt the old woman's feelings. "Maybe I should go to one of those reproduction shops instead."

"Much good they would do you if time's the problem," the shopkeeper said, brushing off a layer of dust as she lifted the lid. "Besides, how do you know what you can afford until I tell you how much it costs?"

"Well, I—"

"Here you go. Just what you need," she said, extending the box to her. "What do you think?"

Annoyed at the interruption, Gillian was fully prepared to reject whatever ancient trinket she had unearthed. Then she saw the watch nestled in a bed of white velvet, and all thoughts of refusal flew from her head.

Fashioned out of lapis lazuli, the engraved Roman numerals etched in gold and mother of pearl, the watch was the loveliest thing she had ever seen. The oval case was rimmed with seed pearls, and the tiny stem had been carved to look like a flower. No, a thistle, she corrected, picking up the watch and studying it closely.

"It's beautiful," she whispered, a feeling of intense longing washing over her as she cradled the watch in her hand.

"It's a pendant watch," the older woman said, indicating the tiny gold loop above the stem. "You can wear it suspended from a chain or a velvet ribbon. That's how the original owner wore it."

"The original owner?" Gillian asked absently, still entranced by the elegant beauty of the watch.

The shopkeeper picked up the watch and turned it over, handing Gillian a jewelers loupe so she could read the words delicately etched into the back of the case.

L. Culross
Number 6 Half-Moon Street
London 1848

"She had her address engraved on it?" Gillian asked, puzzled by the action. "How odd." She would have had the watch engraved with some old-fashioned sentiment, she decided, brushing her thumb over the words. Or else the name of the man who had given it to her. She knew, somehow, that the watch had been a gift from a man.

"To you, perhaps, but that was the sort of person she was," the older woman replied, turning the watch over so Gillian could continue studying it. "Now, as you can see by the thistle, the watch was made in Scotland—Edinburgh, most likely. The thistle is the symbol for Scotland."

"I know," Gillian said, smiling at the memory of the lectures her grandfather used to give her about her Scots heritage. "My maiden name was Ferguson."

The shopkeeper gave her a surprised look. "Was it now? Perhaps that would explain it."

"Explain what?"

"A great deal," came the cryptic reply as the shopkeeper eyed her with professional interest. "Well? What do you think? Will it suit?"

Gillian wanted to say no, certain she could never hope to afford the watch. She was in England to celebrate the first year anniversary of her divorce, and her budget was limited. There was no way it could stretch to cover something so expensive. "It's very nice," she said at last, giving the watch a wistful look, "but I'm afraid I can't afford it."

"Even when you don't know what I'm asking?"

Gillian's heart began pounding with hope. "How much *are* you asking?" she queried, praying it was so far above what she could afford that she wouldn't be even slightly tempted.

"Fifty pounds."

Fifty pounds! Gillian did some swift calculations. The price wasn't so low as to make her suspicious, and it was also within her budget . . . if she didn't mind living on soup and tea for her last three days in London. She glanced at the watch again and took a deep breath.

"I'll take it."

"Of course you will." the woman said, smiling as she plucked the watch from Gillian's hand. "Just give me a few minutes to set the time for you, and then you can be on your way."

While she fussed and muttered in the back room, Gillian counted out her traveler's checks, and fought against buyer's remorse. She knew her ever-practical family would be appalled by what they would term her frivolous waste of money, but she didn't care. She was used to their disapproval by now, and in any case, she had finally taken to heart the lesson it had taken her twenty-nine years to learn. This was *her* life, not theirs.

The shopkeeper soon returned, the watch dangling from a ribbon of dark blue velvet. "Here you are," she said cheerfully, handing it to Gillian. "Just put it on. That ought to get it running."

Gillian did as she was told, slipping the soft ribbon over her head, and placing the watch between her breasts. It felt oddly right there, and she smiled as she gave the face a loving stroke with the tip of her finger. As if the watch had been waiting for only that, the minute hand began to move—but much to her amazement the hand moved backward, not forward.

"Wait a minute!" she exclaimed, watching as the hour hand began to move as well. "This watch is running backward!"

"Of course it is," the shopkeeper said, sounding pleased. "It has to catch up, doesn't it?"

"Catch up to what?" Gillian demanded, beginning to feel dizzy as the hands spun faster and faster until they were a blur.

"Why, the correct time," she heard the other woman say, her voice echoing as if she was speaking from a great distance. "That's where you said you belonged, isn't it?"

Gillian felt a wave of dizziness wash over her, but she was unable to tear her gaze from the spinning hands of the watch. She closed her eyes for a brief moment, and when she opened them again she was horrified to discover that everything about her had vanished in a brilliant explosion of light and color.

Two

"Madam, are you all right?"

A man's voice filled with concern penetrated the thick fog swirling in Gillian's mind, and she felt the tentative touch of a hand on her elbow.

"Madam?" The man repeated anxiously. "Shall I summon a constable?"

Gillian forced herself to concentrate on the voice, using it as a lifeline to pull herself out of the sticky dizziness that clung to her. She took a deep breath and shook her head, blinking her eyes to clear them. It took several seconds, but at last the man's features swam into focus. And when they did, she stared at him in shock.

He was tall and quite handsome, with wavy light-brown hair and a pair of lustrous blue eyes that regarded her solemnly. But it was his clothing that made her stare; clothing that was at least one hundred years out of fashion.

When he saw her eyes were open, the man ventured a cautious smile. "Do you feel better now?" he asked solicitously. "You will forgive me for being so bold as to address you, but you looked so unwell I feared you were about to swoon. Would you like me to send for a physician?"

"I . . ." Gillian's voice trailed off, her mind searching for some logical explanation for what she was seeing. Finally she realized the man was an actor in period costume, like the men in Elizabethan dress she'd seen wandering around the Pageant at the Tower, and her shoulders slumped in relief.

"No, I'm fine, thank you," she said, feeling slightly foolish at her initial response. "I'm just a little hungry. Guess I should have had more than an Egg McMuffin for breakfast," she added, shooting him a rueful smile.

He looked slightly confused. "An Egg McMuffin, madam?"

This guy was really good, Gillian thought, and was about to compliment him on his performance when she was jostled from behind. She turned around, and was confronted by two other people also in period dress. The man was dressed similarly to the one standing before her, while his companion was wearing a wide-rimmed black bonnet edged with white lace, the full skirts of her gown making her look like a walking bell. Gillian stared after them, her astonishment mounting when she saw that everyone around her was wearing the same old-fashioned clothing.

The man saw her reaction, and his expression grew more concerned. "Are you quite certain you are all right?" he asked, his brows meeting over his nose as he studied her pale features.

"Oh, yes, I'm fine," Gillian returned tautly, swallowing nervously as a black and yellow carriage with large yellow wheels clattered past them on the cobblestone street. Maybe she'd wandered onto a movie set, she thought, struggling to remain composed. It was the only explanation that made even the slightest sense.

She tried to think of what might have happened to affect her memory, but her last clear recollection was of being in the antique store. "Can you tell me where Mrs. Tippleton's shop is?" she asked, deciding it was best to start looking for answers there. "It's an antique shop somewhere near here."

He looked thoughtful for a moment, and then reluctantly shook his head. "I am afraid I have never heard of it," he said, frowning. "Are you quite sure it is in the area?"

"Of course I'm sure!" she protested, a cold drop of terror beginning to trickle down her spine. "I just stepped out of it when you spoke to me!"

He arched his eyebrows in an eloquent gesture of skepticism. "You stepped out of that shop, madam," he said, pointing in back of her with a gloved finger.

She turned around, her jaw dropping when she saw the discreet sign displayed in the window.

Wilson and Son
Bespoke Clothing for the Discerning Gentleman

"But . . . but I don't understand," she stammered, staring at the sign in mounting confusion. "It was an antique shop a few minutes ago! It's where I bought my . . ." her voice trailed off as she glanced down. Instead of the burgundy sweater and black and navy blue windbreaker she was expecting, she saw an expanse of lilac-colored silk, lavishly trimmed with black lace. And instead of a pair of faded jeans, her legs were hidden by a full skirt in the same lilac silk. Her purse was also gone, and in its place was a small cloth bag dangling from her wrist.

She lifted her hands, staring at the pair of black lace gloves with the fingers missing that covered them. "This isn't real," she heard herself murmur, as a feeling of unreality washed over her. "This can't be happening."

Her rescuer began frowning, his look of concern giving way to one of vague alarm. "Perhaps I should summon assistance after all," he said, taking a cautious step closer to her. "It is obvious you are unwell."

Unwell didn't even begin describing how she felt, Gillian thought, hysteria bubbling up inside her. She wanted desperately to believe she was dreaming, but she knew herself to be wide-awake. She was trying to think of some response when she saw the man suddenly stiffen, his blue eyes narrowing as they rested on her chest.

"Where did you get that?" he demanded hoarsely.

Gillian was momentarily non-plussed by his transformation. "Where did I get what?"

"The watch you are wearing," he said, showing no signs of his earlier gentleness. "Where did you get it?"

Gillian spared the pendant a puzzled Look. "From the antique shop I was telling you about," she replied, more confused than ever. "Like I said, I'd just stepped outside when you—"

"Do not play me for a fool!" he interrupted, grabbing her arm in a rough hold. "Tell me how you came to be in possession of my wife's watch, or I will have you taken up as a thief!"

A thief! The fear and disorientation Gillian had been experiencing vanished under a wave of furious indignation. "Just try it, buster!" she snapped, meeting him glare for glare. "You even *think* about having me arrested and I'll sue you for every cent you've got! Now let go of my arm or I'll deck you."

His jaw clenched so hard Gillian wondered it didn't snap, and for a moment she thought she would have to make good on her threat. She was preparing to use the self-defense she'd learned at the local community college when he finally dropped her arm and stepped back.

"Very well, madam," he said stiffly, his voice as icy as his piercing blue eyes. "If that is the way you wish to play it, I suppose no harm will come in humoring you. You will kindly accompany me."

"Accompany you where?" Gillian demanded, resisting the urge to rub her arm where he'd been grasping it.

To the Royal Institution. I am on staff there, and am to give a lecture in less than an hour. Were it not for that, you may be certain I would not hesitate escorting you to the nearest police station and laying a charge against you."

Gillian decided she'd had enough of his little charade. She was just about to tell him where he could put his stupid threats when a man dressed in an old-fashioned bobby's uniform walked up to them.

"Is everything all right, miss?" he asked, his dark eyes full of suspicion as they rested on the man's face. "This here gent ain't botherin' you, is he?"

Gillian might have had a great many faults, but being slow on the uptake wasn't one of them. Recognizing salvation when she saw it, she grabbed hold of it with both hands. "Oh, officer, thank heavens you are come!" she exclaimed, batting her eye-lashes and over-acting for all she was worth. "This . . . this masher accosted me, ordering me to accompany him to his rooms!"

To her delight the man's face instantly turned a bright red. "That is rot, officer!" he snapped, blue eyes blazing. "I am a respectable citizen, and I assure you I was not *accosting* this woman!"

"Were you not, now?" The constable rocked back on his heels, folding his arms across his massive chest. "Then you weren't commanding her to go with you just as I was walking up?"

The man's face grew even redder. "I suppose I may have done so," he conceded through clenched teeth, "but—"

"Arrest him, officer!" A heavyset woman with a huge feathered bonnet cried, her jowls quivering with outrage. "A fine thing when a decent lady can not walk down the street without being assaulted by the likes of him! Ha! I knew no good would come from that foolish exhibition. Only look at the riff-raff it brings to our city!"

Another woman added her agreement, and Gillian turned in surprise to find a sizable crowd had gathered around them. Once again she was quick to recognize an opportunity when she saw one, and while the man was vociferously defending himself, she slipped quickly into the crowd. Not knowing what else to do, she began walking toward Picadilly, praying that when she got there things would be restored to normal. She knew Londoners liked their pageantry, but she didn't think even they would go so far as to block off one of the busiest streets in the city to let a bunch of Victorian enthusiasts run amok.

She continued walking, and the closer she got to what she thought was Picadilly, the more worried she became. A sign bolted to the side of a brick wall assured her she was still on Dover Street, yet it wasn't the Dover Street she had walked down earlier. The buildings were essentially the same, but the businesses they contained were different than those she remembered. Another thing that worried her was the lack of street noise. The blare of horns and roar of traffic were as much a part of London as the ancient buildings, but nothing—not even the shriek of a police siren—could be heard above the rattle of harnesses and the rhythmic clop of hooves on stone.

She drew nearer to her destination, her heart racing with sick fear when she saw that, like Dover Street, Picadilly was thick with horses and carriages. This had to be some kind of recreation, she told herself, battling hysteria as she gaped at the crowds of people flowing past her in their old-fashioned clothing. It was either that, she decided wildly, or London had been caught up in some kind of cosmic time warp.

Time warp. The ludicrous notion leapt into her mind, followed immediately by a memory of the shopkeeper's whimsical remarks about time. And then she recalled how the hands of the watch had run backward when she'd placed it around her neck. What was it the other woman had said? she mused, brows wrinkling in thought. Something about the watch needing to catch up to the correct time. . . .

"Paper, miss?" A grubby urchin appeared before her, waving a newspaper with a commanding air. "Cost ya ha'penny, is all."

She stared down at him, thinking dully that he looked like he'd just wandered off the set of OLIVER! Hadn't she read somewhere that one of the theaters in the West End was mounting a revival? She bit back a jittery giggle as she envisioned him breaking into a rousing chorus of "Food, Glorious Food."

"Well?" The young entrepreneur was glaring at her with decided impatience. "Does ya want 'un, er not?"

She fumbled with the bag dangling from her wrist, and was relieved when she found a collection of coins inside. Extracting one of the smaller ones, she handed it to the boy.

"You can keep the change," she said, hoping she hadn't been either wildly generous or miserably cheap. Apparently she had been neither, for the boy simply handed her the paper and turned away. Gillian unfolded the paper, scanning it quickly to find the date. *July 2, 1851.*

She stared down at the date, feeling the world crumbling about her. She glanced up, but the boy had disappeared into the crowd. Maybe it was a set-up, she thought, her hands shaking as she refolded the paper. Somebody was just trying to gaslight her, that was all. It was like the old TV series where they would perpetrate elaborate jokes on people, and then leap out at the last minute and yell "Smile!"

Clinging to the thought, she began walking, looking for the hidden camera or some tangible bit of proof that would assure her she hadn't lost her mind. She found none. She did see several other newsboys, and acting on impulse, she flagged one down.

"Is this today's paper?" she asked, gesturing at the one he clutched in his ink-stained hand.

"O'course 'tis, miss," he said, dark eyes regarding her with obvious derision. "A fat lot o' good yesterday's 'ud do me."

Gillian handed him another coin, a much larger one if his words of thanks were any indication, and shook open the paper. *July 2, 1851.*

She stared at the date, a feeling of cold horror washing over her. It was true, she thought, gazing at the headlines with unseeing eyes. The first paper she could dismiss as a fraud, but given all the newsboys running around central London, how could whoever was behind this know which one she would select?

There was no denying the truth anymore, she realized at last, taking a shuddering breath as she allowed the enormity of that truth to sink in. However bizarre it sounded, however much it contradicted everything she had been raised to believe, she knew she could no longer ignore the facts. She was indeed in 1851, and she had no idea how she got there or how she could get back to her own time again.

Three

Gillian spent the next hour absorbing the sights and sounds of the strange new world in which she now found herself. She walked up and down the teeming streets, her stunned shock giving way to a numbed acceptance, and then, incredibly, a mounting sense of excitement. She was where and when she had always wanted to be, and she was suddenly eager to see and experience all that she could. It was like Disneyland, only infinitely better, she thought, watching wide-eyed as a brightly painted mail coach rumbled past her. Disneyland was a pretty, plastic lie; but this, this was as real as it got.

It took another few hours of exploration before her excitement dissipated, and the myriad problems facing her began making themselves known. Food was her first priority, followed by a place to stay and some means of earning a living. She didn't know how long she'd be trapped in this time, but she decided it was wise to plan for the worst.

A quick search of her purse . . . reticule, she corrected herself silently, revealed she had a little over fifty pounds cash; exactly the same amount she'd had in 1995. She wasn't sure how much that would translate into in Victorian days, but she thought it should be enough to last her for a few weeks if she was very, very frugal.

In the end, locating a respectable boardinghouse that would accept a single woman with no luggage proved more difficult than she could have imagined. After several attempts ended with the door being slammed in her face, Gillian threw her conscience to the winds, spinning the wildest yarns she could think of before finally hitting pay dirt at the sixth house she tried.

"You mean to say you lost your luggage when thieves made off with the entire mail coach, horses and all?" The landlady, a Mrs. Kingston, asked, clutching a shaking hand to her breast as she regarded Gillian with wide eyes. "You poor child! What a dreadful welcome to England you have had!"

"And so ironic, when you consider I had crossed the entire continent of America without seeing so much as a single Indian," Gillian agreed, mentally congratulating herself for her decision to pass herself off as an American traveler fallen on hard times. She knew her accent precluded her pretending to be a British subject, and further reasoned her nationality would explain any gaffe she was likely to make. Even in 1851, she was certain English snobbery would have her being regarded as little more than a barbarian.

"Painted savages," Mrs. Kingston shivered in terror and delight. "One hears the most *dreadful* stories, but you say you saw not one of the devils in your travels? How disappointing."

"Not on my trip *back* from San Francisco," Gillian corrected, more than happy to give her landlady whatever details she wanted. "But on the journey out we were positively beset by the creatures. One of the men in our party was even scalped."

Mrs. Kingston shivered again, and then to prove the English could be no less bloodthirsty than American Indians, proceeded to tell Gillian of every vicious murder that had been committed in London in living memory. Such tales horrified Gillian, and put an end to more than a few cherished misconceptions of the Victorian period. So much for a kinder, gentler time, she thought, trying not to wince as Mrs. Kingston gleefully described how a man in the Wapping Docks area was said to have murdered an entire family in their sleep.

"Of course, that happened years ago. And the villain took his own life, so you need not fear being troubled by him, my dear," Mrs. Kingston said, patting Gillian's hand. "You are quite safe here, I promise you. This is a respectable household."

The respectable household consisted of the landlady and her dour-faced daughter, Minerva, as well as three other women who had come to London to seek employment. Gillian met them over dinner that night, and listening to them talk provided her with an uncomfortable glimpse of what she could expect in her new life. England in 1851, it seemed, did not look kindly upon unmarried females without the protection of their families.

The five pounds a week she paid for her room also provided her with the services of a maid, and Gillian was quick to discover why, in the era of laced stays and horse-hair crinolines, servants were a necessity, not a luxury. The next two days were spent purchasing a few gowns, and discreetly searching the papers for a job she thought she could perform. She was sitting in the parlor circling possibilities when Miss Merriam, one of the newest lodgers, came in to join her.

"Pray do not pay me any mind, Miss Brooke," she said, her eyes flashing behind her spectacles as she lowered herself onto the chair facing Gillian. "I have just come from an interview with the most difficult man, and I find myself actually grateful he did not offer me the position."

Gillian set aside her paper, intrigued by the other woman's reaction. One of the first things she'd observed was that women of the period rarely if ever showed strong emotion, and she wondered what could have made the normally staid woman so upset.

"Really?" she asked, reaching what seemed to her the only possible conclusion. "Did he . . . er . . . try anything?"

"What?" Miss Merriam looked momentarily perplexed, and then her thin face suffused with color. "Oh! My heavens, no, Miss Brooke!" she exclaimed, regarding Gillian with horror. "How could you even think such a thing! Indeed, it was nothing of the sort, I assure you. I am a lady, after all, and for all I fear him to be a Bedlamite, Dr. Culross is a gentleman."

"Culross?" Gillian echoed, unconsciously grasping the pendant as she recognized the name. It was the same as the one engraved on the back, and she wondered if it meant something, or if it was just a coincidence.

"You have heard of him?" Miss Merriam sounded surprised. "I did not know he was known in your country, as well."

"I . . ." Gillian tried to think of some plausible explanation,

but before she could succeed, Miss Merriam said, "Oh, I'd forgotten, you must have seen the article in this morning's gazette.
Have you ever read such nonsense in all your life? Time and
electricity being somehow intertwined," she shook her head in
gentle disgust. "And the great pity is that the poor man truly
believes his silly theory! That is why I can not work for him, you
see. It is obvious grief has cost him his reason."

"Grief?" Gillian's heart began racing at the mention of time.

"Oh, yes," Miss Merriam provided with an eager nod. "That
would not have been in the papers, for it is old news now, but I
recall hearing he lost his dear wife some three years ago. The
cholera, you know. Her name was Lydia."

L. Culross, now Gillian knew it was no coincidence. It couldn't
be. She licked her lip nervously. "Does . . . does he live on Half-
Moon Street?"

"Why, yes, he does," Miss Merriam said, eyeing her in surprise. "He and his little girl. The position I mentioned is for that
of governess, and the salary is tempting. Quite tempting," she
added with a sigh, "but I must not be swayed. My dearest papa
was a vicar, and I am sure he would never hold with such progressive theories as the good doctor advocates."

She continued chatting with Gillian for a few more minutes
before finally leaving. The moment she had gone Gillian began
tearing through the newspaper, tossing the sheets on the floor
until she found the article Miss Merriam had mentioned.

Astonishing New Theory! The headlines screamed.

> *At a recent lecture at The Royal Institution, Dr. Ian Cul-
> ross amazed those members and their guests in attendance
> by putting forth a most remarkable theory. The scientist,
> well known for his work with the esteemed Dr. Faraday,
> hypothesizes that time, rather than being an abstract, is in
> actuality an element, and like an element, can be measured
> and controlled. He further speculated that an object, prop-
> erly charged with electrical particles, could be propelled
> forward in time, and stated he had been conducting experi-
> ments to that effect. The audience, it is said, was under-
> standably skeptical."*

The paper dropped from Gillian's hands. If fate had brought her back in time, then she reasoned it had also just handed her the only chance she had of finding her way home. The question was: Did she want to go? It took her less than a moment to make up her mind.

After three days in this time, she had mastered the intricacies of traveling by horse-drawn carriages, and less than an hour after dashing out of Mrs. Kingston's lodging house, she was standing on the doorstep of Number Six, Half-Moon Street. The butler who answered her knock was tall and cadaverously thin, his dark eyes suspicious as he regarded her over his beaked nose.

"Yes?" he asked, his rich voice dripping with condescension as he gave Gillian a measuring look.

"I've come about the position as governess, if I'm not too late," she said, putting on the demure facade she'd learned to adopt over the past few days.

One of the man's bushy white eyebrows arched at her accent. "Unfortunately, you are not," he said, his tone indicating this was somehow her fault. "The other applicants the agency sent have proven most unsatisfactory, and the master is quite displeased. You are not English, Miss . . . ?"

"Brooke, and I am American . . . sir," Gillian provided, gritting her teeth at his superior attitude. He reminded her of Mr. Dillford, the persnickety little man who was the head of her company's payroll department. Apparently obnoxious, officious little twits were as much a problem to the Victorians as they were in her time, she thought, wondering what he'd do if she gave in to her impulses and gave him a swift kick in the rear.

"Indeed?" The other eyebrow rose to meet its fellow. "Well, that can not be helped, I suppose. As you are here, I see no reason why you should not be admitted. You could hardly do worse than the last two creatures." He opened the door and stepped back. "This way, if you please."

He led her through the surprisingly spacious hall to a small, sunlit parlor decorated in a symphony of yellow and cream. "You are to wait here," he ordered, his manner as imperious as ever, "but do not trouble removing your cloak. I much doubt you will be remaining."

"Yes, sir," Gillian replied, deciding she'd kick him some place infinitely more painful.

He gave her a sharp look, as if sensing her unladylike thoughts. "I am called Clares—*Mr.* Clares, to you, should Dr. Culross choose to engage you. And I must warn you that I expect the highest level of performance from my staff. You will be accorded no special favors merely because you are an upper servant. I trust you take my meaning?"

Gillian imagined him doubling over in pain before speaking. "Yes, Mr. Clares."

After he'd gone, she entertained herself comparing her elegant surroundings to Mrs. Kingston's fussy, overcrowded parlor. She recognized the chair and side table as being Sheraton, and unless she was mistaken, the mantle over the fireplace could only have been carved by Adams himself. She was studying the stunning rug beneath her feet when the door was suddenly thrown open, and she turned around to find herself face to face with the man who had accosted her on the street outside Mrs. Tippleton's shop.

The man's jaw dropped, and then snapped shut as he recognized her. "You!" he exclaimed, his eyes narrowing with fury as he advanced toward her. "What are you doing here? How the devil did you get into my house?"

After the shock of traveling through time, Gillian would have sworn nothing could surprise her, but apparently she was mistaken. "Mr. Clares let me in," she said weakly, too stunned to form a coherent thought.

The incredible blue eyes she remembered all too well flashed with scorn as Dr. Culross stalked over to the rope pull. "Then he can just let you out again," he snapped, reaching for the rope. "You've caused enough mischief, and I'm dashed if I'll let you cause any more."

Gillian realized he was about to throw her out, and stumbled to her feet. "No! Wait!" she cried, dashing across the room to grab his arm. "You can't kick me out of here!"

He glared down at her. "Can I not?" He sneered, jerking his arm free. "You're mad if you think I'd let you anywhere *near* my daughter after what you've done!"

"I don't care about your daughter!" Gillian snapped, then

stopped when his eyes narrowed dangerously. "I mean," she amended hastily, "I'm not interested in being a governess. That was just a ruse to get in to see you."

His expression didn't change by so much as a flicker, but Gillian sensed he was no longer quite so angry. "If you didn't want the position, then why would you wish to see me?" he asked, his tone frankly suspicious as he studied her upturned face.

Gillian nervously wet her lip, her heart pounding in terror of the huge risk she was about to take. "I . . . the first time we met, you . . . you asked me where I got my watch," she stammered, forcing herself to meet his eyes. "Do you remember?"

His gaze flicked to the watch hanging about her neck, and then he raised his eyes again. "I remember," he said tersely.

She drew a deep breath to steady herself. "Instead of asking where I got it, I think it would be better if you asked me *when.*"

He looked startled, then gravely inclined his head. "Very well," he said slowly, "when did you get the watch?"

She straightened her shoulders, her chin coming up as she answered her own question. "June 10, 1995."

Four

Dr. Ian Culross stared at his beautiful visitor in disbelief. "You're mad," he whispered, his voice shaking as his thoughts flew to Deidre, playing peacefully in her room. He did not think the woman dangerous, but then he had not thought her mad, either.

Seeing the expression on his face, Gillian turned away with a heavy sigh. "I wish I were," she said, rubbing her forehead with a weary hand. "Believe me, being crazy would be preferable to being here."

"Here?" Ian asked, brows wrinkling as he struggled to follow her twisted logic.

"In the past . . . or the present . . . whatever," Gillian gestured helplessly with her hand, realizing she was right back where she started. Since that first night when she'd lain awake sobbing, she remained perilously close to tears, and it took all of her strength not to give in to them completely.

It was watching her fighting those tears that succeeded in relieving the worst of Ian's fears. Mad, she might be, but he would wager his last pound she meant no one any harm. Laying a gentle hand on her arm he began leading her to the settee. "You wish me to believe you are from the future? From 1995?" he asked, wondering if he should send for his good friend, Charles Mawton. Charles was a physician who specialized in treating cases of hysteria, and if anyone could help this poor woman, it was he.

Sensing she was being humored, Gillian whirled back around to face him. "Do you think I don't know what this sounds like?" she raged, deciding she had nothing to lose by telling him the rest of it. "How do you think I felt when I realized I was sent back in time? That this isn't some kind of bizarre theme park?"

"Theme park?" Ian was at a loss, once again.

"I . . ." she paused, then shook her head. "Never mind," she said, her shoulders drooping in defeat. "You'd really think I was insane if I tried explaining Disneyland to you." She sighed again, searching for the words that would somehow convince him.

"Look," she said, forcing herself to meet his gaze, "I don't know how I can make you understand, but I *am* from 1995, and I don't have any idea how I got here. All I know is I want to go home, and you're the only lead I've got."

"Me?" He exclaimed, beginning to wonder if *he* was the mad one. "How can I how help you?"

Before she could answer, there was a tap on the door and Clares walked in the room, his expression censorious as he saw his master and Gillian standing close together. "Is everything all right, doctor?" he asked, his tone making it obvious he was hoping it was not.

Realizing he was treading dangerously close to impropriety, Ian took a hasty step back from the woman. "Yes, Clares, everything is fine, thank you," he said, struggling for a calm that seemed just beyond his reach. "You may go now."

Clares was far too well trained to display so much as a flicker of disappointment. "As you wish, sir," he said, executing a deep bow as he began backing out of the room.

Ian hesitated a moment. "Clares, wait!"

"Yes, sir?" The butler shot him a hopeful look.

Ian studied his visitor's white face. "Have Mrs. Cookson prepare a tray for us," he ordered, knowing he was risking scandal. "Miss . . ." he glanced at her for assistance, unable to recall her name.

"Brooke," Gillian supplied, hope beginning to stir in her heart. She'd been certain the doctor would order her tossed from the house, but if he was willing to hear her out, there was still a chance he would agree to help her.

"Miss Brooke has agreed to join me for a cup of tea," he said, turning back to Clares. "Be so good as to fetch it."

A spark of what might have been emotion flared in Clares's

eyes and was gone. "Very good, doctor," he said, shooting Gillian a wary look. "Er . . . will Miss Brooke be joining staff?"

Ian also glanced at Miss Brooke, never so unsure of anything in his entire life. "I'm not certain, Clares," he answered heavily, truthfully. "The tea, if you please."

When they were alone once more, Ian crossed the room to the cellaret and poured himself a healthy dose of brandy. He did not usually indulge in strong spirits so early in the day, but then, he did not often meet a lady claiming to be from the future. He felt a burning excitement shimmer through him at the possibility. Feeling her gaze upon him, he glanced up to find her watching him with wide, gray eyes.

"You must forgive me, Miss Brooke," he drawled, gesturing with his glass, "but I fear I am at something of a loss. The prospect of speaking with a traveler through time has somewhat overset me."

"Time traveler," Gillian said, thinking he sounded like a sexy David Niven when he spoke like that. In the next moment she was shaking her head at herself for indulging in such idiotic fantasizing when her entire life was hanging in the balance.

"Madam?"

"The correct term is time traveler . . . I think," she said, struggling to recall every episode of *Star Trek* she'd ever seen.

Ian set his glass down with a thump. "Such things are possible in the future?" he demanded, wide-eyed at the thought.

Gillian's cheeks grew red at the misunderstanding. "Well, maybe in the distant future . . . *my* future," she said, feeling foolish. "I was speaking metamorphically. Time travel is mostly science fiction at the moment, but some day . . ."

Ian wondered what science fiction might be, but decided to save that particular question for another time. He retrieved his glass from the sideboard and took another sip, his expression thoughtful as he considered what she had just told him.

"If what you are telling me of yourself is true, Miss Brooke," he said, fixing her with a measuring look, "one may only assume that *some day* is now. You said you have no idea how you came to be in this time." Before she could speak he added, "but surely you must have *some* notion. Tell me precisely what happened."

Gillian, who'd had several days to consider the mechanics of the situation, did just that, telling him everything she could remember about her fateful visit to the small antique shop. He frowned several times, and when she took off her watch and handed it to him, he looked particularly grim, but he never interrupted her. When she finished speaking, he was holding the watch cradled in the palm of his hand.

"I bought this for Lydia to celebrate our fifth anniversary," he said absently, rubbing his thumb over the face of the watch. "When it vanished, I thought it lost forever. I suppose that is why I was so shocked when I saw you wearing it."

"Whoever stole it must have hocked it," Gillian said, feeling a pang of sympathy at the sad expression on his face. "I mean, I guess that's how it ended up at Mrs. Tippleton's. Although, after a hundred forty years, I suppose it really doesn't matter."

He raised his gaze and gave her a confused look. "The watch was never stolen."

"But you just said it vanished—"

"Yes," he interrupted, the watch still held tightly in his hand. *"Vanished.* One moment it was in the bell jar I was using as a conductor, and the next, it was gone."

She digested his words and all they meant in silence. "When did this happen?" she asked, struggling to believe that like her, the watch had somehow passed through time. And not once, but twice. It was an incredible thought.

"Three years ago."

She frowned at the stark reply, and then remembered what Miss Merriam had said about his losing his wife at about the same time. She wondered if the two events were somehow related, and then decided they must be. What else but a terrible tragedy would make a man want to manipulate time?

The maid arriving with the tea cart provided a much needed relief, and Gillian was somewhat embarrassed when it became obvious she was expected to serve. Hoping she didn't make too big a muddle of it, she managed to pour them each a cup without disgracing herself. She thought she'd succeeded, until she raised her head to find Dr. Culross watching her with those magnetic blue eyes.

"I take it tea is not consumed in the future," he commented, raising his cup to his lips. "Pity. As a beverage, it has much to recommend it."

Gillian glowered at him, her cheeks pinking because he had been snide enough to comment on her awkwardness.

"I'm an American," she muttered, taking a quick sip of her own tea. "We drink pop."

"Pop?" He frowned over the unfamiliar word.

"Yes," she began, then shook her head again. "Never mind, it would take too long to explain. But if it will help ease your mind, tea is still served in England; although they charge an arm and a leg for it. I had a tea just like this at a hotel in Mayfair, and it cost over fifteen pounds."

He choked on the mouthful he had just taken. "Fifteen pounds?" he wheezed, hastily setting down his cup. "For tea? Good heavens, that's ridiculous!"

Gillian gave him a smug smile. "That's what I said, but those fancy hotels really hose the tourists."

He tried to imagine why someone would wish to put hose on tourists, and then decided it was of no importance. He was only now coming to the unimaginable conclusion that he was actually taking tea with a visitor from another time, and he realized he had a thousand different questions. But before committing himself irrevocably, he thought it might be best to test the veracity of her claim. He wasn't entirely convinced she wasn't a Bedlamite, and a few pertinent queries seemed in order. He took another sip as he marshalled his thoughts.

"If you are indeed from 1995," he remarked, idly crossing one foot over the other, "I daresay there is a great deal you could tell me about the future . . . or the past, as the case may be. Where would you like to start?"

Gillian stirred uncomfortably in her chair. Although not a huge fan of science fiction, she'd seen and read enough of it to know that time travelers weren't supposed to mess with past events. The old conundrum about going back in the past and killing the person who would be her grandfather came to mind, and after a thoughtful pause she said, "I really can't tell you about the immediate future," she said, praying she wasn't cutting her own throat. "Number one, because I'm American, and even though I'm something of a Victoriana nut, British history was never my forte. And number two . . ." she hesitated, choosing her next words with care.

"Number two?" He pressed gently.

She set her own cup down and met his skeptical gaze with cool conviction. "Number two, because telling you of the future could alter it, and if I alter it even a little, I could change everything that ever was or ever will be."

Ian felt a frisson of excitement shoot down his spine. Her remark was eerily close to his own hypothesis; a hypothesis he had never discussed with anyone for fear of being ridiculed. So the past and the future were separate halves of an intricate whole, he mused, his mercurial mind racing off in another direction. If that was indeed the case, then perhaps time could eventually be controlled or even harnessed, as vaporous gas was being harnessed to provide light. Perhaps—he broke off the intriguing line of thought when he saw her frowning at him in obvious concern. Promising to jot down his theories in his work book, he picked up his cup and took another sip.

"An intriguing possibility, and one I will accept, for now," he said, leaning back in his chair to study her. "Since you can not tell me of the immediate future, tell me what will happen a hundred years from now That should not alter the past or the future, as I will be dead long before it becomes a reality."

Gillian paused and then began cautiously to tell him of the horrors of two world wars yet to be, seeing the sadness on his face when she spoke of the Blitz. She also told him of the wonders of modern medicine and television, eagerly describing for him a hot July evening in 1969 when Neil Armstrong took a small step for all of mankind.

"A man on the moon," Ian said, his voice full of awe as he tried to imagine such a thing. "It seems impossible."

"Actually, within this century an Englishman will write a book about a flight to the moon," she said, smiling as she remembered reading H.G. Wells in high school. "He'll also write about a time machine; something I'd always thought of as pretty far-fetched . . . until now." She ventured a slight smile.

"My Lord!" Ian's teacup rattled as he suddenly sat forward. "It's all true, then! You *are* from the future!"

"That's what I've been trying to tell you!" Gillian exclaimed, torn between exasperation and exultation. She'd finally been able to convince someone of the truth, but he didn't seem willing to do anything about it.

"But do you know what this means?" Ian rose to his feet, his teacup forgotten as he began pacing. "If my charging the watch with electricity somehow affected time by bringing *you* back, then it logically follows it can be affected to bring someone else forward in time!"

"I know that!" Gillian snapped, rising to face him. "That's why I came to you. I want you to do whatever you did, and send me home. Now, are you going to do it, or not?"

Ian stopped pacing, taken somewhat aback by the asperity in her voice. "Certainly I shall endeavor to return you to your own time, Miss Brooke," he said, fairly insulted she should question his integrity. "If I am correct, and my experimentation with the watch is responsible for your presence here, then it is only proper I should do everything in my power to assist you."

"Good."

"Your coming here under the guise of applying for a post as a governess was most fortuitous," Ian continued, ignoring the sarcasm in her voice, "it will allow you to remain with me without eliciting undo suspicions from my neighbors."

"Undo suspicions?" Gillian repeated incredulously.

He gave her an admonishing look. "Naturally, as a widower I could not allow an unmarried female to reside under my roof without her being either a servant or a relative. You are unmarried?" He added, scowling as he considered the matter.

She paused, trying to remember how Victorians felt about divorce. They weren't overly fond of it, as she recalled. "Yes," she admitted, deciding it was the truth. "But—"

"Then there is no impediment, is there?" He gave her a smile which, under any other circumstances, would have had her taking definite notice.

"Impediment to what?" Gillian asked, beginning to feel as bewildered as she had when she'd first been thrust back in time.

"Impediment to our renewing the experiments, of course," Ian said, crossing the room to summon the butler.

Clares must have been listening at the door, because Ian's hand had scarce released the rope pull before he was bowing his way into the room.

"Yes, doctor?" he intoned, dark eyes watchful as he glanced at Gillian.

"Ah, Clares, there you are," Ian gave him a pleased smile. "Be so good as to show Miss Brooke to her room, will you? She has decided to join us—for the time being, that is." And he gave a chuckle that made Clares doubt for his employer's sanity.

Five

Gillian's things were delivered while she and Dr. Culross were closeted in his study going over the notes from his original experiment. His drive and intelligence amazed her, and she thought it a pity he would be an old man before the things he theorized about became a part of everyday life.

"Well, no one *really* understands how electricity works," she said at one point, feeling decidedly harassed by his countless questions. She'd made the mistake of telling him electricity was the primary source of power in the next century, and he'd been plaguing her for explanations ever since.

"But surely someone must have some notion as to its application," Ian protested, frowning in disapproval that citizens of the future should be so hopelessly ignorant.

"Sure, scientists and the power companies. The rest of us just hit the switch and hope for the best. It's like TV; it either works, or it doesn't."

Since she'd already explained television to him, he allowed her comment to pass without remark, although he made a mental note to quiz her on the matter later. While they continued talking, he gave her a curious glance, wondering if she was a true representative of the women of her time. If so, he much envied the men of the future.

It was not that she was beautiful, he decided with the objectivity that served him so well as a scientist. She was taller and more slender than most of the ladies he saw on the streets, and he supposed her light brown hair and gray eyes could be accounted as lovely, but there was something more, something else that attracted him to her more than he considered proper.

Perhaps it was her confidence, he thought, tapping a finger on the polished surface of his desk as he continued studying her. She'd reluctantly told him women of her time voted, held elected office, even, he recalled with an inner shudder, served in the army in times of war, so he supposed that would explain her cool insouciance. As a gentleman, he'd been raised to believe that ladies were the weaker sex, and ought to be protected from the ill winds of the world. God knew he'd tried his best to protect Lydia, for all the good it had done. As they always did, thoughts of his late wife made his lips tighten in pain.

Gillian saw the grim look on his face and wondered what had put it there. He was such an enigma, she thought, hiding a quick smile. Her fault, she supposed. She'd always assumed men of another age would be simpler and easier to understand than the men of her own time.

Ian sensed her watching him, and stirred restlessly in his chair. "I will review my studies at the laboratory tomorrow," he said briskly, not quite meeting her eyes. "In the meanwhile, I will introduce you to Deidre." He did meet her eyes then, his expression implacable. "Naturally I must ask that you not tell her the truth about yourself. It would only confuse her."

Gillian flashed him an impatient look. Apparently men of all times were the same, she decided, her chin lifting with pride. They were all jerks. "Give me credit for having a few functioning brain cells, Doctor," she said, her voice edged with irritation. "I won't tell her a thing without your permission."

Her incivility made Ian blink in astonishment. "There is no need to be so snappish, Miss Brooke," he protested, his own temper beginning to stir. "I was but making an imminently sensible suggestion."

"You were treating me like I didn't have a brain in my head," Gillian corrected, rising to her feet to challenge him. "I don't like it. My ex-husband used to do that to me, and—"

"Your husband?" Ian surged to his feet to gape at her. "You told me you were unwed!"

Gillian cursed herself for letting her temper get the better of her. "I am, now," she said, trying to repair the damage she'd already done. "I'm divorced—a common state of affairs in 1995, so you don't need to look at me like I'm some kind of Jezebel."

Ian sat back down, wondering how many more shocks he was supposed to endure. To him, divorce was a disgrace beyond comprehension, and it was several seconds before he could trust himself to speak. "I hope I have not given the impression I regard you so slightly," he said, choosing his words carefully as he shifted his beliefs to accept what she had told him. "But you must do me the courtesy of allowing me time to consider what you have said. You must admit it is . . . disquieting."

Annoyed as she was, Gillian supposed she could concede his point; not that she intended admitting as much, she decided with a flash of rare obstinacy. "As you wish," she said, finding it safer to fall into the rigid propriety of the period. "Now if you'll excuse me, I'd like to go to my rooms and lie down for a while. I'll meet Deidre tomorrow, if that's all right with you?" She lifted her eyebrow in unconscious challenge.

"Tomorrow would be fine," Ian agreed gravely, wondering if he was making a mistake in exposing his young daughter to such a recalcitrant creature.

Gillian inclined her head and started toward the door. Her hand was closing on the handle when she suddenly thought of something, and turned to face him. "Oh, Doctor?" she drawled, sending him a sweet smile. "Do you remember I told you women could be elected to public office?"

"Yes," he said warily, not certain he trusted either her smile or the sugary note in her voice.

"One will be elected Prime Minister of England. Goodbye," and she was gone before he could close his mouth.

Gillian's first full day in Ian's household was spent settling in her new rooms and becoming acquainted with her charge. Deidre Culross was a delight—a lively six-year-old with her father's luminous blue eyes and a mop of wild red hair she had inherited from her mother. Gillian had always longed for a little girl of her own, and she found it painfully easy to lose her heart to the enchanting chatterbox.

"*Grandmeré* says children ought to be seen and not heard," she confided to Gillian within minutes of their meeting. "But Papa says it might be better if *Grandmeré* wasn't seen or heard altogether. They don't like each other, you know." She added this last with a confiding whisper.

"It sounds like it," Gillian agreed, wondering if a proper Victorian governess would have admonished the little girl for gossiping. Ah what the heck, she decided a few minutes later as Deidre went on to tell her about the parlor maid and the footman kissing in the hallway. Everyone knew how emotionally screwed up the Victorians were. It would probably do the kid a world of good to get some good ol' 60s laid-back values.

They spent the morning going over the assignments drawn up by Deidre's last governess, and Gillian had to bite her tongue to keep from making some pithy comment on what Deidre was being taught. It made her think of her cousin, a college professor and a feminist who had done her thesis on sexism in basal readers. Leslie would have a stroke if she saw some of this crap, she thought, setting one particularly cloying book aside.

"Of course, being a wife and a mother are important things," she said, giving Deidre an encouraging smile. "But sometimes I think it might be fun to be other things, as well. Wouldn't you like to be an explorer or a scientist?"

Deidre's blue eyes grew wide. "Like Papa, do you mean?"

Before she could stop it, an image of Ian Culross looking amazingly sexy despite his stuffy black jacket and old-fashioned cravat flashed into Gillian's mind. "Sure," she answered with false brightness. "Wouldn't that be fun?"

Deidre cocked her head to one side. "I suppose," she said, her tone thoughtful. "But I am a girl. Girls can't be scientists; can they?"

It was on the tip of Gillian's tongue to tell her girls could be whatever they wanted to be, but then she remembered that in this time and place, they weren't even regarded as citizens. "Well, maybe not a *real* scientist," she temporized, "but we could study science, if you'd like. What do you think? Wouldn't that be better than studying French and sewing all day?"

Like any child, Deidre was eager to try anything new, and they spent the rest of the morning going over the few books on nature Gillian could find in the schoolroom. The little girl was as sharp as a tack, and it quickly became apparent that she'd inherited more than her father's sky-blue eyes.

"That's very good, Deidre," Gillian said, praising her young pupil for correctly naming some of the more common elements. "Your father will be so proud when I tell him what a good student you are."

That first day set the course for those that followed, and by the end of the week Gillian realized Deidre's mind had outstripped the meager contents of their small library. After a great deal of soul-searching, she decided it was time to go to Ian . . . Dr. Culross, she corrected, determined to follow the rules of her new society, and ask him for some new books. After all, she reasoned coolly, how could he possibly object to furthering his own daughter's education?

She learned from a still disapproving Clares that Ian was hard at work in his study, but as he'd already given her permission to enter whenever she needed to speak with him. She walked in after a quick tap on the door. "Doctor, I'm sorry to disturb you, but I——" she stopped abruptly, her eyes widening when she saw him.

Ian turned at her entrance, eyebrows raising at the expression on her face. "Is something wrong, Miss Brooke?"

"I . . . you . . . you aren't wearing your jacket," Gillian stammered, and then blushed in embarrassment. God, she sounded like one of those ditzy women in Deidre's lesson books, she thought struggling for control.

Ian felt his own cheeks redden at being caught in his shirt-sleeves, but he sternly suppressed his reaction. "It is rather warm today, and I saw no harm in being comfortable while I work. However, if you are offended . . ." he began reaching for his jacket.

"No!" She held up a hand to stop him. "Really, it's all right, I was just surprised, that's all. And I know what you mean about it being hot; I'm roasting." she plucked at the high neckline of her gown for emphasis.

Ian wasn't entirely convinced. "If you are certain," he said, reluctantly lowering his arm. He remembered some of their earlier conversations about her life in the late twentieth century, and shot her a confused look. "Do the men of your time not dress more casually in the heat?" he asked curiously.

Gillian thought of thong bikinis and nude beaches and managed a weak smile. "Oh, they've been known to loosen their ties every now and again," she said, then quickly told him the reason behind her visit. When she finished, he was looking more perplexed than ever.

"But why would Deidre need any more books?" he asked, frowning slightly. "Miss Lancaster, her former governess, bought several boxes of books shortly before leaving us. Deidre could hardly have read them all."

Gillian, who had been expecting an immediate agreement, gave him an indignant scowl. "Why not?" she demanded, placing her fists on her hips. "She's your daughter, isn't she?"

Ian stiffened at once. "What is that supposed to mean?"

Gillian realized she had offended him, and set out to correct the mistake. "It means Deidre is bright—really bright," she said, her voice more even. "And she needs more of a challenge than those stupid books can give her."

Ian grew even more rigid. "Those stupid books are the best money can buy," he said, smarting under her hint that he was somehow derelict in his duties as a parent.

Gillian gave up attempting to placate him. "They're crap . . . uh . . . drek," she amended hastily. "Have you read any of them? I know she's only six, but giving Deidre those gaggy improving books is like giving Einstein a Dick and Jane reader!"

"Einstein?" Ian was not familiar with the name.

"A scientist; one of the most brilliant men who ever lived," Gillian explained, and then sighed. "My point is that Deidre is fascinated with science, and none of those books Miss Lancaster bought even mentions it. All I'm asking is that you let me order some for her."

Ian relaxed as soon as he realized her only concern was his

daughter's well-being. "I suppose that would be all right," he said after a thoughtful pause. "I want the best for my daughter, and if you think new books will be of benefit to her, then you must by all means order them. She is interested in science?" He added this last with a smile, pleased by the notion.

"She loves it," Gillian assured him, smiling at his pleasure. "Like I said, she's your daughter. I just wish this was a few decades from now—I could take her to the Museum of Natural History. She'd love it."

Her mention of a museum made him remember something, and he gave her another searching look. "Actually, Miss Brooke," he said, clearing his throat uncertainly, "I was going to suggest this earlier, but I got so caught up in my calculations I quite forgot. Do you think she would enjoying seeing the Exhibition?"

Gillian's eyes lit with interest. "The Royal One?" she asked, thinking of the many articles she'd read in the papers praising the display of science and domestic technology.

He was amused by her eagerness. "Is there another?"

"Not that I know of," she said, too excited to take offense at his indulgent tone. "Oh Ian . . . Dr. Culross, I mean, that would be wonderful! She'd have a blast."

The euphemism pleased him, almost as much as her use of his Christian name. "I take that to mean she would not find the prospect displeasing," he teased, his eyes dancing as he studied her face. She was so animated, he thought, so honest in her every thought and emotion. So different than Lydia, who hid every devious thought behind a sweetly smiling facade . . . his smile vanished at the thought as if it had never been.

"She'll be in seventh heaven," Gillian replied; seeing once more the bleakness stealing into his eyes. "When will you be taking her?"

"I thought to take her . . . and you there tomorrow, provided I am able to obtain vouchers," Ian said, forcing the dark memories from his mind. "If you wish to go, that is," he added, lifting his eyebrow questioningly.

"Are you kidding?" she gave him an incredulous look. "I wouldn't miss it for the world!"

"Then we shall go," he said decisively, his spirits lifting. She had verbally shown him much of the world from which she came, and he found he was eager to return the favor. Suddenly he was as anxious as a schoolboy anticipating Christmas Day, and he could not wait for the morrow.

Six

The morning was hot and sunny when Gillian finally awoke. Last night had been a difficult one for her, and sleep had been as elusive as a chimera. Although she'd done her best to keep thoughts of the future and those she'd left there at bay, last night those troubling worries had come rushing in, and she'd spent most of the night staring at the ceiling.

She wondered if she'd been reported missing yet, and what her family would do about it. Her father would probably start calling his congressman, while her step-mother would shake her head and say she hadn't expected anything else. Her friends and her cousin would worry the most, and she wished there was some way to let them know she was all right.

A tearful smile touched her lips as she imagined their reaction when she suddenly reappeared. She couldn't tell them what happened, of course, she decided, wiping a tear from her eye with the corner of the sheet. Not unless she wanted to land on the front pages of the tabloids, that is. She figured time travelers must rate right up there with crop circles and the latest dirt on the royal family.

She was still brooding about her family when the door to her room was flung open, and a red-haired whirlwind flew across the floor and landed on her bed.

"Are you awake, Miss Brooke?" Deidre demanded hopefully, bouncing up and down on the mattress. "Papa says we can have breakfast together if you are awake!"

Gillian smiled at the little girl's excited chatter. "I'm awake, sweetie," she said, giving a tangled curl a gentle tug. Deidre was wearing a white starched dress tied about the waist with a yellow ribbon, and Gillian thought she looked as adorable as one of the porcelain dolls her neighbor collected.

"I have been up for *hours!*" Deidre informed her proudly, still bouncing up and down. "I have played with my dolls, and the cards *Grandmeré* sent me, and I even did my sums."

"Sounds like you've had a busy morning," Gillian gave her an impromptu hug and then set her gently to one side. "Now, why don't you skedaddle while I get dressed?"

"Skedaddle?" Deidre's brows met in a perfect imitation of her father's puzzled frown as she stumbled over the unfamiliar word.

"An American word," Gillian explained, feeling a sudden burst of affection for the little girl flooding her heart. "It means move it."

"Oh!" Deidre gave her a bright smile, and then leapt down from the bed and raced for the door, calling out for the maid as she ran. "Annie! Annie! I know an American word!"

Thirty minutes later Gillian was walking into the morning room struggling to draw a deep breath. She and the middleaged maid who had been assigned to her had all but come to blows over how tight to lace her corset, and although a compromise of sorts had been reached, Gillian still felt as if she was being slowly cut in half. Some of her discomfort must have shown, because Ian's face was full of concern as he rose to greet her.

"Is everything all right, Miss Brooke?" he asked, his blue eyes searching her face. "You look a trifle unwell."

Gillian wondered what he would say if she told him her underwear was killing her, and managed a polite smile. "It's just the weather," she said, taking her seat with care. "I can't believe how hot it is, and it's barely ten o'clock."

Ian resumed his seat, sensing she was being less than honest with him. "Yes, it is unseasonably warm," he agreed, signaling the footman to begin serving them. "Perhaps we should put off our visit to the Exhibition until it is cooler?"

Gillian saw Deidre's bottom lip tremble and quickly shook her head. "No, there's no need for that," she said in a firm voice, picking up her napkin and laying it on her lap. "I'm sure I'll be fine once I've eaten something."

Ian merely raised his eyebrow and they began eating, each lost in their private thoughts. It was impossible to eat in silence, of course, as a wound-up Deidre kept up an endless stream of questions and comments. Annie had said the queen would be at the Exhibition, would she be wearing her crown? Why not? What good was it to be queen if one didn't get to wear one's crown? By the end of the meal Ian's head was reeling, and after his daughter had dashed off to wash her hands, he flashed Miss Brooke an apologetic smile.

"You must forgive me, Miss Brooke, for allowing my daughter to prattle on so," he said, grateful the maids and footmen had withdrawn to leave them alone. "I do tend to overindulge her, and I fear she may be becoming spoiled. I trust she has not given you a horror of her?"

"Oh, no, Deidre is an angel!" Gillian assured him, thinking of some of the obnoxious brats she'd seen in restaurants. "And as for your overindulging her, I wouldn't worry. You're just a little ahead of your time, that's all."

Ian considered that a moment, and then smiled. "Thank you, ma'am. I must admit I am reassured to know I am doing Deidre no harm. And I will also own to being pleased that my advanced methods meet with your approval. I have always regarded myself as a progressive thinker."

Gillian's heart gave a skip at that warm and all too intimate smile. To cover her confusion, she lowered her gaze to the table and began fiddling with her teacup. "Speaking of progress, how are your experiments coming?" she asked in a falsely bright tone. "Any luck?"

Ian thought of the many frustrating hours he'd spent in his lab and gave a disheartened sigh. "Not as yet," he admitted, hating the feeling that he was disappointing her. "I have repeated the experiment numerous times, recreating it to the smallest detail, and yet I seem unable to get the same results." He paused a moment and then added, "I have been thinking of confiding my difficulties to Dr. Faraday. The man is a genius, and if anyone can be of assistance, it is he."

That brought Gillian's head snapping up, and she met his somber gaze. "Do you think that's a good idea?" she asked, and then bit her lip, fearing he would think she was criticizing him. "I mean," she amended, "if you tell him about the time travel thing, wouldn't you have to tell him about *me* as well?"

Ian had already weighed the danger of that and decided it was a risk they would have to take. "I fear there is no other way," he said grimly. "If we have any hope of returning to your own time, we will need help. And you needn't worry he would tell anyone of you; the man is renowned for being taciturn."

Considering she'd never heard of a Victorian time traveler, Gillian was willing to concede the point. And at any rate, it wasn't the possibility of discovery that had her hesitating. It was the sudden and shocking realization that she wasn't so sure she *wanted* to go back. After last night's bout with despair, the idea was enough to jolt her, and she quickly raised her head to find him watching her.

"Well, if you're sure you can trust him, I guess it would be all right," she said, relieved to hear Deidre returning. "I just hope he doesn't think you've gone off the deep-end, and dismiss you."

Ian wondered if going off the deep-end meant what he thought it might, and decided it was an apt description for what was happening to him. If ever a man could be said to be in over his head and sinking fast, he admitted with a sigh, it was him.

Despite her turbulent emotions Gillian enjoyed the short ride to Hyde Park and the site of the Exhibition. This was the first time she'd been farther than Picadilly Street since moving into Ian's house, and it was all she could do not to press her nose against the window of the carriage he'd rented for the occasion.

Ian watched her indulgently, enjoying her reactions to everything about her. "This must be quite different than what you are accustomed to," he remarked, leaning back against the cushioned seat and smiling at her obvious excitement.

Gillian saw a wagon, heavily laden with wine barrels, cut in front of a cart stacked high with boxes. "Oh, I don't know about that," she remarked as the cart driver shook an angry fist and shouted a string of curses at the wagon. She'd been back in time for a little over a week, and she was still amazed to discover that while some things seemed completely alien to her, others were quite familiar.

It was just the trappings, she decided, a rueful grin touching her lips as she saw a man waving a sign denouncing Free Trade. Take away the horses and carriages and the clothing, and the entire scene could easily fit into the 1995 London she had first seen. She wondered if in another one hundred forty-four years beyond 1995 time the same thing would apply.

Ian remained silent, content to sit back and study Gillian as she chatted gaily with Deidre. In her modest gown of forest-green and black plaid, a matching bonnet perched on her curls, and a black shawl of Norwich silk draped over her shoulders, she looked much like the other ladies they passed on the streets. And yet, there was an undefinable something that set her apart from the others. A something that had her creeping into his thoughts at the oddest times of day, and stealing into his most secret dreams at night . . .

The admission startled him, filling him with frustration and shame. Gillian—he could now admit he no longer thought of her as Miss Brooke—was a guest in his home; a traveler from another time and place who was dependent upon him for safety. The thoughts he harbored about her did neither of them credit, and he vowed he would keep his desires to himself.

Gillian's first glimpse of the soaring expanse of glass and steel that was the Crystal Palace had her jaw dropping in amazement. She tilted back her head, trying to take in everything all at once. "It's beautiful!" she exclaimed, eyes wide with delight as she gazed all about her. "This is nothing like I expected it would be!"

"And pray, what were you expecting?" Ian teased, tucking her hand beneath his arm as he took Deidre's hand. He'd already had a stern word with his exuberant daughter, warning her that if she dashed off just once, the excursion would end then and there.

"Something heavier, more ornate," Gillian answered vaguely, refraining from telling him that in her time, "Victorian" was often synonymous with hopelessly ugly.

Ian presented their passes to the officer in the booth, and they walked through the arched glass doors. The sheer size of the place astounded Gillian, but what impressed her most was the sight of three huge elm trees that towered above the floor. She mentioned this to Ian, and he gave a wise nod.

"You have a Colonel Sibthorp to thank for that," he said, giving the trees a speculative look. "He kicked up such a dust in Parliament about them that Mr. Paxton, the architect, was forced to design a transept to enclose them."

"Papa," Deidre tugged on her father's sleeve, clearly bored with all this talk of trees, "might we go see the elephant now?"

"Elephant?"

Ian smiled at the expression on Gillian's face. "A stuffed one only," he said, giving her hand a gentle squeeze as they began pushing their way through the crowds choking the wide aisles. "It comes all the way from the museum at Saffron Walden, so mind that you give it its proper due."

They did see the elephant, and several other things as well, including the Hope Diamond. Its owner had brought it to show the queen, and Gillian gazed at it so wistfully that Ian was unable to hold back a chuckle as he led her away.

"I know I promised you a souvenir, ma'am," he teased, "but I fear my pockets are not quite so deep as that."

Gillian gave the deep-blue hued stone a final gaze over her shoulder. "That's all right," she said with a sad sigh, "it's got a curse on it anyway."

There were a dozen other sights to dazzle the eye, and Gillian soon forgot all about the diamond. It was really like a World's Fair, she decided, as they walked past a display of statuary from Belgium. It was obvious a great deal of work had gone into its planning, and she knew most of the credit lay with Prince Albert, the queen's consort. It appeared there was a lot more to the old boy than a can of pipe tobacco, she thought, then came to an abrupt halt when a familiar object caught her eye.

Ian felt her stop, and was about to ask her if she wished any refreshment when he saw the tears shimmering in her soft gray eyes. "Gillian!" he exclaimed, unmindful of the crowds as he lay a gentle hand on her cheek. "What is it? What is wrong?"

Gillian blinked rapidly, her breath hitching in her chest as she struggled for control. "It's my flag," she said, her voice breaking. "It's my country's flag."

Ian gazed up at the red and white striped flag with its rows of stars on a blue field, and he felt his heart constrict with pity. He'd always felt he understood what she must feel to be so far away from all that was dear and familiar to her, but until this very moment he hadn't fully comprehended the enormity of her suffering. His hand closed convulsively on her chin.

"Gillian, I—"

"Problem, sir?" One of the strolling constables had paused in front of them, his sharp gaze resting on Gillian's tear-stained face with professional interest.

"Not at all, officer," Ian replied, slipping a protective arm about Gillian's shoulder. "My wife is an American, and she is simply overcome at seeing the flags."

Gillian stiffened, shocked as much by Ian's possessive touch as by hearing herself referred to as his wife. She gave a loud sniff, trying to force her frozen brain to function. "I . . . yes," she stammered, her emotions as wildly chaotic as her thoughts. "It seems forever since I left, and I suppose I am more than a little homesick."

"No explanation necessary, mum," the mustachioed officer replied with a toothy grin. "I'm from the West Country meself, and many's the time a lark's song has brought a tear to me eye. Enjoy the exhibition." He touched his fingers to his hat in a brief salute and then wandered away.

Fearful they had already attracted undo attention, Ian hustled them toward the exit, ignoring Deidre's vociferous protest that she wished to stay to see the queen. Several minutes later he had them safely bundled in the back of a passing hack, but if he thought that was the end of the matter, he had not reckoned with an inquisitive six-year-old with very big ears.

"Papa! Are you and Miss Brooke married?" Deidre exclaimed before the coach had scarce pulled away from the curb.

Ian's cheeks flushed a dull red at his daughter's probing demand. He had no idea what madness had made him claim Gillian as his wife, but he was already regretting the impulsive slip of the tongue. "No, Deidre, we are not," he said between clenched teeth, fervently wishing himself elsewhere.

"But I *heard* you!" Deidre insisted, red curls bobbing as she bounced up and down on the seat. "You told that police officer Miss Brooke was your wife!"

Ian's flush deepened, and he stole a quick glance at Gillian's face. "You are mistaken," he informed his daughter curtly, wondering what thoughts were hidden behind Gillian's frozen expression. "Now, let us hear no more of this."

"But—"

"Deidre!" Ian's voice was unusually sharp. "I said no more!"

Deidre's lip protruded in a mulish pout as she flung herself against the plush cushions. "Well, I heard you!" she repeated, folding her arms across her chest. "And if you and Miss Brooke are not married, then that means you lied to that policeman. *Grandmeré* told me if you lie to the police, they take you away and lock you up in the tower for a hundred years!"

Ian laid his head against the seat and closed his eyes in weary defeat. "A hundred years," he told Deidre with a heavy sigh, "ought to be just about right."

Seven

The next three weeks passed quickly for Gillian. Since attending the Exhibition, Ian saw that she got out several times a week, and soon she was as familiar with Victorian London as she'd been with her hometown of Portland, Oregon. At first the dirt and grinding poverty appalled her, but she reluctantly came to accept them, reminding herself that homelessness and hunger were problems even in her world.

As the days progressed it became more obvious that Ian's attempts to return her to her own time weren't working, and she had to face the very real possibility she might never get back. She grieved to know her family must think her dead, and in a way, she supposed they were right. If she remained trapped in the nineteenth-century, she would be dead long before any of them had been born.

But if she mourned for what had been lost, she also rejoiced in all that she had found. She adored Deidre, loving her as much as if she were her own child, and nothing gave her greater pleasure than when the little girl came running into her room each morning excitedly calling her name. The thought of never seeing her grow into womanhood was painful—almost as painful as the thought of never seeing her father and friends again, and Gillian felt bitterly torn between the two times.

Then there was Deidre's father to consider. Ian haunted her nights, stirring feelings inside her that were as confusing as they were powerful. It was absurd; they hadn't exchanged so much as a single kiss, and yet she found herself drawn more and more to him. She tried telling herself it was mere desire, or even infatuation, but in her heart she feared it was a great deal more. It was like being swept back in time, she decided, and was human enough to resent the fact that once more she was at the whim of a force beyond her control.

When she'd been in his house for a little over a month, Ian surprised her by asking her to accompany him to his laboratory on the following morning. She must have looked as surprised as she felt, because he gave her one of his slow, teasing smiles.

"You seem shocked," he drawled, those blue eyes she spent far too much time fantasizing about dancing with laughter as he leaned against the doorjamb of the schoolroom. "Surely we haven't kept you so imprisoned that the very thought of freedom has rendered you speechless?"

Gillian shot him a resentful glare, wondering how he could attract and irritate her all in the same moment. Doug had never had that effect on her, and they had been married for over five years. "Of course not," she responded coolly, putting on the stiff mask of politeness she'd learned to don over the past few weeks. "It's just that I've come to think of your lab as the holiest of holies, and I'm surprised you're allowing a mere woman to darken its doorstep."

Her snappish reply made Ian's eyebrows climb in surprise. In the weeks since astounding him with her true identity, Gillian had told him much of her world and the role women played in it. He knew the bounds his society placed on her occasionally chafed, but he'd thought she'd been adapting. Apparently he was mistaken, he decided, his stomach sinking at the realization.

"Not another lecture on Victorian chauvinism, I implore you," he teased, still amazed he could think of his own time as a historical period. "I realize you are not accustomed to such restraints, but that is no reason to condemn all of us out of hand. Besides, it may interest you to know that ladies have always been welcome to visit our Society."

Gillian recognized the truth of his words, but the resentment simmering inside her temporarily spilled over. "Yes *visit*," she said, emphasizing the word with an angry toss of her head. "But I bet it would be a different story if I got up on the podium and started lecturing your esteemed colleagues about black holes!"

Ian spared a quick glance at Deidre who was playing on the carpet nearby and doubtlessly eavesdropping. "Considering that neither they nor I have the slightest idea what a black hole might be, I daresay you are right," he said soothingly. "However, as it happens, I have a reason for asking you to join me tomorrow. Dr. Faraday wishes to meet you."

The news melted the last of Gillian's anger. "He does?"

Ian nodded, recalling the conversation he and his mentor had had earlier that afternoon. "Yes," he said, his gaze stealing once more to his daughter, "he feels our experiment may meet with greater success if you are there."

Gillian also glanced in Deidre's direction, her heart breaking as she realized that if the experiment succeeded, she would never see the little girl again. For a moment she wanted to tell him no, but she fought back the impulse, telling herself she had no other choice. "That would be fine, Doctor," she said, blinking back tears as she turned to face him. "What time should I be ready to leave?"

Her singular lack of enthusiasm shocked Ian almost as much as the tears he could see shimmering in her gray eyes. He'd have thought she would have leapt at the chance, however remote, of being returned to her own time. Indeed, had he not spent the past few weeks preparing himself for just such an eventuality? And yet, now she seemed reluctant to go. His heart pounded as he wondered what her reasons might be.

"Dr. Faraday likes to work on his special projects early in the morning, before others are about," he said, forcing his voice to remain cool. "Will eight o'clock be acceptable to you?"

Gillian closed her eyes against the wave of desolation washing over her. "Eight will be fine, Doctor," she said, opening her eyes to meet his somber blue gaze. "Will you be joining us this evening, or will you be dining out?

A daring plan suddenly leaped into Ian's mind, and much as he tried to reject it, he found he could not. He knew it was probably as ill-conceived a thing as he had ever done, but for the first time since Lydia's death, he knew he would follow his heart rather than his head.

"Actually, I am promised to attend the theatre," he said, his manner purposefully indifferent, "and I was wondering if perhaps you would care to join me? McCready will be doing *Macbeth* for the final time."

Gillian didn't have a clue who McCready was, and Macbeth was her least favorite of all of Shakespeare's plays, but she knew she couldn't resist spending what might be her last night in this time with Ian. "I would like that very much," she replied softly, her pulse racing with anticipation. "What time will we be leaving?"

Before he could answer, Deidre abandoned her toys on the floor and was standing beside him. "Might I come, too, Papa?" she asked, slipping her small hand into his and gazing up at him hopefully. "I shall be ever so good, I promise!"

Ian scooped his daughter up in his arms and deposited a regretful kiss on her rosy cheek. "I am sure you shall, sweetest," he said gently, "but children, however well-behaved, are not tolerated at the Haymarket. I am sorry."

Deidre pouted prettily. "May I go with you tomorrow morning, then?" she asked, her tone so wheedling that Ian instantly suspected that had been her real goal all along. Like mother, like daughter, he thought, and was ashamed of his own bitterness.

"No, you may not," he said firmly, dropping another kiss on her cheek before setting her down. "Now, run down to the kitchen and tell Janie I said you may have two biscuits for tea." He gave her backside a loving pat.

Deidre was evidently too practical to push her luck, because she dashed out of the room with a delighted squeal. Gillian watched her go, unaware of the tears sparkling behind her lashes.

"I'm going to miss her," she said, her breath catching in her throat.

"As she will miss you," Ian replied, aching to admit that he would miss her, as well. "But she will forget you soon, as she has forgotten her mother."

Gillian turned to him, her pain at leaving temporarily forgotten. "What makes you think she's forgotten her mother?"

The demand made Ian frown in surprise. "Because she was but three when Lydia died," he said, wondering at the sharp note in her voice, "and she has never mentioned her mother to me."

"So?" Gillian snapped crossly, recalling her own pain and frustration when her mother died. "I was only five when my mom died, and I *still* remember what she looks like! Don't assume that just because Deidre doesn't mention her mother that she doesn't remember her! And as for Deidre not mentioning her mom, do you ever mention her mother to her?"

Ian's face stiffened at once. "I do not discuss my late wife with anyone," he said, his voice clipped with fury. "Now, if you will pardon me, I need to attend to some things. We will be leaving at seven o'clock, if that is acceptable to you?" He raised a dark eyebrow inquiringly.

Gillian managed a mute nod, stunned by the agony she had glimpsed on Ian's face. He must have loved his wife a great deal if he couldn't bear speaking of her, she decided, watching in dejection as he strode away. Terrific. Not only was she living the life of a Victorian governess, but she'd also fallen in love with her employer—a man as haunted by his late wife as the brooding Mr. Rochester. If it hadn't been for her fear of tempting karma, she would have wondered what could possibly go wrong next.

Some three hours later Gillian stood in front of her mirror, staring at her reflection in a mixture of amusement and disbelief. If she'd earlier compared herself with Jane Eyre, she now felt decidedly like Scarlet O'Hara—give or take a few years and a few thousand miles. She held out her arms and turned sideways, causing her full skirts to flare out.

"Are you a good witch, or a bad witch?" she asked her image in a flutey voice.

"Miss?" Alice, the little maid who'd been assigned to help her, gave her a confused look.

"Nothing, Alice, just an American expression," Gillian replied, having learned that embracing her nationality was the best way to explain what she knew the staff viewed as her "odd ways." "I was admiring my reflection; that's all. Thank you for all your help."

Alice's pasty cheeks grew bright with pleasure. "You're welcome, miss," she said, fussing with the puffed sleeves of Gillian's midnight-blue evening dress. "I only wish I could convince you to do more with your hair. I know all the latest styles, and it would be no trouble at all." She gave Gillian a hopeful look that reminded her of a Moonie confronting a possible convert.

Gillian gave a discreet wince as she thought of the torturous arrangements of braids and curls that she knew to be the current rage. She'd rather shave her head then go out with her hair twisted into one of those monstrosities.

"That's all right, Alice, thanks," she said quickly, easing the sting of her words with a warm smile. "You forget I'm a governess, and I wouldn't want Dr. Culross to think I was getting ideas above my station." The servile words almost choked her, but they must have been convincing because Alice gave a wise nod.

"You're probably right, miss," she said with a sigh. "It will cause talk enough if anyone should learn the doctor took his daughter's governess to a *play.*"

She made it sound like Ian was taking her to a live sex show, and Gillian told herself that such ridiculous prudishness was one of the things she'd miss least once she was back in the twentieth century. The thought brought another stab of pain to her heart, and she masked it by turning away from the mirror to pick up the fan and black lace mitts the disapproving housekeeper had deigned to lend her.

"I would not have you disgracing this house by appearing without the proper accessories," the older woman had told her stiffly as she'd offered her the items. "Perhaps if you intend accompanying the doctor to other events, you will wish to purchase such things for yourself?"

Gillian had gritted her teeth and thanked the old witch for her kindness, adding that such expense would be unnecessary as she doubted the doctor would ask her anywhere else. Her reply seemed to please the pinched-face housekeeper who dismissed her with an arch warning about the dangers of young ladies of modest birth having their heads turned by dubious attentions. It had been all Gillian could do not to gag.

She popped into Deidre's room to show off her finery, and

then cautiously made her way down the stairs to where Ian was waiting. He was dressed in formal evening wear, a silk-lined cape flung carelessly over his broad shoulders. Gillian took one look at him and came to an abrupt halt.

Ian glanced up when he heard Gillian coming, his pleasure turning to puzzlement when he saw her stop, an expression he could not name freezing her lovely face. "Is something wrong?" he asked uneasily, fearing his valet had neglected to fasten something important.

"Wrong?" Gillian echoed in a high voice, wondering if Victorian women called men hunks. "No, everything is f—fine, thank you," she stammered, then mentally gave herself a stern shake and started forward again. "I'm just excited, that's all," she added, hastily pinning a smile to her lips as she reached the bottom of the stairs. "I've always wanted to see a London play."

As he did so often these days, Ian wondered what she really meant. He'd learned Gillian hid most of what she felt, and he supposed he could not fault her for her caution. Still, he thought, smiling as he took her hand and allowing his gaze to linger on her, it would be nice if just once there was no artifice between them. But there was no trace of such wayward thoughts on his face as he favored her with a low bow.

"Then I hope you will not be disappointed, Miss Brooke," he said, aware the butler and several maids were listening to their every word with unabashed curiosity. Much as he longed to compliment her on her beauty, he knew he dared not. He'd already exposed her to enough unpleasant speculation as it was. Later, he promised himself, with a secretive smile. Later.

Eight

The evening was everything Gillian could have asked for . . . and more. She found the acting to be melodramatic and overblown, but the fact she was sitting in the same theatre as Queen Victoria more than made up for any histrionic shortcomings. Afterward Ian again surprised her by suggesting they stop at a friend's house for a post-theatre party.

"It has occurred to me that you have had little opportunity to meet other people," he said, his tone oddly formal as he gazed down at her. "And I think you will find these friends of mine most interesting."

"That sounds lovely," Gillian agreed, somewhat perplexed by his distant attitude. Since leaving the house he had grown increasingly rigid and cool, his manner so unyieldingly correct she couldn't help but think she must have offended him. A thrill of fear shot through her at the thought he'd somehow guessed she had fallen in love with him, and she vowed to keep a better rein on her emotions. Two could play at this prim and proper game she decided, her spine stiffening with pride.

Ian's friends lived in a lovely town house on Portman Square. After introducing her to her hostess he confounded Gillian by abandoning her to her fate and disappearing into another room with his host. At first she felt a sharp pang of betrayal, followed by a flash of anger and then a simmering resentment as it became obvious few of the guests were inclined to converse with a simple governess. She was standing in a corner by herself, wondering if Victorian protocol would allow her to leave on her own, when Ian finally rejoined her.

"Why are you standing here alone?" he demanded in a low voice. "I thought you wished to converse with other people."

The injustice of the remark made Gillian burn. *"I* might have wanted to converse," she retorted through clenched teeth, "but your stuck-up friends have other ideas! Apparently they don't consider a mere servant worthy of so much as a 'Hey, how about those Trailblazers?' "

"Trailblazers?"

"Forget it," Gillian gave a heavy sigh, "I just meant your friends haven't exactly been friendly."

Ian's jaw clenched at the thought that she had been snubbed. The Mellingtons had been more Lydia's friends than his, but he'd always thought of them as decent enough. He was trying to think of some way to rectify the situation when the melodious strains of a waltz caught his ear. Without pausing to consider the matter, he reached out and captured Gillian's hand.

"Come, let us dance," he said, as he began dragging her toward the ballroom.

"Dance!" Gillian exclaimed in genuine alarm, struggling to keep up with his longer strides. "Wait! I don't dance!"

Ian ignored her weak protests, guiding her into the ballroom where other couples were already spinning about the crowded dance floor. He turned to her, slipping his arm about her waist and taking her hand in a firm grasp.

"Now," he began in the tone he reserved for lecturing his students, "there is nothing to fear about the waltz. It is a simple matter of mathematics."

"Mathematics?" She scowled up at him, remembering the disastrous ballroom dancing class she'd taken as a sophomore. The professor had promised her a B if she agreed not to come back for the rest of the quarter.

The feel of her in his arms was having a decided effect on Ian, and he had to force himself not to pull her even closer. "Certainly," he said, sweat beginning to bead on his upper lip, "one has but to concentrate on the numerical sequence of the notes. Can you hear it? One, two, three," and he swept her away and into the whirling throng.

After a few missteps and embarrassing stumbles, Gillian

caught the rhythm of the enchanting music. Following Ian's lead
was a lot easier than trying to coordinate her movements with
some nerdy chem major's, and she was soon ensnared by the
magic of the waltz. The rustle of her skirts and the light cascading
down from the shimmering chandelier filled her with an overwhelming sense of enchantment, but it was the brush of Ian's
body against her own that made her tremble. She knew that if
she ever did make it back to the twentieth century, this was the
one moment she would never forget.

Ian was also caught up in the sweet sorcery. His original intention had been to dance one dance with Gillian, and then prevail
upon one of his friends to partner her next. He reasoned that
once others saw her dancing they would accept her into their
midst, but now he knew he could not do it.

The very thought of another man holding Gillian in so intimate
a manner touched on the raw pain inflicted by Lydia's casual
infidelities, and he knew he could never tolerate it. The admission
made his arm tighten about Gillian's waist as he grimly accepted
what he had been denying almost from the moment of their first
meeting. He loved Gillian. God help him; he loved her.

The realization astounded, horrified, and finally delighted him
as he allowed it to sink in. He'd been terrified Lydia had killed
his ability to love, and he could have shouted with joy that it was
not so. But as quickly as his spirits soared, they plummeted to
the ground again. How could he love a woman who could vanish
from his life as mysteriously as she had appeared?

"Ian?" He felt her pull slightly away from him. "Is everything
all right?"

He gave himself a mental shake, chagrin darkening his cheeks
when he realized they were standing in the middle of the dance
floor, the object of several speculative gazes. He took a quick
step back, his arm dropping from about her waist as he pulled
his dignity about him. "Everything is fine, Miss Brooke" he
replied, his voice curt as he struggled to master his emotions.
"But the hour is late, and we should be going."

Puzzled and more than a little annoyed by his autocratic manner, Gillian allowed him to escort her from the floor. After saying
their goodbyes, they collected their wraps from the maid and

hurried outside where Ian flagged down a passing hack with an imperious wave.

Gillian flung herself into the darkened cab, her arms folded across her chest as she fought to control her temper. She didn't often get mad, but she could feel the hurt and resentment welling up inside her, and after a brief struggle she decided to hell with it, and turned her head to give him a frosty glare.

"Look," she began, her voice tight with fury, "I know I'm not exactly Ginger Rogers, but that doesn't mean you had to hustle me out of there in disgrace! What did you expect them to do? Start throwing tomatoes?"

Lost in his own dark thoughts, Ian hadn't the slightest notion what she was saying. "What?"

"You heard me," Gillian retorted, her chin coming up with pride. "I embarrassed you, and you couldn't get me out of there fast enough!"

Ian gave her an incredulous look. "You're mad!" he exclaimed with conviction. "You most certainly did not disgrace me!"

"Then why did you all but drag me out of there and stuff me into the first available cab?" she demanded, in no mood to be placated. "And don't try telling me you didn't," she added when he opened his mouth in protest, "because I have the bruises to prove it!"

Ian paled in horror. "I bruised you?" he exclaimed, his voice hoarse. "Where? Show me." He pulled her into his arms, brushing her cape aside with hands that weren't quite steady.

Embarrassed, and feeling more than a little guilty, Gillian made no move to fight him off. "Nowhere," she said at last, her voice slightly breathless as the feel of Ian's hands made her senses hum. "I—I was just being melodramatic, that's all."

In the flickering light of the jet lamp her skin gleamed like the most expensive of velvet, and Ian's breath caught in his throat at the enticing sight. Desire, potent and sweet exploded in his veins, and he was unable to resist the temptation to taste what his hands were caressing. He bent his head, his lips brushing over her flesh in a heated caress.

"Gillian," he whispered, his voice shaking with a passion that surpassed even his iron will.

Caught in a sensual whirl every bit as devastating, Gillian's arms closed around Ian's neck, pulling him closer. After five years of marriage she'd have thought she knew all there was to know about desire, but Ian's touch was showing how wrong she could be. The feel of his lips was shattering her control, and she gave herself up to its power with a sigh of delight.

"Ian," she whispered, her hands sliding up to bury themselves in his thick hair. "Kiss me, please kiss me."

Inflamed by her breathless demand, Ian levered himself over her, his fingers shaking as he brushed them over her flushed cheeks. He gazed down into her passion-darkened eyes, and seeing an echo of his own need reflected there, he bent his head and took her lips in a burning kiss.

Her mouth parted at once, welcoming the bold invasion of his tongue, even as she welcomed his heavy weight as he pressed himself against her. The taste of him was as heady as she knew it would be, and she trembled to think he wanted her as much as she wanted him.

He continued kissing her until they were both gasping for breath, and only then did he draw back. "You are so beautiful," he whispered, his voice shaking with passion as he pressed a string of kisses across her jaw. "I've wanted you forever!"

His words filled her with a fierce, feminine pride, killing the last of the lingering pain her ex-husband had inflicted on her with his cutting words about her lack of sexuality. She'd never felt more a woman than she felt now in Ian's arms, and the knowledge made the love inside her burn even hotter.

They continued kissing and touching each other, hampered by their clothing and the small confines of the hansom cab. It was worse than being in the front seat of a Volkswagen, an errant thought that made Gillian chuckle. She was about to share it with Ian when the sudden cessation of movement registered on her whirling senses. Ian stiffened also, and just as he was lifting himself from her, they heard the driver call out.

" 'Ere you are, guv!" he said, his voice suspiciously loud. "Number Six, 'alf-Moon Street!"

Ian pulled Gillian's cloak over her clothing, helping to hide her mussed appearance as he helped her from the carriage. Clares was there to admit them, and uncertain what she should do, Gillian turned toward the curving staircase to go up to her room. But before she could take a step, Ian laid a detaining hand on her arm.

"A moment, Miss Brooke, if I may," he said, his eyes as flat and expressionless as his voice. "I should like to speak with you in my library, if you would be so good."

Taking her cue from him, Gillian gave a cool nod. "As you wish, sir," she said, her tone diffident as she was aware Clares was hanging on their every word.

In the library the fire had been allowed to die down, but the coals still glowed a dull red. After lighting the lamp on the side table, Ian crossed the room to the fireplace, using the poker to stir the embers to life. He stood with his back to her, staring down at the fire a long time before finally speaking.

"I am sorry, Gillian," he said, his voice strained as he continued studying the flames with unseeing eyes. "I . . . I forgot myself. I had no right to touch you as I did."

Gillian flinched at the remorse evident in his husky voice. "Even if it was what I wanted?" she asked, laying her pride on the line with more courage than she knew she possessed.

Ian hesitated, then turned around to face her. "Especially if it was what you wanted," he said, his eyes meeting hers. He'd been giving the matter a great deal of thought, and painful as it was, he knew it was time he and Gillian both faced the bitter reality of their situation.

"We both know you are here in this time through no desire of your own," he continued, keeping his expression controlled with considerable effort. "If all goes well tomorrow and our experiment succeeds, you will be sent back to where you belong. It would serve no purpose for us to complicate matters now." There, he thought, taking grim comfort in his cool reasoning, he'd said it. With luck, she would never know what the prosaic words had cost him.

At first Gillian couldn't speak, pain making speech impossible. A complication? she thought, struggling for calm. Was *that* how he regarded any relationship between them? If so, she wondered if he had any idea how much like a man of the late 1990s he sounded. And as for where she belonged, where was that? Heaven knew she no longer had any idea.

"I see," she said carefully, determined to be as cool and unemotional as he. Not for anything would she tell him how much his words hurt.

Ian frowned at her cold tone. "You must understand it is for the best," he said, somewhat nonplussed by her cool acceptance of his words. He'd feared offending her, and given what had just passed between them, he felt he could not fault her. Instead she seemed as unconcerned as if they had done no more than exchange the most indifferent of handshakes.

"Yes, I understand that," she agreed, with that same maddening nonchalance, "and you're right, of course. This time tomorrow I could easily be back in 1995 London, and I certainly wouldn't want to leave things *complicated.*"

His frown deepened. "Gillian—"

"Do you know what I like best about this time?" she asked suddenly, making him blink.

"What?" His tone was wary.

"That you consider yourself a gentleman," she said in a sweet tone he now recognized as sarcasm, "and as a gentleman, you have no choice but to let me retire to my room. Good night, Doctor, I'll see you tomorrow." And with that she turned and walked out of the room, leaving a very angry and frustrated Ian to glare helplessly after her.

Nine

Ian awoke the following morning bleary-eyed and heavy-hearted. He'd spent an almost sleepless night coming to terms with his feelings for Gillian, and in the end he decided he had been right to say nothing. In the event he and Dr. Faraday succeeded in returning her to the future, he didn't want to burden her with the knowledge of his love. And in the event they failed, he didn't wish her to regard him as her only option in this time. He'd already gone through a similar experience with Lydia, and he knew he couldn't bear for Gillian to remain with him out of mere convenience.

Downstairs he found Gillian waiting for him, her lovely face composed and her gray eyes shimmering with an emotion he could not name. Knowing the servants were doubtlessly eavesdropping, he gave her a cool nod as he took his seat.

"Good morning, Miss Brooke," he said, his tone formal as he signaled Clares to begin serving. "I wish to thank you once again for accompanying me to the laboratory. It is very good of you to agree to translate the doctor's notes into German."

Gillian raised an eyebrow at the glib fabrication. So *that* was how he meant to explain her presence, she thought, trying to appreciate that once again he was doing all he could to protect her from servant's gossip. But given the fact that she was still furious with him, she wondered if she'd be able to eat her breakfast without dumping her tea over his head.

"You're welcome, doctor," she replied, striving to match his even tone. "I am happy to be of service."

He gave her a startled look, clearly uncertain how to take her remark. They ate their meal in a tense silence, and then set out for the Institution. As it was only a few blocks away, Ian proposed they walk, a suggestion Gillian was more than happy to agree with.

They hadn't gone but a block when he said, "Do you intend maintaining an injured silence for the rest of the day, ma'am? If so, it will make working with Dr. Faraday devilishly hard."

Gillian stopped walking, her eyes bright with fury as she glared up at him. "How dare you!" she exclaimed, although she was careful to keep her voice low-pitched. "After last night I can't believe you'd have the nerve to say such a thing to me!"

Ian flinched at this reminder of the passionate kiss they had shared. "I have already apologized for my ungentlemanly conduct," he said, forcing the words past his clenched teeth. "Now, I would suggest the less said of the unfortunate matter, the better. We have other considerations at the moment."

Gillian was surprised to find she was perilously close to tears. She knew she was being unreasonable, but she couldn't seem to help herself. She loved Ian so much, and to have him reject her hurt more than she could bear. She drew a deep breath, taking a careful step back from the emotional precipice she was tottering on. "You're right, of course," she said, keeping her gaze fixed on a point over his broad shoulders. "Shall we go now? I'm sure the doctor must be waiting."

They continued walking, and had just reached Dover Street when Ian suddenly stopped. "Have you ever been able to find that shop?" he asked, peering down the narrow, cobblestone street.

Gillian gave a disheartened shake of her head. "No," she said, recalling the many trips she'd made going in and out of the shops, but never finding the one she sought. "I've been past where I think it should be, but it's never there."

"Perhaps it is the wrong time?" Ian suggested, thinking carefully.

"No," she shook her head again. "I remember the sign in the window saying the shop was founded in 1851, so it *should* be there." She gave a heavy sigh and made a weak stab at humor. "Maybe it's from an alternate universe or something."

"Alternate universe?" Ian looked much taken with the notion.

"Just an expression," Gillian assured him, not up to explaining quantum physics, even if she understood them.

They continued walking another block before turning down Albemarle Street. The Institution was located in a Greek-style building, and Gillian had a vague memory of wandering past it on her first day in London. After signing in with the porter, Ian escorted her to the building's basement where he introduced her to the man many would one day call the father of electricity.

"So you are our time traveler," Dr. Faraday remarked, his hazel-colored eyes dancing in amusement as he studied Gillian's face. "Dr. Culross failed to mention you were so lovely."

Gillian's cheeks grew rosy at the compliment, and a quick glance at Ian's face showed he was almost as embarrassed. A chance to get back some of her own shimmered tantalizingly before her eyes, but she managed to resist the impulse.

"And none of the articles I've read about you mentioned you were so charming," she returned, offering him her hand. "It's a pleasure to meet you, sir."

Dr. Faraday gave her a surprisingly impish smile. "You must know I have a thousand questions," he drawled, escorting her to a long, flat table that was covered with equipment, "but Dr. Culross has explained why you can not answer them. Pity, I daresay you could have taught me much."

That was the end of anything resembling a personal conversation as Dr. Faraday and Ian threw themselves into the matter at hand. Morning became afternoon as the two men labored over their experiments, both seemingly oblivious to Gillian's presence unless they had a question for her. She did everything that was requested of her—holding the watch after it had been charged with electricity, and even agreeing to having a small current zapped through her. But in the end, it was obvious their efforts had been to no avail. Both she and the watch remained permanently stuck in 1851.

"I am so sorry, my dear," Dr. Faraday finally said, his shoulders drooping in defeat as he studied Gillian, "but I fear that is all there is to be done. I can think of nothing else to try."

Gillian dredged up a weak smile, wanting him to know she

appreciated his efforts. "That's all right," she said, laying a comforting hand over his. "I've known from the start that this was a long-shot. Thank you for trying, at least."

"You are content to stay here?" Dr. Faraday asked, his brilliant eyes searching her face. "You will not mourn for those you loved and will never see again?"

The question made Gillian hesitate as she wondered what the eminent doctor would say if she told him those she loved most were already here in this time and place. She'd miss her father and friends, certainly, but if she could have Ian and Deidre in her life, then she knew she would be more than content.

"I'll always miss my family," she admitted at last, choosing each word carefully. "But I'm here, and it looks as if I'll remain here for the rest of my life. So, I guess it doesn't matter how I feel."

Ian felt a sharp pain stab through his heart at her bleak words. He'd hoped she would accept her fate, if not with happiness, then at least with some small measure of tranquility. Now he wondered if she ever would.

After promising to continue working on the problem on his own, Dr. Faraday left, leaving Ian and Gillian alone. There was another strained silence, and then Ian spoke.

"Would you like to take a carriage back?" he asked, guilt eating him at the pensive look darkening her eyes.

She gave a distracted shake of her head. "No, I'd rather walk if you don't mind," she said quietly. "I—I need to think."

Ian flinched at the subdued note in her voice. "Of course," he said, reaching for her cloak. "Shall we go?"

They walked for blocks, wandering without purpose until they reached Green Park. Fearing she might be tiring, he led her to a bench, and sat silently beside her as he struggled against the emotions warring inside him. Unable to bear the pain a moment longer, he turned to face her, his jaw clenched in anguish.

"I am sorry, Gillian," he said, reaching out to take her hand in his. "This is all my fault. I have failed you."

The remorseful words startled Gillian out of her fog, and she blinked at him in confusion. "Failed me?"

"I know how unhappy you are here," he said, his gaze fixed

on their joined hands. "I know how you have longed to return to your home and family. You never asked for this incredible thing to befall you, and I wish with all my heart that I could make it right again, but I can not." He raised his head, his eyes bleak as they met hers. "Can you ever forgive me?"

"There's nothing to forgive!" Gillian protested; horrified by the tortured look on his face. "This isn't your fault!"

Her generosity made his lips twist in a bitter smile. "Isn't it?" he asked with a hollow laugh. "Had I not been playing with elements I had no right disturbing, none of this would have happened. The watch would never have been sent forward, and you would never have been pulled back."

Gillian glanced down at the watch she now wore about her neck. She lifted the case, turning it over so that she could see the words engraved on the back. "Why did you start experimenting with time?" she asked softly, running a thumb over the scrolled gold. "You must admit it's an unusual concept for this era—even for a scientist."

Ian thought a long moment before giving her the simple, unvarnished truth. "I wanted to change the past."

Already suspecting as much, Gillian swallowed painfully. "Has this anything to do with your wife's death?" she asked, then steeled herself to listen to his impassioned words of love for another woman.

Ian gave a vague nod, recalling the emotions consuming him that day as he conducted his first desperate experiments. "I thought if I could make time go back, I could stop her from defying me and going about the city when the cholera was raging," he said, a fresh wave of anger and grief washing over him at the memory. "But I doubt now that I could have changed anything, even if I had miraculously achieved my goal. Lydia never listened to anyone."

There was such an undercurrent of rage and longing in his deep voice that Gillian felt her own eyes mist with tears. "You must have loved her very much," she said, wishing there was something she could do to help ease his pain.

To her shock he drew back his head and gave her a puzzled look. "What makes you say that?"

"I . . ." she stared at him in confusion, unable to think for a moment. "You tried to change time to save her!" she protested, recalling his confession. "Of course you loved her."

Ian shook his head. "I regret her death, certainly, for she was but twenty-six when she died," he admitted, too upset to guard his tongue, "but I did not love her."

"But—"

"Don't you see?" he demanded, his eyes blazing with anguish. "It wasn't her death I was trying to prevent, it was my son's!"

Her head snapped back as if he'd struck her. "Your *son?*"

Ian was not ashamed to feel tears stinging his eyes. "Egan," he said brokenly, still scarcely able to speak his son's name, even after all this time. "He . . . he was only six months old when Lydia contracted the cholera and died. The disease spread to him before we could stop it, and in a day he was gone. I thank God Deidre was out of the city staying with her grandparents, else I may have lost her as well."

Even though she knew it went against every convention of the day, Gillian pulled him into her arms and held him tightly. "Oh, Ian," she whispered, brushing a loving hand through his dark hair, "I am so sorry, my love. I had no idea . . ."

Ian closed his eyes, giving in to the grief he had held inside for so long. "It was never in the papers," he said, reveling in the healing magic of her touch. "There were so many deaths at the time that children were seldom mentioned, and in any case I wished to keep it private. It was my pain, my fault."

She cupped his chin with her hand and gently raised his head. "How could it be your fault?" she demanded, brushing the tears from his cheek with the pad of her thumb. She'd never loved anyone as much as she loved him now, and she was finding it impossible to keep from telling him so.

Ian pressed a soft kiss to the palm of her hand, unmindful of the shocked whispers of the people passing by their bench. "Because I didn't do more to stop her from going out," Ian said, confessing what was to him his greatest shame. "In truth, I recall being happy she'd decided to go out that day, despite the danger. We'd been quarreling, about my work, as usual, and I remember her saying if I didn't take her to the gardens, she would find another escort."

"Lydia saw other men?" Gillian asked, surprised to find she was actually shocked by the thought.

Ian nodded, and in a stilted voice he went on to describe the wasteland his marriage had become. When he finished speaking, they were sitting side by side, their hands still joined. He searched her expression anxiously, looking for any sign that she'd found his confession reprehensible.

"You do not mind?" he asked, half-afraid he was misreading the emotion that was turning her eyes to silver smoke. "You aren't shocked to know I was considering a legal separation?"

Gillian couldn't help but smile. "When *I'm* divorced?" she said, recalling his initial reaction when she'd told him. "Of course not. Maybe my generation makes divorce too easy, but in some cases, it's the only solution. My husband cheated on me, too," she added, deciding that if he could be so unflinchingly honest then so could she.

Ian pressed a gentle kiss to her cheek. "I'm sorry, darling, I know how much such a betrayal can hurt, even when you do not love the other person." He paused, then gave her an anxious look. "Did you love him?" he added, his heart pounding with hope.

Gillian's heart was also pounding, and once again she felt herself on the edge of a soaring precipice. "By then?" she asked, her eyes meeting his steady blue gaze. "No. And now I wonder if I ever did. I never felt about him the way I feel about—" Her voice broke and she glanced away, her courage deserting her at the last moment.

Ian's hand wasn't quite steady as he gently turned her face to his. "About what, my sweet?" he insisted softly, happiness making his spirit soar.

The endearment gave Gillian the confidence she needed, and she bravely met his gaze again. "About you," she confessed, all her fears and doubts falling away at the love she saw reflected in his aquamarine eyes. "I love you, Ian."

Those eyes flared with emotion as he continued caressing her cheek. "Are you certain, my heart?" he demanded in a rough voice. "Because, God help me, I do not think I have the strength to let you go should you change your mind. I love you, Gillian. Please say that you will marry me."

They kissed passionately, endlessly, whispering vows of love between each fevered kiss. Finally Ian drew back, his voice shaking with rueful laughter as he pressed a final caress on her soft lips. "We'd best stop, my love, else I fear our reputations will be even more tattered than they are now," he whispered, painfully aware they had attracted a large crowd of gawkers.

Gillian's cheeks grew bright red when she realized he was right. Her hands flew to her hair, and she began frantically trying to stuff it back into its tidy chignon. Finally she gave up the effort, and concentrated her wrath on the large woman whose pinched expression made her look as if she'd just swallowed a particularly sour pickle.

"What's wrong with you, lady?" she demanded in her most belligerent manner. "Haven't you ever seen a man propose to a woman before?"

A loud cheer went up from the crowd, and Ian wasted no time in hustling her out of the park. Once they reached Picadilly, they turned toward Half-Moon Street, and in less than fifteen minutes they were safely tucked in Ian's study where they resumed their passionate kissing. Their caresses grew even more fevered as they continued exchanging pledges of love, and when Ian repeated his plea that she marry him, Gillian gladly agreed.

"You must know this will delight Deidre beyond all bearing," Ian told Gillian a short time later as they cuddled on the settee. "She loves you almost as much as I do."

"And I love her," Gillian said, her eyes misting in delight that Deidre would soon be her daughter. "When Dr. Faraday asked me if I would mourn for those I loved, I almost told him that the ones I loved were already here."

Ian's hand stroked her hair. "I wish you had, my love, for it would have spared me a great deal of anguish," he said, recalling the torment he had suffered. "It killed me to think my tinkering with time had brought you here against your will."

Gillian's fingers played with the gilded buttons on his waistcoat as she mulled over his words. An idea had occurred to her several days ago, and the more she considered it, the more sense it made. "I've been thinking," she said carefully, raising her gaze to his, "and I don't mean to knock your experiment, but I don't think that's what brought me back."

He moved his head back a fraction as if in surprise. "Then what did bring you back?" he asked curiously.

"*I* did," she said, smiling as she finally accepted the incredible truth. "Mrs. Tippleton asked me what time I belonged in, and I told her this time. I put the watch on, and it brought me back here to you and Deidre. Where I belong," she added in dazed wonder, her eyes shining as they met his gaze, "where I really belong."

Ian didn't speak for a moment. As a man of science he knew he should reject such a fanciful notion, but as the man who held the woman who had come through time to be his love, he knew he had no other choice. He lifted her closer for another kiss, and then drew back.

"Are you certain, my dearest angel?" he asked, his heart so filled with love it threatened to burst. "You are content to remain with Deidre and me?"

"More than content," she assured him firmly. "Even if I could go back, I wouldn't. I've found my life here, and this is where I want to stay. Forever."

The last of Ian's doubts melted away, and he gave her a tender kiss. "Forever," he repeated, settling her against his heart. "Through the whole of time."

Two weeks after their marriage Ian and Gillian, accompanied by a delighted Deidre, were taking a leisurely stroll down Dover Street when something brought Gillian to an abrupt halt.

"What is it, love?" Ian asked, giving his wife a worried look.

In answer Gillian pointed a shaking finger at the painted shop window.

The Keeper of Time
Elizabeth Tippleton. Prop.
Estab. 1851

"It's back," she whispered, raising fearful eyes to his. "What—what do you suppose it means?"

Ian didn't know how to answer. His first impulse was to grab Gillian and run as far from the shop as he could, but in the end, he knew he could not. Even if it killed him, he knew there was only one person who should make that decision. He reached out a gloved hand and gently touched Gillian's cheek.

"I think you should go inside," he said, praying he was doing the right thing.

Panic flared in her gray eyes. "But I told you, I don't want to go back!" she exclaimed, her voice shaking with fear. "I want to stay here!"

Mindful that Deidre was now watching them with wide eyes, Ian was careful to keep his own voice even. "I know that is what you told me when you thought you had no other choice," he said, ignoring the pain ripping his heart to shreds, "but the situation has apparently changed. You must go inside, Gillian. It is the only way I shall ever be certain you are staying here because you wish to, and not because you have to."

Gillian bit her lip, knowing that he was right. If he thought she was trapped against her will it would always be between them. But if she could prove him wrong . . . she gave the wooden door a nervous look.

"Mama? Papa?" Deidre's light blue eyes were worried as she slipped her hand onto Gillian's. "Is something wrong?"

Gillian gave herself a mental shake and then bent to give her daughter a loving kiss. "Nothing is wrong, sweetie," she said, brushing back a bright red curl from Deidre's forehead. "Mama has to go into that shop for a moment. Will you wait for me?"

Deidre's curls bobbed as she gave a vigorous nod. "I'll wait, Mama," she vowed firmly. "I'll wait right here until you come out again."

Gillian gave her another kiss and then straightened to meet Ian's gaze. "I love you," she told him, her voice shaking with emotion. "I'll always love you."

"And I shall always love you," he assured her, his voice not quite steady. "Now go quickly, before I change my mind."

The bell above the door gave an off-key jangle as Gillian

pushed it open and stepped inside. As before, the shop was dusty and dark, and she thought herself alone until she spied a familiar-looking figure perched on a stool behind the counter. Drawing a shaky breath, she took a hesitant step forward.

"Mrs. Tippleton?"

The white-haired head came up at the sound of her voice, and a pair of shrewd green eyes studied her approach with interest.

"Oh, it's you," she said to Gillian in the abrupt manner she remembered so clearly. "How is your watch working? Is it keeping the correct time, or do you wish to exchange it for something else?"

Gillian gazed over her shoulder where she could see the outlines of Ian and Deidre through the grimy bowed window. Her heart swelled with love and an odd kind of peace as she turned back to Mrs. Tippleton. "The watch is keeping perfect time," she assured the proprietress with a tremulous smile. "I love it."

"Good, good," Mrs. Tippleton gave a pleased nod. "A happy customer's a satisfied customer, I always say. Come in again if you need anything."

"I will," Gillian promised, although she knew she'd never have need of the shop's unique services again. "Goodbye." And with that she turned and walked out the door to where her future and her world were waiting for her.

About the Author

Joan Overfield has been a published writer since winning the Golden Heart Award from Romance Writers of America in 1987 for her novel, *The Prodigal Spinster*. Since then she has written a total of sixteen books including her newest work, *The Door Ajar*, her first time travel, which will be released by Zebra in November 1995.